THE MONSTER AND THE MAGPIE

BRIANNA FENTY

BLOODHOUND
— BOOKS —

For Sam, my biggest cheerleader
(and Oliver's #1 fan)

CHAPTER ONE

A FARMER IN BANFFSHIRE

One might be surprised how many murderers ply their trade in Scotland. One would be shocked, however, to discover just how many don't do their own shopping.

Whether you were the heiress to a Greek shipping magnate or the American corporate lawyer expatriated abroad, the Highlands offered ample space to dump bodies where they would sooner rot than be found. There were a few exceptions, of course. A deer stalker might stumble upon a corpse left on the heather moors. A coastal crofter might uncover a pale face in the sand at low tide. But even if the authorities identified the victim, even if the victim was buried with everything from the murder weapon to the clothes the killer killed in, not even the most diligent detective would ever find the perpetrator. Hope was too good at her job.

Midnight in Aberdeen, where the River Dee empties into the North Sea. Across the harbor, the city's gold lights winked along its endless beach, home to endless people sleeping in endless granite flats. All was dark south of the river, where a crumbling old fort stood sentinel over the water and, more importantly, where few of those people wandered past twelve on a winter weeknight.

In the passenger seat of the pickup truck, Hope rubbed the invoice between gloved fingers, imagining the fuzzy scratch of overhandled paper. The requested cargo had been odd this month. Even for him. It was a consignment that had demanded bribing, smuggling, and a threat to a sketchy curator at the Swedish Museum of Natural History who had the misfortune of being on her radar. She was about to unfold the note—not to review the order, but to admire the handwriting—when the tailgate slammed shut and the driver's door popped open. Mr. Charles slid behind the wheel. He kept the door open as if he were seated beside an untrained dog and might need a quick exit. The dashboard dinged away at an otherwise silent night.

"We're square now, eh, Magpie?" After a week's worth of Scandinavian sing-song, his brash Aberdonian was near unintelligible. "Squared up?"

"That depends on your ability to keep your mouth shut, Charlie," she said. "Wouldn't wanna owe me another favor. Unless..." She swung an elbow atop the center console and leaned in close, putting on a sardonic smile. "Are you... No, you wouldn't be a *masochist*, now, would you?"

Mr. Charles stiffened. Hands on knees, eyes straight ahead, jaw double knotted.

"What a scandal that would be, huh, bud?"

His breath came in clipped clouds; hers wafted his face and made his cheek twitch. She closed her eyes, pretending to savor Charlie's fear as if it were tiramisu. As it happened, Hope rather disliked tiramisu. Coffee belonged in cups, after all. Not dessert.

She dropped the act, reclaiming the deadpan stare her face naturally relaxed into. Once she'd checked to make sure her guthook knife remained safely tucked in her boot, she slipped the invoice in the pocket of her peacoat and slid out of the truck.

"Go home to Marcie and the girls," she said.

Hope shut the door, smacked it twice, and Mr. Charles peeled down Greyhope Road, leaving naught in his wake but a pallet stacked with crates and the silhouette of a man, leaning in the ancient archway of Torry Battery. The figure descended the small hill to the dirt parking lot. There was no swish of grass, no crunch of gravel. An Irish lilt, smooth and deep, crooned to her from the dark.

"You took your sweet time."

"My time's money," Hope replied. "Better have enough for what this load cost."

Killian Glass stepped from shadow to starlight: blue eyes, black hair, and a snow leopard's smirk. "I have more than enough, little Magpie," he said, rapping a knuckle on the top crate. "Always do."

"Always smug."

"And you always secretly enjoy it," he said, adjusting silver glasses. "I've probably paid the tab and then some on those new earrings, eh? Bulgari, is it?"

"Buccellati." Her American accent, which hadn't faded after fifteen years traipsing about Europe, butchered the name. She'd never been good with Romance languages. "Well? You know the drill."

Killian retrieved a fat envelope from inside his herringbone overcoat. Hope knew the piece well. She'd purchased the original from an octogenarian tailor in Stavanger, Norway, and later had it modified with hidden pockets by a mute seamstress in Trucios-Turtzioz, a village in the Basque Country, at the dreadful height of summer. She'd slid it off his shoulders once, too, straddling him in the backseat of his Beemer. But that was a long time ago.

Hope caught the envelope he threw and counted the wad of bills inside. Killian approached the crates and hefted one of the locks.

"Code?" he asked.

"One-eighteen ten."

The date-turned-password earned her a split second of side eye. She tried to hide her grin. Poking Killian's patience proved an amusing, if risky pastime, but so long as her stick was big and his temper deep enough in hibernation, what damns remained giving?

For a while, there was only the click-click of metal keys and the strep throat hiss of waves on rock. Then the telltale *snick* as the first, the second, and the third and fourth crates revealed their wares. At first leaning away from the stink, Killian's smile eventually found its phoenix, and its rebirth was a mild thing. A sinister thing. A negative energy version of him Hope recognized instantly by the spark in his cyan eyes and deeply, thoroughly disliked.

He rummaged through the contents. Didn't flinch from a puff of dusty fur. Seemed to inhale it, almost, like nitrous to a man mid root canal.

"You cut your hair again," he said. "Don't you keep it long until spring?"

Hope suppressed the urge to run a hand through her choppy platinum bob. Killian had always been keenly attuned to body language—hers most of all—and this was more an inquest than genuine curiosity or casual conversation. She'd forfeit no data for analysis, deferring instead to the invoice and ignoring his comment completely.

"Three Scandinavian grey wolf pelts."

He lifted one from its coffin, drawing mouth to maw.

"Two taxidermied paws, claws attached."

He hefted them, bigger than his palms.

"One upper and lower mandible."

One in each hand, he fitted the jaws together.

Hope licked and bit her lower lip, eyeing the final item. He'd thrown in an extra thousand euros for it, a hazard pay bonus that padded her wallet but did nothing to still the nervous quiver in her chest.

From the smallest crate, which wasn't a crate at all, but a hard, medical-grade plastic tub, came an exhaust of something foggy and cold. Liquid nitrogen. Dry ice, maybe. Hope didn't know, didn't want to know and hadn't watched as her contact at a World Health Organization satellite office packaged it cautiously, pneumatically sealed inside a glass lab. Her jaw clenched, watching Killian pluck the vial from its foam bed and hold it to his face. Moonlight refracted through the glass. It cast a toxic glow.

"Ten cc's of *Rabies lyssavirus*," Hope said, burying her discomfort under six feet of practiced apathy. "Twenty-two-gauge hypodermic included."

With utmost care, Killian replaced the vial, sealed the tub, and returned it to its place of honor upon the pallet. A cloud of fur floated to the dirt, silvered in the starlight. Hope suppressed a sneeze. Killian was unfazed. Forever unfazed, forever watching her with a cocked head, pocketed hands, and an expression edging between amused and analytical. Wind whipped the black priest's cassock under his coat like curtains over an open window.

Hope cleared her throat. "Staging a mauling, are we, Father Glass?"

"When have I ever offered up the details of my affairs, Hope?"

Her name on his tongue made pretzels of her gut and released butterflies in her stomach, nausea and excitement in equal measure.

5

"It's for your own protection," he went on. "One would think you'd appreciate the concern."

Hope unwound the knots. Squashed the butterflies. Stepped forward—one step. A bold step. "Wolves were just reintroduced to the Highlands, what, two months ago?" she said. "They're gonna be blamed for whatever it is you plan to do with these... parts."

"Perhaps I dislike wolves."

"C'mon, who doesn't like wolves?"

"A farmer in Banffshire," he said, "whose son will be killed by one."

A dense *clunk* as he punched the last lid shut. Hope watched him roll the pallet to his car and load each crate into the BMW's trunk without so much as a grunt or groan. Killian wasn't a large man, nor a particularly tall one, but underneath his vestments Hope knew were ropes of muscle earned not through bench presses and bicep curls, pull-up bars or tricep dips. His strength was won through more barbaric means. Bloodier, uglier, more preternatural means. Instinct forced her to take a step back. She huffed at her lack of self-control, planting her feet and hardening her face.

I'm not scared of you, she told herself, as Killian shut the trunk. He rolled the empty pallet into the sea, dusted his legs, and cleared his throat, setting his diagnostic gaze upon her. *I am not afraid.*

"Well!" Killian clapped his hands. "Care for a coffee, darling?"

"At 1 in the morning on a Thursday?"

"Bethesda Bean is open twenty-four hours," he said. "You of all people should remember that."

"That was fifteen years ago. The hours have probably changed."

"They haven't." He didn't need to add the fact that he'd checked.

Hope eyed the silver Beemer, its obvious claim to wealth painting a target on its windshield for desperate low-lives or inebriated undergrads bound to discover the incriminating payload in its trunk.

"How d'you think you're gonna drive that thing down High Street?" Hope asked. "Let alone park it?"

"We always find a way."

"We used to," she corrected.

Killian dipped his head in acquiescence. "Still, the side streets are dead this time of night. Fancy a trip down memory lane?"

Hope saw her hand misspelling Killian's name in black Sharpie on the first cup of red eye coffee she'd served him a lifetime ago at the Bean. She remembered his second. His third. Fourth, fifth, twentieth. Eventually a smiley face joined his name, and then a heart, and then her phone number jotted along the rim of the lid where he put his lips. She sometimes wondered if that was her life's grand mistake. Her point of no return. She more often wondered what dirty alley she'd be whoring in without making said mistake, or on which corner she'd shake paper cups of change at leering passersby. She smelled fresh-ground coffee and steamed whole milk, heard frothers whizzing and shouts for more caramel syrup at station two. Calls at the pickup counter for Scott with the soy latte, Nial with the mocha frap, Karen with the flat white, extra whip, and three Splenda.

Killian with the red eye. No sugar. No milk. Nothing but black, black ink for the post-grad Divinity student fresh out of Seminary, on his way to lecture at five.

Opening her eyes after failing to realize they'd been closed, Hope shook her head. The temptation to keep her attention fixed on the ground was strong, oppressively so, but she resisted the urge and met his stare tit for tat.

"No," she said. "Can't."

"No?" Killian raised a brow at the assertion of her refusal. "And why can't you, my dear? Some dazzling fundraiser's ball to attend with someone new on your arm?"

Emboldened by his patronizing tone, Hope tore and tossed his invoice. The wind snatched the pieces, ferrying them to locales unknown. Likely the sea, where most things wound up; where they would dissolve and never be read again.

"Because ex-fiancées don't go on coffee dates."

A change in his face. A minute one, apparent in the post-forty lines crow-footing his eyes, the sides of his mouth, the posture of his lower lip. The kind of change only a longtime lover—a close friend, an almost-wife, or a bitter, bitter enemy—would notice.

"Enough of your reminiscing, Father. I've got a day job to get to. Gotta run to Cartier."

"There are no Cartiers in Aberdeen."

Hope sashayed down the sloped path to Greyhope Road, refusing to look back and glad of her choice of boots over heels.

"Damn right." From her pocket she retrieved a boarding pass, a dark blue passport, and a clearance card for a private flight. She flashed them over her shoulder. "But there's one in Bordeaux!"

She stopped at the intersection of the street and the path. She looked up at Killian, leaning on the hood of his car. Relief flooded her chest, warm and serene, at the canyon of space yawning between them.

"You know how to reach me," she said, unsure why. "Next time..."

"Next time I need you, darling."

Killian offered what looked, to the unpracticed layman, like a reassuring smile as welcome as sun on a frigid day. Hope, on the other hand—a woman well-versed in his minutiae of movements and their subtle diction—saw the smooth smirk for what it really was.

Dangerous.

CHAPTER TWO

LANGOUSTINE

Lounging in the leather seat of the private Learjet Liberty, Hope shook out *The National*, savoring the musk of newspaper and ink. An attendant approached with folded hands and a properly amicable face.

"We'll be departing for Keflavík in just a few moments, madam."

"That's swell," she said. "Malbec, please."

"Pardon me, but we're banned from serving alcohol prior to takeoff—"

"Malbec, please and thank you."

He paused. He nodded. "Right away, madam—"

"Hope," she said. "It's just Hope."

"Right away."

She wondered what profanities he rattled off to his coworker upon reaching the kitchenette. Thoughts of *Rich, entitled bitch* and *Self-absorbed skank* made her smile before returning her attention to the paper's obscene headline.

CROFTER'S SON SAVAGED: ANTI-WOLF SENTIMENT REJECTED
IN RURAL RATHVEN

Hope snapped the paper shut as the attendant returned with a glass of red and a napkin. "Mind the takeoff, madam—"

"—and be careful not to choke." Hope offered a gracious beam fit to charm a monkey of its fruit. "Thanks... Aron," she said, peeking at his embroidered nametag. "Sorry for the attitude. It's been a long week. Hellish, actually. Frenchmen are exhausting, aren't they?"

He straightened with a sweet smile. A duped smile, coated in the sugar of false courtesy. "We've all had our days. Just so you know, it will be a three hour and forty-five-minute flight to Iceland."

"Perfect. I'm overdue for a cat nap."

She matched his smile until he left. Her face fell, having accomplished its task.

After watching the highlighter-vested workers wave highlighter-colored beacons on the tarmac for a spell, Hope snatched the paper from where it taunted her on the tray table. The engine purred as the craft pulled from the jetway, stirring her wine.

Horrified as she was by the murder's every detail—rabid foam crusting the boy's mouth; wolf jaws superglued to the kid's head; paws sewn on his hands and pelts arranged like wings from the raw meat of his flayed arms, where he hung from a barn's rafters by the wrists—she couldn't help but admire Killian's finesse. It was a fitting end for the degenerate teen who had taken a shotgun to a den full of sleeping wolf pups.

The National, naturally, hadn't included a photo. The scene had been too gruesome even for Scottish sensibilities. Any sensibilities. So as the jet taxied down the runway, as her Malbec swayed in its glass, Hope closed her eyes. She pictured the victim: a canid angel crucified from the beams of his father's barn, his own gun poised between his legs and aimed, fully loaded, at his fifteen-year-old cock.

Bang.

The jet hit the runway. She jerked awake, checking her watch.

"You haven't had your wine," said the attendant, as the craft inched towards the airport.

She glanced at the newspaper. At the window. The Malbec she hadn't had because it looked too much like blood.

"Aron," she said groggily, smacking *The National* against his chest and ignoring the secondhand guilt blooming like buttercups in her own, "please get me off this fucking plane."

———

Hope was surprised to see Andresína holding the sign at arrivals instead of her usual chauffeur. At the sight of her wavy brown mane and clever fox's smirk, Hope couldn't help but laugh.

"Your limousine awaits, Ms. Rippa," Andi cooed.

"Is that the Lincoln or the Cadillac?"

"Um..." Andi twirled her chestnut eyes up in mock thought, searching for answers in the ceiling. "The Toyota?"

Hope dropped her carry-on and pressed her grin to Andi's, nipping her bottom lip in greeting. Where Hope's were jerky dried by a week of French wind, Andi's were soft and sweetened with cherry Chapstick. She broke the contact only to chide, "Unacceptable, Ms. Hammershaimb," at which Andi giggled and resumed their hungry kiss.

"How was Bordeaux?" she asked, receiving a light hand slap when she attempted to snatch Hope's luggage. "Is that new client of yours still an unbearable cow?"

"At least you can eat cows. This bitch gives me a blank check to buy three necklaces from Cartier and sends 'em all back in a huff. *Emeralds, I said!*" Hope exaggerated a bougie French accent, gesticulating wildly with her free hand.

"*Emeralds, 'ope, not sapphires!*" She plucked an invoice from her leggings' microscopic pocket. "Take a look."

"Let's see." Andi appraised the bill, typed on minimalist Rippa Royale letterhead. "Three sapphire chokers."

"Three. Sapphire. Chokers." Hope snatched the invoice, balled it up, and lobbed it in a trash can. "Models," she scoffed. "Who the hell needs a sapphire necklace, let alone three?"

"Models."

"Why the fuck did I get into this business?"

"So you could buy me fancy langoustine dinners?"

"Right..."

Hope's day job was much in the same vein as her night job, only her day job didn't require shady meetups, questionable contraband, and elaborate networks of contacts either blackmailed or IOU'd into her no-questions-asked supply chain. Acting as the Magpie—an acquirer and launderer of occupational accoutrements for some of the continent's wealthiest serial killers—lined her pockets nicely, but her steadiest income stream came from Rippa Royale, LLC: the premier personal shopping agency in Northern Europe, of which she was founder and CEO. The agency's clientele were models and millionaires, business people and trust funders. Decidedly less criminal, or at least less violent, but no less demanding. Sometimes, in fact, the murderers had better manners.

The pair crossed the garage hand-in-hand, blown by a bitter breeze. The Corolla beeped, flashing its headlights hello. Hope plopped her luggage in a trunk crowded with boxes of alcohol swabs and stethoscopes, sterile equipment and bandages, wound pads, sanitizer, catheters, and gauze, the tools of Andi's hospice nurse trade. Hope frowned. She thumped it shut, turning to where Andi stood by the driver's side door. Her face lit up, unfazed by Hope's withering gaze. Eventually, it shattered her resolve. She had somewhere to be tonight, but dinner shouldn't take long.

"Fine," she said through a laugh, escaping Andi's squeal of delight by slipping inside the car. Empty coffee cups and Red Bull cans littered the console. "But we're sharing dessert."

Andi flopped behind the wheel. The abused car chugged to life with a concerning rattle. She ruffled Hope's hair; Hope smacked her hand away, frantically rearranging carefully arranged waves.

Andi pressed a kiss to her fingers and mushed them on Hope's cheek. "You're too good to me, Monkey."

As Andi pulled from the lot, Hope watched her intently. The barely veiled excitement playing her face, the pulse of her carotid betraying her happy buzz. Eyebrows arched with joy. Eyes buoyant with energy. Jaw clenched to suppress a smile that never seemed to fade.

You're too good to me.

Hope looked out the window, watching the airport speed by. She clutched her coat sleeve, letting her nails dig crescents in her palm. Andi didn't know that tonight's dinner came not at the expense of a forgetful model in Bordeaux, but instead one of the deadliest men north of the Mediterranean—and his penchant for morbid performance art.

You're too good to me.

Meanwhile, Hope lied more than she spoke truth, spent more time abroad than she did at home. Focusing on the broken landscape of black, volcanic rock fields, Hope sighed under the weight of her shame. Even now, six months and change after she and Andi had made their relationship official, all she could think of was Killian Glass.

———

Andi froze when Hope caught her in the act of sucking butter from her finger.

"What?" Andi defensively swiped her mouth with the linen napkin she hadn't spread on her lap. "Must I remind you every time we go out that your love for me stems from my good looks and dazzling personality, and not my table manners?"

Hope laughed through her nose. "Don't forget your ass."

"That too." She slurped a final chunk of langoustine, plopped its remains on a mound of shells. She reclined back with a groan. "Now that was a dinner."

Hope banished an image of Killian gracefully daubing the corners of his mouth after sipping a tumbler of Tullamore Dew. In its absence, she took note of the violet bags under Andi's eyes, the thinness of the neck above her blouse, the breakable wrists covered by rolled-down sleeves despite the sheen of sweat on her forehead.

The waiter removed their mess and took an order for chocolate cake. Andi's cheer set a stone in Hope's gut. She could tell it was forced. She saw it in the faint frown lines framing Andi's heart-shaped mouth and the sudden exhale of breath as she rubbed her stomach for half a second. Bloated with discomfort, like a starved woman after a too-big meal.

"Actually, we'll grab the check," Hope called.

The waiter's confusion mirrored Andi's.

"But you said—"

"We'd share. I know." Hope went to grasp Andi's hands, to enfold them with love and care. Thinking better of it, she set them back down on the table. "Andi..."

Andi reached out. Hope pulled back.

"Won't you look at me, at least?" Hope did. She tried. She immediately looked away. "Monkey?"

"If you need to go puke in the bathroom, feel free."

Hope needn't have looked up to see the hurt contorting her

partner's face. She felt it like a policeman's flashlight aimed through a window at a traffic stop.

"What are you—"

In a burst of fed-upness, Hope slid Andi's sleeve up to the elbow. Diners glanced over, averted their eyes, whispered under their breath. Hope didn't give a damn. She eased back in her seat and stared at Andi's untouched wine glass. Waiting. And when the waiting proved fruitless, she looked at the yellows and greens bruising Andi's arms, at the little red dots pitting the skin.

"I know you relapsed, Andi. You're a terrible actor, y'know. Taking me here to try to prove you're fine, but you're barely able to keep your dinner down."

Andi's eyes teared. The heat of those tears and the intensity of her guilt was borderline unbearable as she pulled down her sleeve.

"You don't have to pretend," Hope said. "I understand—"

"Understand?" Her shout disturbed the diners, ushering a brief silence to the nearby tables. When the ambient chatter resumed, she reiterated: "You *understand*?"

"I—"

"You have no clue!"

"Andi—"

"No!"

Andi shot up from her seat. The chair skidded back and toppled. Hope's chest filled with barbed wire as the diners zeroed in on the disturbance.

"You don't get to understand," Andi spat. Even her anger was subdued, undercut by a deep current of exhaustion. "You don't know who I am. You don't know what I deal with. You fly around the world buying expensive clothes for crappy people who don't need them, sipping wine you never drink in your fancy private jet, driven from Chanel to Dior by guys in suits and little black caps!"

Hope tented her fingers over her mouth to keep from saying something cruel. Something her no-nonsense nighttime self might say. If only Andi knew. If only Hope's lips weren't permanently stitched because they had to be.

"How dare you try to embarrass me? You have no idea what shame is, Hope."

But she did. And to protect her nighttime clients and her nighttime self, she had to be cruel. "Leave."

"What?"

"Go." Hope's hands slid from her face into a pile on the tablecloth, revealing an unaffected stare. "Go on and shoot up in your car, Andresína. But do me a favor?" Tense silence, taut as bungee cord at the base of a jump. "Do it *after* you make the drive home."

Disgust and pain made awful dancing partners on Andi's face—stepping on toes, waltzing without rhythm. She swept a glass from the table. It shattered on the wall. She stormed out without a word, trailed by judgmental stares.

Hope brought her hands once again to her lips, studying the stains on the tablecloth, the broken glass of Chardonnay Andi hadn't sipped once. A woodchipper filled her stomach, stocked with bricks and salt.

You're too good to me.

The waiter approached with caution, setting the black check folder on the table's edge.

"Whenever you're ready, madam," he said in a scandalized hush. "Whenever you're ready."

CHAPTER THREE

EVEN REYKJAVÍK HAS ITS MONSTERS

H ope was a master at salvaging situations she was equally adept at ruining in the first place. She'd smacked down some cash, run out into the night, and caught Andresína in a two-armed grip that obviously hurt her fresh track marks. As her girlfriend sobbed on the snowed-in sidewalk, tears made tawny by streetlamps and glittering Christmas lights, Hope shifted her hold to the wrists. Gentle and apologetic. Firm and unrelenting. Preventing Andi from escaping to her Toyota, to her needles, to wherever she hid the Dilaudid.

"I can't just stop," Andi cried aimlessly.

"You can."

"I can't do it."

"Of course you can."

Andi ripped her wrists from Hope's grip. "You know nothing!" she shrieked, before collapsing in the grey, boot-churned snow, shielding her face from the world. Hope reached out, but her hand was slapped away.

"No."

"Andi, please."

"No."

"Goddammit, Andi!"

The searing anger in her voice brought Andresína's tirade to a screeching halt. Hope wasn't sure she'd ever used that tone with Andi, the one once reserved for Killian in fits of impassioned fury. She regretted using it. No going back now.

"You're a mess!" Hope said, watching Andi stand. "You're a mess, An—no, Andi, don't you walk away from me, don't you dare. Get back here and look at me. At yourself. Do you see?" She jutted a finger at their reflection in the Corolla's window, spackled by a fresh curd of birdshit. "Well?"

"Of course I see! I have to look at it every day." Mania punched Andi's voice into higher octaves. "Y'know what I see? The way you touch those scars of yours whenever you're naked in bed with me. Staring at the ceiling like I'm not even there."

"Stop."

"I'm the mess, *I'm* the mess when you're still pining over some prick you broke up with half a life ago, a prick who cut you up like a Thanksgiving turkey whenever he screwed you!"

"That's enough."

"You won't even tell me his *name*. Six months and you won't even tell me that much! I always come second, don't I? Tell me I'm wrong. Go on! I bet he's who you think about whenever I stick my face between your legs—"

"I said that's enough!" Andi cowered. Hope swallowed. Breathed. She folded her rage and ripped it up so she wouldn't feel it anymore. "Just... just stop, okay? I need you to calm down."

Andi offered nothing but a whimper and a sidelong glance before she broke down fully, collapsing again to the sidewalk, this time on hands and knees. Hope watched her for a time. The pathetic display reddened her cheeks, made her want to turn tail and walk, no, run away. She had to pause and remind herself that she cared for this woman, and this woman was in pain. Struggling. So she didn't leave. She knelt to meet Andi on the ground, tipping her chin upward.

"I'm with you. Not him. And I'll stay that way, Andresína, because I want to. But this..." Hope ghosted a hand over Andi's forearm. "This has to stop."

Andi buried her face in the crook of Hope's neck, wetting her skin. Hope tensed and tried to stop tensing, attempting to soothe her girlfriend. Rubbing her back. Stroking her hair. It felt unnatural, alien—something everyday people did in everyday relationships with everyday problems. Still, she tried. She had to try.

She cared for this woman. This woman was in pain.

Ignoring the spot Andi chose to cry on was an Odyssean feat of will. It was once Killian's favored real estate: the tender hollow just above Hope's right collarbone, where he'd left behind a patchwork gloss of bitemarks that hadn't faded twelve years after their separation.

Hope held Andi's head there, grimacing against the memory, how he'd tainted a stretch of her own flesh. She hugged Andi tight, not just to comfort her, but to erase the permanent bloodstain of Killian's teeth with the presence of another lover.

"How about the park then, Andi?" she suggested. Self-hate boiled in her gut. "Yeah? The one across the road. C'mon. Let's take your mind off all this."

Let's take my mind off all this.

Hope hoisted Andi to her feet.

———

Hope stripped her coat and shed her blouse to expose small breasts cupped in tasteful lace. Straddling a half-naked Andi in the icy grass of Elliðaárdalur park, she unhooked Andresína's bra and tossed it aside. Winter gnawed at them. A half-frozen stream chugged over nearby rocks. Gold lamplight lined the path and park bench from which they barely hid. Amid breaths stolen in pauses from their ravenous kiss, Andi asked: "Are you angry?" and Hope answered: "Yes," digging her thumbs into Andi's injured elbows.

The other woman gasped. "How angry?"

Though she'd been born petite and thin—the veritable runt of the litter—Hope's years of sidestrokes in the pool made yanking the larger woman upright an easy task. She forced their chests together, their skin to touch, their hot breath to mix as mist in the bracing cold.

"More than you realize." Their lips car crashed. "More than you care." Their waists embraced. "More than you know, Andi —more than you'd ever fucking know."

She swung her arms over Hope's shoulders. Hope scraped her nails down the back of Andi's head, the nape of her neck, burning red trails down the skin of her back. Andi moaned and Hope pushed her down to the dirt none too gently, craning down to lick a path from collar to nipple: blush pink, small, hardened by the chill—the thrill—the undeniable lunacy at play in their actions. Holding Andi's body to hers, feeling her clammy sweat, her conflict, Hope lost herself in the moment as a child in the woods. Grass on her knees. Frost on her legs. Andi's flesh on her flesh, hands and slender fingers, smooth bellies, and spider silks of hair caught between mouths. Forgetting, forgetting, so close to forgotten—

Hope felt a presence. A radiator heat at her back. She ignored it, indulging in vulnerable Andi, at least until she became aware of the presence, too, and the tryst came to an abrupt end.

"There is a man," she whispered, sitting up. "Hope. Hope, there's a *man*."

Frantic, Andi pawed her shoulders, her head, the ground,

gathering her sweater to protect whatever dignity there was left after being caught mid-foreplay, outside, in December. Hope glanced behind her, annoyed—and froze.

A deer that hears the snapped twig too late. A hare that undershoots the dive to its den. Hope didn't have a chance to catch her breath because her breath was nonexistent, replaced by a vacuum crinkling her lungs to raisins.

Andi went to replace her bra. Hope shook her head, helping her slip the sweater on without it. "Go to your car and—"

"*What?*"

"I'm serious." Her tone dipped low. "Don't wait for me. Head home." Strain and fear tightened Andi's face. Hope softened hers, the only reassurance she could safely offer. "It's okay. Just follow the path. I'll call you. Now go." Hope squeezed Andi's hand. "Stay on the path."

Blessedly, Andi nodded. She stood, coat bundled in her arms, and gave the man a wide berth before hurrying from the park.

Hope waited in the dirt until the sound of Andi's boots scrunching pebbles and snow was far out of earshot before slipping her bra straps back where they belonged. Unbothered by the chill in the air, or at least pretending to be, she left her shirt and coat behind and strolled up to the man in black. The man in the priest's collar, whose lamp-glazed lenses hid the secrets in his blue, blue eyes.

"I didn't realize you'd be needing me so soon," Hope said.

"And here I thought you were relatively aware of my punctuality, Magpie."

"I figured you'd go to the dead drop at the tip of Bakkatjörn. The stone in the reeds—"

"—shaped like a horseshoe, yes. We used that location last. Don't you recall?" Killian appraised her body from the waist up, everything between belly button and brow. "Falling behind on the logistics planning, are we, darling?"

Hope gave a nasal sigh, lighting a cigarette pulled from a pack of American Spirit that had magically stayed in the back pocket of her leggings. Killian sneered ever so slightly at the smoke, enough of a reaction to breathe a puff of wind back in her sails.

"Hell of a catch, huh? Bet you always wanted a piece like that. Bit more meat on her bones, tits bigger than half a handful."

"You shouldn't speak of your body with such disdain," he said. "It's an affront to the Lord's efforts."

"When's the last time I listened to one of your orders, Father?" Her words were hoarse with smoke. "Besides the ones on your grocery lists."

"Cut the act, Hope." Killian plucked the cigarette from her mouth, ground it to the gravel under a wingtip shoe. "You know I don't fall for it."

"You used to."

"In a way. But you're forgetting one thing." He reached a hand up. Halted in midair. Hope's lack of objection translated to permission, one of their many unspoken rules, and he brushed an index finger under her neck from tensed jaw to soft, fragile chin, pressing his mouth so close to her ear his exhale tousled her hair. "Back then, it wasn't an act."

With that, a release. With that, an end. Hope stood shirtless on the path in the park, lighter in hand, gooseflesh pricking her arms. Ire and desire soured her insides. The line he'd traced on her skin was red hot, when everywhere else was ice cold. Their mutually agreed upon no-contact policy led Hope to forget what his touch felt like—and react viscerally during rare moments of weakness, like this, when she allowed it to be broken.

A faux-mink coat draped itself on her shoulders, retrieved from the shadows. She didn't turn to face him. He didn't step in front of her. She didn't dare move, and when she didn't, the danger of it all became delectably poignant. It reminded her of the beat in her chest. The air in her lungs. How easily both could be snuffed.

"Be careful, little Magpie. The hour is late, and even Reykjavík has its monsters."

He walked away, the crunching gravel growing quieter. Farther. Hope whipped around, holding her coat closed. "Wait!"

Killian stopped. Turned halfway. Hope bit the inside of her cheek until her professional persona responded to the summons, bringing her voice level. She cleared her throat. "Don't you have an invoice for me?"

"Never mind it, darling." He needn't raise his voice. Despite its soft baritone, his voice carried far. "It was a sloppy draft, either way."

Hope wasn't sure what to make of that. "Where we meeting?"

That gave him pause. Only a moment's.

"Come to my village and get some fresh air in those black lungs of yours. It really is lovely this time of year."

Watching him climb into a car obscured by skeletal trees and pull off into a night shrouded in Nordic winter, Hope searched for a threat in the offer and came up empty. Yet still. A tingle in her stomach. An unsettling, a tectonic shift, like an abandoned beaver dam breaking loose and flooding a town in the nearby valley. Killing the sheep. Drowning the children. It told her one thing for certain.

She'd made a mistake.

CHAPTER FOUR

MY FIRST

Hope's Range Rover rumbled up the packed silt road. She eased the brake pedal before a gargantuan sign. *Velkomin til Fjöðurfjall*, no doubt hand carved from stained birch by the first crop of villagers. Some might have been shivering in the wake of delirium tremens, others unsteady with the methadone shakes. Whatever it'd been, it gave the chiseled letters a unique homespun roughness. Hope grudgingly admired what the tiny village stood for: recovering addicts housed in a self-sustaining community, working and living together away from the temptations of the city alongside therapists, medical staff, and volunteers with full hearts. But the black wooden church cherry-topping the town was as irremovable a stain as wine on white velvet.

It was as much Killian's domain as the Ninth Circle was Satan's. Here, he held fragile minds in his hands, muttering spiritual guidance to the vulnerable and God only knew what else.

While Fjöðurfjall wasn't in their rotation of meeting places, where invoices and down payments were clandestinely exchanged, it wasn't unfamiliar. Hope had been here several times. She'd attended a service once. Fed injured birds in the sanctuary. Balanced on a crate to spy through a high window as a nurse administered Narcan to a screaming patient in the treatment center.

As she drove into the village lot, that same resident waved Hope's way, lugging a box of small melons on healthy, childbearing hips. Hope faked a smile. The woman was blond-haired, blue-eyed. Nothing like Andi, yet Hope could picture no one else.

She parked.

It hadn't snowed southeast of the city, or maybe it'd melted overnight. The grass looked like wheat, combed over by wind and thicker than straw. It toupéed the cottage roofs, snaked up buildings painted in weathered reds and browns alongside dead climbing vines. Here, a garden of clumsy sculptures; there, a glen of wooden windchimes. All handicrafts. Projects. Art therapy in all its forms—creating with one's hands, manifesting the power of God with one's own fingers, carving, sculpting, making music. Painting, weaving, learning self-forgiveness. These things, along with the clean air and exposure to nature, were as imperative to recovery as medicinal treatment. At least that was what Killian once told her.

A lot of it seemed like bullshit.

Hope watched koi tango around a cluster of lily pads in the pond on Fjöðurfjall's northwestern border, wishing for breadcrumbs. She sat on the edge of the slatted bench standing sentinel by its shore, snowy slate mountains rising in the distance. They cupped the valley, flattened first by open plain, then lumped by lava rock, lastly ascending, with gusto, into inhospitably gargantuan bluffs. The weak winter sun was on its way to touch their tops, its light diffusing sideways through a layer of cloud.

"Quite the view," Killian said.

"Your village is such a drag."

Killian sidled up to the shore, tossing a handful of flakes in the water. An orange tornado ensued. He settled on the opposite end of the bench to maintain a respectful distance. Hope appreciated it. Despised it. The line he'd traced on her jaw still burned.

"It may be a good option for—"

"Don't," she said. "Don't even say her name."

"I wouldn't dream of it, darling. Though this place could certainly provide a suitable cage for your canary as she recovers. The caretakers here are—"

"You're one of 'em."

The thought of Andi isolated here, outside Reykjavík, beyond Hope's reach and a cottage or two away from Killian—it was enough to catapult her from the bench and into an outburst. But she didn't move. She pretended her backseam tights were welded to the wood and would rip if she so much as sneezed.

Killian continued feeding the koi. "Well, you know how to reach me, should you reconsider. Our services are rendered free of charge."

"How'd you even know she was an addict?"

Killian seemed to take in everything from Hope's taut frown lines to her wrought iron grip on the bench's lip, from her toxic glower to the vein no doubt bulging in her neck. She refused to look away, weathering his examination to deny what little satisfaction he might exhume from nervous body language.

"The same way you must have, though I am trained to spot the signs." He offered a handful of flakes. "Fish food? It's organic."

"You saw her for *two minutes*. We've been dating for—" She bit her tongue.

Killian's eyebrows lifted in a caricature of curiosity as he popped a pinch of flakes on his tongue. "For?"

It was none of his business. He shouldn't care. They'd come to an end long ago, and yet…

And yet.

"Six months," she said, snatching a dash of fish food. Her fingertips grazed the calloused mound of his palm. Stomach in active freefall, she threw the flakes at the pond. An octagon free-for-all started underwater. "Does it matter?"

"Of course not." Killian rose, dusting his hands over the water. "As much as it saddens me, we are neither here to exchange pleasantries nor updates on our romantic goings-on."

"Glad we agree." Hope stood and held out her palm. "Well?"

Killian slipped a folded piece of notebook paper into her waiting hand, careful not to skim her skin. He faced the pond, the plains, the tabletop mountains beyond—turning his back— and outside of his periphery, Hope felt secure enough to remove her attention from his body, as if he were a Swiss Army knife left open on the bar in an empty pub.

She slipped a legal pad from her coat, reviewing the invoice with feigned disinterest. There would be time to ogle it later behind her Rover's tinted windows. She secretly looked forward to it, in fact: the script writ in 4B graphite, in a style fit for apothecary bottles and turncoat letters.

Something on the list caught her eye. Stopped her pulse.

The delivery spot.

"Reykjavík?" she breathed. "Killian… Reykjavík?" Hope snatched his arm, pulling his whole body off-kilter, too panicked to care about their no-touch policy. "What do you mean, Reykjavík? The walking bridge over Tjörnin… Are you insane? Killian, are you fucking *insane*? Did you lose a marble under the altar, maybe the whole collection? Do you need help looking? *Jesus*, Kil, I can scrounge up a flashlight, and I've got little hands, I'll help you look for 'em!"

"Relax."

"Relax?"

"Yes. Relax."

"Tell me to relax again and enjoy living as a goddamn amputee!" She thwacked his shoulder with the legal pad and her heart crimped—one didn't thwack leopards with legal pads —but irradiated anger refilled her with brave blood. "You..."

Hope stared at the grocery list, fixated on the transshipment point. *Pedestrian bridge between Monument, City Hall. Lake Tjörnin. Reykjavík.* 64°08′45.3″N 21°56′29.1″W. "Why?"

She thought of herself. Of Andi. Their lustful park affair cut short by Killian's arrival. It'd been selfish and petty, untimely and unwise, so incredibly unwise.

Killian must have seen the dust devil of worry stirring her face. "Don't," he said.

"Don't what?"

"Trouble yourself."

"How can't I? We live in the same country, hiding from the same things for the same—for *similar* reasons. I take your cash. I get your shit, I fill your orders. But always, *always*..." Her grip wrinkled the paper in her hands. It took all her mustered men and scrambled jets to meet his solid gaze without faltering. "I always deliver your crap to another city. Another *country*, Killian. Fuck's sake, shipping your deliveries pays twice my rent, most months, wherever you choose to do what the hell it is you do."

"So this is about the money?"

Hope's fuming silence formed an almost audible *No.*

Killian sat down. Leaned forward, elbows on knees. He watched the tall grass dance about the pond's edge, the breeze rippling a surface streaked by fleeting silver sun. Hope felt half a dollop's worth of shame as she admired a profile chiseled by prehistoric flint. Fine. Keen. But however tapered and honed, however she'd once touched and kissed and loved that face, she couldn't, wouldn't allow it to soften her loaded question.

"Who are you gonna kill?"

Whooper swans drifted. Eider ducks gathered. Wind iced the small gold hoops dotting Hope's ears and reddened her nose, but she refused to turtle inside her scarf.

"It isn't you," he said. "Nor your canary. Spend your concern at a different carnival."

Hope had known Killian for half her life and in that time, he'd never lied. Not once. She calmed, to an extent; her body, never one to trust her trickable mind, remained steel-tense. This was risky for them both. Giddy terror pirouetted on her brain's stage, whipping and twirling as a carousel at speed, balanced on slim heels, slim legs, and even slimmer notions of *We'll be fine*.

"Why now?" she asked.

"It seemed like the right time."

"Here?"

"My first," Killian confirmed.

"The police will come for you."

"Only if you set them upon me."

"They're gonna figure you out."

"Only if you divulge my secrets."

And she had every reason, including self-preservation, to keep them.

But an Icelandic murder, one of Killian's caliber? The country wasn't ready for such a thing—no one in it was. Her penmanship went sloppy as she estimated the price of the tools he'd use. She dropped the pen just as she finished scrawling the €8,000 cost for a single item on the list. Her vision swam, black at the edges, and she staggered, but before she could fall Killian caught her arm. One hand rose to her face, tender yet firm and forcing her to look at him even as she struggled—*don't touch, don't touch*—until she stopped fighting.

"I swear, Magpie. It's not you."

"Use my name."

"I swear, Hope. On my own mother's well-kept tomb."

He let go, retrieving her pen from the grass. She returned to the bench and he followed suit, respectable distance re-established. Minutes came and went as Hope scribbled figures and legalese, never quite able to soothe her galloping heart, or fully tear her attention away from the tingling sensation left in the wake of his touch. The sun began its dip, the swans and ducks their evening retreat. Sunset bathed distant crags in gold and struck wildfires in the grass, casting long shadows across the village. Mackerel clouds heralded rain.

With a polite thank you, Killian reviewed the final statement, and as it left her hands, her adrenaline and anxiety left with it.

"I'd always been quite fond of your name," he admitted, stroking the letterhead. "*Rippa*."

"Mama named me Hope as a joke, y'know." She curled her knees to her chest, watching a dispute between two terns over a fish. "She didn't realize it was a joke at the time, but the universe and I had so many plans."

"I don't think she meant it as a joke." Killian pocketed the invoice and folded his hands on his knees, a chaplain if she ever saw one and a priest if she ever smelled one, like a dog smells cancer on a dying man. "A prophecy, maybe. One you continually decide to deny. At every point in your life when it extended its hand, you slapped it away and made it light your cigarette instead."

"Speaking of." Hope smacked a Spirit from its pack and waggled it between manicured fingers. "Do a girl a favor?"

"Smoking is bad for you."

"*You're* bad for me."

"Actually, I do believe I'm worse."

"How's that?"

Killian struck a match and raised it to her lips. "Because I light your cigarettes, darling."

"Stop callin' me darlin'," she said, mocking his accent.

Hope took a drag and dragon-gazed through the smoke. Merlot lipstick kissed the filter, the same that once stained his priest's collar minutes before his sermons. She half-smiled, remembering the locked drawer he'd once dedicated to spares in his office desk at the back of the little church in Aberdeen: his first post before, more fittingly, becoming a prison chaplain before the move north.

"Are you smiling at me?" Killian asked, dressing his confusion in the colors of amusement.

Hope thought she spotted a spark in his eye. A whale's tail from the sea, or the silver flash of a herring. Something nameless. Something gone in an instant.

"No," she said, unhappily. "I'm smiling at someone you used to be."

"You always had a talent for sneaking my heart under your boot heel, you know." Killian shook his head. Sucked his teeth. "Six months..."

"Twelve years," Hope countered.

She neglected to mention that Andi was the first person she'd attempted a romance with beyond casual sex in the twelve years since she and Killian broke their illicit engagement. And while any engagement to an ordained priest was a sham by default in the eyes of Catholic law, it had been as real to Hope then as was the air in her lungs, the sun in the sky, and the gravity keeping her tethered to earth.

"Twelve years." Killian nodded, removing his glasses—the same rectangular silver frames he'd always worn—and cleaned their clean lenses on the edge of his off-duty button-up. Hope suppressed the urge to ash her cigarette on one of the lenses. To give him something to really clean. Something to ruin his white, white shirt.

"I've always been the man you see now, Hope. Albeit in better lighting."

A brief quirk of the lips betrayed his mindset, nostalgic and stuck in a better past. She knew the feeling intimately, vastly, and knew it for what it was. It was a trick, idealizing good times long gone and bittering the present with cod oil and capers. It left one yearning for simpler times—and vulnerable to resentment.

Darkness descended over him. Hope could see it. Feel it, like something quick and slimy brushing her leg upon wading into the waves. Killian chucked the glasses as if offended; they bounced off her knee and fell to the ground. She dropped her cigarette in surprise.

"Perhaps you need these more than I. Until Monday, little Magpie."

Killian vanished into shadows cast by the village buildings. His sanctuary. His church. The sculptures in the garden. Hope's chest went tight. Not from the hit, no—they were glasses, not kettlebells. She looked down at them: cracked, broken things on frost-hard earth, discarded without regard for the things they'd seen.

When she finally mustered enough energy to leave the pond, Hope retrieved her cigarette stub and Killian's fractured glasses. Nothing remained of their meeting but a shard of lens and a scorched blade of grass. Back in the lot, she tossed the butt in a garbage can and pretended not to see Killian disappear inside the church, and as she settled behind the wheel of her Rover, Hope cradled those glasses, swearing her watery eyes came from a place of anger and nowhere else.

She threw the truck in reverse and sped off.

CHAPTER FIVE

MEET-CUTE

Two weeks had passed since the rendezvous with Killian on the pedestrian bridge at Lake Tjörnin. She'd rented a small moving truck for the oven and hired three Filipino fishermen grounded by rough seas to muscle it up and out, offering wads of cash in exchange for never having seen her face. Nothing on the news, but nothing was good. Blessed by a rare day off visiting the homes of the dying and enough energy to brave the world, Andi accompanied Hope's morning rush to the café.

"You didn't have to come," Hope said.

"I wanted to." Andi exuded joy, but Hope felt the lag in her step. "Didn't you want me to?"

"Well, yeah, but—"

"But?"

"—but maybe you shouldn't be out right now."

Andi fixed Hope with a glare fit to sunder worlds. "Am I slowing you down?"

"No," Hope lied.

"Am I being a burden?"

"No," she lied.

"Would you rather be alone?"

"No," she lied again, chewing the inside of her cheek. "Look, just—"

"Just what?" Andi stopped short on the dark, cobbled street. Hope instinctively scanned for alerted pedestrians, but the streets were deserted before seven in the morning. Andi snorted. "I knew it, look at you! You're ashamed, aren't you?"

"Andi!" Hope seized her elbows, careful not to touch the healing tracks. The mad spark in Andi's eye dissolved before it could catch fire. "I want you here, okay? But I understand if you can't be, that's all." She swept a tear from Andi's cheek before it met the curve of her jaw. "You kinda look like defrosted roadkill, honey. Not gonna lie."

After a dense pause, the tension went slack with a shared laugh. Crisis averted, Hope flicked Andi's shoulder. "Let's go mainline some caffeine, huh?"

"But you hate coffee."

"Tea's a thing."

"You're the only barista I've ever met who hates coffee, y'know that?"

"Good thing I quit that racket years ago."

They cut through a park that was more an overgrown, frozen bog, boots clomping across a wooden walkway raised above the reeds. The café sat ahead, an unassuming hole-in-the-wall made of lacquered wood and bay windows. Crossing a pebbled trail before their heels touched blacktop, Andi asked, "Do you see yourself?"

"Hm?"

"Across the counter."

"Any time you'd like to make sense, I'm all ears."

"When you get your tea in the morning from the barista, does she remind you of who you used to be?" Andi clarified. "In Scotland?"

Hope opened her mouth to say no before pausing to puzzle over the question. Almost always the café's first customer, she had developed a habit of watching the barista's every move. How high she filled the boiler, how snug she fit the cup sleeve, how much loose leaf she tapped into the infuser and how long she let it steep. Would Hope do things differently? Would she practice as much care? She'd never taken much pride in her dead-end shift at the Bethesda Bean, never put much stock in the palates of racoon-eyed university students or their tired professors. Was she polite to the clientele, offering toothy retail grins? Flipping through a dusty phonebook of long archived memories, she was disturbed to recall only ever smiling at a single customer out of thousands.

He was the only one she remembered at all.

JANUARY, 2007

It'd been half past four when a very average man with a very not average face stumbled into Bethesda Bean. A dark suede blazer was tastefully tailored to meet the waist of faded jeans, but the state of his tartan scarf and windblown mane produced an in-a-hurry bearing unsuited to what might normally be something like elegance or class. One of his cap toes was untied. His leather satchel, half buckled. Hope, more interested in her lollipop than a customer, didn't look up until she noticed him standing at the counter. Unmoving, unspeaking. Usually people just talked at her. Soy latte this, large cappuccino that, and do the pretty leaf thing with the foam, would you? This status quo departure bade her glance up from her phone at an androgynous thirty-something with cheekbones fit for an Old Norse queen and eyes too light a blue to be human.

Before she could come up with some barbed quip about his

state of affairs, she noticed his predicament: one hand held his wallet while the other pinched glasses to his face. The tape joining them at the bridge had decided to come undone. A bruise lavendered his cheek. Three scratches bloodied the skin from clean-shaven jaw to Adam's apple.

"Get punched in the face, bud?" Hope asked.

"Whatever might have given you that idea?"

"Those don't look like the fun kind." She nodded at the scrapes. "Plus," she gestured vaguely in his direction with the lollipop. "All that."

It wasn't sheepishness or shame reddening his cheeks. It was something similar, but something decidedly else—something that pegged him as a man born into status or at least wealth, as if the quality of his clothes hadn't already accomplished the task.

Mildly injured pride. That was it.

"We close in five minutes," she said.

"The sign says twenty-four hours, if I read correctly."

"How'd you read the sign if your glasses are busted?"

Tension around his lips. They were nice lips, Hope decided. "Do you make red eyes or not?"

"Reddest in Old Aberdeen," she said. "Joey! You heard Rockefeller over here."

The pizza-faced teen scrubbing coffee stains from the Formica counter behind her threw his rag in the sink with an angry wet smack. "And why the fuck can't you do it then?"

"I've got a pair of glasses to fix. Be a good lad." Hope stuck the lollipop back in her mouth, patted Joey's nest of mousy curls, and crooked a finger at the stranger. "You. Come with me."

In the dingy room behind the kitchen, Hope popped her locker and emptied her handbag onto the break table. Her wallet flopped open. Her keys jangled out. Makeup tumbled across plastic until, at last, an eyeglass repair kit.

She went to work in silence. He watched her in silence. His look was abrasive, but not steel wool abrasive—not sandpaper or stained carpet or cheese grater abrasive. It was abrasive like rope burn when you're tied down to a bed.

"I take it this is merely your day job." His Irish accent was thick, but it wasn't the buttery timbre of it that glued Hope in place. It was the words themselves, and the complete and utter conviction they carried. "At night, you must be someone entirely new."

"What makes you say that, Sherlock?"

"Everything."

Hope crunched down on the lollipop. Spit the soggy white stick.

"You have key cards to three different hotels in your wallet, one to the penthouse at The Scotsman in Edinburgh. Four different shades of lipstick—dark brown, Barbie pink, black, and cherry red make a rather curious assortment, I'd say. Not to mention they fell from a brand-new Gucci handbag which I can't imagine a barista's wage could buy, and then—" He analyzed her open locker. "I spy with my little eye red-bottom stilettos peeking from your duffel bag, next to a slip of what must be the world's smallest silk dress." He turned back her way. "Lastly, that." He pointed at the eyeglass kit. "You don't wear glasses, as far as I can tell."

"I'm wearing contacts."

The man leaned in, examining her green eyes with the scrutiny of suspicious mothers and private school principals. "No you aren't."

"How about I have a go? You must be from the Divinity College," Hope jeered, packing her belongings. "You lot are always the judgiest. Lemme guess. You're a grad student trying to style himself a theologian in open rebellion against daddy and his oil money?"

"Close enough to the mark, it may as well be a bullseye." He laughed through a set of straight white teeth. "But you misunderstand my intent. I've no reason to report a call girl going about her business. We all do what we must to survive, don't we? You'll find no judgment from me... Hope," he said, reading the nametag tacked to her apron. "Only curiosity."

"Well..."

"Killian."

"Well, Killian. Take your curiosity, roll it up in a nice, tight little ball, tuck it up your keister and mind your own fucking business." Hope smacked the repair kit and mended glasses against his chest. "And get your red eyes somewhere else from now on, 'kay bud?"

The next day she'd forgotten him, preoccupied with a newly acquired hickey and a ghastly sore throat, wondering if money was worth such trouble. She'd forgotten him, at least, until 4:15, when a very average man with a very not average face strolled into the Bean: shoes tied, scarf neat, satchel double buckled.

"I told you to get your coffee somewhere else."

"And I told you I was curious," he said, setting vascular, rough-knuckled hands flat on the counter. "And I'm nothing if not honest, darling."

She smiled.

"Earth to Hope," Andi sing-sang. "Your presence is requested back in the mortal coil."

The chime jingled when she opened the café door—and out poured a waterfall.

The stink of burnt coffee was tougher than an uppercut. Thunderheads of smoke greyed out the chandeliers inside. Stepping over the flooded threshold, Hope's leather Manolo Blahniks splashed in a shallow sea of coffee stretching from wall to wall. All the percolators shook as they boiled and overflowed. All the machines rattled, spurting endless espressos on the floor. All the toasters burned bright orange, charring grease and panini crumbs. A thousand teabags floated like drowned beetles in the tepid ocean, and as Andi waved her arms about in panic, struggling to pull Hope from the wrecked café, all thought received an eraser-heavy makeover from the whiteboard of Hope's mind. In red Sharpie, in block letters, a shaking hand wrote one thought, one word, one name.

Killian.

CHAPTER SIX

ECHO

E ventually, Hope found Saga the barista in the kitchen behind the bakery counter.

"Stay here," she'd commanded Andi. "Call the police."

Hope had dashed into the café, wading through the black lake to pull the fire alarm, only to find it smashed. She called Saga's name. Shouted it. Yelled it. Checked under the tables, in the break room, in the bathrooms and the supply closet, every locker in the locker room. No answer. No corpse. Nothing, no one to be found, but still one place to check, the place Hope knew she'd be.

One industrial oven. Forty inches. Five cubic feet.

She vaulted over the counter.

Fifty pounds of Costa Rican coffee.

She ran for the double doors.

Orthodontic jaw wiring.

She shouldered through against the tide.

Bottle of superglue.

She crashed into the flood.

One sledgehammer.

In the kitchen, the tide was red.

Andi barged in behind her—Hope turned—Andi screamed, tearing her hair in horror as Hope fought to wrestle her back into the front room. They tussled across the seating area, overturning a table and two chairs before finally crashing into coffee-stained, smoke-smudged heaps on the sidewalk.

While Andi sobbed, shielding her face as if her palms could banish the image, Hope stared blankly at the black sky. Crows cawed. Gulls shrieked. Police sirens whined in the distance. Though she was aware of these sounds, their cacophony growing closer, she didn't hear them. Not really. She couldn't hear because all she could do was see. See Saga the barista's bones broken at the wrists, the elbows, the knees, the ankles, the hips, the shoulders, and even the spine until her busted body pretzeled just so to fit snug in the industrial oven. Door open. Racks removed. Unplugged and never turned on.

The oven hadn't been his weapon. It'd been her coffin.

Shattered limbs contorted inside its metal confines, Saga's head had been positioned perfectly straight and precisely upright so her mouth could be wired open to transform her jutting, unhinged jaw into a skin bag brimming with coffee beans. A suckling pig with an apple, waiting for the spit. But of all the gory details, it wasn't the splintered bone, the dried cascades of blood, or the dislocated mandible that pressed the branding iron to Hope's memory, searing the image there permanently.

It was the eyes.

They'd been glued open. The right was glazed with milky death. The blood vessels in the left had been thoroughly burst, splotching the whites bright red.

Do you make red eyes or not?

The police arrived.

———

After several failed attempts to resuscitate her from catatonia outside the café, Andi was admitted to the hospital under observation. The constables attempted to question her while she was slack-faced, prone, and strapped to the bed with medical restraints before Hope chased them out with all the furor of a lion driving hyenas from the den. They took the opportunity to interrogate her in the cafeteria. Hope saw Saga's eye reflected in the dirty linoleum, in the vinyl table, in the spit-shine on the constables' badges. The first's upper lip hid under a wispy attempt at a handlebar 'stache; the other sported a two-haired mole jutting from the crease of his nostril.

Could they get her something warm to sip—coffee, perhaps? It took ten seconds of languishing under her vacant stare to realize their own absurdity. They asked if she spoke Icelandic, she nodded, and then the questions came.

"What time did the two of you arrive at the café?" asked Sad-Moustache.

"I dunno. Bit before seven, I guess."

"Did you know the victim?" asked Beetle-Mole.

"She makes my tea."

"You charged into a flooded, smoking building in a mad search for this woman," said Sad-Moustache. "Clearly you must have been close."

"I knew her name, if that's what constitutes *close*," she said. "Look." Hands down on the table. "Handlebar. Bugface." She addressed them individually, leaning from one to the other. "I've bought my London Fogs from that barista every weekday morning at 6:55 for the past two years."

The constables exchanged befuddled glances at their new nicknames, perhaps coming to a mutual realization that they'd failed to introduce themselves.

"She wasn't a friend. She was barely an acquaintance. She was just a constant in my life who happened to make the best

43

cheap tea within a mile of my office. Of course I went on a *mad search* for her." Hope huffed back in the plastic chair. "I wanted my fucking tea."

A pause to doodle notes in their flip pads.

"And where were you, Miss Rippa?" Sad-Moustache asked. "Before seven, of course."

"The hell's that supposed to mean?"

"Simply standard procedure, Miss Rippa."

"Dotting i's, crossing t's," said Beetle-Mole.

"I was with my girlfriend all night. Y'know, the one you were barking at for half an hour while she drooled at the ceiling?"

"Can she corroborate that?" There was no threat or menace in Beetle-Mole's voice—it *was* standard procedure, dotting of i's and t's—but the fact did nothing to cool the rolling boil in Hope's gut.

"Gee, officer, I don't know." Hope rose from her chair. Loomed across the table, teeth clenched. "Why don't you try asking once they take her off sedation to keep her from trying to gouge her eyes out, you bumbling, brain-aborted cock jockey. But just so you're aware?" She checked her Tiffany watch, undid the clasp, and shoved it in their faces. "Visiting hours are over."

Hope left the hospital, abandoning the €10,000 timepiece she'd purchased with Killian's paycheck in a curbside trash can.

———

If she screams loud enough and the acoustics are just so, a woman lives for a moment after dying.

Killian had told her that once, a few years back, when she dug too deep into his darker life with derisive questions— striking bedrock, breaking the shovel. As Hope walked the befogged streets of Grandi, cornered equally by old fish warehouses and barren fields of dirt, the memory tar-stuck between folds in her brain.

Bludgeoning worked best. Blunt force trauma to the head. Be sneaky, but not so sneaky she doesn't hear you coming. Fast, but not so fast the fear doesn't spark. And then the scream. The blow. The blow kills her, cuts off the scream—but the echo, well, the echo keeps screaming, doesn't it? In a tunnel, perhaps, or under a bridge. An abandoned building, one with high ceilings. A church, she'd thought then, as they'd conversed inside his at Fjöðurfjall, back when it had been sparkly and new.

That echo hangs in the air, he'd said, like the ghost of the girl gone. A memorial of sorts. One last taste of this world before the ferryman to the next pushes off the shore. She lives after dying, if only for a second.

Would Hope's scream echo too? Or would the mist muffle it, leaving the hammer to snuff her existence easy as a candle flame? She wondered if this was knowledge Killian had gained in his early days, his experimental teenage days before his crimes became meticulous works of macabre art.

Spotting the sparkle of the bay and the great black box of a building where her loft roosted, Hope unknotted her fists, letting the waves lapping at sea rock lull her into a cautious calm as she made her way home.

She'd asked why this only applied to women. Men didn't scream, Killian had said, and before she could roll her eyes, he'd amended: "Men rarely scream. They blubber for their lives, then their mothers. Such mewling rarely echoes."

Hope shut the apartment building door, basking in the foyer's light. The door buzz-locked behind her. Before ascending the steps to her fourth-floor nest, she looked back onto the expanse of Shore Walk, where the fog was too thick to see shadows. But she saw one anyway. She always saw one, every night, standing just there.

A shadow in a priest's collar with a hammer in his hand.

After entering her flat, quadruple-locking the door, and throwing her bag down on the polished oak table, Hope discovered through the worst means—a routine flipping-on of the TV to the evening news—that blood loss had not been Saga's cause of death, but rather a combination of drowning and boiling from the inside out as coffee was forcibly funneled down her throat.

Hope rushed to the wall of floor-to-ceiling glass facing the sea, tore open the sliding door, and ran out onto the balcony, gulping ocean air until the salt spray slowed her hyperventilation. The elderly neighbors' cat squeezed through the metal banister dividing their balconies, figure-eighting through her legs.

"Hey, Biscuit." The shaggy tabby beast kneaded her shins until Hope hauled her up. The purring engine against her chest helped melt the lump of lard stuck in her throat. "You won't believe the day I've had. Wanna chat over kibble and tea?"

She carried Biscuit inside. Once she'd spent an hour in the tub scrubbing off a layer of skin, trying and failing to be rid of the stench of coffee, Hope fixed her tea. She managed three sips before vomiting in the sink.

CHAPTER SEVEN

LA PIE VOLEUSE

A week went by.

Peering past climbing ivy through the time-stained glass of Fjöðurfjall's bird sanctuary, Hope watched Killian soothe a half-blind sea eagle. He stroked its head with gentle compassion, one in direct contrast to those other things he did with his hands.

Killian fit in with the raptors and corvids. From his sharp face to his sharper gaze, his predatory eyes and dangerous curiosity, Hope had sometimes considered him more animal than man. She absentmindedly stroked the magpie feather tattooed down her arm. She closed her eyes. The goosebumps and the ink. Fresh mud on the wind. They carried her back in time to a shift in their lives: a transshipment point that'd carried their old selves away in exchange for newer, stranger identities. Years after leaving him, when they'd both begun earning certain reputations, they'd reconnected.

OCTOBER, 2012

"You know why they call you the Magpie, don't you?"

47

They strolled down Old Aberdeen's High Street, pre-dawn. The ancient cobbles reached up to trip Hope at every corner, but Killian knew better than to steady her. To touch her. They'd been doing business together for the past year via snail mail, but this was the first ground rule she'd set before physically allowing him back into her life in a strictly professional capacity.

"Your... clientele?"

"My clients are idiots," she said.

"But you do know why they call you—"

"Cus magpies steal shiny things," she mocked. "Collect stuff, like tiny dragons with tiny hordes." Killian opened his mouth to speak, but Hope cut him off. "It's not even true. It's all that old French play's fault. *La Pie Voleuse,* the one where the servant's accused of stealing silverware and almost gets executed, but really it was a magpie all along? Y'know they did a study with a bunch of magpies, and even when they did go for the bauble over the food, which was only, like, twice out of sixty-something tries, they dropped it. It's a myth. The nickname is stupid—my clients are stupid. Plus, I pay for everything."

The clack of his Oxfords; the tap of her sneakers. Hope squinted up at Killian's quiet smirk.

"What, didn't expect me to know pedantic nineteenth century trash? Forget what I *used* to do for a living when the sun went down?" she grumbled. "Rich old men love to talk when they're happy."

"Right. Forgive me." Killian chuckled, humorless. "I suppose you'd be strutting about in stilettos rather than trainers, were that still the case."

"Hell, I wouldn't even be here. Look at the state of the street. Bound to break an ankle." She kicked one of the road's ancient, jutting bricks for emphasis. "You'd be surprised how many johns think they can impress a down-home country gal with pompous crap. Like, you're already paying how much cash to get between my legs? Shove me down and get on with the show, bud, and let me go home when it's over. I mean, it's not like the girth of a wallet makes its owner's bullshit smell less like a pigsty."

Hope was keenly aware of Killian's dislike for her former livelihood, however high end or well paid. She smirked at his discomfort, at what she knew was jealousy that'd persisted after their breakup. She knew, in his mind's projector of an eye, he still saw some fat cat from London or Edinburgh strip off his tie, unbuckle his belt, and pull down her hosiery on 500 thread-count linens just waiting to be ruined every time she brought up the subject.

"Do what you love and let it kill you," he said.

"Do what you're good at," Hope countered, "and never love again."

"Words to live by."

"Thinking that way makes the living part easier, at least."

They'd stopped. When she noticed Killian looking at the ruby-crusted ring dangling from the chain around her neck, she re-tucked it behind her shirt.

"It looked better on your finger," he said.

"You looked better when I didn't know what you were."

Sadness was a rare animal on the face of a murderer as proficient as Killian, so whenever it emerged from the brush, it was bright as day despite the smile designed to hide it. "You should come with me. To Iceland."

The sudden proposition puzzled Hope quiet until she decoded the words. "Why the hell would I go to Iceland with you?"

"I've become your best client with no signs of slowing down. Why wouldn't you? Might save on petrol and airfare."

"And lose everything I save on leasing office space."

"As if you're not hemorrhaging overheads in Edinburgh already," he scoffed.

"I ain't your dog. I won't follow you around like one."

"All hungry animals follow the herds and hands they eat from, and none are as generous as mine," he said. "Think of all the assets you launder through the fishing boats here. Forget Fraserburgh and Peterhead—imagine Neskaupstaður, Vestmannaeyjar, Grindavík instead, plus all the barren fields and storerooms your scheming heart desires. Not to mention making it simpler than ever to service your Scandinavian clients. Don't think that uptick in northeast-bound flights has gone unnoticed, neither by me nor your logistics team. The Swedes get more and more ambitious every year, do they not? You can't use your agency as a cover forever. Not from here."

Hope bit the inside of her cheek, searching for the ulterior motive lurking behind decent rationale.

"My business acumen may not so much as approach par with yours, darling, but I do know a thing or two about steering clear of the legal radar's line of sight. It's time to flush your team clean, build up a new front, and embrace a change of scenery to stay abreast of Johnny Law."

"Why wouldn't I just fuck off to Sweden, by that logic?"

"Sweden may be a safe haven, but Iceland's a utopia right here on Earth. Who would think to look for creatures, there, such as you and I?"

Before she could dig yet another crater in the pocked moon of her inner cheek, Hope continued walking. It kept her from having to look at his face while she digested the idea. The opportunity. The trick she knew it was—and the temptation to fall for it, even now.

"It still suits you, you know," he said.

"What does?"

"Your alias. Magpie."

"Oh yeah?" As they turned down Meston Walk, Hope ghosted the quill of the feather tattooed on her arm. "How you figure?"

It took a spell for Hope to realize Killian had stopped walking. When she turned, his stare burned ultramarine by way of the lamplight on the corner. A second-story window glowed in the cottage across the road. Neither moved to close the yards between them. Hope's shoulders stiffened to protect the back of her neck. She eyed the dark windows. The empty sidewalks.

"Magpies are vicious," he said. "Magpies are predators."

"Don't—"

"Magpies murder baby songbirds when their parents are away."

"Stop."

"The mother returns to the nest to find nothing but feathers and blood."

"I'm not a killer."

"Does the magpie eat the baby? Was she hungry, or bored, or driven by instinct, by nature? Measurable in the biology of her black heart—"

"I'm not like you, Killian!"

The cottage curtains stirred—Hope held her breath—and then the light went out.

Trembling, she reiterated softly, "I'm not you."

Killian watched her for a beat. He scraped his middle fingernail against the pad of his thumb. Space-time froze. The sunrise stalled. Even the gulls stopped their trilling, as if the weight of his coming judgment brought the Earth's spin to a standstill.

"No." He returned his hand to its pocket. "Not yet."

Hope's heart made quick acquaintance with her feet. The sunrise cast Killian in bloody bas-relief, spawning a shadow long enough to touch the tips of her toes as first light stretched between the flats.

"What're you on about, not yet?"

"Magpies are misunderstood. Mistreated by common thought and myths perpetuated over hundreds of years." He stared ahead at a thing she couldn't see before returning his attention to her. A spotlight. A target. "And when the sun strikes them? Well." A soft, breathy laugh, insidious in every way. "Then they are stunning creatures, indeed."

Killian vanished around the corner and back down the High Street, leaving Hope blinded by crimson rays. It wasn't until he was gone that she realized he hadn't answered the question. He likely never would. It was his way to make people answer questions for themselves.

As the northern sun warmed her back, and as she clawed her tattooed arm, Hope released a shuddering breath to dispel the memory. Peering through waxy leaves and roses, she watched Killian ease the injured eagle back into its cage. She caught sight of his arm slathered in red through patinas of yellow-green pollen and water stains. He hadn't worn a falconry gauntlet or glove. The eagle's beak went unmuzzled. Injured though it was, the beast could have plucked Killian's eyes, torn artery from neck. Hope wondered absently if the creature knew the nature of the man handling it, caring for it—wondered, then, if Killian's innate savagery formed an unspoken bond of understanding. Could the eagle sense it, the bestial equality between them? Was that why Killian never cared for loons or for plovers, ducks or swans or gulls?

Hope turned her back on the sanctuary. She ached for the bluster of the sea by her loft. What was she doing here? Why had she come?

She imagined the same hands that had just caressed the eagle's head jamming a screwdriver through the hyoid bone of some unsuspecting bastard; the tongue, the hard palate, the skull and then the brain inside, squelching, crunching, gushing red.

She imagined those hands tracing trails down the small of her back. His palms clutching her hips. His fingers grasping her thighs. The moan in her ear, the hot breath on her neck, the grip on her waist as he thrust inside her and the gasp she unleashed as he groaned her name.

Her real name.

"Hope?"

She jolted. She hadn't heard the sanctuary door nor the swish of shoes in amber grass. Killian offered his palms in placation, stopping three yards away. Blood slicked his skin where the eagle had perched. It soaked his rolled-up, black cassock sleeve, revealing a forearm banded with lean muscle, black hair, and dark-green veins.

"I wasn't expecting you," he said. "There's coffee in the cafeteria, if you'd like."

Smoking toasters. Rattling percolators. A broken barista stuffed in an oven.

"I don't drink coffee."

"I know." He lowered his hands. "But there's tea as well."

Heated needles pricked the backs of her eyeballs. They teared. She blinked. She rolled her eyes up and laughed, as if a laugh could disguise the confused emotions fiddle-playing her face off-key. "Got any Moroccan mint?"

For a moment, Killian looked as if he'd extend a hand to lead her there.

He didn't.

"I always keep your favorite here," he said. "Just in case."

53

———

The cafeteria was spartan, just sizeable enough to accommodate Fjöðurfjall's modest population of 102. Bleached winter sun streamed in through the windows, spotlighting Hope's hands as she wrung them, white-knuckled, on a table spotted with rings. Steamed mint perfumed the air.

Watching Killian's back as he rinsed his arm clean in the sink, the thought crossed her mind that he might slip cyanide in her tea. But as quickly as it came, it went. Poison wasn't his style. He liked to use his hands.

The talon wounds kept dribbling as he set a mug down in front of her. A droplet reddened the tea. She'd never been less thirsty. She'd never been more thirsty. She settled for warming her palms on the mug, letting the aroma sauna her wind-chapped lips.

"I'd ask what brings you down from Reykjavík, darling, but I fear I wouldn't receive a straight answer," Killian said, settling across from her.

"Why's that?"

"Judging from the look on your face, you don't seem to know yourself."

"You got blood in my tea."

"Twelve years might've healed the bite marks, but I happen to recall you enjoying the taste. You'd get this wild look in your eye, like a jackal. Red on your lips and your teeth. Your smile."

The blood sank and dispersed. She slurped, mint and iron. She burned her tongue but kept it down; she'd been practicing her tea-drinking after what the media had dubbed The Coffee Pot Incident. Incident, not murder. Murder was a dirty word.

"Why don't you wear gloves when you handle the big birds?" She regarded his arm, its burnish of talon scars. The fresh punctures had mostly stopped bleeding, but she regretted asking. It was too easy to imagine it wasn't his own. "Having a go at self-flagellation?" she asked, dunking her discomfort in a thick coat of sarcasm.

Killian's smile hid behind the rim of his own mug, but the lines in his face were unmistakable. She'd traced them so many times, lounging in his bed. They'd been deepened by age, of course, but while faces changed, expressions seldom did.

"Such a practice would imply I've done something wrong," he said, sipping his red eye. "Have I?"

He'd replaced his discarded glasses with a carbon copy. Hope despised their thin, shiny frames, their perpetually polished lenses. They should've provided some sort of bulwark from the pierce of his stare, like glasses were wont to do, but their sheen served only to sharpen his laser sight.

In response to her silence and refusal to look away, Killian removed his priest's collar and loosened the buttons on his cassock. "These birds have suffered," he said. "And they have suffered enough without hoods on their heads, or leather under their feet." He absentmindedly rubbed the cuts honeycombing his arm. "They deserve compassion. Kindness." He went to sip his coffee but stopped an inch from his mouth. "Contact."

"Or maybe you're just trying to hide defensive wounds."

"You think my playthings stand a chance to land so much as a scratch?"

"I dunno, Killian." Hope set her tea down with a decisive smack. "That scrape on your wrist suggests some might."

His smirk fell. "You know what I do, Magpie. You help me do it."

"I don't help you. I take your money and look away."

"I'm relatively sure playing the supplier makes you an accomplice, under most interpretations of the law—"

Hope slammed her hands down on the table and leapt to her feet. "You killed Saga!"

His eyes didn't flit to the open windows as she'd expected. He didn't lean back not even half a millimeter, didn't tense or flinch as she hoped he might. Her explosion had no effect except for the hardening of his face. He adjusted his glasses as if her outburst had thrown their balance.

Wilting under the weight of his non-reaction, Hope whispered, "Her name was Saga," and flopped back in her chair. "Did you even know that?"

Quiet passed between them for an age, an eon. Crows croaked outside. Feet shuffled on the sidewalks as the village slowly woke from its midday siesta, citizens making sluggish beelines for the church. Killian's church. The thought of him preaching peace to mushy minds brought bile to her tongue.

"She was a barista at Café Svartur on Miðborg. Everyone at the agency gets their coffee from some... some ridiculous, bougie shithouse charging 900 króna for flat whites that taste like watered-down sewage, but Saga made the best coffee for less than half the price. Best tea west of Hallgrímskirkja too." Hope studied her reflection in the lukewarm piss in her mug. "She was *eighteen years old*."

Hope thrust the mug. Moroccan mint splashed Killian's cassock, his neck, the hollow between his collarbones. This time, he flinched. She couldn't even savor it; anger stole her satisfaction. She tossed the empty mug aside and it shattered on the floor.

"I'm not blind, Kil. I sure ain't stupid." Hope rose again from the chair. Slow, now. Methodical. "Don't expect me to believe you picked her name from a hat."

"I don't wear hats, darling. Only glasses."

Again, she slammed her hands. Her palms tingled.

Blinking tea and perhaps a drop of blood from his lashes, Killian appraised Hope, hands folded, as a millionaire might appraise a mare whose spirit he intended to break. She felt her resolve waver. Killian's serenity in the wake of her outburst chilled her to the marrow. Animals—no, predators, after all, were most composed before the killing blow.

"Please, sit."

She didn't.

"Fine." He drank his coffee. Dabbed tea from his face as the church bell gonged. "I don't choose, Hope. Victims choose themselves. And on a small, cold rock like this?" His eyes pulled an orbit, as if to address Iceland at large. "They are bound to be someone you know."

Killian stood, collecting his mug and ignoring the ceramic shards on the floor.

"Lunch is served after Mass." For a moment, he lingered. "Will I see you there?"

Hope gathered her nerve. "No." She meant it to be strong, but it came out a mumble. "Saga makes better tea than you."

Her walk to the door, through the exit, and down the path to the parking lot was a quick one, but not quick enough to escape Killian's compulsive need for the final word.

"Made," he said. "She *made* better tea."

CHAPTER EIGHT

HANNA

Hope had initially refused to fill Killian's next order due to its record-breaking size, remote location, and a hefty dose of plain, old-fashioned fear. Saga hadn't been a coincidence. The parallels were too stark. Too obvious. He could claim it was happenstance until the sun rose in the west, but she knew the murder had been a show for a one-woman audience, and she had the only ticket.

Something like that couldn't happen again, not if Hope wanted to protect herself. She was half an inch from arriving at the decision to never fill his orders again, at least until she more closely examined the delivery coordinates on the GPS.

Private airstrip. He was leaving.

It took sixteen days to gather the items under the scrutiny of Reykjavík's panicked police force, but time was not an issue. Time was a cost concern shouldered by clients well aware of the difficulty of procurement, plus inevitable incidentals. Incidentals like increased maritime security and the tripling of officer presence on nighttime side streets, all as Christmas and the new year came and quietly went. Three SUVs, two horse trailers, and one unmarked church van later, Killian's goods arrived on a skinny runway east of Sólheimajökull, an outlet glacier just unimpressive enough to be unpopular with tourists in January at 3am.

Hope patted the van driver's hand. The poor sod was visibly shaking behind the wheel with a black bag over his head after the ordeal of obeying blind directions for the past several miles. She promised him a carte-blanche favor in exchange, told him to wait for a lapdog named Gisli to relieve him from his post to the passenger seat, and swung from the vehicle.

Killian waited by the jet in a maroon tweed suit, at once shaded by its wing and gilded by the airstrip's articulated yellow lights. He watched her cross the tarmac with eyes she couldn't reconcile as human or demon. Something in between, or beyond. Something worse.

"You took your sweet time."

Amusement revealed the better angels of his smile. Hope ripped off their wings. "And you damn well know why." She spat her half-smoked cigarette at the shiny toes of his shoes. "This is ridiculous, Killian, this whole situation—"

He cut her off with a cigarette stomp. Not so much as a sizzle escaped before filter became one with pavement. From the breast pocket of his dress coat, he pulled a rubber-banded roll of hundreds twice as thick as a Wall Street cigar.

"Your expert handling of this ridiculous situation has warranted a bonus well beyond expectation. I assume you're fine with stretching your fee into two installments? This will more than tide you over until then, I believe."

Hope stuck out her hand without answering, feeling like a dog on its back. "Care to explain the *ridiculous* bit? All this fuss, Killian, and for what? It's..."

"Ridiculous?"

Hope huffed. The roll dropped into her glove. Not

bothering to count the bills, she tucked it down her bra without an ounce of modesty, a joey to its pouch.

"Your worry lines have always been like beacons at sea, you know," he said. "Hard to miss, even before the years made them mainstays."

"Is that a poetic way of saying I've aged?"

"We all age, darling. Look at me."

Older, certainly, forty-five to her thirty-three, but still beautiful—and beautiful was the exact right word, stuck as he was in the sweet spot between masculinity and effeminacy. She said nothing, however, and gave nothing away.

"Listen, I'm heading off—"

"No shit." Hope lit another cigarette and used its tip like a laser pointer to address the jet, whose engines had begun to whir.

"Going on a bit of a European tour," he continued. "Waiting for the proverbial heat to cool."

"What, you on spring break? And here I thought it was January."

"You know well what I mean," Killian said under his breath. "And you know it'd be wise to consider a similar strategy."

Were she a wolf, her hackles would rise, but Hope was human, unbearably so, and to account for her shortcomings she glowered at full nuclear power. "I'm not leaving Andi here." The force of her own commitment caught her off-guard. "I won't."

"The decision is yours, darling. I merely want the best for you. But I needn't be the one to tell you that the longer you stay, the worse things will get."

"I don't need you to tell me anything. What I need you to do is leave the country."

The smoke she blew in his face didn't provoke so much as a blink.

"All set, sir."

Hired muscle had finished loading the plane. Three men formed a line of bulging biceps and cut quads beside the cargo bay. Taking in their blindfolds and the wet cotton plugging their ears, Hope wondered how well these Mister Universes were paid. Maybe they'd soon be subject to a one-man firing squad just to be sure they didn't quack. Somehow she doubted it. With two senses revoked, how they loaded the plane in the first place was a mystery, and likely involved training too expensive and time-consuming to dispose of so carelessly.

Killian looked to them, and back at her, eyes narrow in thought.

"I'll be fine," she grumbled. "I'm good at my job."

"You are," he said, sincere to the letter and, in a microscopic way, sad. He surveyed the empty land beyond her. Something, *there*—not beyond her, but behind his glasses, in the creases of fine crow's feet was something uncatchable, even with the most effective of dredges and trawls. An undiscovered species of expression. "That you are."

They went their separate ways. Then:

"Killian?" He stopped. "For once, I haven't got a milliliter's worth of wanting to know what the fuck you're up to. But I swear, if you do anything, I will find whatever it is you love and set it on fire. I'll watch it burn, spit on its ashes, and leave a tape recording of whatever mewling, pathetic sound it makes while it dies playing on a loop on your fuckin' pillowcase. You hear me? I *swear*."

A pause passed in the rush of the jet's priming engines.

"To what?" he asked. "To God?"

Hope whisked across the tarmac, holding the threat close to her chest to keep her resolve from crumbling. She climbed into the back of the church van. Twisting on her heels, she crouched on the vehicle's lip just as rain began to spit.

He wouldn't be able to hear from his perch on the jet's collapsible staircase, but Hope knew he could read lips. "To *your* God."

She slammed the sliding door.

————

The phone rang the moment Hope sank into the desk chair in Rippa Royale's corner office. She rested her chin on laced fingers, watched the city lights trace jetways to the dark bay, a veritable end-of-universe void unlit by a moon rendered nonexistent by clouds. Beyond the black, a grey smudge of mountain stood as a barely-there reminder of the world's existence beyond the pulse pounding in her ears. She checked the watch she no longer had, then glanced up at one of four time zone wall clocks. 6:14am.

Brrrrring, brrring brrring.

"Go for Rippa," she told the speakerphone. Without her assistant to screen calls, she hadn't thought to check the caller ID.

"Hope, don't hang up." She was about to do just that, finger hovering over the key. "It's Hanna."

"I know that much. Fuck off."

"Give me four minutes."

"No."

"Two?"

"One. Make it interesting."

The first time they'd met, the younger woman—a plain-pretty, red-maned Pole freshly interned to the nation's top newspaper—had been seated in the intentionally wonky seat opposite Hope's desk, stuttering through an interview for a feature in the biannual cover edition of Iceland's Who's Who. The second time, Hope had pulled into the lot at Fjöðurfjall to fetch a last-minute invoice from Killian just as evening Mass let out, and atop the flood of villagers waterfalling back to their cottages, she'd seen Killian with a hand on Hanna's shoulder, radiating patriarchal warmth. She'd seen Hanna simpering, perhaps under the weight of his priceless spiritual wisdom, but more likely beneath his rapacious presence. A good Catholic girl in search of a good Catholic priest beyond the reach of the city's sins. It was no small wonder she'd be there. It made sense, but the sight had tightened Hope's grip on the wheel, and one year later she could still hear the leather squeal under her gloves.

"You were at Café Svartur when—"

"Is this on the record?" The chastised silence on the line said *Yes*. "I'm hanging up."

"No!"

The word had a taste that gave Hope pause. Bitter lemon, the tang of biting coins with a mouthful of silver fillings.

Desperation.

"Please, I just need a statement. One little quote."

Hope had been a peon once, crushed beneath the boot heels of totalitarian managers and onerous clientele. While Hanna had been promoted from intern to associate reporter at *Fréttablaðið* two weeks after their interview, any cursory glance at the paper's middle pages confirmed she'd been thrown into the inescapable ball pit of fluff journalism. The Coffee Pot Incident could be her ladder. Hope might be a demon, but she wasn't the Devil. It wasn't Hanna's fault she'd been caught in Killian's floodlights. The girl didn't know how to hide. Didn't know she had to.

Hope sighed. "Go on."

The relief was plain in Hanna's muffled guff of relief. "The girl. Um, the victim. You knew her?"

"A bit." Hope offered an edited version of what she'd told Killian regarding Saga's tea-making skills and tragic youth.

"And how—how..."

"How, how what? How'd she bite the bullet?"

Hanna's voice deflated. "How are you?"

Hope squinted at the phone. Opened her mouth. Closed it. *How am I?*

"How are you doing? O-off the record, I mean."

A tear fallen from cheek to paper blurred ink on some document, firing Hope from one dimension to the next. "I'm..." She blinked, blotting the drop with a tissue. The ink smeared, erasing the name of an employee she'd intended to check on. "Why you asking?"

"Hope—"

"That's my name, yes."

In her deep breath in and slow breath out, Hope heard Hanna gather her grit. David facing Goliath: dropping his sling and stone in favor of peace with the beast.

"I know you dislike me, even if I don't know why," said Hanna. "But as much as *Fréttabladið* paints you Queen of Mount Business Management, I know you're human. Just like me. And humans who see, the... the things you've seen? Sometimes they're not okay. And that's okay. So I just wanted to know, I guess," she said, meek as a mole rat. "How are you?"

Another tear came as a surprise, banishing the sardonic, knee-jerk laugh that involuntarily rose in her throat whenever normal folk assumed she was normal too. The things Hope had seen... experienced... did and continued to do.

It wasn't just the foul sex she'd endured for cash at an age when she should've been in school. It wasn't the weight of saggy old men grunting and sweating on top of her that haunted her more than Saga's dead eyes. It was the grunting and sweating of one particular old man, the best-paying Old Man, the Old Man who had wrapped her hair in pigtails, dressed her like a private schoolgirl, and called her Bunny when he pressed her down on the bed.

When she'd returned home from her very last night of prostitution, pale-faced and nine hours late, the concern in Killian's eye had nearly broken her. He'd slipped out of his priest's collar, having just returned from the night shift tending the depraved souls of HMP Barlinnie, back when he worked as a prison chaplain in Glasgow. The concern became suspicion when she refused to speak, couldn't speak—when she curled up in the bath and didn't unlock the door when he knocked and said her name so softly it cracked her already shattered heart. But he was never one to pester. He'd let the matter drop. Hope recovered. They never spoke of it, not once. Killian still didn't know what happened that night, the only secret she'd ever kept from him.

What happened to Saga—what Killian did to her, what Hope had helped him do—was a shock. A terror, to be sure. But Saga was nothing compared to what Hope had found fourteen years ago in a barber chair in the Old Man's padlocked office.

"Hope?" Hanna pressed. "Are you still there?"

Hope wanted to crush the phone. The desk. Throw the leather chair, break the window walls, burn the magazines arranged in an immaculate fan on the coffee table and then the table too.

How am I?

The question was so foreign, so unfamiliar as to be unpalatable. Spoiled caviar. Chunky milk. Ipecac by the quarter cup, but she needed to purge, and the need to purge broke her like she would have broken her office.

How am I?

The secret scorched the tip of her tongue, but she swallowed it. Hers was a secret never meant to see the light of day, never meant to touch another's ears. She erased the Old

Man and the barber chair from her mind, focusing on the now, how was she *now,* and was both surprised and ashamed at the answer she found. It snapped her voice in two as she admitted it, for some reason, to a woman she irrationally hated.

"Not so great."

———

"Miss Rippa?"

Hope's longtime assistant prairie-dogged through the office's open door at seven sharp. She hugged a pink sequin folder to her chest, the whites of her eyes bulging like marbles. Despite having served at Hope's side since Rippa Royale's early days in Edinburgh, Ellie had never used her boss's first name and never seemed to be comfortable even using her last. Hope never encouraged her to do or feel otherwise. Not because she disliked her assistant, not because she thought her inferior—she wouldn't have purged everyone from the company payroll except Ellie during the transfer to Iceland if that were the case—but because she rather *did* like her and didn't want to entangle Ellie in the spiderweb of her nighttime ventures. Even if it meant being a bitch.

"M-Miss Rippa?"

Hope roused from a sleeping slouch in her chair, sucking oxygen through her nose until she oriented herself. *Office. Office Building. Reykjavík. Iceland.* She straightened. Heard the dial tone of a phone line gone dead. Had she fallen asleep venting to Hanna about the rumbling percolators haunting her dreams?

She hung up, restoring the silence and quashing her self-disgust. There was nothing to blame the moment of weakness on other than her own lack of composure.

"Miss Rippa, there is worker too... ah... *kirurgia*?" Hope waited. "*Helvetti.* Marie, she, er... Marie is—"

"*Puhu*, Ellie! Christ's sake."

"Marie is very ill, Miss Rippa."

Hope switched to her assistant's native Finnish with some effort. "How bad?"

"Bad enough to be in hospital, I suppose."

"Admitted?"

"Undergoing surgery, I'm afraid."

"Guess her drinking habit finally caught up with that heart defect of hers."

Ellie's nose wrinkled the way it always did when Hope said something uncouth. They'd been colleagues for over a decade and the girl had only ever spoken out of turn twice. She wondered if Ellie went home to the English husband she thought Hope knew nothing about and cursed her to *helvetti* in their flat in Breiðholt on bad days.

Hope tapped her pen on the tear-wrinkled document stuck to her elbow. Marie's assignment was crucial. "Right. Marie was supposed to fetch half a wardrobe's worth of lingerie for that whore in Milan."

"The... actress," Ellie squeaked.

"And the only reason you'd be bugging me with this is...?"

Ellie retrieved two private flight clearance cards from her bedazzled folder. Her hand shook as she presented them like condolence cards rather than tickets to Italy.

Hope hated Italy.

"All the other agents are overseas with clients," Ellie mumbled. "Logistics said—"

"To give it to me. Of course they did. Dick-juggling trash, aren't they? Don't answer that."

Hope waved her over. She wanted to snatch the passes but believed in the innocence of the messenger. Ellie's ramrod posture sagged in relief when the exchange came to a peaceful end. The boarding pass demanded her presence at the airport in three hours.

"It's okay," Hope said.

Despite Hope's reassurance, Ellie backpedaled—a quart-sized penguin from a pint-sized polar bear that hadn't yet spotted the easy meal.

"Take the day off, Ell." Hope used the desk as a crutch to rise. Exhaustion announced its presence with trumpets and fanfare. Blinking hard, she uncapped a fountain pen and wrote a sloppily initialed note. "If anyone gives you shit, slap 'em in the face with this."

She collected her belongings, sluggish and slow. Ellie read the note. Her Scandinavian skin strawberried. *Day off, piss off,* it read in English, Icelandic, and textbook Arabic, to cover all the bases that could possibly arise in the office.

Hope assured Ellie she'd send an actual agency-wide email for the office to expect her absence. "Go home."

"Thank you," she said. "Safe travels, Miss Rippa. Please take care of yourself."

Hope stopped in the hallway, turning just in time to catch Ellie sticking the note to her folder's inside flap as if it were a treasure. Did Hope really look enough like yesterday's lunch to earn a well-wish from her penguin assistant?

Saga was eighteen years old—the same age Hope had been at the Bethesda Bean when she'd met Killian—and while Ellie was only a few years behind Hope, she came off as much younger. She was a disturbingly easy target.

But Killian was away from Iceland for a few weeks. Maybe months. Hope clung to that reassuring fact, strutting past cubicles and ignoring *Hellos* and *Good mornings* as she left Rippa Royale, LLC, climbed into her truck, and drove home to pack with wasps in her chest.

CHAPTER NINE

A CONFESSION

Eleven days dashing about Italy buying Chantilly bustiers, lace bodysuits, and precious gem jewelry for a B-list nympho's star-studded swinger soirées had left Hope picked to bare bones. She was as good at her day job as she was at her night job; her name on the agency attested to the fact. Obedient but persistent. Subservient yet unintimidated, unafraid to argue in favor of style over extravagance without purpose. Sometimes, her clients even listened.

Despite having a knack for prescribing fashion to ornery fashionistas, she hated her day job with a passion. At least her midnight clients were doing something productive. Getting exercise. Reducing the population. What did these actors and models and self-styled socialites do with their free time besides bellyache over the difference between mink and fox fur?

The flight back to Iceland hadn't exactly been a nirvana of airborne luxury either. The stupidly long walk from Keflavík's private gate to the parking lot had done no favors for her good humor—not that she'd had any left. Removing her forehead from the steering wheel's horn, Hope started the truck, revved the engine, and rolled from the airport at 6:12 in the morning.

Andi had called on Hope's tenth day in Milan. The barbed wire of bad timing continued to prick and poke even now, as she drove to Andi's apartment two blocks from Hallgrímskirkja. They'd spoken as Hope chucked her clothes in a suitcase at the Hotel Dei Cavalieri, sluggers of suede and satin gaining torque the longer their conversation dragged on.

"You left me," Andi had said.

"Not by choice."

"You could have stayed."

"I had to work."

"Your name's on the letterhead," Andi rasped. "You could have said no."

"Not if you want more langoustine dinners," Hope said in an attempt at light-heartedness. "Chocolate cake?"

"I don't want dinner."

"Brunch, when I'm back?"

"Not hungry. Not thirsty. Coffee…"

"Andi, when's the last time you ate?"

"I don't remember…"

"Why do you sound like that?"

"I don't… I…"

"Andi?" Hope had stopped packing, a fistful of denim balled in her hand. "Andi!"

She'd paid a massive fee calling international from the hotel suite's phone to the private home of a doctor in Kópavogur who owed a no-questions-asked favor. He paid in full that night, having arrived at Andi's home by way of the spare key taped under the stairwell railing to find her clam-cold and close to comatose on the floor of the apartment. After administering Narcan and IV fluids and stabilizing her in bed, the doctor picked up the cellphone he'd dropped upon discovering the scene.

"She's okay," he'd said. "I'm disposing of her… supplies."

Driving there now, Hope still tasted blood in her mouth, having bitten clean through her cheek listening to the muffled sounds of crisis through the doctor's discarded phone, powerless in a hotel room thousands of miles away.

You're going to be fine, Andresína, I'm here to make sure of it. Just stay with me. Let's do this together. Okay, Andi? I'm right here. I'm not going anywhere, not until you're okay. Look at me. Look at—good, that's good. Here we go, Andi. Okay. There it is. See? Breathe, Andresína. You're fine. You're okay.

Hope's breath stalled. Backfired in her lungs. She fought to keep the wheel straight, to follow the lines on the road and the streetlights in the infinite winter dark as the ghost of the doctor's words assailed her.

You're fine. You're okay.

She was speeding past the striated shark tooth of Hallgrímskirkja when the massive church's acoustics amplified a scream from inside. Her foot hit the brake. The Rover skidded on a patch of ice. The oxygen crushed from her chest. She waited in the cab of the horridly quiet truck, now cockeyed on Skólavörðustígur's barren street with the windows rolled down. Goosebumps rife. Fresh air cold. Waiting, waiting—

Another scream.

Hope kicked the door open and fell from the cab, skinning palms and knees. She scrambled up and skirted the headlights, sprinting past Leif Eriksson's statue, across the paved courtyard, and through the church's open double doors.

Its innards were architectural bliss, ivory ceilings sailing higher than the skies. Its pews were simple and clean. Its floors, grey stone. The organ hung high overhead, a beautiful monster of polished metal and wood. Hope had always preferred big churches to small: so grand, so sturdy, oozing status and presence. Killian's acid could never crumble their walls. Big churches were safe. Big churches were good. Big churches were too tall to topple, too powerful to poison—and yet the snake had slithered inside just the same.

Hope slowed to a jog. A walk. A stop. An older woman, presumably a caretaker letting herself in to straighten the Bibles and sweep the floors, kneeled in the aisle before the pulpit. She could've been praying, but instead she wept. Felled by hysteria, her whole body met the ground, and Hope saw clearly the construction obscuring the altar.

Inside an extravagant confessional booth erected before the pews, the naked corpse of an elderly woman cowgirled the naked corpse of an elderly man seated in an ornate Toscano chair. A mulberry silk curtain was tied aside to expose their shame. The booth's housing was Gaboon ebony, expertly fashioned; the doorknob to the empty penitent's side was aluminum, cheaply wrought; the metal lattice separating the sides was iron, woven by hand. The victims were likely local. They were pale, yes, but paler than pale, nearly grey as the stone outside, grey as the floor and the city sky at noon. Hoods covered their heads, as if to hide their sin from God.

They'd been cut with a scalpel. Carotids clamped. Blood drained through arterial tubes connected to embalming machines. Hope knew the method as well as she knew the material. She knew every rivet holding the booth's joints in place. Bloody handprints spotted the confessional's innards. Walls. Hips. Waists. Necks. All the places one touched in the throes of sex. But Hope couldn't imagine these corpses having such vigor. Wrinkles, crepes, spider-veined legs—neither appeared younger than eighty, and the woman's wrists were restrained behind her back with rosary beads.

"How do you normally do this?" Hope breathed in the crook of Killian's neck, straddling his lap. His strong arms worked behind

her, trussing her wrists with rosaries at the small of her back.
"Where do I start? Forgive me?"

"No. Repeat after me..." The crucifix hanging from his collar bit her bare chest. "'Bless me, Father.'"

"Bless me, Father."

"'For I have sinned.'"

"For I have sinned."

One last jerk and her hands were tied.

"'It has been forever...'" Killian grabbed her thighs. "'... Since my last confession.'"

"It has been forever—" Hope bucked as he held her hips down firm, forcing her to take him all at once and fast "—since my last confession."

Killian demanded she confess her sins.

Up.

"I've fornicated with men."

Down.

"I've fornicated with women."

Up.

"I let a priest fuck me in a confessional thirty minutes before Mass."

Killian wound her long hair around his wrist, leveraging it like a leash to seize the back of her head. He yanked her close.

"You forgot one, darling."

"What?" she moaned. "Which?"

He nipped her neck. Licked the small cut clean. In a husky rasp dripping with menace and need, Killian pressed his lips to her ear and murmured, "You're going to take the Lord's name in vain." Calloused fingers caressed the curve of her shoulders. "And you'll do it over and over until I'm done with you."

. . .

Hope staggered backwards until the outside air claimed her. She gagged. Coughed. Puked on the stone. She knew the method as well as she knew the material.

She'd purchased it.

With a tortured gasp echoing the caretaker's wail, Hope bowed to her knees as a penitent before the cross. Nails in her scalp and gravel in her throat, she realized for the first time what she should've always expected.

Killian never had any intention of leaving Iceland.

CHAPTER TEN

INSPIRATION

Hope sped into Fjöðurfjall's village lot that evening, not bothering to park or kill the engine before sprinting up the black church's steps. Like the gate to Hell at the end of days, the double doors cracked open with a thunderous *bang!* and Hope was the first demon through.

"You dirty fucking liar!"

Killian looked up from a sawhorse erected in the chancel at the foot of the altar stairs. He dropped the coping saw just as Hope wrenched the collar of his work shirt and charged him against the wall. The plank he'd been cutting clattered to the floor, sending a storm surge of sawdust to sweep their shoes.

"You *lied* to me! You piece of—you... you..."

As rage congealed to gelatin in her veins, she realized whose button-up she clenched in her fists, whose body she pinned below stained-glass windows. The saw on the ground. The hammer on his toolbelt. Hope relinquished her hold. Anger turned to fear, fear to fatigue; she shook her head, met his eye, and said, in a hush, "You've never, *ever* lied to me."

"I didn't lie."

"Liar."

"I went on a tour of Europe!" he exclaimed. "I visited my sister in Belfast. Aoife. Remember her?" Hope stepped back. Killian pared his back off the wall, moving slowly so as not to spook the quarry. "I had my yearly physical with my doctor in Helsinki. Smidge of hiking in Lapland. Saw the aurora."

"You can see that here."

"It's different, there. You've got to earn it." Killian lowered his hands. Hope eyed the hammer. He undid the button-clasp so it dropped on the floor. "I hunted red deer in the Cairngorms, south of Auchallater."

Hope swallowed, nibbling her inner cheek in a desperate bid to regain composure. "Stayed near Braemar, did you?"

"Yes. The cabin. Do you remember it?"

Of course she remembered. New Year's Eve, 2009. A lodge in the woods. A table draped in blood. *It's where I taught you how to dress a stag,* said his eyes, *and then fucked you beside the body.*

Red on her chest. Red on her stomach. Red on her cheek, peeling curls of beech from the planks with her nails, bent over the table. From her periphery, Killian's right hand grappled the antlers for leverage.

"I remember."

She remembered moaning, arching her back in madness. She remembered inhaling iron, fur caught in her throat. She remembered turning toward the stench and watching the deer's dead eyes watch her.

The breath before the bullet.

Hooves hushing through the ferns.

Squatting in the dirt—the *clink* of the rifle bolt, the fog and spitting rain—the color of the bathwater when she scrubbed herself raw, crying quietly so Killian wouldn't hear as he seared venison steaks in the kitchen.

Most of all, she remembered the squelch the stag's viscera made, slopping onto wood floor.

Killian nodded slowly, as if he were a therapist helping a patient come down from a manic episode. "And then I brought lilies to my mother for her birthday. Here. Luckily enough, you were just a few hours too late to spoil the reunion."

A bitter edge to his voice, barely there; Hope followed his line of sight outside. Modest rows of tombstones and an undertaker's shed caught her eye through a window depicting the fourth station of the cross. She recalled that Elizabeth Glass had once been an addict too.

But Hope wasn't here to mourn a woman she'd never met, and she could give fewer damns for the inconvenience of her presence, because—

"You murdered *here*, Killian!" she hissed. "Again. Again! After all that nonsense, all the flaming hoops I jumped to get that order to the plane on time—"

"And it wasn't for nothing," he insisted. "Where would I store all those items, eh? Where could I possibly put them out of prying eyes' reach? Best to take them with me. Yet better to keep them quashed under my thumb."

"Quashed." Hope quivered with new courage, Molotov-sparked by the sting of deceit. "What, like me, you mean?"

"If you were under my thumb, darling, you'd be chained to a grate in that cabin's cellar, lamenting the loss of your tongue."

The warning was delivered like liquid smoke. Men like Killian never needed to shout. Never hid behind bluster, red cheeks, or bulging purple veins. Over her life, Hope had dealt first in sex, companionship, and coffee, then in murder, fashion, and blackmail, and in doing so she'd met men from one spectrum's end to the next. The Old Man was their king.

Could you remind me what my one rule was, Bunny?

Don't go in the office. Never go in the office.

Hope crammed the fourteen-year-old memory in an oil barrel and rolled it into her mental river.

The spectrum, in any case, was null and void when it came to Killian. He wasn't anywhere close to being on it. There *were* no men like Killian. He was an altogether new breed of dragon.

"I didn't lie to you," he said. "I would never dream of it. I did indeed tour Europe, my dear—I just didn't kill anyone along the way."

"You're being reckless. So stupidly, unbelievably *reckless*. Can't you see that you're putting us both in danger, or did that doctor forget to check your eyes? Huh?"

"Your lack of confidence in my abilities is bordering on insulting, darling."

"I'm not fuckin' kidding."

"Neither am I. This isn't my first time holding a gun at the shooting range, fumbling with the safety like an amateur. Don't you believe I'd practice an extra degree of care and self-restraint working from home, as it were?"

"In what world is this restraint?" Hope asked, incredulous. "Didn't your mama ever teach you not to shit where you eat?"

The stern force of Killian's glower rolled her tongue back down her throat like a carpet. Hope reminded herself what he was capable of.

Rosaried wrists. Bloodless bodies. A confessional booth where it didn't belong.

What had the old couple done? How did they piss him off? They didn't, she told herself. They'd just had the audacity to exist.

Hope ached to hunker down and dissolve through the floorboards. Her angry confidence sputtered. She opened her mouth to reignite it, continue contesting, fighting to open Killian's eyes to the risk of his actions, but what was the point? She stewed in silence, suddenly exhausted. Killian would do as Killian pleased, and she'd given him the tools to do it all.

"Come," he said, ascending the stairs to the altar. "Might as well drink something hot if you're rooted in place, and you've never quite warmed to the idea of my fixing your tea out of sight. It appears you could do with some, in any case. Do what you like, stay or follow—"

"I'm not a dog."

"I know." He waited. She didn't move. "Very well. Do try to keep it in the cup this time."

———

Killian emerged from the sacristy with a mug of rooibos. "No more mint. We've weeded it from the greenhouses, as it tends to strangle the other plants. Good for the odd stomach-ache, but it also makes mojitos, which we tend to avoid here."

Curled up in the choir's nest, Hope accepted the mug without acknowledgment. The church was a cozy beast built by modest hands. Small. Quiet. The tented ceiling reached as high as the valley's brutal wind allowed—a *Thomas the Tank Engine* statement: the little church that could. It stood stalwart against the gusts, air whistling past like trains whisking by the church's station. Candles warmed chestnut walls. The pews were cushioned. The kneelers, more so. Economical, functional, and incredibly upkept. The adoration of its parishioners was apparent in the dust-free floor, the spotless keys on the tiny organ. The Bibles. The hymn books. All stacked and tidy. There wasn't a single screw loose from the grand construction of Killian's lie.

He crossed his arms over the pulpit, surveying the pews as a lion would its pride. In the custard light he appeared a Roman sculpture: creases and violet eye bags, furrows and shadows dug deep by time. Hope thought she must look much the same. He the sinner, she the bystander: the enabler, the Eve, the wind in his foul wing. She sipped her tea to scald vulnerability from her mouth.

"You used to come to church in fishnets," Killian mused.

"And you used to grin when I did." Hope retrieved a cigarette from the pocket of her jeans. "Funny how twelve years changes things."

"Don't light that in here."

"Or what?" She lit it. "Gonna put *my* name in tomorrow's headline?"

"Most of these people are recovering addicts. You might try thinking of someone other than yourself for a spell."

"Oh, that's richer than caviar, coming from you."

"What are you still doing here, Hope?" Killian asked. "Shouldn't you be off buying fur coats and diamond rings? Perhaps a few axes and a roll of plastic tarp, given the hour?"

"I want you to stay away from Andresína," she blurted. "I don't know what game you're playing. But I know you're gonna kill here again. That list was a lot longer than some expensive wood and autopsy equipment. I don't care who... I don't care *what* you do or who you do it to. You know that. Just..."

"Just?"

"Yeah. Just."

"Don't worry, little Magpie. I wouldn't dream of making your canary sing."

With the belt and tools all put to bed in a supply closet, Hope felt more comfortable, if not safe. She stepped down from the nest and approached the pulpit one stair at a time, making a note to neither cross herself nor bow. Like she used to.

"How'd you know I'd find them?" she asked.

"Who?"

"The pair you butchered in the church. *Fréttablaðið*'s

calling them The Penitents." She took a drag from the cigarette. "How'd you know I'd be there?"

"Frankly, darling, I had no idea you'd be there. I would lay the blame on the shoulders of cosmic timing, but you make it sound as if it were my intent for you to find them."

"How couldn't it be?"

"News of double homicide travels fast in this country. You love your newspapers. It's a simple deduction. You'd find out about them eventually, likely as soon as you returned home and flicked on the television. Truly, your stumbling upon my installation was either a stroke of luck or misfortune, depending on your perspective."

Hope gnawed her inner cheek, measuring the probability of coincidence against the possibility of a Killian-class lie. She dashed the thought. Backtracked.

"News travels even faster when it happens barely a month after your first little display," she said. "What were you thinking?"

"I killed four times consecutively in Lithuania back in October."

"In *Lithuania*," she said. "The highest homicide rate this side of *Russia*. What're you doing, Killian? Honestly? Cus if you're trying to send a message, I can't read your handwriting. I'm right in front of you. If you got somethin' to say, just tell me to my face."

"What makes you assume it's for you, if there is a message at all?"

"Don't play dumb," Hope snapped. "I saw them. Up close. The booth, the rosary, the... position. The bloody handprints too." Walls. Hips. Necks. "Where they were."

"You've a sharp memory."

I remember everywhere you've touched me.

A pillar of cigarette ash singed her finger, making her jump. She took a puff.

"Let's just say I've been feeling... inspired," Killian said.

"Inspired? You're a goddamn lunatic if you think your little surge of inspiration won't land us both in jumpsuits."

"Icelandic prisons are rather well-appointed, I hear."

Hope sighed, roughly massaging her temples. She would've flopped face-first on the altar in frustration would that not expose the back of her neck. When she looked up at Killian, his brow was lined with concern.

"I told you, Hope. I swore it wouldn't be you."

"I know," she muttered, gouging the pulpit's edge with her nails.

"I have never lied to you. I never will."

"That might've been your first. How can I be sure?"

"I'm afraid that's entirely up to you, darling."

Exhaling smoke, Hope studied his lines, searching for sincerity. But Killian wasn't just a closed book, he was an antiquity locked in a temperature-controlled room somewhere in the Vatican, one only exorcists and archbishops even knew existed. She could contest his claim. Argue until she went blue in the face. But frankly, after the week, morning, and night she'd had, Hope couldn't scrounge the energy to do much more than breathe it out. Let it happen and pray the police were too overwhelmed by the scope and magnitude of the murders. She couldn't convince him not to keep going—and she surely couldn't stop him.

"You've got a lot more toys lying around, if I'm remembering right." Hope crossed her arms. "That grocery list went on for miles. I don't suppose you're going back to Lithuania either."

"You suppose correctly."

She suppressed a sigh, a scream, the urge to pummel his chest. The urge to beg him to stop killing here, to kill anywhere else but here, on her hands and knees. It would do nothing but strip her dignity. As usual, she was powerless.

"What are you gonna do with the, um..." She consulted her memory of the enormous invoice, the supplies she'd delivered to the jet. "*Industrial-sized vacuum sealer*? And what the hell'd they do to rustle your feathers?"

A smirk transformed his face. "As you know, my dear—" he leaned over the pulpit Bible "—I never kiss and tell."

A shiver xylophoned her spine. She shook her head in disdain; it was the best she could muster. "Fork over the rest of my payment, Father Glass. I'll be on my way."

Hope accepted the envelope, the second and final payment for Killian's massive order, pulled from the pages of *Revelations*. She caught a snatch of upside-down text—*I will explain to you the mystery of the woman and of the beast she rides, which has the seven heads and ten horns*—before the cover thumped.

Seven heads. Ten horns. Upon reaching the church doors, Hope turned, and saw only one of the former and none of the latter. But she knew they were there.

"Judging from the size of that invoice," she said, "I guess we won't be seeing each other anytime soon."

"I expect what you're holding will be the last debit from my account for some time."

Killian strolled to the bedroom door behind the sanctuary, pulling his shirt over his head. Hope averted her gaze to avoid studying the tapestry of scars she'd painted so many years ago, having lionessed his shoulder blades every time they made love, or war, or something as yet unnamed.

"But it is a small country," he called. "We'll cross paths sooner or later, darling."

The door thunked shut. But for the sputter of candles, the church was silent. Eerily hollow. The fourth station window filtered starlight in shades of blue and green, submerging Hope underwater, lost in a kelp sea. There were sharks. There were eels. There were unknowable things with sharp eyes and sharper teeth.

Hope discarded her cigarette butt in the bowl of holy water by the entrance.

Hiss. Sizzle. Silence.

CHAPTER ELEVEN

CORVID

K nuckles on the Rover window launched Hope from one blurry nightmare to the next, and this one wasn't a dream. Her lower back. Her knees. The side of her neck. All protested an evening spent upright. She'd camped out overnight after leaving the church in a misguided attempt to stake out Killian—to see if he snuck out to indulge his darker impulse— while parked none too subtly in the shadow of a birch copse.

He stood outside the driver's side, now, decked in an extravagant, emerald-green chasuble and matching stole, chased with gold thread.

Sleep had claimed her with chloroform, apparently, stamping any recollection of having witnessed suspicious behavior. Now it was dawn. Well past dawn. The church bells were clanging, splitting villagers into tidy tributaries to their respective workstations, assignments, and therapies. As Killian windmilled a finger to suggest rolling down the window, Hope noticed no blood crusting his fingernail. No red on his collar. No scrapes on his wrists or scratches on his cheeks.

She cracked the window an inch.

"I'll take your presence here with a grain of salt and do you the courtesy of withholding my questions," he said.

"How generous." She grunted, cracking her neck and knuckles. "The fuck do you want?"

Killian surveyed the state of her car: the dust on the dash, the butts in the tray, the open envelope spilling a few hundreds on the passenger seat. "I would have offered you a bed if I'd known you were planning to spend the night."

"Your bed's a bit small for the two of us."

"Come on out," he said, shrugging off her sarcasm. "I simply want you to stretch your legs."

"Scandalous, Father."

"Smidge of fresh air, eh?" He squinted into the meager winter sunrise. She must have overslept. "You look overdue for a dose of therapy. Care to see the birds?"

"Any of your meth heads gonna be there?"

"The villagers," he corrected, "have other duties until lunch. Come."

"I'm not—"

"Not a dog," he affirmed, trudging through ankle-high grass without a care if she came or went. "I know."

———

"Would you like the glove?" asked Killian. "Falcon talons aren't everyone's cup of Earl Grey."

Hope shook her head, looking around the verdant greenhouse that doubled as a bird sanctuary. She was in no mood for the disparaging smile he'd give if she accepted, and the creature was a small thing, besides. Would've been pitiful, what with the cranial scars turkey-balding its head, except that she admired the slate blue of its wings, the sunflower yellow of its feet, and when Killian transferred it from his hand to hers, the grip, the flap, and the squawk from its hooked beak reminded Hope she was holding a raptor and not a finch. Light abrasions, as it settled. Two pricks of blood. The merlin calmed, shushed by Killian as if he were the goddamn bird whisperer.

"What's her name?"

"Gita."

"Got another named *Bhagavad*?"

"No."

"What happened to her?"

"Hunting dog," he said. "Skittish, stupid. Went for the wrong quarry."

"Skittish and stupid, maybe, but fast enough to catch this little broad."

"Nature is, at times, cruel in its chaos." Without warning, Killian tossed a strip of raw meat. Gita snatched it from the air. "I can't say I've seen such unease crease that lovely face of yours in quite some time. What became of your sense of adventure, darling?"

"I've channeled that energy into staying alive."

"And do you have something to live for?" Killian stroked the head of a nearby raven with a broken beak. "Do you find life as fulfilling as before?"

"Fulfilling?" She barked a humorless laugh. Gita screeched. "At least I'm not supplementing my barista's salary with a prostitute's wage anymore."

"So that's the fire under your feet?" A gyrfalcon with a bandaged leg trilled to his left. "Money?"

"Let's call it financial independence."

"Aptly put."

"Is this your middle-aged version of adventure?" Hope watched a long-eared owl with half a wing shift in the grass. "Bandaging up birds? Curing junkies with the light of God?"

"Oh, little Magpie." Killian glanced up from the raven with

a smirk that could crack spines. "You know exactly what I do for fun."

Crushed joints. Coffee beans. Rosary-bound wrists and pallid old skin. Hope had always taken an intellectual sort of pleasure in assembling the penultimate image of his murders based on details offered as scraps in the papers and online news. It was a sort of puzzle, a paint-by-numbers to which she'd shut her eyes and color, filling in the blanks with her knowledge of him and how he worked. Pleasure was the wrong word. Satisfaction? Accomplishment? Success, upon completing the painting, and beholding the grotesque work she'd helped construct?

Helped construct.

Killian took Gita. Hope picked her way through waist-high ferns to the greenhouse window, dusted with chartreuse pollen and spores. She watched a platoon of villagers flow through a regimen of Tai Chi in the courtyard. They streamed from one movement to the next, unmoved by the blustering wind, unfazed by the polar weather. They looked happy. Somehow peaceful, here, maybe fifty yards away from Europe's most prolific serial killer and his bitter accomplice.

No, she told herself. That's not who she was.

What are you, then?

The group bowed to one another at the end of the session.

"Why do you do all this?" Hope thought aloud. She scoured a hand through tangled locks, giving up halfway down her head as calcified hairspray refused to unravel the knots sleep had made. "You're a monster, and then you just, what, stop? Slap on an angel's hat and do all this?"

"That's called a halo, I believe."

"Why do you do it?" she asked, when the real question was *How?*

"Balance, I suppose," Killian said thoughtfully, for the first time in a long time sounding half an ounce uncertain. "At night, I take—"

"Take and take."

"—and during the day, here, I give. I tend to believe we are what we give away."

Hope's heart leapt when she turned around. She backed into the window. The glass was freezing. In the presence of injured predators in cages, on perches, and curled, asleep, in manmade nests, she'd forgotten the healthy dragon lurking among them—and he'd drawn close without making a sound. Hope was exhausted down to the metatarsals in her toes, so much so she hadn't the energy to chastise herself for reacting to Killian's approach or for turning her back in the first place.

There were no weapons in his hands.

"We are what we give away, huh?" Hope cleared her throat, trying to sound casual. "And what's that make you, Father Glass?"

Killian's eyes flicked to the delicate chain vanishing beneath her sweater's neckline. "A man without a heart."

The pit in Hope's stomach widened. She focused on his priest's collar instead of his face. "Not the wisest thing to give away."

"I'm inclined to agree."

"Where is it?"

He inched closer. She inched back. Their eyes met—lightning to its rod—and in its unspoken strike he asked permission and guaranteed no ill intent. Hope would have nodded, but she didn't have to. They never had to.

When Killian lifted the chain from her collarbone, the brief shock of skin-on-skin forced her eyes shut against an onslaught of sensations long archived to the reference section of her memory. Skin-on-skin that lasted longer. Grabbed harder. Caressed softer, rougher, sharper, stranger. The warmth of his fingers pressing an altar wafer to her tongue—the kiss of his thumb swiping her lower lip clean of sacramental wine—the heat of his palms on her shoulders and hips as he pulled her astride him on the altar.

"Well?" Hope asked, waking from the fever dream to watch his hand. "Where'd you put it?"

Killian trailed a finger down the chain. He lifted the payload from its hideaway behind her shirt: a platinum ring studded with rubies. They caught sunrising rays, intruding through the greenhouse glass to refract rainbows of blood.

"Around your neck."

A hollow ache sundered her chest. "I tried to give that thing back," she said. "You always insisted it was a goddamn gift."

"And it was." Killian stroked her cheek as he'd once done after releasing her wrists from the rosaries' hold; as he'd done after she'd drifted from the cabin bathroom to the kitchen for a dinner of deer; as he'd done a thousand times before. "It just so happens I lead a more productive life without it."

His own engagement ring snatched the light. One he'd never removed. Hope fought to control the quiver in her deepest gut, the itch to gnaw her already mangled cheek. She struggled to keep her voice on an even keel. "So you feel nothing now? Nothing at all?"

Killian lifted her left hand, looping the ring around the tip of her fourth finger. He closed his hand gently around hers before it could settle and find a home there again. "If you were to have a vital organ removed, while somehow still kept alive, would you feel nothing?"

"It'd hurt."

"It would hurt. Indeed." Killian lifted the ring away, flipping it like a magician's coin from knuckle to knuckle. "What would you do about all that hurt?"

The reply came without thought. It was pulled from her: a fish hooked and yanked from the sea. "I'd probably kill myself."

"And if you couldn't?"

"I'd fill it, I guess," Hope answered. "Fill the hole with something else. Anything else."

"Nails?"

"Yeah."

"Kitchen knives?"

"Sure."

Killian slid a hand through the short hair at the back of her head, pulling her in when she failed to resist. Her heart drill-bored for release from the cage of its ribs and met nothing but impenetrable sheets of foot-thick steel. On his collar were scents of church incense and aftershave; on his neck, the sandpaper prick of shaved stubble.

"Guthook blades?"

The ends of her nerves split and frayed. Her stomach clenched like a fist. The knife in her boot went so leaden she feared it might fall out. Might reveal itself. Did he know about it? About the Old Man, the barber chair, the secret she'd die to keep? No—he couldn't possibly. She searched his face for any hint of conspiracy, of knowing malice, and when she found none she realized just how close he really was.

Hope tore herself free from his grasp, wrangling the bucking bronco of her breath.

The chain zipped down Killian's fingernail. The ring landed on her chest. She re-tucked it, hidden like a shameful secret from the world—one she'd been unable to discard into the misty oblivion of the past. Through her clenched fists and clenched teeth, through her suppressed shaking and suppressed shivering, Hope looked up to find a smile playing Killian's lips. A pleasant smile.

A sad smile.

"Now you're catching on, little Magpie," he said, turning away. "Now you're catching on."

On her zombified march back to the Rover, Hope bumped into the blond-haired, blue-eyed resident, the one she'd once watched flail in the infirmary bed and, more recently, carry melons down the road. Hope mumbled a distant apology.

"Oh, it's okay, dear," the woman said.

It was only when Hope checked her cloudy mascara in the mirror and saw her drawn face, her green eyes gone matte, that she realized the resident had thought she was a new addition to the recovery village. She sped down the road to Reykjavík, cranking the radio to quell rampant thoughts on the way home.

CHAPTER TWELVE

FOUR

N ails. Kitchen knives. Guthook blades.
I'll do anything. Please. Please don't kill me!
Hope leapt awake in a queen bed fluffed with fleece and faux fur pillows, gasping for air with a throat full of razors. She grabbed the blanket, grabbed the headboard, took deep breaths —*one Mississippi, two Mississippi, three*—grounding herself in her loft's bedroom: the end tables, the lamps, the mirrored walk-in closet; the open door, the balcony, the sweet sea beyond. She didn't bother with a robe before rushing outside. Her bare feet froze on the stone. Her naked stomach prickled, splashed by fine spray. Bracing against the balustrade, Hope gulped ocean air until the shakes subsided and the compulsion to sob found another fox to chase.

The Old Man and the barber chair may have been things of the past, but they found new life in her dreams every night.

A muffled meow behind glass, one door and fence to the left. At half past noon, the sun had decided to show up to work, making concussion stars of the water and silver plate of the neighbors' window wall. Hope was desperate for a shower and enthralled by the temptation to play hermit for the day, but she couldn't ignore Biscuit's pitiful howling.

"I'm coming, you greedy bitch." She hopped the rail dividing the balconies. "Gramps forgot to feed you again, huh?"

Hope picked her way around it before inching open her neighbors' perpetually unlocked door. "Gunnar?" she called. "Katrin?"

The couple often held long conversations outside as she sunned herself shirtless on the balcony in summer, so Hope had no qualms about traipsing around in her bra and shorts. She still valued privacy behind closed doors, however, and was reluctant to trespass.

"Anyone home?"

The only response was a long, demanding meow. The television and lights were on—Gunnar and Katrin were often forgetful—but no one was in.

"Okay, your Majesty. Let's get us both some breakfast."

Biscuit's dish was empty. Her water was down to the last half inch, a bloated speck of kibble floating in what remained. Hope grumbled, refilling the bowls, but Biscuit seemed more interested in the cup of strawberry skyr she nabbed from the fridge than the wet food spooned in the dish. She pawed at Hope's wrist. Pawed at the spoon. Finally swiped the rim, knocking the yogurt from the counter.

"You gonna clean that up?"

Biscuit hopped down to lap skyr from the floor.

"How kind."

Kneeling to dab the excess from the black pebble mosaic tile with a wad of paper towels, Hope fought a memory bubbling at the edge of her awareness.

"Kneel."

Hope daydreamed past Killian's shoulder, studying the modest cross hung between the arched windows of the Aberdeen church.

"I don't kneel for God anymore," she said, shifting her attention his way, to where he sat on the chancel steps. "Not even yours."

"That's not what I asked."

"You said to kneel."

"Not to God," Killian said, standing. "To me."

He unbuckled his belt.

She held the memory's head underwater until it drowned. It'd been nearly three days since her encounter with Killian in the bird sanctuary, but his phantom presence was a constant in the haunted halls of her head.

A gust roared through the open door, tossing the chandelier before a particularly furious wave splashed spray clear across Shore Walk and into the fourth-story flat. Nearly slipping on skyr, Hope rushed to slide the door shut against the sudden windstorm. In doing so, she caught a glimpse of the muted TV screen. The ticker scrolled by:

MORNING TOURISTS TRAUMATIZED BY GOLDEN CIRCLE'S 'RUBY RING': GRISLY NEW ADDITION TO BOWERBIRD KILLINGS

Hope dashed to the floral couch, searched its cushions for the remote, and amped the volume until Biscuit hissed and fled from the noise.

"After exiting the exclusive *Perla hjóla* bus touring the Golden Circle to catch the spectacle of the Strokkur geyser erupting during a winter sunrise, a small group of tourists were shocked instead by a horrifying sight. A ring of seven people, bound in..." The newswoman looked to her co-anchor. "B-bound at..." Looked to the teleprompter. "They..." To her papers. "Um..."

Live on air, she glazed, greened, and excused herself offscreen.

The other anchor attempted to salvage the broadcast by piping over the sounds of his partner's violent sick. "Bound at the Geysir Hot Spring Area in several hundred meters of wire and suspended over Strokkur by, er..." He consulted the documents. Sheafed them, tapped them. "My apologies." A strangled laugh.

The silver-haired, spry-minded newsman with over a decade of screentime under his belt pinched the bridge of his nose. As long as Hope had watched the news, she'd never seen such an atrocious take.

"We're still live?"

"Yes," whispered the cameraman. "Do something!"

The newsman flicked his wrist, shaking his head in speechless defeat. Run the reel, his hand seemed to say, and it ran. Hope fixated on the 'LIVE' glowing bright in the screen's corner. Snippets of the atrocity's aftermath peeked over a field reporter's shoulder. Cops and journalists milled about. One of them approached a male colleague in the background: a bonfire of frizzy red curls, wind-chapped cheeks.

Hanna.

Hope kneeled in front of the television, drawing nose-to-screen. She dug her cellphone out of the pocket of her shorts.

It rang.

And rang.

And rang.

The field reporter straightened her mustard blouse,

flustered and oblivious to the fact that she was live on air until the cameraman said so.

"Oh! Good morning, we're reporting to you live from—"

Hi, you've reached Hanna Maslany at Fréttablaðið! Please leave your name, number, and a detailed message, and I'll be sure to—

Hang up. Redial.

"—police have since transported the witnesses to Reykjavík to gather statements, but with forces stretched thin by the recent chaos in the capital, not much could be done to hide the horrifying—"

Onscreen, Hanna tossed her hands. Her mouth went O-shaped in a shout, ending a heated argument with her colleague. She dug around in the back pocket of her jeans.

"That's it," Hope said, watching Hanna fumble with the phone. "Good girl."

"Hello?"

"Hanna?"

"Who is—*Hope?*"

"You're on TV."

The redhead scanned her environment, a rabbit searching the tundra for wolves. Hope's stomach somersaulted when Hanna's eyes met a camera lens not meant for her. She scurried offscreen.

"What channel?" Hanna asked.

"Does it matter?"

"Well, no, I suppose not, but my boss—"

"Screw your boss. What's going on?"

A pregnant pause, full of unsaid jabs like *Can't you read the ticker?* and *Don't you hear the reporters?* that Hanna Maslany was far too polite to say. Yes, Hope *could* read the ticker, *could* hear the reporters, sure, and they were so loud, crashing as waves in a cave at high tide, thundering and big, wrecking her

97

limestone walls with salt, water, and blood. But the news wouldn't divulge the kind of detail Hope needed to know.

The field reporter prattled on. "Seven Reykjavík residents were discovered dead today in what many are calling the nation's most vicious multiple homicide to date." A quaver, a tremble, a consultation of notes. "This incident alone has catapulted 2022 to a record high in terms of the national homicide rate, with the greatest number of people killed in one year since 2004, when a total of five citizens were killed in a then-rash of violence, now a memory of safer times here in Iceland."

Hope struggled to keep her voice level. "What's going on, Hanna?"

"Seven people!"

"I know—"

"Seven people, can you believe it?"

Hope couldn't see Hanna any longer, but she didn't have to look at someone's face to tell when their emotional dam was breaking. Hannah's voice went thick with emotion, saying, "I didn't sign up for this. There aren't enough reporters! There isn't enough anyone."

"I know, I know."

Gone was the sun. Lightning struck the sea. Thunder rumbled the loft, making Biscuit growl; she darted to a haven hidden in the shadows, the carefully curated sort so often claimed by cats.

"What happened to the victims?"

"Hope, I can't divulge that sort of—"

"Fuck off. Yes you can. Look at the scene and tell me what you see. I know they haven't cleaned it up yet."

"You..."

"No, you. *You're* the one who called the other night, all false concern—"

"It wasn't false!"

"—to get me to spill details on the café crime scene. Time to return the favor."

"I still can't—"

"D'you wanna keep your job, Hanna? Wanna get shipped back to Poland? Romania, Latvia, whatever fucking '-ia' it is you're from? Huh?" Borne of sheer impatience, the threat was as empty as it was cruel. "I've got an officer at the Directorate of Immigration who owes me a no-strings favor."

"You don't mean that."

It was a spongy backbone, but it was still a backbone, one Hope hadn't heard support the floppy ribs of Hanna's voice since they'd had the misfortune of meeting.

"No," Hope said. "I might not, but *maybe* I do, and it's for that reason you're gonna tell me what you see, got it?"

Biscuit's gold-green eyes stared from an open cabinet, brimming with the sort of feline judgment that felt almost supernatural.

"Please," she added, appealing to Hanna's nature. "I need to know who they are."

It was an age before Hanna spilled her secrets. Almost did, anyway.

"They haven't released the identities of the—"

"Ma'am, we're going to need you to clear the area."

"I'm a journalist," Hanna told the speaker. They sounded like a cop.

"We need you to clear out. This is a crime scene."

"That's why I'm here."

"Nevertheless."

"Excuse you!" Hanna stepped back into frame, ripping her arm from a constable's grasp as if she'd been groped by an alleyway drunk. "Sorry, Hope, I have to go."

"No. Wait." Hope pressed a palm to the TV, rising on her

haunches. The screen sizzled under her fingertips. She tried to count the emergency personnel and vehicles on-site. It was easy enough—they were hardly on top of one another. *One, two...*

"I've got to go!"

Three...

"I'll call you when I'm back in the office, Hope."

Four...

"Wait!"

Four constables and two patrol cars compared to six ambulances and ten medics in-frame, seven dead bodies somewhere off it, and God knew how many witnesses.

The math didn't track.

"Hanna, where're the police? There's barely anyone on the scene."

"The force is divided. Haven't you heard?" Hanna shouted over the wind as it tore the plain. "They identified The Penitents. It was all over the 9am news!"

"I overslept—who were they?"

"I need to hang up—"

"Hanna!" Hope shouted. *"Who were they?"*

"Gunnar Guðmundursson and Katrin Jonsdottir!"

Shit.

The door to the balcony, ten feet ahead. The door to the hall, thirty feet behind.

Boots on the stairs—she strained to listen—two floors down and closing fast.

Before she could make it out onto the balcony, the front door banged open and Hope stifled a scream.

"Reykjavík Metro Police!"

CHAPTER THIRTEEN

DETECTIVE SUCH-AND-SUCH

The two-way mirror reflected a pathetic, cornered creature, but cornered creatures often proved the most dangerous. This is what Hope told herself, staring at the short waves flopping a tumbleweed over her face, at brown roots streaking through blond, at the horsehair blanket draped haphazardly over her shoulders by the arresting officer. The cuff ring on the table, to which she was shackled, denied her third attempt to reflexively unsmudge the previous night's makeup. Something sticky on the table sucked at her forearms.

The interrogation room's insular silence was oppressive. Whether the bumblebee buzz of the fluorescents made that silence more or less tolerable was a thought she pondered, discarded, and returned to many times, as unable to ignore the noise as she was unable to soothe her boredom. That's what she was calling her fear to keep herself from panicking, resorting to simple arithmetic whenever she teetered too close to the edge.

"I need to piss!" Her shout bounced back at her. She pulled at the restraints, steel on unused steel. "I'll sue you to hell and back when this is over!" When she tugged again, her wrist bones sang. "Think I'm bluffing? Check my file, motherfucker!"

The squeal of a rusty hinge announced a man's entry. Slicked hair, leather jacket, insomniac-chic eye bags. Hope groaned at the walking stereotype until it opened its mouth.

"Do you really think all that yelling is conducive to proving your innocence?" An unusual voice delivered the question in a package of genuine perplexity. One arm carried a fat manila folder while the other remained casually pocketed. "Ma'am?"

When Hope denied his existence with a deadpan stare to the mirror, the cop's sigh went husky with a dollop of exasperation. "Icelandic or English?"

With no response to field, the man harrumphed into the chair opposite her, interrupting Hope's eye contact with herself. He replaced her greens with sunken, chocolate lookers, an angular jaw, and a forehead ridged by a quartet of lines that went smooth once his brows fell. The last name on his badge was undeniably Icelandic, but the accent playing musical chairs with his words was sandpapered at the edges, as if he'd spent one too many years wintering in the American Bible Belt—must have, what with the complexion not quite tan, but at least a couple notches south of Nordic white.

In English, he asked, "Do you actually have to use the restroom?"

In Icelandic, she answered, "Is that the only reason you came in?"

The file whacked the table. A fist pressed to his mouth. The officer observed her over a mountain range of red knuckles while the index finger of his free hand tapped the table.

Tap.

Tap.

Tap.

Each little thump struck a match under Hope's ass until a blowtorch heat made her squirm. The tapping stopped. She fumed at the smile poorly hidden behind the detective's hand, too reflexive to be an act. Maybe he was amused. Maybe it was a tell. Either way, that smile divulged something important, an advantage Hope tucked away in the arguably small arsenal at her disposal: Detective Such-and-Such was cursed with a face so expressive it might as well be a billboard advertising the goings-on in his gray matter.

"As a matter of fact, it's not," he said in Icelandic.

"What a crying shame," she said in English.

The linguistic tennis match left Detective Such-and-Such's smile discarded courtside. A gulp of lukewarm coffee from a Styrofoam cup revealed a tremor in his hand. Nerves? Low blood sugar? Withdrawal?

Hope inhaled, searching for a slug of Scotch in the cop's coffee, but it was clean. She saw Saga again. Jutting jaw, splintered joints.

"I'm Detective Chief Inspector Oliver Ragnarsson." He settled on English, where a hint of American influence hardened his Icelandic accent. "Do you—"

"That's a redundant mouthful, ain't it?" Hope mused. "Detective Chief Inspector. Christ, pick a word."

"Do you know why you're—"

"Say, did someone cum on this table and forget to squeegee? It's sticky as hell."

"Ma'am—"

"So, Ollie, where'd you get that scar?" Hope pointed to the mauve streak beveling a perfect *c* above his upper lip. He folded his hands, waiting with stern, teacherlike patience for her to be done. "No?" She frowned. "How about the one on your neck?"

The tension was subtle but instant. Hope ogled the ghastly, uneven scar curling behind the cop's neck all the way from left to right. She tilted to the side to get a better look at the silver centipede in the mirror, winding over his cervical spine, sincerely wondering what kind of weapon caused the wound. How he'd survived, how he'd rehabbed, who did it and why. Detective Such-and-Such cleared pavement salt from his throat.

"Must be real grateful to the doc who fixed you up so good," Hope said. "Can't imagine life as a bobblehead being too fun."

His face darkened ever so slightly, but it wasn't enough to get a rise out of him. She'd crossed her fingers for someone like Sad-Moustache or Beetle-Mole—but instead she got a DCI.

"All finished? Great." He cracked a one-sided smile devoid of humor. "So. How're you feeling, Miss Rippa? Care to explain why you were slinking around half naked in an apartment belonging to the victims of a double homicide?"

"Care to explain why your buddies broke down their door like a bored teenager called in a bomb threat?" When he didn't respond, she said, "I feed their cat."

"You feed their cat."

"Yeah, I feed their fuckin' cat."

"What's the cat's name?"

He smoothed the front page of his notepad. Hope snorted.

"Gee, I dunno, sir. Wouldn't wanna snitch. Is she a suspect, Constable Such-and-Such?"

"Detective—"

"Detective Such-and-Such."

A hoarse sigh through a pinched nose was always a good sign according to Hope's master dictionary of Exhausted Body Language. As they rattled through standard-procedure questions and confirmed her address, Hope honed in on his eyes, trying to sus out the person behind them. Though separated by a distance of only two or three feet, Detective Such-and-Such felt miles away, as if his thoughts lived in a distant and claustrophobic world. A quiet trauma lived there with him, one entirely distinct from recent events.

"Maybe you should grow out your hair," Hope suggested as he jotted down notes.

"I didn't cart you in for fashion advice, Miss—"

"To hide the scar. I mean, it obviously bothers you. If you grew out your hair, less people would notice, and less people would stare, so..."

"Where were you the morning of the twenty-fourth, ma'am?"

"Where were *you* the morning of the twenty-fourth, bud?"

"If you'd be so kind as to answer the question."

"You first."

The pencil strained in Oliver's hand. He relaxed his hold before the tip could snap as if he knew its breaking would be a strike against him. The scoreboard remained tied. 0-0.

"Guess I'll come back in another two hours." He grunted to his feet, pulling an odd contraption from his jacket pocket: a hard-angled mess of polished rosewood and shiny metal. "Maybe a little while longer without a bathroom break will jog your memory."

He rapped his knuckles twice on the table and turned his back, sidling towards the door while he clicked away at the puzzle box's convoluted joints.

Hope grumbled to herself. She could play the petulant hag for hours on end, but at the end of the day, *he* wasn't the one in handcuffs. He could get up and leave when his bullshit tolerance hit its ceiling. She had the option of waiting out the end of his shift in the hopes for someone less capable to take up the interrogation, but that was still a gamble—and in truth, what with ten dead, she wasn't positive his shift *had* an end.

Hope piped up before he touched the doorknob. "And if I want my phone call?"

He reoriented to face her, lips pursed in an expression equal parts dubious and thoughtful. "Depends who it's for, I'd guess."

"A lawyer," she said, "unless you come sit with me. Can't you see I'm already agonizing over the loss of your company?"

Cautious optimism shuttle-bussed him back to the chair. He slowly unzipped his jacket as if he were shedding a bulletproof vest in front of an armed lunatic. Heat swelled in Hope's chest. Back to it.

"All right. I'll play." He set the puzzle box down and picked up the pencil. The tremor in his hand was still there, but his even voice betrayed no sign of nerves. "So. The twenty-fourth."

"I was in Italy the whole week, Ollie."

"Yet you were first on the scene."

"Second," Hope corrected. "Listen, I may not be a good Samaritan, but that doesn't mean I'm someone who just ignores it when a woman screams her lungs off at the crack of dawn while some psycho's on the loose."

"Fair enough, I suppose, but pump the brakes." He squinted at his notes, humming. "Didn't you say you were in Italy?"

"Jesus, don't you have the statement I gave your pals?" Oliver blinked vacantly, then spread his hands as if to say *I don't know where it is*. It was Hope's turn to pinch her nose and sigh, but she resisted the urge. "Yes," she continued, theatrically slow. "I was in Milan, and then I was here. I was on the way back from the airport when I heard the caretaker—y'know what? Let's make this simpler for you. Check with anyone in the logistics department. *My* logistics department. At *my* company. I bet you'll find 'em more than cooperative and we can all go home, sipping hot cocoa, blissful in the knowledge we did all we possibly could to find your adorable little killer."

Oliver was smiling, and despite his shiny badge and late thirty-something age, he seemed more like a teen, in that moment, agonizing in anticipation as his bully fell into the flypaper of a well-laid prank.

1-0.

Hope kicked herself for letting herself be fooled into thinking the DCI was an idiot. She combed through every word she'd just said to figure out which were responsible for his shift in attitude, but came up empty.

"In my experience, Miss Rippa," he leaned forward, "it's usually a mistake to assume you're the smartest one in the room."

He picked up the puzzle box. *Click, click, click.*

"So you think you're smarter than me?"

"Who, me?" He chuckled. "No, ma'am. Just because I color myself an optimist doesn't mean I'm deluded. But I did just so happen to mention your name to the chief inspector before waltzing in here, who then immediately and *loudly* regaled me with all manner of wild, truly fascinating stories—all I'd ever need for twenty lifetimes of dealing with degenerates like you."

"There are no degenerates like me."

"Are you saying you're not a degenerate, or that you're a unique degenerate?"

"I'll let you puzzle that one out, Poirot."

"Funny you should say that about your, uh... What was it? Logistics department. Hey, did you eat breakfast this morning? *I* ate breakfast this morning. French toast. I don't usually eat breakfast, see, but I made an exception for my little girl's thirteenth birthday. Set some butter and syrup in front of that kid and she goes to town till she's blue in the face." Hope checked his finger. Wedding ring. "Turns out it wasn't the best day for all that. I puked it up at half past eight this morning. And let me tell you, Miss Rippa, it doesn't taste quite so good the second time around."

He shook his head as if it was his life's greatest tragedy, then abruptly clapped his hands, too loud in the too small room.

"Well! I'd offer you a bucket for *your* breakfast's second coming—I'm a gentleman, you see—but something tells me you won't be needing one." He flicked the case file open with his handy dandy pencil. "Something tells me you've never needed one."

Like a blackjack dealer serving cards, Oliver slapped a corporate headshot on the table and the corresponding crime-scene photo beside it.

"Erla Sigursdottir."

Another pair.

"Kristján Arnarsson."

Another.

"Amelia Symanski."

Another.

"Lilja Ragnarsdottir, Cecilia Kristofersdottir, Khadiija Ali, Jon Jonsson. Recognize them?"

Seven smiling faces in smart business suits next to seven red, steaming skulls, their features summarily snuffed by Strokkur's boiling hot water and steam. The entire logistics department of Rippa Royale, LLC looked up at Hope, wondering what they'd done to deserve to die so horrifically.

"Maybe you should've rethought your alibi before you went and murdered it."

What little skyr Hope had managed to scarf that morning went sour in her stomach. Rancid bile bubbled in her throat. It wasn't just the horror of boiled face-meat hanging in strips off cheekbones and chins, steamed moist and probably tender, fit for stew—it was the fact, the undeniable *knowledge* that Killian wasn't merely playing with his food. He was playing with her life, and he had it by the throat.

Her barista was a taunt. Her neighbors were a threat. Half of her employees? What else was that, if not dousing her in gasoline and waving the match under her nose?

Hope swallowed the reflux and reality along with it. She couldn't afford to be distracted by the gravity of what Killian was doing. This wasn't the time or place. She'd have to worry about that later; right now, her defenses needed reinforcement. She wasn't really being questioned about the murder of Gunnar and Katrin, who she'd found staged the morning of the twenty-fourth—she'd just happened to be in their apartment after their bodies were identified by police. No, she was being investigated for the murder of her employees... who Killian must have nabbed sometime during the week she was in Milan. It was the only explanation as to why she hadn't noticed their absence.

She took a steadying breath. "If I'm smart enough to warrant a warning from your boss," she ventured, "then surely I'm smart enough not to kill my get-out-of-jail-free cards."

"Or maybe you're cocky enough to bet on that rationale as your excuse. What do they call that? Reverse psychology? Deflection? A serious Hail Mary? I wouldn't know," Oliver said, exaggerating an *I give up* shrug as he lounged back in the chair. "I'm not as smart as you, after all."

Hope was used to those with whom she made eye contact being the first to break it. Oliver was made of sterner stuff. She nearly cracked a fake smile, but the photos seized her attention again. The geyser-boiled heads looked like blistered cherry tomatoes, basted in blood instead of oil. She looked away, searching for something else to focus on—defenses, defenses—and chose instead to appreciate the fit of Detective Such-and-Such's black V-neck.

"I'm up here."

"Sure you are. But I prefer what's down there." Hope cocked a brow at his abdomen as if she could X-ray through cotton to see muscle underneath. It appeared to be the lean sort, like the relatively new bulk on the brittle bones of former addicts who'd found the light. She recalled the shake in his hand. "Sober... no. Clean, right?" It was a wild stab in the dark. "Four years? Three?"

"Miss Rippa—"

"Cocaine? No. Meth, maybe." Not to mention a more than likely dash of PTSD. The silver scar winked from the side of his neck. "Still can't quite get rid of that tremble."

Hope shrugged the horsehair blanket off, revealing a petite body covered in goosebumps. Oliver rolled his eyes away, but the pink in his cheeks betrayed his inner core of Southern Christian modesty.

"See, you act like such a gentleman, but the reality is, Detective Such-and-Such—"

"Oliver."

"—reality is, Ollie, your buds wheeled me in here wearing my itsy-bitsy bra with my itsy-bitsy wrists cuffed behind my back. Sure, so you had Sad-Moustache and Beetle-Mole fetch this flea-ridden rug to wrap me in, but you've had plenty of time to notice a few things from behind that fancy mirror of yours, I'm sure." Hope bent forward until the table's edge pinned her breasts. "Did you take little old me into custody to talk about poor Katrin and Gunnar, the untimely passing of half my office..." She sprawled back, making a spectacle of scanning her marred stomach and thighs, "or were you just curious how I got *my* scars?"

"The only wounds worth my attention are recent ones, Miss Rippa."

"So you did look? And didn't even offer me a shirt. Tsk, tsk. How about a second glance?" She dropped the mockery for a sterner tone. "Take a good, hard look, and then ask yourself how a tiny gal like me could murder ten people in less than two months, build some contraption big enough to support a party of seven, and hoist it above our beloved country's most hyperactive geyser without a single defensive scratch, splinter, or burn, when I'm obviously unafraid or maybe even fond of a little personal injury?" Hope snuck a look at a photo of the full construction: a wooden crane of sorts, dangling a circular chandelier of silver wire, the bodies bound horizontally so their heads stuck out in intervals along the ring. "Or a degree in engineering, for that matter?"

Oliver crossed his arms tight enough to ride his shirt sleeves up, revealing the grey fringes of tattoos from another life. She focused on them instead of the photographs, instead of how she recognized the wire and the wood, the nails holding it all together; saw in each joist and rivet the hand of the demon who'd built it.

"Frankly, Miss Rippa, you've driven me to a point where I don't care about your scars, your status, or anything but the fact that you vanished from the country on a conveniently private flight, your employees went missing soon after, and today, every single one of them turned up dead. Do you have any idea how nine—well, counting..." He consulted his notes. "Saga Sigrúnsdottir, ten—how *ten* of your personal acquaintances have been brutally murdered?"

Neighbors, colleagues, staples of her routine. Dead. All Hope could do was summon words that didn't belong to her. "On a small, cold rock like this? They're bound to be someone you know."

"Cute. I cannot express the degree to which that simply isn't good enough."

"I assume you're still working on getting your paws on the security footage of me at the airport." And probably figuring out how to apply for a warrant to search her company's records. "So what the hell is it you want to hear from me while we wait for the bureaucratic red tape to loosen, huh?"

She meant for it to come out condescending and hard, but her uncertainty bled through, weakening her words. Oliver narrowed his eyes. Had she truly fucked up? Slid on the ice and busted her ass? She tucked her thumbs in her fists, watching him study her, trying to decipher whatever conclusion he was or wasn't coming to, but she didn't have this man's Rosetta.

Rosetta or no, Hope realized with a start that she didn't have to eat procedural bullshit. She had the killer's name.

CHAPTER FOURTEEN

THREE YEARS AND A BIRTHDAY

Hope opened her mouth—and promptly snapped it shut.
Compromising Killian meant compromising herself.
She laundered his supplies with utmost care, but he was
unpredictable. What was stopping him from admitting to it all,
just so he could bring her down with him as an accomplice?
Hope didn't know why he'd done all this, what his motivation or
endgame could possibly be, and for that reason she couldn't dare
mention his name.

"Miss Rippa, we've both had a long day," said Oliver. "Tell
me how your colleagues wound up like this."

"I told you I don't know. I was in Italy."

"And who can corroborate that besides the folks we have to
bury? Unless, of course, you want to fork over your records."

"Get a warrant."

"Figured as much."

Hope had the system configured to purge the drives every
night at 11:59. The only copies kept were paper, secreted away
in boxes upon boxes, nighttime trips mixed with daytime travels
according to a meticulous code only she understood. If it were
up to her, she'd burn all the hard copies, incriminating and

legitimate alike, for simplicity's sake. But that was bad for business. The ability to use them as blackmail kept her afloat—and safe. Recordkeeping, whether illicit or legal, was an evil necessary to thwart auditors or murderers should they ever come knocking. Plus, compared to the tidy digital filing systems to which they'd grown accustomed, crate upon overstuffed crate of folders tended to discourage the former.

"So what now, officer? Gonna slap me in chains? Oh, wait." She tugged at the cuff bolt. *Chink!*

Oliver gathered the photos, arranging them in two neat stacks—headshots, forensics—before tapping them straight and tucking them in the case file.

"What're you doing?" Hope asked.

"It's my daughter's birthday."

"And?"

"And I'm not wasting any more of it on you, ma'am."

"Am I invited for a slice of cake?"

"Hardly." Oliver stood, folder tucked under his arm so he could continue struggling with his puzzle box. "We're authorized to hold you for twenty-four hours before sending you to the judge. I'd advise you enjoy your stay, but considering the sort of luxury you're used to, this room may as well be North Korean solitary."

Tipping an imaginary trilby, Oliver bade her goodnight.

"That won't work on me again," Hope said, nodding at the jacket he left hanging from the chair. "Forgot something."

"Hm? Oh, no. You'll need it. Gets real cold in here 'round six."

Hope dug her nails in the table at the squeal of the doorknob. As the door screeched open, pouring police station light into the dim room, she came to a sudden and strangulating realization—that the room was a cell with no windows, that she had no clothes, that she was restrained and vulnerable and without defense should monsters crawl hungry from the shadows. It cast the fog of pretense from her mind and forced its gears to turn.

"Wait."

"I'm done waiting, Miss Rippa."

One step through the door. One more and her freedom would disappear. She couldn't stay trapped in here while Killian was out there, scheming whatever came next in his baffling plan.

"I can prove it," she said. "I can prove I wasn't here."

Oliver stopped in the doorway.

"Ellie." Hope ground the name out like meat through a masher, hating herself for giving in, but she'd been left without any other option. "Call my assistant. Ellie Lehtinen. She can prove where I was."

Oliver traveled a backroads route up Hope's legs, belly, chest, neck—somehow not lewd in the least—reaching her face with an abject tiredness, as if the visual journey had exhausted the gas he kept in reserve. What kind of creature did he see, she wondered? What did he make of its teeth? He made to leave again, but this time, he nodded.

Nodded and tossed the solved puzzle box, now a perfect cube, on the interrogation room table.

———

The slink-and-clatter of handcuffs falling to the table jolted Hope from her doze with such force that Oliver nearly fell over. Scorching him with as mighty a glare as she could muster, she rubbed her wrists. Free at last.

"Mind warning a girl before you touch her while she's asleep? Aren't you a cop?"

"Fair enough. You just looked—"

"Tired?"

"Well, yes."

"Whose fault is that?"

"Yours. You think I want to be here?"

He looked as if he wanted to toss the handcuff key—no, chuck it at the window or the lights, something that'd make a nice, loud sound—she could hear it: *clank! bang!* But a quick jaw-grind session seemed to calm the impulse. He slid the key onto the ring dangling from his belt.

"You're hardly off the hook, anyway," he said. "No travel. Investigation's ongoing. Consider your passport frozen until further notice."

"You sure know how to charm a girl." Hope busied herself with the sticky stain on the tabletop. "Am I free to go? Relatively speaking?"

She was so drained, so preoccupied with the mystery stain that she didn't sense the presence behind her or the thing it carried until it was nearly upon her, but she felt it just in time, and she twisted, turned, shooting up and staggering back, back, back into the table.

"What the fuck—"

"I'm sorry—"

"What the fuck do you think you're doing?" Hope snapped, a flush of heat warming her face.

She seized the table's edge in a death grip before realizing Oliver's intent. He held the blanket she'd shed. Only when she recognized the brown horsehair between his fingers did Hope feel the cold and shiver.

Weak.

"Sorry," he said sincerely.

When he offered the blanket at arm's length, Hope snatched it. Cocooned herself, but not too eagerly. She was closest to the door now. Was it unlocked? Could she run for it, lock him in, and escape the understaffed station? Flight instinct tugged her toward the exit, but Hope rooted her bare feet on the concrete. That instinct was a knee-jerk, and she couldn't afford to give in to rash impulses. She was free, after all, if only conditionally. Why test it?

Once-overing an embarrassed Detective Such-and-Such, Hope asked, "How long you been clean?"

Oliver surprised her with an honest answer after some hesitation. "Your second guess."

The wild stab had been right. "Three years?"

He nodded.

"You're pretty normal for an addict."

"Former addict."

"To what?"

"Second guess."

"You American?"

"Half."

"Where from?"

"Charleston," he said. "By way of Stykkishólmur."

"Hell of a combo."

"Consider my dad's doorstep your complaint box."

"Daddy issues, huh?"

"We've all got them," he said. "Even those of us who love our fathers."

"Must be an Iceland thing."

"Having daddy issues?"

"Loving your fathers."

Oliver seemed to search the room for an adequate response. He found none.

"What's your daughter's name?" Hope prodded.

"I'm not telling you that."

"Even if I was the killer, would a thirteen-year-old fit my profile?"

"Don't know, don't care. That's a line that doesn't need crossing."

"You say that like it's been crossed before."

"You say that like you wish it'd been."

"And wish harm on a kid?" Hope opened her mouth to protest, then thought better of it. How many orphans had she helped make? "Yeah, fine. I wouldn't give you my kid's name either."

"*You've* got kids?"

"Don't sound so surprised, Ollie." A pause. A huff. "No."

Something reminiscent of a smile twitched his thin lips. Silence ruled, for a time. Emptiness too. Just them. No superiors behind the glass, no bud in his ear, not that he'd had one to start with. The duality was almost comfortable, and that comfort was too strange a thing for Hope to let live.

"So Ellie came through?"

Seconds ticked by on the clock overhead, sluggish and drunk, before Oliver offered a nod.

"Not gonna shoot me on the way out, are you?"

"I'm unarmed."

"That wasn't a no."

"After you, Miss Rippa." Oliver motioned to the door.

She'd count her blessings when she was home. Hope turned the knob and breathed deep when it opened, washing the interrogation room clean with sterile white light.

Ready to be rid of the stuffy room, she still couldn't help but look back at Detective Such-and-Such—seated once again at the table he'd straightened—thumbing through the crime-scene photos. Fingers dug trenches in his hair. Nails carved into his temple. Hope knew the position well. She knew intimately the doubt that came with it as she pored over invoices for murder weapons, wondering if what she was doing was worth it. Was redeemable, was...

Whatever it was, she molted free of it and stepped into the hall.

"That's an interesting ring around your neck, Miss Rippa."

Hope froze.

"Unique," Oliver said.

He wanted her to turn. Gravity wanted her to turn. The telltale wibble-wobble of the photo he held up wanted her to turn. She did.

"It makes a statement," he said, "doesn't it?"

Seven bodies twined in silver. Seven heads jutting from wire. Seven heads now bulbous, bright red, and melted, swathes of skull shining through like patches of pus where the skin had sloughed off. After figuring out how to move it somewhere out of Strokkur's range, forensics would've had to take individual photos from the underside of the great wooden gallows suspending the ring of death above the geyser, contrasting hues of horror against the irradiated backdrop of the sky.

An abyssal maw yawned inside her chest. The scene looked like a lunatic's interpretation of the ruby engagement ring on her chain, and that fact hadn't gone unnoticed.

Oliver watched Hope, perhaps waiting for a cruel laugh to bubble up from the witch's bog in her throat. Watched... That was the wrong word. No, he examined her with a searchlight stare picked up through years of experience, likely overseas dealing with South Atlantic devils. That stare slowly dissolved away as Hope's expression failed to take a turn for Evil Queen. It took every ounce of resolve she had left to keep from crumbling.

Finally, he put the photo away, having made his point.

You are not safe. You are not free. I know you're involved, I just don't know how yet.

Unleashing a grim sigh, he rubbed the back of his neck. A wince made topographic maps of his face, as if the old wound still hurt—and it did, probably. Not physically. Hope had a few of those. Like acid flashbacks. You see it. Feel it. Hear it, smell it. All over again, and again and again, every time you touch or graze or spot it in a freshly washed window walking down the street. Evil of such a magnitude never found satisfaction in haunting only nightmares. It bled into the waking world, too, and it was always hungry.

"I do have one more question, Miss Rippa." This was not DCI Ragnarsson. This was Oliver. Ollie. The man behind the badge, tortured brown eyes, and faded ink. "If you don't mind my asking, where *did* you get those scars?"

Those tortured brown eyes were too sincere to lie to, or maybe she was too tired to bother. "A man," she said. "Someone who's nothing like you, Detective Such-and-Such."

"It's Oliver."

"Ollie."

"Should I take that as a compliment?"

Hope considered Oliver's character thus far, analyzing the cobweb-ridden ceiling tiles as she did so. "Promise not to call me Miss Rippa again, and it might be."

"As long as you stop calling me Ollie."

"You prefer Detective Such-and-Such?"

"Makes me feel less like an eight-year-old."

Hope snorted. "Well, if that's all, I'm gonna go send Ellie a thank-you note."

"My card's up front with your cell. Detective Tinna will drive you home. If you remember something, if you're contacted by anyone, if *anything* changes—"

"Yeah, I get it."

Hope looked back at the man who dared meet her eye unbothered. "I'm keeping the blanket," she said.

"I'd be offended if you didn't, ma'am."

CHAPTER FIFTEEN

THE CHURCH OF FEATHERS

4:00pm.
    Dread cinched the corset of Hope's ribs tighter with every step from the safety of her truck to the great unknown of Fjöðurfjall's church. She looked upon the doors and turned to stone.

The cable-knit sweater she wore was an antique scrounged from a go-bag in the trunk of her Rover. After Detective Tinna dropped her off, Hope had lurked outside her apartment for an hour. Too tired to brave four stories on unsure legs, not to mention the active crime scene next door, she'd diverted to last resorts. Watching her balcony, watching Gunnar and Katrin's balcony and imagining Biscuit's lonely yowls, she'd slipped into tights, skirt, and last the faded olive sweater, just as the sky cracked an egg of rain on the street's cold skillet. Enduring the drive to the village in damp clothes had done nothing to cool the coal in her core.

The church doors. Amok with splinters, bleached by salt, battered by wind. And calling, crooning for her fingers to wrap around their rusty handles. A beckoning to open. To enter. *Here, kitty kitty.* The doors always protested being doors upon opening, but Hope had come to appreciate the shriek of their hinges. Fjöðurkirkja cried into its own chasm: *I am here.*

It was alive. Wary of its master, aware of its penitent. But Hope had no use for prayers tonight.

She stormed down the aisle. The draft rustled Bible pages and tossed leaflets like she was the Devil herself come to ravage God's sanctum. Biddies in the pews might've clutched their pearls, priests might've rushed to escort her outside, altar boys might've whipped out their phones to film the ordeal, but the church was empty. And so she stomped her way inside, stared down Christ on his cross, and screamed the godforsaken name that haunted her so.

Gold-leaf sunset streamed through the windows, gilding a path he seemed to vampirically avoid. He emerged shirtless from the back bedroom's gloom, caught shaving: half smooth-jawed, half Santa-Claused with foam. Taking one look at the sodden creature panting on the runner, he retreated to whence he came as if Hope weren't there at all—knowing it would only serve to further ignite her fire.

He didn't close the door.

"Hey!"

The boards shrieked with every step. But as Hope stalked through the nave, as she drew nearer the buttery lamplight pouring from the room, Hope's hurricane met its eye. The squalls stilled.

In the three years they'd loved one another before the crueler devils of his nature made themselves known, she'd watched Killian shave with no small contentment from hotel chaises and cabin beds and even, sometimes, from bathroom floors. It'd always been oddly fascinating. The precision, the care, the steady hand demanded by the task, because old school to the bone, Killian had never opted for the inelegant plastic wands found in pharmacy aisles. He preferred the straight razor. Freshly stropped.

Hope didn't have to imagine the glacial sting of the blade's flat on her skin, nor the cut of its business end as it glided across her stomach, prodding a piccolo song from her nerves. She didn't have to imagine because she knew. She remembered, to some degree of muted shame, having enjoyed the experience. Having asked for it. She remembered the pain, and the blood, and the glint of delight in Killian's eye whenever she hissed.

He'd only ever cut with consent. Now that he'd assumed an active role in the demolition of her life, would consent lose all meaning? Tip-toed steps brought her to the bedroom threshold. Tectonic plates of muscle shifted in his back as Killian leaned over the sink, scraping snow from his cheek.

I swear, Magpie. It's not you.

Murdering her acquaintances was one thing. Framing her for the crime was another. All Hope had was the fifteen years of trust between her throat and his fangs, and his recent antics had rendered that trust feeble and him more volatile, more dangerous than ever. Still, she had to know. Why now? Why like this?

Why?

Hope stepped into the bedroom and closed the door behind her.

CHAPTER SIXTEEN

STRAIGHT RAZOR

No windows. No knick-knacks. Just dim yellow lamps in a dim wooden room, spartan but for the cross above the bed, a shelf of worn tomes, and a framed family photo. His mother Elizabeth. His sister Aoife. His father. What was his name? Killian was notably absent; in his presence, the family might not have smiled.

Hope dragged her nails along the cedarwood desk in the center of the room. Flakes of French manicure chipped away. She considered and discarded first words before settling on a statement suited for segue. "The papers have started calling you The Bowerbird."

Killian tapped the razor on the sink's lip, plopping foam and stubble into the hot running water. "Did you know they speak not of me, but you?"

"Bowerbirds build these ridiculous little houses to attract the ladies. Twig domes and archways, berries sorted by color. Architects, they call 'em. Is that what this is to you? Some sick love letter written in blood and ostentatious bullshit?"

"I suppose that depends entirely on if it's working, darling."

Even after years of loving and hating him, Killian's silver-spoon tone and impassive face had always made it difficult to tell when he was joking—but there, a twitch in his lip.

"This isn't funny."

"Oh, dear. What a tragic miscalculation on my part," he said. "Here I thought I was the comedian of the century, ready to schedule my first appearance on *Good Morning America*."

Killian resumed his task. Hope's anger flared, propelling her across the room, nullifying her fear. She slammed him against the wall. The razor nicked him. A bead of blood pearled on his chin. Hope steel-gripped Killian's wrist, the razor inches from her cheek, her eye.

Breath came after breath. Hard and afraid. Close. So close. He could end her right there, right then, with a shove and a slash.

He didn't.

Killian's right hand relaxed, slipping the razor into hers. Its horn handle fit snug in her fingers, loaded as a gun with fatal possibility. She could do it. Do it now. He was only inches away. Jugular. Carotid. Hope imagined the give of soft skin and tough muscle as she plunged the blade through his throat, felt the blood ooze down her arm, Rorschach her chest, drip syrupy from her elbows.

Her gut churned.

"You swore, Killian," she said instead. "Swore on your mother's grave that you wouldn't—"

In one lithe motion he reversed their roles—pinned her to the wall, snatched the razor back, and tucked it beneath her jaw. "That I wouldn't kill you."

"You're framing me," Hope spat. She focused on her breath, fighting for control over her thundering heart. "You may not have a gun to my head, but you're still gonna destroy me if you keep this up."

"I never made any promises on that account, now did I?"

Splinters in the wooden wall tickled the small of her back. His left hand settled beside her head. When was the last time mere millimeters separated their lips? When had his eyes shined so blue—when had his body heat been so oppressive—when had she been so ready to at once slit his throat and submit to his will until the villagers woke to moans echoing from their church?

Resist. Give in. The two used to wage a constant war. Only now did Hope realize that war had never ended; the paradox persisted and refused to be explained, unraveled, or brought before the court of common sense. How could there be room for anything but hatred for the man setting her life aflame?

"You're crushing me," Hope said.

"I'm awakening you."

"You're a condescending fuck."

"Condescending or no, someone has to fuck you."

The door was shut. The light rich. His tone exhilaratingly obscene. Their no-touch pact had evaporated atom by atom in the amber ambiance, in the nuclear light of impassioned rage.

"Do you remember when you loved me?" she asked.

"I never stopped."

"Then why?"

"Why what?"

"Why *what*?"

Hope swiped his pinning arm at the elbow, freeing her hand. The razor clattered into the sink. In its absence she erupted, grabbing his shoulders to flip their positions yet again. His back hit the wall. The church's ribs shuddered.

"Why the hell are you doing this to me?"

Whip-quick, he gripped the back of her head, digging his nails in the tender divot between the base of her skull and the nape of her neck. Alarm bells clanged.

"Killian," she said, half plea and half warning. "You promised."

He leaned in, lip to ear. "Promises can break under the right amount of pressure."

Before her panic could reach a boiling point, Hope was released. She sucked in a breath she'd been holding but didn't give up ground. Didn't break eye contact as she barred a forearm against his Adam's apple.

"I never gave a damn whether you hurt me or hugged me, whether you made me bleed or licked my wounds." The bulge of a gulp traveled beneath her arm. "But this isn't some game of *How much pain can Hope take before she says 'stop'*. Killian, this is my life. Why are you ruining it?"

"Why not?"

"Don't cop out, asshole." Hope applied more pressure, drawing a dry cough out through his smirk. "You've always got something when it comes to me. Maybe not a reason, or a motive, or anything that'd make sense, but an impulse. An urge—"

A kiss, pressed past her forearm. Fireworks burst in her stomach. Snap. Crackle. Boom. Hope pulled away, stumbling back. Contempt, disgust, and the poison thrill of desire marbled inside: a cocktail of oil and milk swirling and refusing to mix. Longing and self-loathing. Nostalgia, potent as ever. She wiped a smidge of shaving foam from her cheek and studied it closely, as if its existence were the oddest thing in the world. It was all she could do, assaulted as she was by memories fond and frightening both.

"You wicked prick," she whispered, blinking away tears. "How dare you?"

"There is no cure for being human, Hope."

Her eyes flicked to the razor. "How about a blade?"

"Not a cure," he said. "But it certainly makes things more interesting."

A tear escaped.

"Would you slash my throat if I kissed you again?"

"I don't know," she said—and for the first time in a long time, she meant every word.

"Let's test the theory then, shall we?"

He waited. She waited. It would be her choice, this time. He would force her to make the decision herself. She could walk away. Wipe her tears, smooth her sweater, and leave it all behind. Get back in the truck. Drive away. Return to normalcy, go home, and forget, forget, forget. But as she'd settle down to sleep that night, tossing and turning among the sheets, even nightmares would evade her as sleep refused to come. Cold sweat would claim her. Every time she'd close her eyes in a futile effort to flee the night, there he'd be—the foam on his cheek, the satisfaction in his eyes, his lips, just there... taunting. Killian was evil in its purest, rawest form, obsidian forged in caves untouched by men and sun.

There was something about those caves though. Despite the dangers and the demons, they begged to be explored.

Stilling her jangled nerves, gathering her courage, Hope approached. She tilted his chin to the left and picked up the razor. With an intimate slowness, she glided up against the grain, over the ridge of his jaw. Once. Twice. Three times. He watched her peripherally in the mirror. She the practiced exhibitionist; he the calm voyeur.

"Y'know," Hope mumbled, forcing her voice onto as even a keel as her fingers. "Your existence really is a burden on mine."

"The fact you've done nothing to correct said burden is a testament to the masochism you work so valiantly to deny. Makes a man wonder if you'll ever tire of playing cat-and-mouse with your own desires."

She could do it now. Right now. The angle of his neck exposed a steady pulse, ready to gush. Hope's own thrummed, a hummingbird in a cage of flesh and bone so eager to be free. And she *could* be free. Forever free from the storm cloud of Killian Glass and the paradox he brought into her life. The paradox he turned her into.

Was she Hope Rippa, or was she the Magpie? Would she fight, or would she flee? Every interaction between them had always boiled down to this—not if she *was* a monster, for he remained convinced she was—but rather, as a monster, what would she do?

Dragging the flat of the blade down his throat, across the slope of collarbone and hillock of chest, Hope wondered if he was right. She could fight by stabbing. Flee by driving home, or to the police station. Killian feared neither outcome, seemed to beg for one or the other as neither death nor imprisonment apparently scared him. Nothing ever seemed to. How, after all, does someone scare the Devil?

One doesn't, Hope decided. One takes him by surprise. One drops the torch and the sword and approaches the beast unarmed.

Hope gave up the razor once she finished shaving him. The slightest hesitation preceded his rinsing it in the faucet, not bothering to towel his face or check for bumps. After folding it shut, he flipped the handle between dexterous fingers. Waiting silently, patiently for her decision.

Hope didn't lunge for the razor. Hope didn't slip for the door.

Killian fracked her eyes, searching for something nameless. He found it. Took her inaction for the consent it really was.

Snick!

Smirking with dark intent, he snapped the razor open.

CHAPTER SEVENTEEN

RUIN

He backed her toward the mirror until the edge of the sink bit her spine. He consumed her with his eyes, an assessment not unlike a jeweler's examination of a gem, deciding how best to cut. How to make it shine. He settled on her thighs. Tipped his head in thought. They were one of his favorite bits of her, second only to her stomach: for kissing, caressing, and cutting deep.

Using his foot as a broom, he swept her legs apart. The razor traveled the length of her inner thigh, hiking the skirt up. Testing the waters. The height of the waves. As he gauged her reaction with a weapon between her legs, Hope refused to let her anxiety manifest on her face. In his own way, a sick way, Killian was asking permission—and in her own way, her sick way, she gave it. Hope grabbed the cross around his neck, yanked the chain until it broke, and discarded it on the floor.

"Do you really want Him watching?"

"You'd know better than anyone," he said, "that I most definitely do."

Skin makes a certain sound when parted by sharp blades. Not audible to onlookers, but heard, rather, on the inside, by the owner of the skin. The nerves sing. One part shock and two parts pain. Stinging and burning linger for the chorus, and then comes the bridge, and the conclusion: a warm and familiar wetness trickling down, down, down.

The first cut, for Killian, was always shallow. A shark's exploratory bite. He slid the razor into Hope's flesh through a fresh hole in her hosiery. Fiber by fiber it ripped, guided by practiced slowness.

The second cut was always deeper. It split the other thigh. Here was the predatory bite—the bite that said *Yes,* that said *This is meant for eating.* Hope gripped the sink, champing her cheek to keep from wincing. Again, the tights tore, nearly hip to knee, bleeding.

Ruined, but not ruined enough. With Killian, things were rarely enough.

He placed the razor's business end sidelong in her mouth *—Hold this for me, would you?—*and ripped the pantyhose from her body. Iron filled her mouth, staining her red lips an even darker red.

"I do hope these weren't expensive." The glare he earned forced a chuckle from him. "Ah, that's right. Wouldn't want to cut that tongue of yours. It has better uses." He removed the blade. "There we are. How's that? Better?"

Slap!

A pink imprint of Hope's hand brightened the freshly opened pores on Killian's cheek. The pleasure of his surprise receded with a surge of the old fear he'd built in her. Subordinate and dominant. Masochist and sadist. But not BDSM. Nowhere close, nowhere near as safe and sensible.

This was depraved. Filthy. Hope knew that—she'd always known that—but the tingle in her deepest gut only intensified.

"I'll take that as a yes."

"Those were Wolfords," Hope said.

"Should that mean something to me?"

"They're worth more than this building."

"Were, darling. Were. And I'm afraid to inform you that doesn't say much, besides."

"Says enough."

"Are you upset I've ruined your pantyhose, or because I've ruined your lovely legs?" He traced the line of her wound with a tender thumb, so tender it almost didn't hurt—at least until he pressed harder, digging not for more blood but for the groan on her tongue.

"You've gotta do more than play dime-a-dozen domestic abuser to ruin me."

"Good thing we're no longer engaged." Killian pressed the thumb to her mouth, smearing blood on the swell of her lower lip.

She dashed the reflex to lick it off. "You're getting soft in your old age, Father."

Hope grabbed the blade. His pulse quickened as she held it to his neck. Killian leaned into the edge. "Are you wearing underwear?"

"Since when do you wait to find out?"

"Since you left me, darling."

For a second split in three, Hope spotted a spark of uncertainty. It was short-lived and small, but she saw it, and for that fractured moment in time Killian's shred of humanity twinkled in the darkness of his night sky.

"I didn't leave," she said. "You forced me away."

"The way I recall it, you threw the ring across the room and said something along the lines of 'We're done here, you psychotic bastard'." The ring went leaden on its chain. "You always did have a poet's soul."

"Prick."

"Case in point." Killian gently pushed the razor away from

his throat. "It does make a man wonder why you're here now, letting me remove your clothes and carve what's underneath. We're both well aware of your historic gluttony for punishment, Magpie, but was this really how you pictured the evening playing out? When you walked through those doors and saw a blade in my hand, did you think I'd kill you, or were you planning it the other way around after all the chaos I've caused?"

"I—"

Hope didn't have time to react. The barber's strop whipped down from its hook, lashed her neck, and spun her back against his body. Air escaped her. Instinct seized hold. She scrabbled at the strop, her neck—reached back for his face, his eyes, wherever they could find purchase. His glasses fell. The strop tightened.

Breathe.

Breathe.

"Breathe!" Killian commanded, and her panic melted from ice to water. Boiling water.

Hope dropped her center of gravity, turned halfway, and grabbed the strop to duck under his arm and away. An elbow to the ribs for good measure—*thump!*

The strop hit the floor.

Killian clutched his side, face split in two by a delighted grin. He retrieved the blade from where she'd dropped it. They stalked one another in a semi-circle until her back was to the sink again—dancers at rehearsal, returning to starting positions.

"The sweet little Magpie remembers how to obey."

"She remembers she's got claws," she rasped.

"Good." A laugh, borderline manic. "Very good. I'll ask you a second time. Will you slit my throat if I kiss you again?"

"Guess you gotta figure that one out for yourself."

Killian grabbed a fistful of hair. She planted her hands on his shoulders. Knee him in the gut. He grunted, abdomen

133

clenching, but his amusement didn't fade and his grip didn't falter. He held her in place. The razor's dull end embarked on a frigid journey between her legs—slow, ever so goddamn slow—and she tensed, swallowed, and lit him on fire with a leer when it found its destination.

"That answers that, doesn't it?" He considered the blade's new wetness. "What else can I ruin for you then, my dear?"

Hope hated herself for the answer pulled forth from her darkest recesses. Her voids, abysses, her hungry black holes. Nothing good or respectable ever came from such places—from the caverns and the tunnels, the damp, dripping places where awful things lived, temptation chief among them, self-destruction the right-hand man.

"Considering everything you've already destroyed," she said, "let's start with everything else."

After tossing the straight razor and undoing his buckle, Killian bent Hope over the sink so she could watch in the mirror as he reclaimed her.

CHAPTER EIGHTEEN

COCKERELS AND OWLS

Seated on the edge of the bed, Hope cloud-spotted images hiding in the blood blotting her legs. A jackal on her left thigh. A rabbit on her right. She imagined them caught in an endless pursuit: the jackal never quick enough to catch his dinner, the rabbit never fast enough to find her den. At least not until Killian, kneeling before her, erased the jackal with an antiseptic wipe. Did that mean the rabbit won? No, Hope decided. The rabbit would soon be gone, too, struck from existence by the hand of God.

"Remember that day in Seaton Park, when we got drunk on sake and found shapes in the clouds for hours, lying in the grass?" Her voice was as distant as the memory.

"You were quite insistent the sake be Nigori, despite it being near impossible to find." Killian threaded a suture needle.

"It tastes better."

"It's sake."

"For a trust-fund fuckstick, you've got the palate of a peasant."

In went the needle. Hope sucked her teeth.

"For the masochistic ex-fiancée of a serial killer, you've got the pain tolerance of a dormouse."

Killian hadn't always tended her postcoital wounds. Many a mauve scar marred her body, having healed by granulation, but at times he insisted. He'd sit her down, retrieve a med kit from some loose floorboard, trunk, or hidden compartment and go to work in silence. This kit he likely retrieved from the hidden room beneath the church, the trapdoor cloistered behind the altar which she knew existed but never approached.

The severity of the wounds didn't dictate whether Killian tended her. Hope never figured out the deciding factor. Perhaps it was the psychopath's version of social grooming among mammals. Maybe it was simpler. Maybe he just wanted to spend more time together.

Do you remember when you loved me?

I never stopped.

"I do remember that day," he said, breaking her trance. "You insisted *ad nauseam* that one cloud was a falcon, when it was clearly a crow." The way he muttered it suggested a trace of spite, lingering even now.

Hope couldn't help smiling. "Was that our first fight?"

Killian tied off the stitch-job. "Imagine how much simpler life would be if all we argued over was the sky."

Simpler, yes. But would it be happier? If they were together again? After the Old Man had seized her life by the throat and saw to forever change it for the worse all those years back, Hope still got to come home to Killian: a different man, a better man who made her feel safe even when she wasn't, even holding a knife against her skin. Made her feel loved, treasured, even when she didn't deserve it. Aware as she was of the toxicity, the manipulation evident in that line of thinking, she couldn't help but feel it. Some things were just true, no matter how sick they sounded. Did that make her broken?

As Killian wiped the rabbit from her other leg, Hope considered the room: the bed, the desk, the floors and walls. She considered the church, and the village, and the bird sanctuary and mountains and the pond with its fat fish. They'd been deliriously happy once. Could they be again?

Then she spotted the splatter on the floor. The bloody handprints on the sink, the mirror. She thought about all those loose floorboards, trunks, and hidden compartments.

She thought about the ten dead bodies. Ten fresh graves, dusted with snow.

No, she decided. Happiness at his side was a thing of the past. Killian was different from the Old Man, and in a way—she supposed—still better. But he was no less evil. He was not an option.

Hope may have been broken, but she couldn't afford to be complicit in her continued shattering.

Andi sprung to mind. How would Hope explain away the hickeys and lacerations? How selfish was she that her first thought leapt to lying, rather than how much the truth would hurt someone she supposedly cared for?

All thoughts of cloud-spotting and sake evaporated like ghosts.

Killian got to work on the second cut. Her eyes traveled about the room for something to fixate on as a distraction and settled for the crucifix over the headboard.

"Do you actually believe in God?"

"I'm a priest."

"That doesn't mean shit."

"Of course I believe in God," he said. "But I also believe there are gods right here on Earth. Men and women destined to be above, designed to look down and never up."

"Did you see yourself as my God?"

"You used to kneel before me and obey my every wish. Is that not worship?"

"Not anymore."

"Indeed. Not for a long while, not even this—*this* was free will. Who is your God now, I wonder?"

"Does it look like I kneel to anyone anymore?"

"I suspect you won't be kneeling for a few weeks. Not with these," Killian said, piercing her skin to weave the wound shut. "But to answer your question, no. I suppose that makes you your own God. We've much in common in that regard."

"I'm nothing like you. I'm just a person. And I say that with as much relief as you've got delusions of grandeur."

Several stitches went by in tense quiet before Killian spoke up again. "It always looked good on you, you know."

"The blood or the scars?"

"The ring." It sat atop her sweater on full display.

"Well," she grumbled, tucking it back under, "you always thought red was my color."

"Actually, blue is more your style."

"Then why rubies and not sapphires?"

"Blue may be your color, darling, but I prefer blood to bruises. You know that better than anyone."

"I wish I didn't."

"The curse of a keen memory."

"As if you'd ever let me forget."

"The past is a cornerstone of our character," he said. "To forget it would mean forgetting a part of yourself."

So much could be dwelled on in the past—happy or sad, angry or frightened—but this was the present, Hope reminded herself. In the present, this here, this *now*, the same man undoing her life brick by brick was sealing cuts stitch by elegant stitch. Cuts he'd put there to begin with because she'd been foolish enough to let him. She'd given in. Debased herself, and for what?

Would he stop killing? She didn't know. Who was next? She didn't know. Would she have an alibi to escape Oliver's clutches again? Hope drilled into Killian's eyes, blasting the seabed with seismic airguns for the truth.

No, no, no.

"You kissed me," she said.

"I did a lot more than that."

"What game are you playing at?"

"I could ask you the same."

Ten dead bodies. *You were foolish enough to let him.*

"No." Hope slammed a hand down on his, ignoring the sting as the needle tore the raw edge of the cut. She angled down into his face. "You've got explaining to do. This? All this? Frame me for murder, tell me you love me, fuck me and lick my wounds as we reminisce? What is this, Kil, Satan's reject script for a Hallmark movie?"

"A love story, then, are we?"

As confused by her own actions as she was enraged with his, Hope slapped Killian from her lap. The stitches tore halfway, spilling fresh blood. She shot up and away so fast he fell back. Surging to his feet, he threw the needle as if it had insulted his mother.

"Just because I let you fuck me doesn't mean I love you!" she cried.

"You'd quickly descend into poverty should you try your hand at poker," he said. "You have a dreadful tell."

"Whatever helps you sleep at night." Hope fought a losing battle to still the twitch in her lip. "Cus I ain't gonna be there to stroke your back."

There was a vocabulary to Killian's movements, but Hope's dictionary was outdated. Like any language the words had gathered new meanings over time, evolving as he evolved into streaks of silver and fine lines. There was, after all, a great chasm between thirty-three and forty-five.

But there were always words determined to stay. The backbone upon which the language builds its body. The look Killian fixed her with now was one of them. The way he scraped his middle fingernail against the pad of his thumb was another. They combined to form a sentence written clearly in the script of his face: *I am unsure. I am thinking. I may come to a conclusion soon, and you may not like what it means.*

It seemed, however, that even permanent fixtures changed. Killian resolved his thoughts much quicker these days.

"You knew I would be there, didn't you?" he said. "You knew I would see you straddling your canary, half naked in the park."

It wasn't a question. It was a test.

Will you try to lie to me?

Are you confident enough in your ability to see if it will work?

Are you prepared for what happens when it doesn't?

Hope wasn't at all ready to test her lies against the sodium pentothal of his stare.

"Yes."

"Didn't quite catch that, darling."

"Yes! Yes, I knew you'd come, I knew where you'd be, I picked that spot so we'd be the first thing you saw. Is that what you want to hear? Huh?"

"I wanted to hear the truth and you gave it to me." Killian regaled her with a ménage of emotions so at war with one another she couldn't tell which were winning or losing. "But you've yet to explain why."

"I don't know why."

"Liar."

"I don't know what I was thinking—"

"Liar—"

"I wanted to rip that smug fucking mask off your face for once!"

Killian smirked without mirth, tilting his head as if to hear her better. "If you don't love me, then what is to be accomplished in wielding jealousy as a weapon against me, at the expense of another? Another you *claim* to love?"

"I owe you nothing," Hope said, moving toward the door. "Not a fuck, not a favor, and not an explanation."

"Good thing I've already received the first."

Killian caught her arm on her way to leave. Hope looked down at it. Up at him. Wrested from his grasp. "This. This is why I don't love you." And then—explosion. "For fifteen years you've terrified me, Killian. Haunting every step I take no matter where I take them, my sleep no matter what pillow I put my head on, every waking moment on the clock and every second in between. You are a *monster*!"

"You're nothing but a cockerel crowing at midnight," he jabbed, "because you always come back for more—case in point." He smudged lipstick from his neck and shoved the fingers in her face.

"And you're an owl hooting at noon!" Hope picked up her ribboned hosiery and chucked it at his chest. "Don't even try to put the blame on me, you fucking hypocrite!"

Killian calmed himself with a tight-lipped sigh and a hand dragged down his face. It came to rest at his chin, holding it in thought. "You know," he started, recomposing himself, "since our separation, you've seen fit to play red-light, green-light with my affection for you. You've always taken pleasure in tiptoeing just up to my line, but at least you had the good sense to never cross it. But that night, you finally lost your balance—and you fell on the wrong side of the line."

"So that's what all this is about?" Hope yelled. "You're setting my life on fire cus you're *jealous*? It's been over a decade since I took off that ring!"

"Exactly. It has been *that long*, and yet you still wear it around your neck. *That long*, and you still flaunt your petty little cruelties every time we meet. Now, I can take cruelty, darling, and I can deal it in spades—I was built for it. Born for it. But you? This? It's pitiful. You play at punisher, mocking me for being a monster to convince yourself you're not exactly the same as me."

"I'm nowhere near the same as you! That's just some horseshit you came up with to keep you company when, really, you're all a-fucking-lone."

Hope rushed out into the church. Killian stalked her down the aisle. Rain pelted the windows, making stained-glass angels weep in shades of blue and green and red, red, red.

"I wasn't jealous, Hope," he called, stopping midway down the pews as she reached for the doors. "I wasn't angry. I wasn't even upset. Do you want to know what I was? Eh?"

Hope wavered.

"I was *impressed*." Killian approached slowly. The jackal and the rabbit. "That night you made an active choice to wet your feet in a deeper inhumanity, and now, this? This isn't me setting your life on fire. No. This is me slash-and-burning the forest you hide in to see what seeds sprout from the ashes. How deep the roots reach. Which rivers feed them. Because denial or no, you and I? We're cut from the same sheet metal. That's what *all this is about*. Lifting the wool with which you insist on blinding your eyes. It's time to wake up, Hope. You can't keep refusing what you are—it is unsustainable."

"How dare you pretend to kill people for my benefit?" She turned on her heel to find him an arm's length away. "You think seeing a little blood's gonna turn me into a leech like you? Huh?

A parasite? Don't act like you're doing this for *me*. Don't even try. You're doing it for you, just cus you wanna see what happens. It's always been your weakness, Kil. Curiosity with no direction. Boredom with nowhere to go."

"Believe what you wish, it's your prerogative. But know this." Killian seized Hope's jaw, fragile as bird bone in his hand. "You are hypocrisy's patient zero, darling, and it's your life's curse to never know it."

Hope smacked him off. Nothing but dust, unwanted and dirty.

"I'm taking Andi and leaving this frozen goddamn rock. I'm done, Killian. With all of it. The meetups, the business, the... *this*, whatever the hell this is." Weakened by rage, Hope's heart shriveled, breaking her voice in two when she said: "I'm done with you. Never contact me again."

She rent wide the church doors. Stepped out onto the landing. As the downpour scoured her cuts, the emotional filth from her hair and skin, the guilt, the shame, the utter disgust with herself, Hope surveyed the courtyard and saw a silver sedan parked beside her truck in the lot on the other side. Standing in front of that silver sedan, holding a floral umbrella promptly dropped in shock, was Andi.

CHAPTER NINETEEN

SKELETON KEY

"I always wondered where you went when you up and vanished," Andi said. "Who knew your big secret was... going to church."

Andi's parka surrendered to the downpour. With the railing as her guide, Hope descended the stairs. Her boot heels sank in the mud.

"Andi?" Her call was snatched by a gust. She jogged across the quad toward the car, using her hand as an awning to ensure what she was seeing was real. She slowed and stopped, keeping her distance. "How... what are you doing here?"

"Is this what you've been planning?"

Hope's heart relocated to her throat. Andi's pupils were blown.

"Exiling me to the hills? Really? What am I, a rebellious filly resigned to pasture? Tell me, Hope, when were you going to say you made my decision for me? Were you gonna tell me at all, or were you going to call a van one day to have beefy men in white coveralls lift me from my house and cart me here? Did you even plan to be there when they took me away?" Lightning. Thunder. They worked to her effect. "I bet you'd hide away in your loft and come visit me once the worst was over, once I wasn't in so much pain that I wouldn't curse you to hell."

"Andi—"

"Well, you've been wasting your time. *I* made the decision first! The hardest decision of my life, all without your help. I called, and called, and called. Every time, I got your voicemail. So I said screw it! I'll call her from the payphone. Write her a letter. Whatever the heck they'd let me do here, because clearly you were busy, the one who never lets go of her cellphone is *busy* with God only knows what—"

And then she saw him.

She saw the blood on Hope's thighs, nearly washed clean by the weather. The tights on her legs, or rather the lack of them. The shirtless man leaning in the church doorway. The marks on her neck. The territorial tear in her skirt that said *I've been here; This, here, is mine.*

Andi's face shattered, rage disintegrating in the rain. Her open mouth closed. It was an easy enough puzzle to solve.

"Ah. I see. Finally. The man in the park wasn't just a man in the park, was he? I didn't get a good look, but..." Her eyes flitted to Killian, and as if violently rebuffed, they flitted away. "Good lord, how can this be worse? Somehow it is."

She backpedaled, tripped on a stone, and fell in the muck. Hope jogged forward and stooped to help but a savage "Get back!" stopped her. Andi's sneer said *Do not touch me, lest you draw back stubs*, but it was quick to melt as she staggered upright.

"You never loved me," she said, no growl left in her voice. There was only room for pain. "Is this him, then? The one who cut you up like a ham, the one you refused to speak of no matter how hard I tried to get you to just talk to me? Don't answer that. Your legs answer that question well enough." Andi's jaw ground. "Love. What a crock. You only ever loved the *idea* of being in love with me, with someone human. But let me tell you something, *Monkey*—" perverted by sarcasm, Hope's term of endearment speared her through and through "—you're incapable of love. What you have? All you have? That's obsession. That's addiction. Take it from someone who knows. It's addiction, poisonous and cold, and it's all you'll ever have with him, yourself, or with whoever the hell else you convince to climb into your spiderweb. And one day? Y'know, one day? That poison you keep swallowing is going to finally kill you. You'll never see it coming, either, you... you unfeeling bitch. All you'll be is the corpse of a monster no one'll ever care to look for, never mind attend the funeral. You're more addicted to that sadistic sociopath than I am to dope! You should be ashamed—"

"I am—"

"Fuck off!" Hope's joints frosted. She'd never once heard Andi cuss, but here she was, mouth filthy with venom. "The only thing I'll remember about you is how forgettable you are, Hope Rippa." After casting a molten glare Killian's way, Andresína Hammershaimb scorched Hope with all the disdain of God watching his favorite angel fall. "And here I was, thinking I was the pathetic one."

"You don't mean that."

Andi ducked, slipping behind the wheel.

"You can't mean that."

She slammed the door.

"You'll never mean that!"

The silver sedan peeled from the court, fishtailed, and shrieked into the distance.

"You're doomed without me. Lost! A wayward junkie slut, lost in the fucking woods!" Hope's screams were answered only by thunder, by the faraway squeal of tires turning toward Reykjavík. "You're doomed," she whispered.

She endured the rain for a long, long time. Her truck was

right there, but even if she thought she deserved respite she would have stayed, stuck to the cobbles, staring into the distance where red taillights had disappeared. They were as final as a wax stamp on a letter declaring war, or an unhappy end to one.

She forgot where she was. Her injuries. Forgot the state of her body, her mind—her *life*—feeling nothing but the cliff-sized loss of a part of that life, gone with Andi's Toyota. And for what? The storm reawakened the pain in Hope's thighs.

For *what?*

Killian plucked Andi's abandoned umbrella from the mud and opened it over her head, having crossed the courtyard without her noticing. "You don't love her," he said. "You never have."

"Oh, fuck you!" Hope blurted, sending anger and grief and loss in every direction: at him, at herself, at all the bastard villagers peeking through their curtains. She smacked the umbrella out of his hands. "Fuck... fuck you."

"You just did."

"That doesn't mean I don't love her! It just makes me—"

"What? A horrible person? A callous, jaded excuse for one? How about a *monster*, incapable of feeling so much as the breeze on your back? Your canary seems to think so."

"I'm none of those things."

"Then what are you, darling?"

"Human!" Hope chomped her inner cheek's chewing gum. "You don't know shit about what that's like."

"I've a pulse. A breath in my lungs, a beat in my chest, and eyes, in my skull, sharp enough to see."

"What the hell in that description makes you any different from a dog?"

"The bit about seeing. Dogs merely watch."

Hope nearly faltered. She was small, and the wind was strong. She was small, and Killian's presence was bulldozing.

But by the glory of gifts granted by sheer force of will, she held her ground, soaked to the socks—channeling energy away from vital organs and into the coal fire inside that had burned for years. Though at times it had faltered, it had never given out.

"So you see through me? That it?"

"No. I see inside," Killian said. "I see a beast restrained by the expectations of men and women. Forced to squat on a stool, swipe at a whip, and jump through flaming hoops to howling applause—not by those men and women, but by herself. You see, Hope, you've convinced yourself for so long that you belong in their world, walking on two legs instead of four, that you've forgotten how easily their flesh would tear beneath your teeth. Perhaps you fear all the blood. Fear all that red soaking your ledger. Well let me tell you, darling: it's already dripping. It's been basting in blood for years, and running from it will never scrub it clean." Killian fended her slapping hands, grabbing her wrists. "You don't belong in their world—" he shook them hard "—but you fit like a skeleton key in mine."

"Put your glasses back on, Father." Hope yanked free. "You're blind."

His hyena's laughter trailed behind as he walked across the courtyard, shaking his head all the way to the foot of the church steps. He ascended them, grasping either handle of the open church doors: a dark Christ, looming tall. One who cheated. Lied. Turned water into blood instead of wine.

"Did you know magpies aren't native to Iceland?" he called over the maelstrom. "You're the only one here. What was that rhyme again? One for sorrow..." He made a show of thinking. "Perhaps you should leave the country, as you planned—but from the view up here, it appears you'll be going alone."

"Screw you, Killian," she said, unable to find better words. "Screw you straight to hell!"

"Hell is where I live."

148

The *crack!* of the closing doors synced with a peal of thunder. Hope spat on the paving stones, wishing they were the cross Killian kept around his neck—better yet, his face—better yet, better yet, better yet...

She climbed in her truck. Clicked her seatbelt. Laying on the horn, Hope screamed into the cab.

Her spit washed away in the rain.

CHAPTER TWENTY

KILLER AND ENABLER

When Hope finally reached the feeble sanctuary of her fourth-floor loft at 3:00am, she struggled to drag a dresser in front of the door. *You're safe. It's over. It won't happen again.*

The mantra was empty. Hope couldn't remember the last time she felt truly safe or certain of an end, of a thing not happening twice.

She collapsed with her back against the drawers. The surface tension of bending her knees to her chest stretched the remaining stitches, reopened her wounds, and made them weep, but the floors were black, her skirt already ruined. She didn't care at all. It hurt, of course. Not in an erotic way; not all pain was pleasure. Most of it was nothing new or exciting when inflicted outside the bedroom. Sometimes pain was just that. Pain.

The burning and stinging pulsed, as if with laughter. *Eat it up, whore,* it seemed to say. *Lick the fucking floor. You like the taste, remember?*

"No!"

Hope ripped a drawer from its frame. Panties and bras went flying.

"I don't want it."

Palms on her ears.

"I don't like it."

Face in her knees.

"It hurts."

"Yet I see it in your eye. A little spark of thrill." Killian *caressed her cheek, resting the knife on the ground. "Of course it hurts, darling. But does it not excite you too?"*

Her instincts flailed in protest. They screamed no, no, no. *But he was beautiful and kind. He didn't bend her over hotel beds and shove her skull to the mattress to muffle her groans, leaving lipstick smudges on linens the maids would sooner burn than wash. He always asked before he hurt, and she had said yes. Every time she said yes. With him, not one dollar changed hands.*

"Look up." Hope looked at the Christmas lightshow of fireflies *waltzing on the dance floor of the summer evening sky. "Imagine yourself up there," he said, slicing into her thigh, sliding his free hand between her legs until hisses turned to moans. "What is flesh and blood, after all, but a barrier between man and heaven?"*

She'd stargazed through threads of yellow blips, feeling life ooze as rivers from her stomach and legs. "I'm not a man," she whispered.

He'd planted his hand on her belly. Her red on his skin formed a sort of pact, one sealed and permanent, though at the time she hadn't known. Back then she'd been a fledgling, perching on branches closest to the nest. Alone. Afraid, until Killian came along with his disarming charm and his knives to teach her how to fly. Maybe she'd already been the Magpie, long before she wedged her foot reluctantly in the door of the business. Long before earning the infamous *nom de guerre*.

But every time they kissed, she shed fluff and grew feathers. Every time they fucked, her beak sharpened and longed for meat. Every time he cut, her talons lengthened, hooked, and became better and better tools to threaten, blackmail, or finesse people into doing her dirty work. The longer they were together, the more Hope had evolved.

What had he turned her into? Why had she let him?

She knew the answer. She pushed it away.

Even when Hope had been oblivious to his hobby, their romance had felt a theater of war. And like all wars, it eventually came to a head.

JANUARY 18TH, 2010

Since she'd traded prostitution for her role as the Magpie, tending the whims of the bloodthirsty few and stocking their toolkits accordingly, Hope had never received a new client request from a maximum-security prison. She wondered who so ached to join the killers there. It couldn't be a prisoner. The nurses were unlikely, the cooks unlikelier, the janitors unlikeliest. Could be a guard, maybe the governor himself.

She'd hesitated at the gates, at first. Imagined the Old Man behind its bars, bearing stained, crooked teeth, snapping like the mad dog he was. If he'd still been incarcerated here, she would've ignored the request. Burned it. Buried it. But she'd checked with a contact in the Scottish Prison service—one she'd secured the minute the Old Man had finally been caught and convicted—

and was relieved to discover he'd been transferred somewhere far away. She didn't bother to check where, preferring the bliss of ignorance. The Old Man was gone. That was all that mattered.

Strutting to the front desk, the men manning it slack-jawed her from toe to tip. She wondered when last they'd heard the sharp *tack, tack* of no-nonsense heels, or seen a young woman working them.

She signed and dated the visitor's log. One-eighteen ten.

After a fifteen-minute wait, two of the meatheads escorted her into an empty hall of visiting booths, narrow and white with fluorescent lighting. The stench of dust and sweat overpowered an undercurrent of bleach.

Hope had committed the request to memory.

Booth three. Wait six minutes. Keep your head down until I sit, and don't pick up the phone until I do.

Commanding tone, clipped words, inflated sense of authority. Probably a guard. Definitely a man.

The pleather stool released a dying gasp when she sat, frothing yellow foam from the split mouth in its side. It was clear the booths hadn't seen much use since the opening of the visiting rooms, where guests and detainees could talk at tables without foggy panes of glass between them. It made for the perfect rendezvous—especially after Hope noticed the security cameras' green lights had gone dark.

Examining the stains and peeling vinyl on the counter, Hope wasn't sure how to feel. Truthfully, she was nauseated. Nervous. This person was an outlier on her client list so far from the mean, he might as well not even be on the graph. And there was something else. Something shapeless and black worming beneath her belly button. Some called it a gut feeling. To Hope, it was a Geiger counter. It kept her alive in a deadly line of work.

It was well in the red, screeching bloody murder. But something kept her in Chernobyl.

A door squealed open. Banged shut. Locked. Slow, measured steps grew louder upon approach. They didn't *thump-thump* like boots. They *tap-tapped* like dress shoes. There was no jingle of handcuffs, no clatter of keys, no swish of synthetic uniform pants. The urge to lift her head was a fierce itch, but she didn't scratch. Hope was a professional. She followed protocol. She'd established them herself, and requests were honored within reason, so she focused on the stains and vinyl of the counter until she heard the muffled huff of ass on pleather.

Killian was the last person she expected to see.

He'd stroked her hair until she woke that morning. Kissed her cheek, her shoulder, the neat grid of slashes recently carved in her hip. She brewed a potent red eye. He fried over-medium eggs. They breakfasted not at the table but on the couch, where she playfully tormented him with cold feet. Setting down his plate and mug, he grabbed her feet as if to warm them, but it'd been a ruse; he used her ankles as levers to spread her legs, and they made love on the couch in the burning brightness of 10:00am sun bleeding through open windows and blinds.

They'd spent the whole day together. He napped. She read. He smacked the book away so she couldn't read; she pounced atop him so he couldn't sleep. When she hissed—the newest addition to her gallery of wounds sticking to the sheets—he retrieved the first aid kit, and while he dressed the wound, he deployed impeccable bedside manner, distracting her with questions like *What's your favorite cocktail?* and *Do you ever miss Georgia?* and *You had a parrot as a kid, didn't you? What was its name again?*

It had been a nice day. A lovely day. And now, squinting at his face through the clouded glass, Hope knew it'd be the last.

Though she knew Killian worked as prison chaplain for HMP Barlinnie's damned, she shouldn't have seen his face until morning, when he returned home from a long night's work.

The cosmic irony was indigestible. Realizing what a blind fool she'd been, every stepping-stone down the path from meet-cute to this moment flooded her system with disbelief. Hope simply couldn't reconcile this night with this morning, this night with the past three years serving as Killian's plaything, a loved and treasured plaything, a plaything with a ring on her left hand in clandestine defiance of the Church. A thousand words seethed on her tongue, hornets ready to roll, and every last one was angrier than angry: each would sting him dead.

But when he picked up the phone, and she picked up the phone, the hornets dove back into her stomach, choosing death by acid over whatever needed saying, even with all those walls and the windows between them.

He spoke first.

"I was under the impression that when you disappeared in the wee hours, it was because you'd resumed whoring," he said. "I never really considered you might be the Magpie."

Hope's throat pinched shut. The Geiger counter broke, and so did her voice when she stammered, "Killian."

"Magpie."

"Don't call me that."

"Is that not your name?"

"You know my name."

"And now I know your real one. Cosmic irony has no sense of boundaries, eh, darling?"

Hope leapt to her feet, unable to corral her self-control. She banged a fist against the glass, but before she could yell or scream he was up, too—he banged the glass, too—he mirrored her and she mirrored him, pain and confusion and fury;

betrayal, broken trust, and love left out like a pint of milk in the sun.

Beneath his fist was a flattened piece of paper. An itemized list, delicately handwritten. Most of her clients typed theirs. An unnecessary countermeasure in the Magpie's hands. Following the loops of his L's, the curves of his S's, the somehow soft spikes of his M's and N's and K's, Hope's grip slipped until she collapsed in a heap on the counter, awakened to the knowledge that her lover cut others besides her.

Only a lot deeper.

"Evil," she whispered.

Killer. Enabler.

"You're evil," she said.

Killer. Enabler.

"Purebred, full-blooded, certified fucking evil!"

Hope tore the ring from her finger and launched it at the glass. It ricocheted, landed somewhere on the tile floor. She felt she should say something. Something to the effect of *It's over* or *We're done,* like they did on the soaps her mother once watched with frantic intensity in the den. But no words rose to the challenge. No words except one.

"Killian…"

It was colored in hues of denial—sepia, maybe mauve. One name could say so much. *This can't be true; you're a priest; you have your vices, but I indulge them and know them well.*

She'd nearly convinced herself that she knew him completely before she looked at the list. "Killian, no."

One ophthalmic speculum.

One melon baller.

One coping saw, one pneumatic drill, three yards of leather lashing, a shovel, gloves, and seven kidney dishes.

Hope hurled the telephone at the glass. Killian kept his glued to his ear. She picked up the phone and threw it again.

Again. Again. The glass vibrated over and over, denying her rage over and over, Killian blinking with each impact. Panting, crying, and pulling apart at the joints, Hope's fire burned out. With nothing left to do or say, she lifted the phone back to her face and managed the million-dollar question.

"You're a *murderer*?"

It was a night for firsts.

It was the first time she saw Killian cry. Two tears, one from each eye. It was the first time his voice hitched. Lost, deprived of its debutant's poise. It was the first time they saw one another truly naked down to the tendons, forced to shed the comfort of their carefully constructed skins and masks and beneath, there were so many ugly scars.

"I..." he mumbled. "I suppose so."

Speculum, baller, saw.

Drill, leather, gloves.

Killer, enabler, killer.

Hope wailed with all the wretched agony the world had on tap that night, dropping the phone to clutch her slashed hips. Her butchered stomach. Her torn thighs. Shock filled her mouth, stuffed it full, no release, choking, strangling. "Why?" she asked.

Killian flopped back in his seat. Once Hope quieted, gulping great lungfuls of air, she met his stare tit for tat and was granted the unfortunate opportunity to witness an evolution. Feeling to nothing. Passion to apathy.

Lover to monster.

"Why?" she asked again, and he answered: "Why not?"

Fear and dread; the byproducts of treachery. They hijack thoughts and lead coup d'états on the brain, leaving behind an irremovable mark. Hope would scrub at it for years. She'd try club soda and bleach. Fire and excision. Hypnosis. Yoga. Tempting fate.

Nothing would work. The stain was permanent.

Why versus why not.

Killian, stroking her hair. Tracing the curve of her legs. Kissing her neck, her back, the ridges her ribs made beneath rice-paper skin when she bent just right. Hope felt all these things, recalled how special they seemed. Hope remembered all the early mornings, mid-afternoons, and hours-past-midnights at once as she stared down the newly minted monster on the other side of the glass.

"We're done here, you psychotic bastard."

She stood and turned toward the door, battling the rapids of square footage from here to there. The ring barred her exit, glittering on the ground.

"Keep it," Killian said. "It was a gift, after all."

Hope considered the space. The locks, the cameras, the guards around every corner with their batons and bad attitudes. "You're exactly where you belong, Father Glass."

"As are you, Magpie. You may not realize it yet, but your fate is irrevocably bound to mine."

"Oh yeah?" she sneered. "How's that? Behind bars?"

"No, darling. At my side." Dusting his black frock, he shook his head at his own proclamation as if it were tragic prophecy. "We are inevitable."

Killian vanished behind the door he'd come from, carrying the bounty of the last word. The list he left behind lied, spread open, on his side of the counter.

Hope stood in that hall for an eon, fighting while standing still. The stain of the night's revelation sank into the meat of her heart. After the tears dried on her cheeks, she made three decisions that would echo through the winds of the rest of her life.

She snapped a photo of the list through the glass.

She plucked the ring up from the floor.

She left.

Hope flipped the ruby ring from knuckle to knuckle, hypnotizing herself to linger in that twelve-year-old night. Feeling the ripples it cast into the present. When the ring fell from her pinkie, she was back in the loft.

The lacerations had clotted. The blood on the floor congealed. The rain and clouds had fled the sky, splashing silver starlight through the glass wall facing the sea. In the absence of the torrential rain's drumming and newly freed from the ghost of breakups past, a noise popped the bubble of Hope's reclaimed self-awareness. Having visited a hospital once or twice in her life, she recognized the steady beeping of an EKG machine. But this was not a hospital. Not even close.

It came from her bedroom.

Beep. Beep. Beep.

CHAPTER TWENTY-ONE

YOUR CHOICE

H er legs peeled off the gummy puddle of blood as she
stood, thighs gelatinous. She crept between the kitchen
table and island, past the mounted ibex skull, wax-crusted
candelabras, hanging baskets of Boston fern and English ivy
until she arrived at the bedroom. Hope usually kept her nest
cozy and dim in gold with a single nightstand lamp, but the
cracked door cast a slice of cyan light across her shins.

Beep. Beep. Beep.

She could run. Should run. But running solved nothing.
Knowing Killian, running was designed to make her look twice
as guilty—was, in fact, a snare trap, wherein the harder she
struggled, the tighter the noose drew.

She nudged open the door.

Blood pressure, 110/70. Heart rate, 76. 98 percent oxygen
saturation, 97-degree body temperature, respiratory rate of 16.

Hanna was alive.

Hanna was alive but Hope didn't know what the IV bag was
pumping into her arm. She didn't know if the solution was
keeping her breathing, killing her slowly, sedating her
permanently or doing nothing at all. The PCA machine read

Continuous, so an unknown amount of an unknown substance would flow into her at an unknown interval for what must be the foreseeable future, or until the bag ran dry.

Hanna was strewn atop the bed in her undergarments. Ruby hair fanned the pillows. Fresh plum bruising flowered on her temple. Tear-streaked mascara traced sewer lines over her freckles, and what first appeared to be smudged red lipstick was really a bloody, swollen lip.

In through the nose, deep. Out through the mouth, long.

Beep. Beep. Beep.

"What the fuck," Hope whispered. "What the fuck, what the fuck."

When had he done this? How? What was his endgame—

No, no, no.

Hope shut down the panic. What Killian had done and why were of no consequence. The only thing that mattered now was how she reacted.

What would a normal person do? Call the police. Oliver. She searched for the phone in her jacket, unlocked it, and shucked his business card from the wallet case.

Oliver Ragnarsson. Detective Chief Inspector, Reykjavík Metro Police.

There'd been a softness to his otherwise sharp-cut face suggesting past trauma, the kind translating, over the years, to a pity for broken things, like cats on death row and Magpies in handcuffs. But that was only part of him. The other, harder half was clear in his words.

You're hardly off the hook.

Hope tossed the phone and crumpled his card in the trash. She was on her own.

Focus.

She scoured the room for oddities as odd or odder than the woman in her bed. In the closet, nothing. On the nightstand, nothing, but there... under the bed, the plunger of an empty hypodermic needle. Hope snatched it, checked under the bedframe, and found an empty vial. The label clipped the elevator cables suspending her heart in her chest.

Hydromorphone. Of course. *Of course* he'd use Dilaudid, but...

There was enough evidence already to incriminate Hope without the needle and drug. Killian left them for a reason. Where else hadn't she checked?

Between the beats of the EKG, Hope tuned in to another channel: a faint *drip-drip* coming from the en-suite bathroom. The door was closed, but from the gap at the bottom came a strip of white. The light was on. Needle in hand, Hope barged inside to find the faucet just barely on, an item on either side of the basin, and a message in Merlot lipstick written across the mirror.

On the left: FIGHT, above a bottle of fentanyl.

On the right: FLIGHT, above a receipt for an unregistered plane seat.

And in the middle, in swooping, elegant script: YOUR CHOICE.

Peering through the O's and C's at her reflection, Hope imagined Killian standing just behind her, stroking her arms from wrist to shoulder and settling at the sides of her neck. Hot breath on her cheek. Smooth lips on her ear. A black velvet whisper: *Which will it be, little Magpie? What sort of monster are you?*

She shook off the mirage but still didn't move. Injecting Hanna with a 150-microgram overdose of fentanyl would cause a severe interaction. Instant death.

"You are small, yet still strong. The ocean is just there. The current is even stronger, more than enough to pull the body down."

Hope fanned Killian's apparition away.

Boarding the flight to Barra, the U.K.'s smallest airport, would sneak Hope to the land where she'd established the vastest networks, safest safehouses, and the most owed favors to carry her away from prosecution.

"*Leave her, darling, don't so much as lift a finger. Run away, far away, so even when she wakes and phones the authorities, not even that lad with the badge and scar will find you.*"

She swatted Killian's phantom, resisting the urge to hyperventilate.

Two options. Two choices. Two spiritual death sentences handing Killian exactly what he wanted no matter which she chose.

What her murderous ex didn't seem to realize, however, was that there was an alternative path. The middle path. The path that was hardly a path at all and the one she'd taken in his bedroom but hours earlier. It hadn't ended well, but it ended better than fight or flight ever could.

When the Devil gives you two options, a smart woman creates a third. Fight? Flight? No.

Hope took a step back, hearing Andi's admonishment over the phone in Milan.

You could have stayed.

She set the empty needle down on the counter.

————

Perched on the foot of the bed, Hope waited for an hour, taking turns picking chips in her nail polish and studying the snap of the bathroom setup she'd taken with her cellphone. Maybe it'd help her case. Maybe it'd hurt it. Maybe it would do nothing to keep her on the right side of Oliver's bars. This was her new normal: smashing a circular peg at a triangular hole until it finally fit—fit because it broke.

A bandage covered the burst-vein bruise on Hanna's arm, wrapped after Hope had removed the IV. She'd considered brushing Hanna's hair, removing her mascara, applying Vaseline to her split lip. But Hope was no caretaker. She cared little for Hanna's wellbeing beyond her being alive—cared even less for her own wellbeing, having yet to scrub the blood candy-coating her legs.

She picked at the raw edges of her wounds. Tied errant stitching into tiny bows.

Hanna groaned.

Hope hopped to her feet, unsure where to move. The clock struck 4:00am. She'd had plenty of time to devise a game plan for fielding Hanna's freakout, but her mind had gone wandering through dark woods instead.

"Who... where am I?" Hanna sat up. Fell back. She poked the mashed strawberry of her lip. "What happened?"

No one in particular was asked these questions. Hope doubted Hanna even felt another presence in the room. There was pawing of blankets and moans of nausea. When at last she ascended the Everest of pillows to sit upright, Hanna noticed Hope—and as if she'd mainlined epinephrine, her eyes went wide and woke her to the reality of her surroundings. Sensing the volcano ready to blow, Hope upturned her palms in supplication.

Hanna squinted at her arm, the machines, her half-naked body in an unrecognizable bed. "Hope?" she slurred. "What'd you do to me?"

It wasn't the question she was expecting. She'd been expecting a *What happened?*, maybe even a *What are you doing here?*

The fear in Hanna's eyes. The racing thoughts.

"No, Hanna, you don't understand." Hope bounced her palms in a gesture she prayed seemed reassuring, taking a cautious step forward. It sent Hanna tumbling over the side of the bed. She stood, stumbled, and stood again, using the bed as leverage. Hope knew it'd be a mistake to help her. "Hanna, relax! This wasn't me, I swear."

"The last thing you swore was to... to have me deported if I don't... if I didn't get what you wanted."

"That was a stupid lie, you know tha—"

"You kidnapped me?"

"No!"

"Drugged me." Blatant fear of what had transpired while she'd been unconscious cranked Hanna's voice to a six-octave squeak. "What else did you do?"

"Nothing, I didn't—"

"You mean nothing *else*?"

"No, I just got home an hour ago—"

"You left me here alone?"

"Christ alive, Hanna, if you'd let me get a goddamn word in—"

"Get those words out of your mouth." It was a shaky warning, molasses-thick at once with terror and righteous indignation. "You've done enough to... to..."

"I didn't do anything to you. I promise."

Finally, a lull in the tension. Hanna sucked in a shuddering breath. Her attention wandered. A good sign. She was secure enough to take her eyes off Hope, the perceived threat in the room. Of course they wandered to the exact wrong place. Something Hope hadn't noticed in her quest for odd things. It was in too obvious a place.

On a loveseat on the opposite side of the bed, piled messily in the corner of the room, were Hanna's clothes.

The remains of them.

A pink shirt was torn from the chest out, as if to expose breasts. A pair of navy slacks was split down the seams, as if ripped off thrashing legs. Hanna clammed. Revolted, *profaned*. One arm over her chest, another clamping her hips.

"I've seen you with that Faroese girl," she muttered to herself.

Panic, hot and inescapable. "No, Hanna. I didn't do this to you."

"Was she not enough for you?"

"Hanna, it's not what it—this wasn't me. None of it."

"Then who?"

Hope's mouth opened. Nothing came out.

"Monster," Hanna whispered. "Lord forgive me, you're a goddamned monster. Hell awaits you. Nothing but hell."

She gave Hope a quick and wide berth, catching the doorframe with her shoulder on her wobbly rush to the main room. Hope followed far behind, both hands tearing hair. What could she say? What could she do? Everything pointed to *you, you, you*.

Hanna reeled to a stop, gaping at the dresser barring the door.

"What is this? Are you keeping me here?" Hanna violently shook her head, the drug's lingering influence making her lids flutter. "Move it," she said. "Move it right now, Hope, or I'll call my boss, I'll call the mayor, I'll call the police." Patting her pantslessness, she amended: "Or I'll... I'll scream and wake all the neighbors. M-move the damn thing. Right... right now!"

"Okay. Fine." Hope got into position to drag the dresser back. "You're not being held hostage, Hanna. I got home tonight and you were just here. I don't know how. Or why. I—"

"Just let me go!"

Hope pulled the dresser back to its patch of floor. As soon as enough space opened up for Hanna to slip through, she fumbled with the four locks, yanked the knob, and wobbled out onto the landing.

"Hanna, wait!" Hope followed her out.

"Leave me alone!" The shout echoed from half a floor down.

"You're naked, you'll freeze."

"And my chance of survival somehow goes up!"

"Hanna!"

No response. Feet padding, lumbering, bumbling down, down, down until the telltale screech of the building door set Hope's teeth to grind. She ran back into the loft and out to the balcony. Looked down over the railing.

"Hanna, stop! You're not safe!"

Hanna teetered into the middle of Shore Walk and reached into her bra. Even from on high, Hope recognized her own phone case. She patted her pockets to no avail. She'd put her cell down somewhere. Hanna had some street smarts after all.

Shit.

Hope considered calling down again, one last plea, but what would it do besides bleed through the static backdrop of whoever Hanna was calling? Instead, Hope leaned over the rail, tilting down to catch snatches of conversation over the roar of the waves.

"... Rippa... Yes... Don't know... No, please, no ambulance... Call the... need a ride... cold."

It sounded like she was speaking to a friend. Not emergency medical, not the authorities—who the hell was Hanna calling? A boyfriend? Her editor? Hope could see her headshot on the front page of tomorrow's morning edition, framed under a slanderous headline. *Former Who's Whoer Faces Shocking Allegations: Kidnapping, Assault, and Murder, Oh My!*

Hanna toddled down Shore Walk, disappearing into the night.

Pacing the length of the balcony, Hope wrestled with what

to do. What *could* she do? Call Oliver to get ahead of any incident reports? With what phone? She didn't have a landline. Freezing at the partition separating her balcony from her neighbors'—from Gunnar and Katrin's—she took in the police tape hanging limply over the sliding door. She could simply go to the next hall over and alert the constable standing guard, couldn't she? Straining for signs of life, for shuffling officer's boots or maybe Biscuit's meow, she heard nothing. The search had been concluded, the force stretched too thin to maintain a watch over the dead couple's residence. How else would Killian have snuck an unconscious Hanna into her apartment if there was a police presence, anyway?

Always two steps ahead, while she was cursed to lag behind.

Hope resigned herself to the fact that there was nothing more to be done. Giving in to exhaustion, she retreated inside, coiling in her teardrop hanging chair.

She waited for the cops.

When they arrived shortly after sunrise, in its fleeting golden moment, they were gentle with her door. Probably because Oliver led the team, because Oliver was the only policeman to come inside and approach the wicker chair, where he found a broken creature covered in blood, cuts, and apathy, sun-honeyed eyes saddened at the state of her—or at least she imagined they were.

She didn't look up when he approached. "Hey, Ollie."

"Good morning, Hope." Oliver took to one knee, pressing his lips together to avoid betraying his pity, or his anger, or whatever maddening mix of feelings he felt as he studied her blood-crusted wounds. A rattle and clank announced handcuffs unhooking from his belt. "I need to put these on you. Okay?"

"Okay."

Zink. Zink.

Oliver glanced over his shoulder. Beckoned with his chin. Another officer shuffled in, handing over a threadbare blanket.

"I brought one with me this time." It came out like an apology. Had Hope not been so lodged in defeated indifference, she might've considered such tenderness suspicious. But the only suspect was her, and Oliver knew that well enough. "Take it. It's all right. At least you've got more clothes on this time, yeah? Let's get out of these guys' way."

Oliver offered an arm, helping Hope to her feet. He made sure to find her boots and let her slip them on before leading her to the stairwell. He didn't spot the guthook knife.

"Do you think I'm guilty, Ollie?" she asked.

"I'm not sure what you are, Miss Rippa." He sighed. "But we'll figure it out."

CHAPTER TWENTY-TWO

EIGHTEEN HOURS

S eated alone in the interrogation room, Hope traced the spine of stitches forcing her lacerations into sideways smirks. She peeled off the dressings.

Oliver had forced her into the ER to get her patched before heading to the station. It was there on the stiff hospital bed, after the doctor had finished sewing the first wound shut, that Hope noticed the cuts were curved. They were blueprinted for maximum pain in every movement: prone to tearing and difficult to scab.

Hope's handcuffs were hidden, at the time, under a moss-green hospital gown. The doctor had clucked in sympathy. He'd said, "Whoever did this to you is a real sick bastard, miss."

She'd made eye contact with Oliver, and he'd looked away.

Across the hours spent wasting away in the interrogation room, Hope eventually graduated from listing in the chair, to pacing its length, to lying on the table and watching her reflection in the two-way mirror, wondering if Oliver watched back. The diffidence Hanna's departure left behind had warmed, defrosting under a space heater of agitation. Hope's brazen self was resurfacing and eager for a verbal spar, for something, anything, another face or body to occupy the space. Anything would be better than wallowing in her own thoughts.

She sprawled, whistling a commercial jingle that'd once advertised a rival coffee shop in Aberdeen. She'd suffered it over her years fixing lattes at the Bethesda Bean, unable to mute the corner TV because the remote had gone missing in action long before she'd been hired.

She whistled the tune, not a care in the world. Not on the outside, anyway. Never on the outside.

Not until this morning. Oliver already had the upper hand with all the evidence for Hanna's assault and kidnapping lighting an airstrip in Hope's direction. Now he was invincible. He'd seen the feeble core she usually donned claws and shamelessness to hide.

When he at last decided to grace her with his presence, this morning's gentleness was so far gone it might as well have never existed.

"Get off the table," he said.

"But I was just getting cozy."

"Now."

Hope sucked her teeth. She shook off the blanket, smoothed her skirt, and settled in the chair. A manila folder took her place on the tabletop.

"The medical examiner says those aren't defensive wounds."

"That's cus nobody was defending anything."

"Nor do they appear self-inflicted."

"Your medical examiner's degree doesn't qualify 'em for much else than shoveling elephant shit at the circus. How good could they possibly be?"

"Excellent, in fact," Oliver said, tapping a finger on a fat casefile. "We've had to call in a specialist from Denmark because of your antics over the past eighteen hours."

"Well, would you look at that." Hope's voice dripped mock appreciation. "Detective Such-and-Such, back on the case, just like that."

"Just like that."

"What happened to the strapping fireman who carried me down the stairs this morning, swaddled in a blanket brought just for me?"

"On leave."

"I didn't know firemen got vacation time."

"Well, Miss Rippa—" the transition from casual first to formal last name stung "—you seem to be the only fire that needs putting out here in Reykjavík, and I give you my full seal of approval for 'well and fully controlled'. If only I had a sticker. One of those little gold stars teachers give to schoolchildren."

"No stickers? I'd file that under police brutality. But alas..." Hope raised her cuffed wrists to emphasize the point. "Controlled is an appropriate choice of words. Tell me, Ollie, what is it you do with fires-under-control? Sweep up the ashes and pray another doesn't catch?"

"I figure out what set them."

"You're seriously telling me, right here, right now, you haven't figured this out yet? Oh boy, oh *boy*—you must've been a force to reckon with back in Confederate country. Look out, ladies and gents, Charleston Charlie's on the case! Bet no one south of the Mason–Dixon fucked with your shrimp 'n' grits."

"I'm vegetarian," he said, unfazed, pulling out and getting to work on another puzzle box, this one shaped like an eight-pointed star.

She was readying a response when a thought balloon-popped in the back of her brain. "Eighteen hours?"

She'd left Killian's village at 1:14am. Got home around 3:00. She'd seen the last of Hanna at 4:04, Oliver took her away at noon, and now it was 7:00pm. Hope had figured the seven-hour wait was just a perfect storm of bureaucratic incompetence, the understaffed state of affairs, and waiting for blood tests to return from whatever backcountry crime lab the police had rented out.

Your antics. Tapping finger. Puzzle box.

"Fuck." She nearly said *his* name but caught it on the K. "It's Hanna, isn't it?"

The finger stopped tapping. There was a twinkle of disillusionment—the last star in his twilight sky chafing to prove her innocence—and then he blinked. Gone. Oliver leaned forward with an *I know something you don't* smile, not much more than a quirk of the lip.

"Ready to spin that yarn for me, Bowerbird?"

Hope shielded her face right before the folder's front flap slapped the table. Wide-eyeing the dark cups of her palms, she listened to the card shuffle of crime-scene photos spreading out in a grid. The thwack of a notebook. The clatter of a pen. A jacket—leather—shrugged off impatient shoulders, catching the back of his chair for a moment and then flopping on the floor.

"Miss Rippa, we received a very distressing call from a very distressed woman. No, not from Hanna. From her boss, Margrét. You know, the award-winning editor-in-chief over at *Fréttablaðið*, with whom my department has worked closely for many a decade. See, Hanna Maslany wasn't the type to up and disappear or fail to send in her work. So, after spending the entirety of yesterday pacing the office floor, wondering where her junior reporter had run off to, Margrét received a similarly distressing call in the small hours of the morning, likely not long after Hanna fled your building. I wouldn't put it past you to entertain ladies on the side unbeknownst to your partner, Miss Rippa—we've all got our vices—but here's the problem." Oliver jutted the pen at Hope's face. "When Margrét arrived to pick Hanna up from Shore Walk, she found nothing but empty street. Can you guess where Hanna is now?"

Hope said nothing.

"Dead and cold on the ME's table, who's trying to determine which killed her first. The flaying of her arms and legs, the splitting of her ribcage, or the house-shaped hole carved in her stomach."

Oliver yanked Hope's forearms down by the chain linking her cuffs, forcing her to look upon the photo front-and-center.

Hanna hung between two trees, Christ without the cross. Crows and jays found purchase on skinless legs while ravens and falcons laid claim to the arms, their beaks stuffed with red ribbons of muscle. A white-tailed eagle, frozen in time, fished an eyeball from its socket, nerves attached and resisting while a gyrfalcon tried its beak at the one nipple that hadn't yet been torn. There were perches plentiful, for her ribcage had been spread-eagled to reveal lungs and heart, both organs peppered with holes from feasts past and ongoing. Starlings and golden plovers waited, quite literally, in the wings for their turn at the buffet: the house-shaped hole in Hanna's abdomen, rid of its viscera, enforced with wood, and fitted with a tray overflowing with sunflower seeds.

"It's not a house," Hope whispered. "It's a birdfeeder."

"She was found by an elderly couple out for their morning stroll," Oliver said. "The wife suffered a heart attack. By day's end, you may have a twelfth victim."

Watching a trainwreck and unable to look away, Hope stuffed a dry heave back down against her diaphragm and pulled the set of photos closer. Each shot studied a different injury, but the crime-scene investigator had accidentally captured Killian's art and framed it in the exact fashion he would have relished. Beams of winter sunset broke through canopies of naked birch submerging the subject in golden-hour light. Meant to be clinical, the snapshots recorded not only the gore, but the interactions between the feasting birds. Here, a merlin snaps the neck of a starling roosting too close on the first rib. There, Odin's two ravens tug-of-warred a hunk of liver atop Hanna's head. And there, a shot of her head from behind, taken seconds later. Both ravens squatted beside one another, and though barely visible within frame, Hope made out each enjoying half the prize in peace.

Predators attack prey because they occupy different rungs on the Darwinian ladder. They cannot coexist: one survives by eating the other. Predators attack predators, too, when the situation demands—but in the end, they're equal. In the end, they might both benefit, and either depart on even terms or form a deadly coalition.

"Get my phone," Hope murmured.

"What?"

"Get my phone!" She banged the handcuffs on the table. "There's a picture of my bathroom. I assume you found it, right? Just get—just look at my goddamn phone!"

Oliver set down the puzzle box. Massaged his temples. Raked both hands through gelled-back hair. The minutiae of his movements stoked Hope's coals, but the meditative way he did them, like he was trying to gather the proper words to divulge a secret, kept her silent and waiting. Waiting for something terrible.

"Miss Rippa." He laid his hands on either side of the puzzle box. "We retrieved these pictures *from* your phone. We found it in Hanna's underwear."

CHAPTER TWENTY-THREE

ALL THAT BLOOD

As Oliver retrieved the bathroom photo from the back of the file, clicking away at his puzzle box once it was laid bare, Hope sank back in her seat. Hanna had stolen her phone. Killian had stolen her phone. No wonder the photos were so artistic—they hadn't come from the clinical cameras of crime-scene investigators. The depth of field, the degree of focus; the framing, the exposure, the lack of noise. She imagined her digital life at Killian's disposal, used instead to snap self-indulgent snuff shots left behind like a taunt. Hope wondered if he'd snooped, but that wasn't Killian's way. He knew all, or at least thought he did. What she truly wondered was what he'd thought when he swiped through the gallery of his work and inevitably found the bathroom picture. Had he chuckled? Tilted his head? Grinned at the impression it'd give police alongside such detailed, macabre shots?

He hadn't deleted it.

Even if Hope *did* out Killian, the police would find no evidence to substantiate her claim. They'd march what measly force they could spare through the gardens of Fjöðurfjall, disturb a middle-aged priest offering the body of Christ to recovering addicts, mid-Mass, and feel ashamed at the intrusion. He'd charm them with his blue eyes, his eloquent words. He'd fix thistle tea and invite them on a grand tour of the village. The officers would leave with gifts of baked bread and greenhouse-grown watermelon in midwinter, and they'd leave confident in the knowledge that Father Glass was neither suspect nor person of interest, just a noble man working hard to heal the troubled masses.

It was then that Hope exhumed a fossil long buried beneath her psyche, one that upturned her anthropological understanding of herself and sent the funders fleeing.

She didn't *want* to out Killian.

She could. She should. Any other person of right mind would. But she touched her stitches, a rollercoaster of stiff nylon, and felt again his touch, their twisted freakshow love-and-hate, and faltered.

Her vocal cords tangled. She could argue her case: that she took the bathroom photo and none of the rest. It wasn't even a lie. Failure, however, was as definite as her defense was paltry.

"Did you check the security camera footage outside the building?" she asked.

"Blacked out."

Hope recalled the twelve-year-old memory of prison cameras gone dark.

"What about the foyer?"

"Dark."

"Stairwell?"

"Nothing."

"Don't you think it's suspicious that all the cameras shut off when this shit was going on?"

"I find it very suspicious," Oliver said. "Which is one of a thousand reasons you're cuffed in a police station."

The DCI began sweeping the photos one by one back into

the folder, as if denying her some morbid satisfaction. At his reaction, Hope shed all pretense. She dipped and leaned until she caught Oliver's gaze on an unbaited hook.

"Ollie, I know how this looks. And I know a lot of guilty criminals probably say 'I know how this looks.' But I see the way you look at me." She lowered her voice and ventured, "The way you treat me when your boss ain't looking. Maybe you didn't know Hanna was dead yet when you picked me up this morning, and that was why you were acting all nice, but I think it's something else. Can you tell when they're watching? Your boss, the... chief inspector?"

His eyes flicked fleetingly to the corner camera.

"I've seen that spark of doubt more than once, and that clumsy kindness you try so hard to keep a secret. Maybe you've played a lot of poker in your time, but I've been fluent in facial expressions since I was six. You can't..." She thumped her wrists down on the last photo before he could slide it into the folder. "You *don't* believe I did this, Oliver. I can see it in your face."

His full name tasted of lemon. Gin. Clear water from a creek. But no matter how candidly Hope spoke his name, Oliver had a job to do. Oliver had bills to pay—family bills, wife and daughter bills. Oliver had a whole goddamn country clambering up his back, screeching in his ears to find someone, anyone to put behind bars, so despite his mug of uncertainty he said nothing at all in response.

And that nothing deepened the black holes in Hope's resolve. What was she becoming? When had her battlements endured such erosion? Who brought the drawbridge into her secret world crashing down, allowing the armies of common men to stalk past the cannons, the bastions, and the buckets of boiling oil?

"You know how implausible this is. Look at the timing. Look

at *me*. It burns you up inside that your buddies can't see what's plain, won't even *consider* that I ain't the Bowerbird." Her throat begged to be cleared, but she powered through, hoarse, when she spotted uncertainty in his eye. "You know I'm being framed."

Her own surprise took her off-guard. Oliver neither confirmed nor denied. He couldn't, not while the tape was rolling. Not while God knew how many of his colleagues watched from behind the mirror.

The sun of opportunity began its descent. There was still a chance. One last chance. Dusk before the dark.

"Look at me."

He didn't.

"Please look at me."

He didn't.

"Oliver, fucking look at me!"

He did, and Hope saw a carpet bomb of doubt detonate behind his mask. Somehow, *this one* was still on her side. It wasn't denial. It wasn't a lack of conviction. No matter how rigid Oliver's tone or hard his words, it was *belief*.

The door flung open and banged against the wall. Hope and Oliver shook out of their mutual trance.

"The kits are back, sir," said the policewoman who'd barged in. "I, er... I think you should take a look."

Their hands. So close. Hope looped her index around his— the first digit, barely a knuckle. He stared. Didn't move.

"You know," she whispered, sure of it this time, sure he didn't believe she was guilty, and then, at last, he acknowledged with the faintest of squeezes before leaving the room.

He may believe, may even know, but one detective's belief was nothing against the need of a nation to put its demons to bed.

Hope rested her chin in a cradle of her hands, staring at the puzzle box left behind.

Perfect square.

————

Hope fell through the veil into a doze rife with nightmares, but before shapes of birds and bodies could emerge from the fog, she jolted awake in tune with the door. Oliver's once motivated stride was gone. He lingered near the entrance, staring at a clipboard, closing the door slowly as an afterthought.

"You were covered in blood when we found you."

"Until you had me dry-cleaned. Ever the gentleman, Detective Such-and-Such."

"All that blood," Oliver interrupted, "and it was all your own?"

"Sorry to disappoint."

He sat, flipping through a flurry of reports. "You sustained your injuries well after Hanna had initially disappeared. That right?"

Hope's first interrogation the previous day had provided the perfect window for Killian to set the scene in her loft, privacy guaranteed by the hours of bureaucratic bullshit keeping her penned inside the police station.

"Imagine how much time we'd save one another if you pulled that badge out your ass and considered I'm capable of telling the truth?"

Oliver's attention shifted from the report to the table, as if with X-ray vision he could see her stitched thighs. "Where did it happen?"

"Last I checked there was plenty of blood on the floor in my flat."

"Pooled blood. I'll ask again: where did it happen?"

"I ain't obligated to answer."

"Who did this to you?"

"None of your business."

"Why won't you let me help you?" He leaned forward, imploring. "You're not simple. You know I'm the only one left in your corner."

"Birdcages have no corners."

Oliver scoffed, pushing back from the table as if in disgust. Shaking his head, he said, "It's amazing you still have feet what with how often you shoot them. You can't even help *yourself*, can you?"

Something snapped inside. A branch over a knee. Maybe it was visible; Oliver's face fell.

"You wanna *help me*?" Hope snarled. "First you wanna protect my modesty, then you wanna pin me for murder, now you wanna avenge my honor—help me help myself? Huh? What's next, fuck me in a hot air balloon?" A blush cherry-blossomed the peaks of his cheekbones. "Listen here, bud. What I do in the privacy of other folks' beds is privileged information —information you're hardly sanctioned to receive, Mr. Wife-and-Kid. You got a healthy eyeful of my scars last time we chatted. How d'you think I got 'em, huh? Playing red-light green-light with a pack of goddamn wolverines?"

"Listen, Hope—"

"Oh, we're back on a first name basis? Praise be."

"I'm not exactly privy to how the whole BDSM thing works—"

"No shit. I had you pegged as a vanilla cone the moment you strolled through that door, Soft-Serve."

"But *those* cuts?" Ollie's stern edge bit Hope's scorn in two. "*Those* aren't normal, no matter what you're into. No matter how much supposed consent you offer. That's abuse. That's *assault*. An inch or two higher and they could've hit the femoral—"

"And just who the fuck are you to decide what gets my panties wet?"

"I'm deciding nothing," Oliver murmured. "You're showing me."

Hope realized her vision was bleary. When she blinked, a tear fell.

There was more dignity in letting it fall than scrambling to catch it. A chomp to her inner cheek flushed the sudden fragility from her system until her eyes dried, but when she cleared her throat to speak, her voice was starved thin.

"Am I free to go or not?"

A gravelly sigh sent Oliver sagging into his chair, rubbing his forehead. "No."

"What the hell do you mean, *no*?"

"There's still a window of time in which we can't account for your whereabouts, between when you left the station yesterday and arrived home last—"

Bang!

A flustered policewoman barged into the room, cracking the door against the wall. "Sir?"

"Chrissake, constable, what the fuck is it now?"

"We've got a one..." She squinted at her notepad, "Andresína... Hammer-shayum? Claiming to have witnessed the, uh, victim between the hours of..." another squint, "3:55 and 4:00am."

An antimatter implosion of shock rumbled the cosmos in Hope's chest. Andi. How had she forgotten Andi? Trapped in the whirlwind that was the past day and night, she hadn't even considered Andi: the breakup, the church, the sedan speeding off in the night. Was she okay? Was she high? Was she here to help or to hinder—to tell the police everything she'd seen in an act of revenge?

"She also claims to have physical evidence not only proving this one's innocence, but implicating somebody else in the murder of Hanna Maslany."

"What kind of evidence are we talking about?"

A third squint. "Dashcam video."

CHAPTER TWENTY-FOUR

VICES

"Andi, wait. At least let me say thank you."

"You're welcome. Now leave me alone."

Hope nearly collided with a pane of glass as Andi pushed through the station's revolving doors onto the street. Hope shimmied into a stile and popped out onto the sidewalk, turning left—no—right. Andi intermittently appeared and vanished in coronas of streetlight punctuating the dark. Hope jogged after her, trying not to slip in the grey slush, maintaining a generous bubble of personal space.

"How did you know?" she called. "That I was in trouble?"

"You're always in trouble, Hope."

Andi climbed into her car. Closed and locked the door. Her window was cracked. Hope laid her palms on it, noticing for the first time the abrasions the cuffs had left behind—and then the dirty glare Andi shot between her fingers.

Her face was drawn. Gaunt. Ashen, even, like a dusting of powdered cobweb splotched onto her cheeks. But her pupils weren't blown. That's what mattered. Hope searched for further signs of recent use. If there were any, Andi's coat sleeves hid them.

A truly hideous part of Hope had entertained the thought of Andi's relapse following their falling-out, but to her surprise the opposite seemed to have proved the case. How hard had that night been for her? How hard was it still? Hope had abandoned her when Andi most needed someone at her side, anyone at and on her side: someone to dab the sweat, run the bath, change the sheets and the buckets of puke. The process was hardly over. It was just beginning. Yet somehow, in the throes of agony Hope couldn't begin to imagine, Andi had found the wherewithal to exonerate the person who'd been most awful to her. Guilt needled at her.

Hope still didn't know how Andi pulled it off. She had no clue what was on the dashcam footage. "Andi, please. How did you know I was—"

The window rolled down. Hope's heart rolled up. Then a newspaper smacked her chest, and up the window went.

"Change your clothes, Hope," Andi said. "You still smell like sex."

Tires squelched through wet snow. The sedan sliced through wintry dark. Hope wondered, absently, how many times she'd see that bumper drive away, or if she'd ever see it again. Either way, the fault lay on no one's shoulders but her own. God, but it was heavy.

This was pain deserved. This pain didn't provoke arched backs and wild moans. Hope deserved every throbbing iota. Her acceptance of it was strange, as if she were committed to the idea of penance and this was the only way she could offer it. Was that what it was? Hope didn't know. Penance implied a toll paid to reach a better place, and she knew she'd never taste Andi's lips again. So why let the pain wreak havoc? Why did she pile on more and more the longer she looked at the brake lights? She could have simply shed it, molt out from under it and move on as if Andi had never happened. But what would that make her?

The newspaper was a copy of *Fréttablaðið*'s evening edition. She'd predicted the cover page nearly to the letter, but instead of a corporate headshot they'd used a paparazzi snap, two summers old, of Hope striding up the drive to a socialite's gated pool house in Bergen, left arm laden with designer shopping bags. Sunglasses, black. Lipstick, Merlot. Heels too high to be anything but insensible.

The headline was snappier.

Iceland *Who's Whoer* or Lawless Loser? Local Mogul Seized in Connection with Bowerbird Murders

Icy street runoff waterlogged the newspaper, blotting Hope's face and name. In a lump of bleeding ink, it clogged a gutter downwind before finally disintegrating enough to fall through the storm drain.

It was cold without that stupid blanket. Reykjavík's city center loomed above and around. Kitchen lights winked on in preparation for dinner. Clubs welcomed locals and off-season tourists beneath their roofs. The breeze made her stitches itch, bare as they were; she drew her jacket tight around her body, disturbed by a squirming maggot of a thought that she needed Andi more than Andi needed her. The tire tracks in the muck proved as much.

Hope wasn't built for love, she decided, flopping down onto the frosty, wet curb. Sadness made her furious. Passion made her violent. Indifference and indulgence filled the empty sockets of her life: never a dull moment, never an in-between—

always off the charts, blowing gaskets, shorting circuits, red all the time, never able to power down.

Hope had broken Andi's heart in a way it wasn't meant to break. Monsters and men. Merlins and starlings. They could feast from the same feeder, but never roost in the same tree. Maybe Killian was right. Maybe she was a—

"If you don't mind my saying…" Oliver sidled up beside her, careful not to approach from behind. "She doesn't seem the type to, uh." He nodded toward her wounds. "To do that kind of stuff to you."

"What are you, fifteen?" Her rancor had lost its fire.

"To cut you. That deep. To cut you at all, really."

Hope took a beat to light a cigarette under her jacket. Smoke in. Smoke out. She crossed her arms, gazing into the abyssal tunnel of the empty street, starred by lamps. "She's not."

"Listen, I know I implied that you were…"

"A slut?"

"No."

"A whore?"

"No—"

"A helpless little jezebel, surrounded by hungry dogs?"

"No, Jesus—"

"You sure do take the Lord's name in vain a lot for a good Southern boy. Did you leave the church on the Easter daddy died and left you behind with a basket of disillusionment instead of painted eggs?"

"You've got a serious flair for the dramatic."

"Then say what you mean, already. Stop letting me interrupt you."

"I'm sorry," he said. "I'm sorry for saying what I did. About the ladies on the, um. On the side. About…" He flailed, almost visibly. "Not being able to help yourself. That wasn't right."

Half of Hope rolled her eyes. The other half relaxed. Then

a car passed, sending a wake of glacial street sludge rolling over her boots.

"You ain't a choirboy anymore, Charleston. Keep your sorries. I'm not in custody anymore—I'm on a filthy side street in the middle of the night wearing a skirt so short I'm left wondering why you haven't pulled out your wallet yet."

"I'm married."

"When has a ring ever come between a prostitute and a cock looking for a change of scenery?"

"You're not a prostitute."

"Shouldn't you be sorrier for putting me in chains and pissing all over my reputation?"

Oliver's answer draped over her shoulders in the form of a ratty blanket she recognized from that morning. Hope ignored it for as long as she could. The wind blustered. The air went gelid. She gave in, wrenching the blanket close. She was sure he'd crouch or sit beside her if she was anyone else, someone who wouldn't snap their jaws at the slightest unsolicited closeness. But he did the best he could with what he had, and so she was glad the darkness hid the night's second tear. She quickly swiped it, wobbling to her feet.

"You look like you could use a drink, Miss Rippa."

"What'd I tell you about calling me that?"

"You look like you could use a drink, Hope."

"You gonna forget what to call me every time this murder-Banksy son of a bitch frames me for murder?"

"I'm just doing my job."

"Then don't call me Hope on your goddamn coffee break."

Hope moved to shove past him but, weakened by fatigue, lost her balance. She would have splatted on the sidewalk if Oliver hadn't reached out and caught her arm. The moment she was steady he released it, showing his palm before she could retaliate. Her cigarette hissed on the wet pavement.

"What's your drink?" he persisted.

"I don't drink."

"You smoke like an Alaskan chimney, but don't drink like an Alaskan trucker?"

"It may be startling to realize there's such a thing as choosing your vices."

Oliver shrugged and ambled toward a black Skoda Octavia whose lights blinked and beeped. "You've gotta drink something," he called. When she eyed him suspiciously, he sighed. "You refused protective custody; you denied a police escort. Consider my motives ulterior. What's your drink?"

"Nothing you could afford on your cop's pittance. Aren't you clean, anyway?"

"Just cus I don't chase dragons anymore doesn't mean I can't enjoy a light beer. Are you coming?"

"No."

"Can't buy your forgiveness?"

"No."

"At least indulge my curiosity. Whaddya drink?"

Hope paused. "Nigori sake."

"Sake?"

"*Nigori* sake."

"What the hell is that?"

"I dunno. Japanese thing."

"Fine. Get in."

"No."

"Are you always this frustrating?"

"Are you always this annoying?"

Hope had spent all her *no*s. If she was being honest with herself, she was starving—and she absolutely could use a drink. She had no clue where to go from here now that her apartment was a crime scene. Even if it wasn't, she didn't think she could bring herself to sleep in the same bed Hanna, now not only dead but brutally murdered and defiled, had been forcibly sedated in not even a day ago. Trying to come up with a game plan on an empty stomach in the cold while coming to terms with the slaying of yet another acquaintance wasn't exactly ideal.

"You know a place?" she asked.

"Well, I dunno about the sake, but they've got a mean sweet potato roll."

Hope reached for her phone to check the time and found an empty pocket. The thing was still in lockup.

"What about your old lady? And your kid?"

It stopped him for a second. He popped the driver's side door; Hope, however reluctantly, approached the car.

"Sleepover," Oliver said. "At our place. You ever tried existing, let alone relaxing after a long day in a shoebox flat on main street, packed in with seven pubescent girls on a sugar high?"

"Does this mean I get to ride in the front this time?"

"Just get in."

"You sound like a criminal."

"A criminal with a badge."

"And a gun?"

"And a gun," he confirmed.

"So I was right about the police brutality. Here I was thinking that was an American thing—oh, wait."

"Sweet Jesus, just get in."

"Is that an order, Detective?" Hope crooned, crossing her arms over the roof of the car with a pout. All Oliver did was laugh, ducking inside.

"What?" Hope swung in and blanketed herself after clicking the seatbelt, inhaling faint scents of clean leather and cologne. "What's so funny?"

Oliver glanced in the rear and sideview mirrors for traffic, and as he pulled from the parking spot, said, "You forgot the Such-and-Such."

CHAPTER TWENTY-FIVE

GUMMY WORMS

T he sushi spot was the king of dives. A strip of a bar ran the middle of the long, narrow wood-paneled room, with barely enough hip space for the hundred-pound slip of a bartender to navigate without knocking glasses. With a single shelf of spirits and three pleather booths on either side, Sushi Mushi was clearly not a popular purveyor of either sake or food, not even with undiscerning tourists. Aside from what smelled and appeared to be a herring skipper hunched on one of the stools, the place was barren.

"I've dined in some pretty sketchy locales, bud, but you've truly outdone yourself with this little gem." Hope followed Oliver to a booth that sank at least five feet upon sitting. "I'll give you points for bravery for eating raw fish where the menu lists more typos than entrées."

"As I've said—" Oliver frowned, fingers fly-papered to the plastic menu card "—I'm vegetarian."

"Does that mean you're paying my hospital bill when I inevitably wind up with food poisoning?"

"Yeah, right."

"Listen here, fuckface." Hope pointed at him. "You've

dragged me to hell and back the past few days, so the least you could do is—"

"Two Nigori sakes, please."

The waitress, a young Eastern European girl, nodded and scurried off.

"You asshole. *'What the hell is that?'*" she mocked.

"You have a mouth more suited to a sailor than a businesswoman." The skipper, barely ten feet away, glowered over a glass of something dark brown and heady. "Uh, no offense."

"And you've got the social constitution of a ten-year-old girl with no friends to sit with at the school cafeteria."

"I choose to believe there's a difference between being polite and being meek."

"If you choose your beliefs as shittily as you choose cards, remind me to bet a fortune if we ever find ourselves playing poker."

They submitted their dinner orders. Oliver fought a grimace when the waitress audibly peeled the menu from his hand, making Hope laugh loudly enough to startle the poor girl out of her skin. Hope offered a waved hand in apology, unable to form words between snickers. Oliver seemed mortified at first, but the longer he watched Hope laugh, the thinner the tension became.

"You kind of remind me of my mother."

Two Japanese carafes of Nigori hit the table. Two adorable tiny cups. Saucers. Paper doilies on the paper tablecloth.

"Well," Hope started, pouring her sake to the brim. "There's something most girls wouldn't want to hear sitting across from a man at dinner."

"No, no." Oliver's laugh was nervous, but not insincere. "Not like that—"

"Relax, Charleston," Hope said, lifting the ceramic cup to her lips. "I'm joking."

Oliver fiddled with his own tiny cup, studying it like a cat with a breakable thing. Hope nearly offered a public service announcement on how to drink before he finally plucked it from the saucer with two index fingers, two thumbs.

"I just meant you have her sense of humor, I guess," he said, losing himself in the cloudy liquid. "And that *look* you give people sometimes. That defiant stare meant to convince everyone in the room you're the toughest, roughest one there, even if you're not."

"Sounds like your mom had impeccable business acumen."

"Well, she was an insurance adjuster."

"She was the..."

"Icelandic one."

"Cheers to the Icelandic One."

They knocked glasses. Sake sloshed, wetting their knuckles. A peace treaty, however tentative.

Hope waited for his reaction upon first sip, and it was a delightful evolution from *What the fuck* to *Oh, okay* to *Wait* and *Damn, that's actually good*. Hope kept her smile tucked in her mouth. She sipped, and—

Memories. Flashbangs of memories, one after the other. Killian here, there, everywhere. No, Hope hissed; she wouldn't allow his presence here, wouldn't grant him entry into this, her split second of R&R. She swallowed all thoughts of Scottish fields, flushed the face with the coral reef eyes, and forgot.

"Tell me more about her," she said.

"Well, there was my dad, the stolid Sunday Bible-thumper from the reddest of all red counties, and somehow he not only tolerated but married my mother. Insubordinate. Stubborn. Not an ounce of respect for his authority and, really, quite loud."

"Sounds nothing like me."

"She didn't need to speak a word to completely undermine

his self-righteous fury. Just a look, that's all she needed to disarm his Jesus bomb."

"Does she offer classes?"

Faraway. That's where Oliver went, with a hollow chuckle. His mother was long dead and probably hadn't gone peacefully.

"My dad always said she had a glass face. Like an aquarium." Reality reclaimed him, and he looked at Hope and she looked at him and he looked slightly down, as if he knew eye contact would reveal all his secrets. "Said you could see all the pretty fish and manta rays rolling around just behind her eyes. But there were other things, ugly things, too, and they weren't exactly shy. Sometimes they'd snap at the glass, he told me. He worried it would crack, one day, and all the water would spill out." Oliver cleared his throat. "Anyway. She knew what she wanted and how to get it."

"And what happened to her?"

"Drug overdose," he said simply. "No one realized how bad it was until—"

Hope's grip tightened around her glass. She wolfed her sake and refilled it, pushing Andi and Hanna to a mental corner where she couldn't see them.

"Sorry. I didn't mean to bring up any—"

"For fuck's sake," Hope droned, forcing her hand to relax around the cup. Forcing herself to relax. "Enough with the apologies already. How do you stand up straight with no spine?"

Oliver grinned. "Pardon me for trying to be considerate after putting you through hell, ma'am."

Hope sighed through her nose, scowling at her sake reflection. "It's not your fault," she admitted. "You're not the one killing folks and blaming me for it. Okay, well, maybe some of it is your fault. But the handcuffs are fun, right?"

He sulked at her. Under the table, she kicked his shin. He

bolted upright and gawked as if she'd called his wife a discount hooker.

"Lighten up, Ollie. You're off the clock." She cracked a cloying smile. "Now you get to deal with the pleasure of my company."

"Bully for me."

Dinner arrived. Hope studied her crunchy tuna roll with a whiff and an exploratory chopstick before deciding it was fit for human consumption. Pouring herself another round, she couldn't help but double- and triple-take at the obscene mess on Oliver's plate.

"What the hell did you order, bukkake on seaweed?"

Oliver spluttered into his glass. "I keep telling you I'm vegetarian," he rasped, "but it doesn't seem to stick."

"Then why take me to a sushi place?"

"You're the one who wanted sake."

"So you're trying to get me drunk?"

"No!"

"How the hell are you vegetarian in Iceland anyway?"

"I have a very accommodating wife," he said, twirling his wedding band. "Who often goes to dinner without me."

Hope cackled. Oliver shimmied out of his jacket, resting a stereotypical dad wallet, beaten and creased, on the table. Handcuffs hooked to his belt rattled with the movement.

"Y'know," said Hope, jutting her chopsticks his way, "if I wind up in bracelets a third time, they better be tied to your bedpost."

The suggestion made dinner plates of his eyes.

"Relax, officer. I'm fucking with you."

"I've got a wife—"

"And kids."

"Kid." Oliver idly twirled seaweed around his chopsticks with no intention of lifting it to his mouth. "Just the one."

"Wanna tell me her name yet?"

"No." A gut reaction. He frowned at his own default response. "Ísadóra," he said. Then, a deep, curative breath, reviving him from the hypnotic mess of his dinner to acknowledge Hope with one of those troubled smiles dads of girls tended to master. "Her name's Ísadóra."

Hope dropped a roll in the soy sauce. She abandoned the chopsticks and used her fingers. "And your wife?"

"Why does that matter?"

Sesame seeds crunched between her teeth. She washed it down with sake: milky, gritty, reminiscent of sweet rice. She popped a dab of wasabi in her mouth, inhaling and exhaling fire. "Trouble in paradise?"

Oliver snuck his hand beneath the table before Hope could tap his ring. "You're just as exasperating when you're unchained, you know that?" he said, not rudely. He tossed a glance over his shoulder towards the closet-sized bathroom. Looking for a place to regroup.

"Wouldn't advise that."

"Why's that?"

"Notice how quiet this place is?"

"So?"

Addressing him with a slip of pickled ginger, Hope said, "So many things are more interesting than silence once you learn to actually listen. You feel me?"

"Not really."

"Consider this Learning to Listen 101," she said. "Focus, and hear all those scandalous little noises the quiet tricks you into thinking aren't there."

Dubious, Oliver humored Hope. A faint grunt. A moan. The muffled hand-over-mouth gasp of an orgasm. Oliver went ruddy and looked over his shoulder at the unisex toilet with a newfound awareness.

"Raw fish and rice wine." Hope shrugged, continuing her meal. "It does wild things to perfectly normal people."

"I had to use the restroom."

"No." Hope skewered a tangle of seaweed salad. "You had to skirt my question."

"It's part of the job."

"You're off the clock."

"But you're not," he said. "Are you expecting me to divulge the great and gobsmacking secrets of your case because we're sitting in a restaurant and not a cozy interview room?"

"You wound me," she said, partly telling the truth. "But you really should consider hiring an interior designer. For your inquisition chamber. Wasting away in there can't be easy for you."

"We hadn't used that room in two years," Oliver grumbled, sipping more sake. "The rookies did their best bleaching the floors."

"I *thought* things were a bit sticky. What was that on the table anyway? Melted gummy bears?"

In defiant silence, Oliver shoveled a bundle of something presumably edible in his mouth. Hope laced her fingers under her chin and happily watched. Chew. Chew. Pause, and another apprehensive chew.

"You took me here cus they had Nigori," Hope said, popping an eyebrow at the wincing man, who very much seemed like a boy, just then. "You're not obligated to eat the gloop."

With a muffled "*Excuse me*," Oliver leaned to the side and spat the green slop into a handkerchief, which he crimped like a dumpling.

"Never eaten here before, have you?"

"It wasn't melted gummy bears," Oliver said, dusting his hands. "It was melted gummy worms."

"Were they yours?"

"We don't allow suspects outside food items. Never know what you might find stuffed in a hot dog."

"So they *were* yours."

"My sweet tooth has been a lifelong burden on both my molars and my dentist, I'll admit. Sexy, right?"

"Consider my panties gone."

A woman emerged from the restroom, straightening a skewed skirt and dabbing creased lipstick. Hope recognized the distant emptiness turning her eyes matte, their sparkle returning only for the time it took to bid the man adieu. She recognized the covert way the woman counted bills at her hip; the way she folded them tight and tucked them down her bra. A man's voice from the kitchen barked something that got her moving into a back room, slipping away like silk through soft fingers.

Oliver, with his back to the scene, noticed nothing but Hope's entrancement. "What memory are you reliving?"

Hope returned to the present. She stalled with a sip of sake. "Hm?"

"Back in South Carolina, I didn't just talk to the bad guys. I spoke with the victims too. They all had that place they'd go to, where nothing could touch them, and you could always tell when they went there."

"I'm not a victim." Hope put a period on the conversation, clanking the cup in its saucer.

"Then what are you?"

Oliver's follow-up came out a smidge too hard, a little too fast. Hope felt a soft pang of warning beneath her breastbone. He'd never actually confirmed he was off the clock, and her gut told her that while Oliver might be treating her to sake in the interest of making peace, that peace was fragile and temporary until the next shoe dropped. He may have believed her in the interrogation room, she may have been cleared—for now—but she was still very much a person of interest.

"What do *you* think I am?" Hope asked. "You don't seem too certain."

Oliver watched her with an intensity that made her want to squirm under the table. At last, he broke the eye contact in favor of more sake. Hope's shoulders relaxed. For the moment.

"You don't make it easy, do you?" Oliver refilled her cup.

"The answer to that question depends entirely on the other person."

"You're like that thing…"

"Ah, yes, that *thing*."

"Kowloon Walled City." Oliver snapped his fingers as he pulled the words from somewhere deep in his memory. "Fifty thousand people crammed in an old fortress. All those levels, buildings, alleyways. Always a fire here, a raid there, a drug deal one block down, but you could never tell where or how to get there. It was a multi-story mess, the world's biggest puzzle box. Screw the aquarium." Oliver nodded to himself. "You're a maze the size of a city."

Hope was familiar with Kowloon in the same way she was familiar with most things older men expected her to be unaware of, but her understanding of it stopped at knowing it had, at one time, existed. Past tense. She wanted to know its fate, but her desire to know fell in line behind her need to seem entirely indifferent, entirely in-the-know. Luckily, Oliver filled in her blanks without provocation.

"It was demolished in 1994."

Unable to stop herself, she asked, "What's there now?"

"A park."

Ponds, gardens, delicately maintained fields of green. Flowers springing from unseen ashes; sneakers squeaking on pebble paths that once were homes.

"Well, while you lose yourself in that very un-victimlike stare of yours, I'm gonna hit the head."

"Look out for cum in the sink."

After standing, Oliver stopped. A baffling mix of concern and suspicion wafted off him like perfume. Whatever he wanted to say, however, went unvoiced, gulped down into an incinerator custom-built to fit the section of throat where questions went to die. He walked off.

Hope stared at her carafe of sake. Uncertainty filled her to the brim. To drink would be to relive the past. To abstain would be to wither in the here and now. Her hand hovered around the pitcher as a bee might before a flower, deciding whether or not its nectar was worth the time and effort.

Grass. Wildflowers. Clouds rolling by. Falcons and crows; *Was that our first fight?*

Wrestling with the urge to knock over the carafe, something caught Hope's eye before she had a chance to give in. It was worn. Laminated. The edge was bent. It stuck ever so slightly from Oliver's wallet.

She stroked its corner. She knew that texture, knew it like she knew the depth of men's cruelty. Rubbing the object between two fingers and knowing it was wrong, she eased the funeral card from Oliver's wallet. Even her weathered heart crinkled beneath the weight of a tragic realization.

Ísadóra Oliversdóttir.

His paternity was evident in the angular cut of the girl's face, but someone else's influence shaped willow-green eyes and a pouty mouth, full and young and raspberry-rose. So happy. So sweet. Such a big grin, bigger than the Charleston police cap sliding off her head.

Beside them the birds of the heavens dwell;

They sing among the branches.
Psalm 104:12

Hope noticed the corner of a second card poking from the wallet, similarly worn, laminated, and bent from overhandling, but before she could think of reaching for it two hands slammed down on the table. Ceramics rattled. Soy sauce spilled. Hope regarded Oliver through a brand-new lens, and he regarded her with a brand-new fury—the sort that broiled the insides so thoroughly Hope could practically smell the smoke.

"What the hell do you think you're doing?"

CHAPTER TWENTY-SIX

NIGORI

"Hey!"

Hope followed Oliver out onto the street. The aurora ribboned the sky with sashes of green and violet. A brittle wind wrested her back as she fought to follow.

"C'mon," she said, "you couldn't expect me of all people not to snoop!"

Oliver rubbed the back of his neck as if he could scrape off the scar. "I expected you to be decent."

"Why the fuck would you expect that?"

"Because you are!" He whirled on her, still scratching his neck. He looked at his palm like he expected to see blood, then shoved it in his pocket to fish for car keys. "At least I thought you were. A tiny bit. Should've known better."

"Clearly," Hope sniped.

Incredulous, Oliver spread his arms wide in a universal *are-you-kidding-me* thrust.

"Is this just what you do?" he asked. "That girl, Andi, *hated* you. Your assistant, Ellie, was *terrified* of you. Every single person we've interviewed in connection to you either froze solid, slammed the door, or snarled like I'd pissed in their skyr. Tell me, please, I'm just dying to know—is this some character you play to stay top dog in the business world or were you just born a spiteful, apathetic harpy?" Noticing how loud he'd been, Oliver lowered his arms. Gentler, he concluded, "Which is it?"

A humorless guff blew from Hope's nose. She gazed past him, down the street—far, far down the street where the cobbles and cement disappeared in the dark. Where she belonged. Not here, debating dignity she didn't have under the light of streetlamps and stars.

"Honestly?" She was talking. Why was she talking? Staying —why not storming away? "I don't even know anymore."

After searching her face for a nameless thing—a lie, a trick— the ire in him drained with a deflated-balloon sigh.

"Was it really her birthday?" Hope asked. "The first time you questioned me?"

A boulder formed in his jaw. "Yes."

"Is that why you came back to Iceland?"

His silence was answer enough.

"What happened to them?"

Oliver shook his head, the flint in his eye saying she'd get no further. *Don't go there.* Still, there'd been no sleepover, no house full of squealing preteen girls, no wife corralling them with bribes of soda and cake. Did he even live in a shoebox flat on main street?

"Why'd you invite me for a drink?" The curiosity came from an unexplored place of sincerity. "Did you not wanna go home to an empty apartment, or were you buttering me up to get answers to whatever questions you still have about me? I can see it. I hear it in the way you talk. At least part of you still thinks I'm not completely innocent."

"That's not true," he lied. "All right, fine. Of course I'm still suspicious. Nothing about you adds up, but…" he trailed off, at a loss.

"Why did you invite me here?"

"Because." Oliver screwed his mouth, frozen in a shrug as if he himself hadn't the slightest clue. "Because I knew *you* couldn't go home after all that ugliness. And because while you definitely don't add up, I don't think you're guilty either, at least not of all this. I thought you were decent, like I said. Decent and in a whole lot of pain." It was something in the way he said it. Decent. Words behind words. "You *are* decent, you just do everything in your power to convince people otherwise. Toughest and roughest, right?"

Hope shook her head in disbelief. "Is talking it out all it takes to earn your forgiveness?"

"I've got enough anger here," he tapped his skull, "to fuel a cargo ship to Cabo. There's no sense in holding on to more."

"I didn't even apologize."

"Sure you did."

"I didn't."

"Hope, there are more ways to apologize than saying sorry."

Oliver cast a look over his shoulder at the exact spot Hope had faded to before admitting her self-ignorance. It was easy to give in to the thousand-yard stare but escaping its hold and returning from it vulnerable—allowing yourself to *be* vulnerable—was a demanding task, indeed. Before she could open her mouth to contest her victimhood again, he waved her off.

"Your loft is still an active crime scene." Oliver fiddled with his keys, thinking. "Is there somewhere I can take you?"

It was tension. Pressure. Not the bad kind, but the sweet, flooding pain of a deep-tissue massage working knots built into muscles you didn't know you had. It was the kind of gravity that clipped the sass from Hope's tongue and replaced it with speechlessness. Watching his hands fidget with the keys, she only snapped from her trance when his wedding ring glimmered, setting her ruby engagement ring on fire beneath her shirt. He must've felt it too—visibly jerking from the shift before finally finding the fob.

"No," Hope said. "I could use a walk. Clear my head. Plenty of hotels around here anyway."

With a lightning once-over, Oliver choked back something probably along the lines of *Be careful.* She couldn't help a tired smile at how transparent he was. It fell into a frown, a genuine one she didn't often entertain.

"I'm..." The words had strong roots: weeds determined not to be weeded. She found a trowel. "I *am*, y'know. Sorry. For snooping."

"I already—"

"I know, I know. Already forgave me, all that. More than one way to... Well, some sorries should still be said out loud, I think."

Oliver looked thoughtful. She didn't fidget under his stare—it wasn't uncomfortable that way—waiting for his turning gears to grind out whatever needed grinding.

"Can I ask one last question?"

Hope shrugged.

"Why Nigori sake?"

"I dunno. It's unfiltered, I guess." She laughed, nearly slipping back into her trench of bad memories. "Makes it sweeter."

Oliver watched her for a length of time that would have been strange under normal circumstances, but under these decidedly abnormal circumstances, it defrosted her chilly bones. He dug around in his jacket pocket and produced a cellphone. She couldn't help her eyebrow cock of surprise, flicking through it; while it wasn't her phone, her contacts had been copied to the SIM card. Before she could say anything, Oliver rounded the hood to the driver's side door. It wasn't a favor, she told herself.

He just needed a way to contact her when the next body turned up.

"I suppose that's goodnight then, Miss Rippa." The car beeped twice. Winked its lights. He popped the door and flashed a lopsided smile, jangling the handcuffs at his hip. "I sincerely hope we never meet again."

"Me too, Detective Such-and-Such."

With a casual two-finger salute, Oliver pulled away from the curb, leaving Hope with two lies hanging in the air for company and a lung-deep emptiness she couldn't explain.

CHAPTER TWENTY-SEVEN

OLD HABITS

The days dragged their feet, spent in a small two-star hotel room with little natural light and much less to do. At less than nine thousand krona a night, it was the last place anyone might expect to find Hope slumming. No one would expect her to slum at all. That's why she'd picked it.

She washed her only set of clothes in the sink with cheap hand soap and freshened her makeup as best she could with an old eyeliner pencil and a tube of crumbly lipstick scrounged from her jacket pockets. She combed snarls from her hair with her fingers and nibbled, nauseous, at granola bars and crisps from the lobby's sparse vending machine. During the day she was glued to the television, indulging a childhood habit of biting her nails, waiting for the news to report on the latest chapter in the Bowerbird's grisly saga, which never came. At night, she hovered by the window, half-hidden behind a curtain reeking of mothballs and geriatric misery, watching the street for shadows shaped like priests.

The morning after dinner with Oliver, she'd noticed an unmarked black car across the street and up-a-ways, a form behind the wheel that looked remarkably like Detective Tinna and one she didn't recognize in the passenger seat. Of course. Oliver wouldn't just let Hope go off on her own with no way to track her down, no permanent address. She might be in the clear for now, it might be obvious that she was being framed, but her personal connection to—and now involvement in—every crime meant she knew the Bowerbird, or the Bowerbird knew her, and the chance to catch them meeting wasn't one the detective would give up just because he had a soft spot for her.

But Killian didn't come. He didn't call.

No one did.

After enduring the evening news for more of the same *No new leads* spiel, some American-import show about bumbling Brooklyn detectives she refused to admit was funny aired. Hope disliked television, and she disliked reruns even more, but—

It was a new episode.

On the verge of dissociation, she wandered into the lobby in a daze. The receptionist informed her seven days had passed since check-in.

Hope checked out.

The friendly streets of nighttime Reykjavík had become aloof in their desolation. Even the aurora above was dim, its verve sapped by the grave state of the city it shone on. She felt like a ghost, haunting backroads and alleys, aimless with no scores to settle or unfinished business to finish, just lost, unsure which door led to Heaven or Hell. After however many hours, Hope stopped in the middle of a four-way intersection.

She had to do something.

When no cars came to smear her on the blacktop—her tail waiting patiently a couple of blocks down—Hope sighed up at the waxing moon. Chewing her cheek to sausage meat, she walked in a familiar direction. There was only one place to go.

———

In the dank building vestibule, Hope paced for thirteen minutes before mustering the gall to press the button next to a label reading *Hammershaimb*. An infernal buzz. Two, three more. Snap, crackle: the intercom choked out rust and dust and a familiar voice said, "Go away."

"Let me in."

"I know you're used to getting what you want, but it's time to sign the reality check and cash in, Hope. Go away."

A click cut off the static as Andi hung up the door phone. Hope thumbed the next button: *Magnússon*, the sweet, senile man with a chronically reliable case of insomnia. Twenty seconds later, the inner door lock thunked open. Two floors later and she was in front of her ex's apartment. On the gloomy landing, the light flooding from under the door onto Hope's shoes seemed a radiant beacon, almost welcoming, and like a lighthouse it went dim as feet approached and waited on the other side. She tried to picture how frazzled she must look to someone scoping her out through a peephole: hair knotted, makeup sub-par, old clothes at peak disarray. A hollow point round of vanity-borne shame slugged her in the shoulder. She shook it off. *God, grant me the serenity to accept the things I cannot change*, and all that jazz.

"You know where I hide the spare key, so why aren't you barging in?" The slab of wood between them muffled Andi's voice.

Hope glanced at the underside of the sticky railing behind her. "I was trying to be polite."

"And?"

"And I imagine it ain't there anymore."

"I'm going to speak with Magnússon in the morning."

"You won't have to, I won't bother you anymore—"

"You're bothering me now."

"I've gotta bother you now," Hope said, planting a fist on the door, her forehead on the fist. "And then I promise I'll piss off."

"Your promises aren't exactly stable currency."

"You—" Hope reeled in a scathing remark, freed it from the hook, and tossed it back to sea. "Look, I'll sit out here all night and day if that's what I gotta do. Can't stay in there forever." No response from the other side, just shifted footing. "I just—oh, for fuck's sake, Andi, just open the goddamn door." She ground her molars down to the root. "Please."

That did it. When rusty hinges finally invited her inside, Hope forced herself to look past Andi's state of satin-robed undress. And though Andi stood aside, Hope found herself confronted by an invisible wall barring her from crossing the threshold.

It used to be so easy. Their chemistry had been so intense before, so reactive and prone to delightful explosion. Now the lab was cold. The beakers were empty. The chemists had been fired, Bunsen burners tossed, the entire building vacated because the grant money ran dry. Hope didn't belong here anymore. Down to the permanent furrow in Andi's brow, every detail announced just how unwanted her presence was. It was only when Andi's annoyed "Well?" spurred her from her thoughts that she wandered inside.

The studio was larger than Hope remembered without its usual clutter of nerd-chic kitsch—the shelves of unboxed Funko Pops and obscure comic books, the *Protomen* posters and sci-fi fairy lights Hope had never understood. *"That one's gotta be Star Wars, right?" Hope asked, pointing at a phonebooth-shaped bulb above from her lounge on the bed. Andi rolled her eyes and straddled Hope, putting her geek culture ignorance to bed with a kiss.*

All that remained was the green couch and the green bed and the coffee table that doubled as a kitchen table. The rest, she assumed, had found new homes in the mountain of cardboard boxes in the corner by the window.

"Moving?" Hope asked lamely.

"Not much left for me here." Andi returned to the kitchen nook, where an octopus-shaped mug steamed on ten whole inches of counter. "Plus, can't rely on you for rent checks on the months I don't break even anymore."

"I'd still help you."

"Oh, I don't doubt it. But you're forgetting one of us has a sense of dignity to maintain."

"Suppose you're glad I never talked you outta your day job."

"Having a sugar mama was nice, but not worth the inferiority complex."

Hope opened her mouth to commiserate and just as quickly shut it. She stuffed Killian back in his cage. She wasn't here for him.

"Anyway, I left the service," Andi said. "Found a cute little cottage outside Raufarhöfn. I'm done with the city."

"Eight hours away."

"Other side of the country."

An arctic spider of worry crept across the skin of Hope's heart, leaving behind an infuriating itch. She found her attention sweeping to the space between the couch cushions, the crack between mattress and box spring, the drawers in the bare television console and the mirrored medicine cabinets behind the open bathroom door.

"If a skipper dumps his dope in the sea, how much would it take to get the whales high?" Andi perched cross-legged on the counter. "A boatload." She scoffed at Hope's failure to crack a smile. "I can see you looking for the hiding places. Save your energy. Whatever smack I had left is either clogging the pipes downstairs or killing fish in the bay. And I won't be alone anyway. Mom's coming from Tórshavn for a while, and... and I don't know why I'm even telling you all this."

Hope watched her take massive gulps of what smelled like chamomile. "Old habits."

"Old habits... what is it? Die slow?"

"Die hard."

"What does that even mean? How do you die hard?" Now she was talking to fill the space, to direct attention away from the elephant corpse stinking up the room. "Can you die soft? Is it like eggs, y'know, soft, medium, hard-boiled death—"

"Andi."

She sipped her tea. They steeped in silence, taut and fraying. When it finally snapped, it did so quietly, like a thread of spider silk whisked from the air.

"You had a bad breakup a long time ago," Andi said, a blanket of ash—the fallout of heartbreak—hushing her voice to a whisper. "That's the only thing you ever told me about him. Didn't even give me a name."

"That's all I wanted you to know about him."

"How long?" Hope hid her shame in the fractures between the floorboards before Andi pressed, "How long?"

"Just once. Just that one time."

Andi's scoff was brutal in its disbelief. "You expect me to—"

"In all the time you've known me, have I ever lied?"

"Constantly—"

"Hid the truth, yeah, but have I ever lied to your face?" Hope watched conclusions come and go in Andi's eyes.

"No."

"It was just the one time," Hope repeated, "and never again."

Andi smacked her mug down on the counter and hopped off. "If you think for one second I'll so much as *consider* getting back together with you, I..."

Her flame seemed to cool to embers when she took a few steps closer. Maybe it was the bags raccooning Hope's eyes, the redness around her stitches. More likely it was Hope's own lack of fire—a fire that had always raged and never faltered, let alone gone out. Coals cool to the touch.

"I wouldn't expect you to, Andi. That's not what I'm here for."

"Sex, then." Andi tried to sound sarcastic.

"No."

"What are you here for, Hope?"

"To..." She cleared her throat. "To apologize."

Hope, there are more ways to apologize than saying sorry.

She supposed Oliver was right, but like plants and sunlight, different types of people required different types of apologies. Nonetheless, it felt unmeant for her mouth, big and sour, with too many angles, and she wielded it with an infant's clumsiness, nearly dropping and breaking it on the ground.

"I'm... sorry." But once it was out, more came. Someone pulled a lever, pressed a big red button and the waterfall drowned the studio. "I'm sorry, I'm so sorry, I didn't—I couldn't—Andi, I'm sorry—"

"Stop!" What an alien sight and sound it must have been, Hope's viper tongue reduced to a blubbering piece of leather. Andi looked on in almost-horror. "Please, just... stop."

Hope stopped. She pretended to cross her arms, but in truth she was hugging herself, keeping the sorries in, keeping the bones and organs and blood in lest they spill out into a shapeless void of meaningless identity, because that was how she felt.

"I'm sorry," she said clearly, slowly, "for treating you like a pet and not a person. For betraying you when you needed me the most." And lastly, before her voice could break: "For not staying."

Andi crossed her arms too. Hugged herself, too, in lieu of

hugging Hope. All that was off the table, now. Another no-touch contract, this one forever unbreakable, even if twelve years passed between them. Hope promised herself—promised Andi —that much.

"Okay." Andi nodded, sniffing.

She looked more ruined than ever, as if the apology had sawed her in two, and perhaps it did. Sorries hurt before they healed, didn't they? Muscles tore before becoming stronger? Reality was a clawing, hungry beast, and admission of wrongs made the wrongs real all over again. Of course it'd make her cry.

"Okay."

Hope returned Andi's weak half-smile of acknowledgement and turned to leave. Before Hope could turn for the door, the cellphone in her coat pocket burst to life and she jumped, having forgotten it was there. What an odd week it'd been, her phone untouched when a typical day had her fielding calls and texts from clients every minute of the hour.

Rooting around as it chimed, she saw her own apprehension reflected in Andi's eyes. Night and day clients lived in the three closest time zones. Who would call at 2:00am? Too far past midnight for starlets sleeping off hangovers. Too close to dawn for killers wrapping up the workday. When at last she pulled her cellphone out, the blue light screamed one word:

FATHER

CHAPTER TWENTY-EIGHT

ASCENDING ORDER

H ope swept the red circle to silence the ringing and lock the screen. Two chimes for texts. One ding for a voicemail. Another chime. Fumbling the phone in frustration, she switched it to vibrate and shoved it in her pocket as deep as deep went.

"It's him, isn't it?"

Hope grimaced. "Forget him."

She wished *she* could. Seeing those six letters appear on the screen at this hour could mean any number of things. It could be good. Could be bad. Could be hands-down, spine-crunching horrid. Had he finally concluded his Magpie experiment, having last seen her pared to the bloody flesh and bone, soaked by rain and mud before his church, blood running down her legs? Had the Bowerbird Murders come to an end? Would he hang up his taste for local fare and attempt to issue an invoice for simpler things, for a simpler place, like Hungary or Portugal or maybe back to Scotland? It was a dream, a lovely dream: populated by puffy clouds, popped champagne, and an overdue good night's sleep. Hope allowed herself to live in that deluded candyland for a few seconds before logic re-staked its claim.

"Just forget him, Andi."

The urge to leave was struck down by a sudden thought. The arrowhead was barbed; Hope couldn't pull it out. A clock, somewhere, had started. But what was it timing?

"Andi..." Hope dropped into a solemn murmur. "Before I go, I need you to tell me what was on that footage."

"Footage?"

"The dashcam footage. The tapes that got me off a prison sentence."

Deep breath in. How much further was Andi willing to be embroiled in Hope's oily affairs? Deep breath out. Just this much more—and then goodbye.

"I don't have them with me..."

"I don't need to see them, just tell me what was on them."

They sat on the couch.

At first, Andi had trouble relaying the events of the night out of a sense of embarrassment. From Fjöðurfjall, she'd initially forged for home before remembering how many vials of Dilaudid were still tucked in the toilet tank. She'd screeched to a full-on stop in the middle of the highway in the rain, taking the key from the ignition. Any driver could have collided with her from either end and snuffed her out right there. A decision had made itself apparent to her, there, in the dark and the cold and the torrential wet: attempt to reconcile, or fall off the wagon hard and maybe crack her skull. Andi couldn't know what irreparable choice she might make if she went to a place flush with stuff that'd take the pain away.

Once twenty minutes passed without being tin-canned by a passing truck, she re-routed for Hope's loft, getting lost along the way. The sobering act of the drive left her in another quandary, as she eventually parked on Shore Walk and stared up at the flat. Go in? Wait? Say screw it and leave? Andi wasn't sure how long she'd waited for her mind to make itself up until a bang and a shout snapped her to attention.

The bang was from the building door. The shout from Hope: *"Hanna, stop, you're not safe!"*

"I was even more pissed, y'know," Andi said. *"Two in one night?* I thought. I was ready to turn around. Actually, I was ready to ram my car into your building, stomp all the way up to that stupid swank pad and punch you in the throat. But... well."

Andi hadn't heard much more of Hanna's phone conversation than Hope did, even with the window cracked. What she did hear, though, was the faint crunch of road grit on tire treads: tires on a heavy car driving slowly. Creeping, even. There was nothing right about that van as it sidled up Shore Walk. Andi said she'd slid down in her seat, and there'd been just enough space between the steering wheel and the console to catch a peek of what happened next.

The van surged forward. The van broke hard. The doors wrenched open and out came a man dressed in black to silence Hanna's scream before it had a chance to alert anyone. He gathered her up and threw her in. He followed in after. Andi heard the doors slam. Thumping and thunking. A struggle, inside. A muffled cry for *Help*! and then a *THUD*! that shook the vehicle and heralded an eerie quiet. The same eerie quiet took hold of Hope, realizing the young reporter had met her end just four floors down from the apartment. And she had walked away from the balcony, too entranced by her own failings to hear any of it.

If she screams loud enough and the acoustics are just so, a woman lives for a moment after dying.

"It looked like... y'know, you used to call them rapist vans. Big, black. Sliding doors. No windows, except that little round one at the back. The license plate was all covered up too."

Of course he'd use one of his church vans instead of his car.

He'd never been prone to slip-ups, so why would he make a mistake now?

Another loud buzz from her pocket.

"Y'know," Andi began, slow and suspicious, "six months might not be too long a time, but I've picked up a few things."

"What have you picked up, Andi?"

"You bite the inside of your cheek when you're upset." Hope released her cheek. "And when you're *scared*. I mean, why do you think I'm moving? For recovery, sure. To get away from you, naturally. But honestly, Hope... if you're not scared, I don't know how. Because *I'm* scared. Everyone who seems to be even tangentially involved with your life is turning up dead in these, these... disgusting, awful ways. And they're getting more and more personal. C'mon. Who's next? Who's more personal than an ex-girlfriend? I don't want to end up like that. I'm, uh... how do they say it? Getting out of Dodge."

"That makes sense," Hope muttered, zoning out of the room to zone in on one sentence that stuck out like cactus on tundra.

And they're getting more and more personal.

Who's next?

"Oh!" Hope launched from the couch and nearly crashed into the opposite wall, peeling out of her jacket to shake her phone from its pocket. "Oh shit, oh shit."

Andi hopped up, hands low, palms down—*Easy girl, don't bite*—and inched forward before almost getting lashed in the face with a coat sleeve. "Woah, woah! What is it?"

But all Hope could repeat was, "Oh my God, oh my God, oh my God," dropping to her knees when at last her phone fell out. She keyed in her code and flew through her contacts. "No, no, no... where are you, Scottish... asshole... jumpy bastard..."

Andi dipped into an uncasy crouch, snapping her fingers to try to get Hope's attention. When she reached out for a wrist, Hope shoved her off.

"What the heck's going on?"

"Ah!" *Ring, ring, ring.* "Pick up. Come on. Pick up, pick up, pi—"

"Hope!"

"I know who's next! I have to stop him."

Ring, ring, ring.

"Wait—*him*? You know who the Bowerbird is?"

"Good morning, Mr. Charles! Yes, yes, my skittish Aberdonian friend, I do happen to realize the hour but whaddya say you give little old me a little old hand with this one, tiny, itsy-bitsy, simple-as-peach-pie task, and after—I said, *right* after —you'll enjoy the lifelong relief of being able to consider yourself completely wiped from my contact list?"

Hope ignored Andi's look of confusion.

"Yeah? Fantastic, Charlie, that's what I like to hear. Now I need you to find me the address of a one Oliver Ragnarsson, Detective Chief Inspector, Reykjavík Metro Police. He's in city limits and drives a silver Skoda Octavia 2017, first three digits of the license plate, MG5... No... It's all I got... I know..."

Andi leaned in on hands and knees with saucer eyes. "Why would he be after that cop before me?"

Hope covered the cellphone's mouthpiece. "Ascending order."

"What does that mean?"

"Ascending ord—look, Andi, I made him promise he'd never touch you. Never hurt you." Hope was borderline hyperventilating now, shuddering with unwelcome adrenaline. "I made him swear."

"All this time you've known? What the hell are you doing getting arrested and—"

"Dammit, Charlie! Just get me the info or I'll crack the lungs from your chest and serve them to your daughters as haggis!"

Andi's perplexity turned into shock, having never seen the Magpie or her talons. Hope made the universal sign for paper and pen. Andi scrambled up and away, searched through packed belongings.

Hope scribbled the address down. "Thanks, Char. Consider our professional relationship well and truly terminated. It's been a pleasure."

She hung up. She stood. Wiggling into her jacket and jogging for the window, she peeked out at Detective Tinna's car parked across the road. She'd have to sneak out the back. She read the address on the slip of paper over and over, running through city streets in her head, through alleys and parks, over old bridges and closes only seedier crowds knew existed. Mapping it out. This route? Too slow. That one? Uphill.

She hustled over to the door.

What about this way? No, that way, no, no-no-no... She grasped the knob, opened the door and—

Andi slammed it.

"What the fuck are you doing?"

"You knew this *whole time*?" Andi yelled. "You let them put you in bracelets, interrogate you for hours, smear your name up and down the news and all this time you've known his name, you've spoken to him, you've made promises with him? All this time... All this... *Why*?"

Weary down to the arches of her feet, Hope stopped fighting to keep up her façade. Deadpan she went, and in that deadpan, Andi uncovered the ghastliest of truths.

For the second time, she asked: "It's him, isn't it?"

"You were right, Andi. About who I am. What I am—completely fucking right. So I need you to get as far away from me as possible, okay? Because you're good. You're better. You deserve someone just as good and better, and... and *safe*. Okay?"

Hope wanted to hold her face one last time. But she

couldn't. Hope had to let Andi go, and Andi had to let Hope go, and that was the end of it. Perhaps Killian was right, in a way; perhaps Hope didn't love her. But just because you're not mad for a woman doesn't mean you don't care for her, don't want to see her hurt or bruised or dead, or crying for you when you don't deserve the tears.

"Find that good and better. Got it? Get out of Reykjavík. Now. Tonight. Pack a bag and send for your stuff later, okay?" Hope faked a smile. *Be strong.* One quick feint later and Andi's cellphone was in Hope's pocket. "No police. Just... just get out of the city. Please."

"Hope..."

"I need you to tell me you'll leave tonight."

"I can't just—"

"Andi!" she rested her hands on the other woman's shoulders. "*Please.*"

Andi stared at her for three agonizingly drawn-out breaths before nodding. Watching her swallow a gulp of fear, Hope knew she'd understood her meaning, heard the words she couldn't commit to speech.

You're in danger.

"Tell me," Hope said.

"Okay," Andi whispered. "I'll leave tonight."

With that, Hope spiraled out into the hall, paper in hand, tearing down the stairs two at a time. She burst out onto the back alley, took two seconds to gather her bearings before hanging a right and sprinting full tilt down the adjacent street.

Please, Ollie, Hope prayed. *Don't be dead.*

———

"Here." Hope smacked a clutch of bills on the cabbie's shoulder. "Here!"

He hadn't stopped, had barely managed to grab the bills and shout about the króna she'd left behind before she poured from the backseat, palmed the door, and ran full-tilt up Sörlaskjól's sidewalk. Suburban houses flashed on her right. A wedge of crabgrass streaked by her left. Rocks melted into a snarling sea, where they suffered the punishment of the ocean's wind-whipped ire. A wave hit the jetty. Sea spray took flight. With water on her ankles and salt in her mouth, Hope huffed down a road without streetlights, guided only by a lit window here and a slice of moonlight there.

In. Out.

The second she'd hopped into the nearest cab outside Andi's, she'd investigated her GPS's rendition of the street.

In. Out.

She'd memorized the two-story rhombus of corrugated metal, its perimeter trimmed by hedges on a street otherwise packed with fences. The ground-floor lights washed the street in gold. The Skoda sat idle in the drive.

In.

She hit her brakes hard. Felt her heart in her airway.

Out.

Hope struggled to wrangle her breath, welded to the property's edge. The front door creaked on its hinges, jostling gently in a breeze fast becoming a squall.

It was wide open.

CHAPTER TWENTY-NINE

OLIVER

A house exudes a certain energy when it's empty.

Hope flew inside, calling his name. Skidding to a stop at the foot of the carpeted stairs between the dimly lit den and pitch-black kitchen, Hope scanned the home for sights, sounds, smells. An electric kettle rumbled on the countertop. A candle on the mantle turned the air evergreen. From the framed family photos on the walls to the shelves of hand-crafted puzzle boxes in various states of being solved, everything seemed to be in its proper place—except for the overturned knife block and the open window above it, crooked in its frame.

Hope searched for blood on the faucet, the panes; she searched for smeared red palm prints on the handles of the blades. Just as she reached to flick on the kitchen light, footsteps shuffled around the side of the house. A garbage bin hit the sidewalk with a heavy metal clang. She whipped around, recoiling.

Too little, too late.

A creak of wood floor. A flash of stainless steel. A shadow in the doorway. Hope crept back, back, back into the confines of the too-small kitchen, pressed further into the home by the silhouette's approach, dodging rays of moonlight and making herself smaller than small until her hip hit a table. Its legs groaned, announcing her presence.

Cornered.

Killian would do more than kill Oliver. He'd *slay* Oliver. Defile Oliver. Make an art installation of his body and a mockery of his soul for all the nation to cover their mouths and cry over, lamenting the depth of their beloved country's devolution to have become ground zero for such deplorable horrors. He'd bathe in Oliver's blood to the elbows, to the shoulders, hand-streaking human red from here, the white pickets of Vesturbær, to the stiff marsh grass cutting Lake Tjörnin's western bank, to God only knows where. Where would the first unfortunate soul find Oliver's skinned hide hanging from? The police station doors? The Leif Eriksson statue? The balcony of Hope's own loft?

Could a body hold that much blood? It only fit so much. Could skin stretch that thin? It only strained so far. She imagined a great flesh balloon of crimson corn syrup. So fragile, wasn't it, without the structural integrity of bone? Hope bent slowly, walking her hands over her sewn thighs, down to her calves and ankles and boots.

She slid the guthook knife from her sock.

Snnk.

The shadow stepped closer.

Crrk.

Knees bent—breathe in.

Arms primed—breathe out.

Ready to claw her way free through the front door—the only door—the only way out to freedom, to life, to one more breath. Hope tensed as each footfall creaked into the house, ready to sneak but more ready to pounce, picturing the jugular, the carotid, the—

"Hope?"

One last step introduced shadow to light. Oliver stood, perplexed, in his own mini foyer, holding a can opener in one hand and an empty tin in the other.

After a full two seconds of stillness, Hope's joints failed, lubricated by an unexpected pump of *Thank God, thank God.* She fell back on her rear. The guthook knife skidded across the floor. Her breath fled in a pathetic huff and in blurry slow motion, an Oliver-shaped amoeba set aside its handfuls and put its palms on display on approach.

"Hope? Holy shit, what are you doing in my house?"

Hope scrambled for an excuse in the wake of whiplash.

"Pro..." Her voice failed. She tried again, breathless. "Protective custody." The words played a concerto of confusion on Oliver's face, no doubt harmonizing with the shock of her sudden presence. "Protective custody. You offered last week. Does the offer still stand?"

"Sorry I spooked you." Each word came slow, leavened with suspicion. His right hand hovered near his hip where a leather holster hung empty. "What are... How did..." Hope stole a split-second glance at the blade, hidden in shadow beneath a corduroy couch. Oliver didn't notice. "How'd you find me?"

His hand also happened to hover near his pants' pocket, where the square bulge of his wallet made itself known.

"Your license," she lied. "I may be a snoop, but at least I'm thorough."

"What's my wife's name?"

"What?"

"You can't open my wallet without her funeral card falling out," Oliver said. A split lapse in nerve snapped his attention to an open safe in the television console, where a service weapon sat unsecured across the room. "So what's her name?"

Funeral card, funeral card. Not his wife's. His daughter's.

Think. Remember. The text beneath the psalm, beneath the photo—*beloved daughter of Oliver and—*

"Belinda."

Oliver's right hand relaxed. Hope struggled to choke down a hairball of deception.

"What, thought I came here to stick a knife in your eye and popcorn-string your intestines around the Sun Voyager? Christmas was a month ago, Detective."

"No." He rubbed his neck, scanning the den and the kitchen and the state of his house. "That's not…"

"Relax, jeez." Hope glared up at her would-be host, relief flooding her senses. "A hand?"

As if forgetting she was on the floor, Oliver rushed in proper Oliver fashion to help Hope to her feet. Their hands lingered. Oliver cleared his throat twice and coughed, disposing of the can opener and the stinking tin of flaked salmon. Cat food. Hope thought immediately of Biscuit, frowning at the thought of her yowling and alone in the neighbors' flat. Someone must have picked her up, she told herself. Another neighbor. A cop. For the briefest of moments, Hope wondered if Oliver himself had adopted the crotchety beast.

"Damn cat, always prison-breaking," he muttered, shuffling past Hope to rinse foul gravy from the can. He nodded to the open window bringing stiff breezes in from outside. "I swear that little asshole only uses me for food and fleece blankets."

"Hate to break it to you, bud, but that's textbook cat behavior."

Hope closed the front door when Oliver didn't. It was clear he'd succumbed to the sudden pear-shaped nature of the evening: flustered enough to scrub the disposable tin instead of tossing it in the bin and, in the process, nicking a finger on a sliver of metal. The kettle growled. The tab clicked. With one last glance to assure her weapon remained out of sight, Hope strolled to his side and poured the water into the cup he'd prepared. Bergamot steam massaged her face, floral and dense.

"It's nearly 3:00am," she said, placing a plastic saucer over the cup to steep.

"So?" Oliver dried his hands with a frayed dishtowel, removed the saucer, and sipped.

Hope couldn't help but wonder how he didn't scald his tongue. "Last time I checked, Earl Grey was caffeinated."

Oliver's eyes darted to and fro over the cup's rim, searching for her point in the steam. "Do... you want some?"

She sighed, leaning back on the counter's edge. The waves and wind behind them did nothing to ease the awkwardness of the silence nor correct the bizarreness of the situation, and it must have been that unbearable tension which prompted them both to blurt the same thought at the same time:

"For a second I thought you were here to kill me—"

"Did you think I came here to kill you?"

Oliver snorted into his tea. Hope suppressed a smile.

"If I was gonna kill you, I wouldn't use the front door. The *open* front door."

"It's been an odd few weeks, Miss Rippa."

"Hope."

"First you're a witness, then a suspect, then a witness yet again. Suddenly you're public enemy number one practically overnight, and then innocent a few hours after that."

"But still involved."

"Intrinsically."

"Is that why you had me followed?"

Oliver's eyes flitted to the door, the bay window, checking for familiar headlights. Detective Tinna's car was nowhere to be seen. "I'm just—"

"Doing your job?"

"Well, yes," he said. "Trying and failing."

"It ain't my fault I've hooked myself a creative stalker."

"Creative," he scoffed. "I don't know what he is, Hope, but creative isn't the first word to pop into the noggin."

"What, then?"

Oliver swirled the tea, mentally freediving into the depths as if the proper word was barnacled to the bottom. "Evil."

A wolf in sheep's clothing, Hope nearly said, and even that image was lousy with inadequacy. There were sheep and there were wolves, but what sheep and wolves oftentimes forgot is that there were butchers and hunters too. Killian was yet above them: a demon dressed in a preacher's frock—unburned by crosses, holy water, or the name of God Himself.

So deeply was Hope buried in thoughts of Killian, she only noticed how troubled Oliver was when he shifted his weight. She dialed in to his body language but was unable to decipher it before he came out and said what was rotting his mind.

"I've never seen you scared before." The statement was such a departure from what Hope had expected—*I really thought you were here to kill me; I thought, just then, that you were the Bowerbird*—that it left her hanging dry. "I've put you in cuffs more than once, let you stew to chowder in the station's dingiest interview room, showed you photos of some of the most gruesome crime scenes I've ever stumbled on in my career. Hell, you found a few yourself. You were startled, at most, and maybe a little sickened, but never afraid."

"That ain't true. I puked blueberry trail mix all over Hallgrímskirkja's sidewalk."

"That's a common visceral response. But you know that. I doubt you're pining for a lecture on the subtle differences between shock and fear, especially from a *layman* like me," Oliver drawled.

"I've always had a sweet spot for professors. Something

about how they grip the lecterns, makes you wonder what else they'd love to wrap their hands around."

"Shock and fear are definitely parked in the same wheelhouse." Oliver cleared his throat, glossing over her comment. "But you get good at telling the difference."

"In your line of work?"

"You make me sound like I'm bragging."

"Even if you were the type to brag, you'd be bad at it."

Hope listened to the distant waves hounding the rocks across the road. A lone car ambled northwest up the street, gilding the kitchen in fleeting yellow. It illuminated a flipbook of family photos arranged on the opposite wall: Oliver pushing a raven-haired toddler on a crooked swing; Oliver grinning at a sleeping tabby cat coiled about her neck; Oliver beside a goddess on the seashore, kissing a porcelain cheek.

"Scared." Hope spat the word like a sour grape skin caught between her teeth. Pushing off the counter, she wandered to the drop-leaf table to fuss with the hinges. The pepper cracker, the salt grinder, the vase of plastic jessamine. "Fear isn't in my vocabulary."

"Then your dictionary must be faulty." To his credit, Oliver didn't wither under the glare she cast. "You weren't just scared, Hope. You were terrified. When I stepped inside the house, you thought I was someone else—and when I wasn't that someone, you were... I don't know. Surprised?"

Hope removed the bouquet, stroking fabric petals. She lifted the faux flowers to her nose and inhaled, as if by doing so she'd teleport back home to fragrant Georgia, landing on the sagging porch of her dead mother's A-frame. Dorothy clicking her ruby red shoes: *tap, tap,* gone, and far, far away.

"Why were you surprised to see me?" he pressed.

"I wasn't surprised." Hope peeled a yellow flower from its

plastic stem and threaded it behind Oliver's ear. "I was relieved."

Oliver peeked at the new accessory from his periphery. Hope swatted his wrist when he tried to take it off.

"Did you think I was next on the Bowerbird's roster?"

Hope replaced the bouquet, fluffing the buds until she was satisfied with the arrangement.

"I got no clue what you're talking about." A car crawled east down Sörlaskjól. Her neck tensed. Headlights rolled an amber carpet under the couch, glinting off the guthook blade. "You just snuck up on me, that's all."

"Is that why you pulled a knife? Because I snuck up on you?" Hope resisted the impulse to glance at the knife under the couch. Oliver set his mug down, loosely crossing his arms. "I may not come off as all grit and noir, but that doesn't mean I'm an idiot. I know you're an old hat at lying with a straight face—how else would you end up a self-made millionaire at the ripe old age of thirty-three? But what you can't seem to grasp, and honestly what I, myself, can't for the life of me seem to understand, is that I can see through you." He pointed harshly, and when he realized he did, he pocketed his hand as if in regret. "Right through you," he added gently. "And this new talent of mine tells me you've only said one true thing since I helped you off the floor tonight." The statement softened the hard angles of his raspy voice. He looked away and back again. "You *were* relieved to see me. You just won't tell me why."

Hope expected some retaliatory remark to cobble itself together in her throat, but in a rare moment she found herself speechless, confused, and unbearably small.

Eventually, she found a few words to mash together. "Can I stay or not, Detective?"

Clawing his fingers through already-mussed hair, Oliver

sighed his way into the den. He flipped on the television and kicked at the couch until it flattened into a lumpy futon.

"The bedroom's at the end of the hall. Just let me shower first."

By the time Hope swallowed enough pride to form a thank you, the water was already running. He left the guthook knife where it was, blue-lit in the gloom.

CHAPTER THIRTY

KNÚS OG GÓÐA NÓTT

T he hollow ache persisted inside her, gnawing like hunger for food that didn't exist. Cars surfed by on the road. Wind whistled against the house's metal shell. On the TV, two newswomen clucked over the horrors of the Bowerbird Murders, cutting to curbside interviews with yet more common hens cock-a-doodle-doing about who and what would come next. Roosters in police uniforms puffed their feathers in response to the threat, fanning false confidence at reporters with shaky hands. At one point, she spotted Oliver in the background of a smattering of crime-scene B-roll, twiddling a puzzle box behind yellow tape as medics rolled a body bag into the back of an ambulance. He appeared deep in thought, as he always did with a puzzle in hand. Hope pondered this quirk of his. It was like he needed a physical problem to solve with his hands to lull himself into a mindset adequate enough to tease the threads of the case, the mystery.

A hot spring of anger bubbled up in her gut when the camera zoomed in on his face, his hands. They didn't *know* him. They provided no context. All the cameras and viewers saw was a senior officer who, instead of hounding his subordinates and stomping around the crime scene with false bravado, would rather play with a glorified Rubik's cube.

Hope shed her jacket, whipping it off with force. She buried her nails into her scalp, holding her head between her knees until all she could hear was the seashell whisper of her own emptiness.

"... following the second release of high-profile suspect and U.S.–U.K. dual citizen Hope Rippa, in what is fast becoming a case of gross negligence and disorganization on behalf of the Reykjavík Metro Police. Lead investigator Detective Chief Inspector Oliver Ragnarsson was contacted but ultimately refused to comment."

Oliver.

I see through you.

Right through you.

How could he? Was there no soul in the way to block the view? There had to be. Calloused and black, but a soul nonetheless. Is that what he saw, or did he look past that, too?

A red thread of gravity led Hope by the pinkie from the den to the hall. The talking heads on the TV slowly gave way to the white noise radiating from the master suite. The bedroom door was open. The bathroom door was cracked. It was the habit, she knew, of a man who had lived alone for too long.

Hope stroked a toe over the crease where carpet met tile. Back and forth. Back and forth. Soon, she lost herself in the hypnotic movement, lulled by the Pied Piper of the showerhead's song. Wandering through her cerebral woods, she didn't bother marking the trail back home, ignoring thoughts and anxieties and apprehensions; her what ifs, whys, and why nots.

It was one of those larger showers with an immovable pane of glass. No door. No tub. Just a drain in the floor.

Oliver braced his arms against the shower wall, head hung,

dark hair dripping, letting the jet pummel the scar on the back of his neck. He was wincing. Here and there, he'd pinch the bridge of his nose. Were she not scattered in her own brain, Hope might have wondered which of his gallery of traumas the night had chosen for him to re-live. Perhaps it was this entrapment in the past, or maybe just the rush of the water that blinded him to her presence. But when Hope padded closer, arms not crossed but wrapped about herself like a shawl, or a ratty blanket, Oliver looked up. When his lips formed the 'O' necessary to say her name, nothing came out.

Sometimes words were the least effective form of communication. Questions took shape on his face, barely visible behind misted glass.

What are you doing?

Why are you here?

Why aren't you saying anything?

To each she answered: *I don't know.*

But there was one plea Hope spotted amid the questions. Bashful yet bold, tinged with loneliness, and it'd managed to steal a millisecond of screen time between his endless queries.

Don't leave.

Hope stepped under the water fully clothed. Her stitches screamed. Her hair flattened. The skirt cling-filmed her thighs while her sweater clung to her chest. An uncertain half-step back put two inches' worth of distance between their bodies. Oliver's back grazed the tile wall. After drifting listlessly over his tattoos and the scars they were tailored to hide, Hope peered up through the steam and the drizzle, wordlessly asking permission. The slightest of nods granted her wish.

Hope traced the ornate letters spelling *Knús og Góða Nótt, Ísadóra* beneath his surgically marred collarbones. She stroked the bouquet of birch trees growing up over the bullet hole in his shoulder. A complex Nordic compass covered a quartet of serrated scars hooking around his ribcage. Hope looped a circle: north, east, south, west. Smoothing her hand up his muscled abdomen, over his chest, her fingers hovered, ghost-like, at the brink of the one scar he refused to conceal. With a gentle thumb, she caressed its edge. Oliver grimaced in pain. Phantom pain. Caught her wrist and her eye—*Don't go there*—and shook his head.

She persisted.

Let me.

Oliver lifted his gaze to the ceiling, to the water, as Hope tenderly wrapped her fingers around the nape of his butchered neck. She ran her nails through the border of his soaked hair. Finally, she removed his hand from her wrist finger by finger and pressed its palm to her cheek, holding it there, keeping it there—and at last, Oliver looked down. The iota of distance between their bodies closed, fitting together as if clay-molded to do so: two of a handmade set, entirely unique and impossible to divide. Her clothes. His skin. Their foreheads, together.

Oliver let Hope feel the fourth and final scar, the pearlescent hook curling down over his mouth, with her lips.

The first was a featherlight touch, hesitant and wary, wary of everything: of complications, and traumas, and agonies inside and out. But the second was deeper. Closer. Rich with abandon. Scalding water rained through their mouths. Clouds of steam rolled on their tongues. Oliver encircled Hope in his arms and kissed her simply and sincerely. Utmost softly.

And he made no attempts to remove her clothes.

She rested her head on his chest, synchronizing to the steady thump of his heart. Clinging to his body, as ruined as hers; clinging to his spirit, as irreparably damaged as hers, Hope let herself cry—really, truly cry—for the first time in fifteen long, dreadful years. And he let her. Resting his chin on her crown of drenched blond waves, Detective Such-and-Such held Miss Rippa in the shower as she sobbed.

They stood that way for a long time, even as the water cooled from scalding to lukewarm. When the shower pulled the plug on itself and divulged an icy rain, they squirmed from its reach, disentangling from the bespoke comfort of one another's limbs. The moment over.

Retreating from the deluge, an expression of comic horror whitewashed Oliver's face.

"Shit," he said. "My water bill's gonna be insane."

CHAPTER THIRTY-ONE

PUZZLE BOX

A fter peeling off her clothes, Hope wrapped herself in the scratchy robe Oliver shoved at her, more out of a grudging respect for his Southern sensibilities than any concern for her own modesty. Freshly dressed in dark jeans and a V-neck the color of a robin's egg, Oliver carried the sodden slop her skirt and sweater had become around the corner and into the kitchen, where the dryer hid in a cabinet beside the dishwasher. Water beaded through his hair, soaking the triangle of shirt between his broad shoulder blades night-sky navy.

"Heard from Tinna?" Hope mocked.

Oliver snorted. "She and her partner deserved a night off. They know you're here with me, and that'll have to do."

Hope hummed, running her fingers over the robe. She couldn't help but relax a bit.

"You *would* own starchy white robes," she said, trading tile for carpet as she ambled into the den, unbothered by the sand sticking to her toes. It reminded her of home. Living in a loft a stone's throw from the sea meant learning to live with the grit and salt.

"Why's that so predictable?"

Hope plucked a half-solved puzzle box from its rack, all cold, geometric angles and impossible possibilities rendered in smooth wood and smoother metal. "Single dads, wayward bachelors, widowers. They've all got the same sense of interior design." She rolled the dodecahedron in her palms. "Must be all that pent-up masculine angst. Add to that your jaded coppiness and you've got a foolproof recipe for the world's stiffest linens."

The dryer chugged viciously, calming to a white noise thud-and-tumble by the time Oliver came over to return the puzzle box to its perch.

"At least I have linens," he said, retreating to a glass liquor cabinet. "And clothes, for that matter. Care for a pair of briefs? They'd make a fetching hat."

Hope crossed her arms, watching Oliver peruse the cabinet for just the right bottle and just the right glass, smiling an unconscious smile that told of the absolute ignorance to the danger he'd been in not an hour before. She tracked the pulse of his carotid, kept tabs on the rise and fall of his chest, counted every blink of his eyes as he poured and downed two fingers of liquid gold that smelled like magic markers. The bulge of his Adam's apple carried the payload down his throat—a throat she couldn't help but imagine bifurcated: slit and sawed so deep the head lolled on a thread to expose esophageal ripples and cervical bone glimmering white through an endless slosh of blood. She heard the gurgling gasp. The death rattle. She followed the streaks on the rug as he was dragged by the ankles by a laughing shadow dressed in priest's clothes.

She hadn't realized she'd stumbled to the kitchen to dry heave in the sink until a hand rested on her back. She jerked away. Oliver presented his hands, cautiously excavating a glass from the cupboard.

"Sorry," he said, filling it with tap water. "I didn't mean to—"

"Stop."

"But—"

"Just stop."

Hope steadied herself on the counter's edge, breathing in through the nose, out through the mouth. She meant to snatch the glass but could only manage a slow and shaky grip that dribbled water on the counter. Basking in the frigid draft drifting through the still-open window, she idly reorganized the spilled knives back into their block. Oliver lingered to her left in that unobtrusive way of his that was so very rare among men.

"Was that the cat food stench or the shower?"

"Neither."

Once the water filled her belly and the knives were sorted, Hope had nothing left to do but speak her thoughts, however unintentionally. "You're the first man to have me half-naked and vulnerable and not rip off my skirt."

"I'll chalk that up to your poor taste in men."

"The men I dealt with wasn't up to me," she said. "I chose none of them."

"That doesn't look like past tense to me."

Oliver scanned her injured legs, leaving rawer words unspoken. Tension stretched like taffy between them: Oliver holding his tongue, Hope reining in a response. She cursed the subtle manner by which he spoke without speaking, leaving no room for rebuttal. Hope might not have known what she was getting into when she spread her legs and let Killian thrust his way into her life, but it was ultimately her decision to reconnect, albeit platonically, and maintain some sort of relationship. That dam of professionalism had been bound to break at some point. Their history prophesized it. Part of her had always known this would happen. Part of her, she hated to admit, had wanted it to. And it had, sweeping Andi away to drown in its tide—and here was Oliver, now, dipping a foot in the rapids.

"You chose someone," Oliver said, voice clipped. "Or maybe they chose you, but you don't seem like the kind of person who just lets things happen without a fight."

The clean swoop of Hope's cuts imparted no signs of struggle, and in the absence of struggle there could only be consent. At least that was what it must have looked like.

Killian over Andi. Killian over herself. Killian over the whole goddamn world.

But it wasn't that simple. Normal folks tended to go about their normal lives and see the world around them through an exhaustingly normal lens. Assuming. Concluding. Clinging to a truth that's true only in their own narrative—because they couldn't peer into the pages of another's book and see just how deeply they were mistaken. Not unless the owner of such a book offered it up: dust jacket, dog-ears, split bindings and all.

She exhumed a volume from her library. A short tome, to be sure, but the root of all her so-called choices. A prologue to all her life's chaos.

"I was young and naïve," Hope said, sinking into the nest of a burgundy lounge chair. "And he wasn't."

Oliver stared, digesting the implications of her words. His face didn't falter, or perhaps it did when he turned away to pour another glass. Settling down in her chair's fraternal twin, Hope was some sort of glad to see in his face a quiet, thin-lipped anger for the woman she was now, and not puppy-eyed pity for the foolish girl she used to be.

Hope said, "I'm not a victim."

"But he *was* an abuser."

"Still is." The pages in Hope's book took flight, as if left open beside a window in a storm. "And he always will be."

She stole Oliver's tumbler, sipped the whiskey, and kept her mouth shut, losing herself in the fireball building mass in her throat before scorching its way down her gullet.

"I thought you only drank sake?"

"Tonight's a night for new things." She gasped lightly for air, coughing through peaty fumes. "Wouldn't you say?"

"It's a night for something. For what, I have no idea."

Hope returned the tumbler. She let out an unsteady breath, analyzing the floral patterns in the rug beneath her feet.

"There's this cabin we used to visit," she started, "way deep in the Scottish moorlands. Smack dab in a forest so small and dark it didn't even have a name. South of Auchallater, outside this village called Braemar, 'bout an hour west of Aberdeen. Pines as far as the eye could see—and you couldn't see far. That forest was an abyss, even at high noon." The air felt close, the home a cozy chrysalis wrapped about them in shades of birch and gold. "I wish I could just go there. By myself, y'know? Poof. No more chaos, no more hiding, just... I dunno." She was talking to herself. Talking to the floor. "Peace and quiet."

The lamplight reflected off Oliver's whisky as he sipped barely half a thimbleful. He held it in his mouth, not so much savoring the flavor as he was using it as proxy for chewing a thought too loaded to voice. With eyes as honeyed as the spirits he drank, Oliver melted deep in the middle distance beyond her shoulder. Lost.

"I would have," Hope blurted. Up came his eyes. Clarity returned to them, confusion its companion. "I would have chosen you."

Oliver's long, heavy silence and half-smile bore all the world's sweet sadness. "In another universe," he said.

"A better one."

Oliver snatched the remote from the coffee table and muted the TV just as the 5:00am news cut to a week-old clip of Beetle-Mole stroking his triple chin, offering priceless professional insights on the bleak state of national affairs.

"Such a raging, herpetic twat," Hope muttered. "Y'know, after the café, he—"

"What really brought you here tonight?"

Hope drummed her nails on her ankle, thoroughly caught off-guard. Lies were a currency toward which frugality never applied when it came to her mental wallet, and the temptation to flash a few bills was intense.

But there was something about tonight. The firefly-jar lighting, the cool drip of water down her neck, and the soft tones in which they spoke made it feel as if they were trading secrets instead of opening up. Connecting. Was that what people called it? Connected or no, she couldn't rightly tell a cop she'd come because she suspected the Bowerbird—whom she not only knew, but knew intimately—was coming to bludgeon him dead in the night.

"I don't know," she said, and it was only partly a lie.

"What do you want from me?" he asked.

"I'm not sure what I want anymore. I haven't been sure for a real long time."

"But something brought you here, and I doubt it was concern for your own safety."

"Misery loves company?" Hope's lame attempt at a non-answer was met with a dubious look. Huffing in frustration, she added, "I dunno, Ollie. Broken attracts broken, I guess."

"I don't think you're broken."

"Why else would I feel like I am?"

"Maybe you've just been told you are so many times that you started to believe it."

"And you're here to tell me otherwise, that right? To show me the light?"

"What? No... No, but I think most of us could use a reminder now and then that whatever we are, it's up to us to decide."

Hope shrugged listlessly. "You can't decide what the world does to you."

"I—"

"And don't give me that bullshit about choosing how you react. Take a look at how you freaked out in the sushi place and tell me that shit ain't coded in your DNA."

"Fair enough."

"Do you think *you're* broken?"

Oliver leaned back, considering the question in the popcorn ceiling's cracks. "I think I'm in that musty back section of the antique store even the owner forgets is there sometimes. But I've still got a price tag, and the odd ones wander in every so often to find something odder than themselves, and see me. Does that make sense?"

"Sort of."

"Either that, or... I dunno. Maybe I'm in the clearance section at Hobby Lobby."

Hope shared his laugh. "Is that shithole really still in business?"

"Last time I was stateside they still had the flimsy stand piled with half-off Jesus lit."

"When was that?"

It was a tragedy to watch his smile fall. An answer was unnecessary to spot the years of psychological distancing from a home that had betrayed him. Surely his wife and kid were buried there, or perhaps had met their end there. And from the subconscious way he prodded the back of his neck, the scar was no doubt how God tried sparing Oliver a lifetime of grief before changing His mind at the last minute. For a moment, Hope wondered if he'd done it to himself. Maybe one day he'd learned how to tie a noose online, found a nice spot in the backyard and strung himself up on a sturdy dogwood. She imagined the hemp friction-burning his neck as he struggled, having misjudged the height of the fall; heard the crack of the tree limb as the heavens said *Not today*.

It was a fine enough theory, but that scar wasn't from rope burn. Hope had as intimate a knowledge of blade scars as she did of her body. If you wanted to kick the bucket by sawing through your skin, though, you'd go for the wrists or throat. Not the back of the neck. Someone else had done it to him.

"How'd you get it?" she asked.

Oliver's hand retreated to his lap, where it twisted the hem of his shirt into knots, recoiling from the question and seeking safe haven in the space between his knees. Hope didn't let up, staring hard, waiting for his clay shell to crack and reveal the tender meat of a secret inside. He was nearly there. Teetering on the edge.

Then the doorbell rang.

A curious cocktail of shame and relief spilled off him as he walked by.

"I ordered some coffees," he muttered.

———

"I woulda thought there'd be more creative juice in a drought than anywhere near you, Detective Such-and-Such," Hope said, investigating a charcoal starling in a sketchbook on the coffee table. "Not bad."

"What can I say." Oliver gulped down the last of a paper cup that smelled like mocha. "I'm more than just a pretty face."

"More than puzzle boxes and PTSD, you mean?"

"Should put that one on a T-shirt."

"Have you ever watched starlings before a bad storm?" Posed as a question, it came out like a thought spoken accidentally aloud. "Pulsing in the air like a black aurora. The way they move, together, in perfect sync—no one bird leading, or guiding, or following. All just... moving." Hope's finger ghosted the curve of an ashen wing. "It's like they're helping the sky breathe. Lungs in the wind. Breathing in," her hand waved left, "and out..." then right, hovering above the bird frozen in flight as if she could set it free. "... In, and out."

"It's called a murmuration," Oliver said.

"It shouldn't have a name. Some things should just stay mysterious."

"Not there to please or serve anyone," he added. "Just there to exist, and maybe be admired."

"Or feared."

"Why not both?"

"Hm." When Hope shifted her attention from the sketch, she caught Oliver watching her from across the room. "I guess it depends who's doing the looking."

He blushed but didn't waver. "Perspective's a bitch, isn't it?"

"No matter what way you slice it."

Hope didn't notice the rapture in the room until a trash bin falling outside broke the spell. A cat yowled.

"Shit. Sorry." Oliver hopped to his feet. "Clothes. I should've gotten you clothes."

"Admit it. You just go banana-pockets for little girls in wet towels."

"That's disgusting."

"Brings a whole new meaning to *dirty cop*, doesn't it?"

Muttering flustered nothings under his breath, Oliver stomped down the hall and into the bedroom. Hope bit the inside of her lip, quirking her smile sideways just as the world's most geriatric meow came from the kitchen window. An ancient orange cat, more dreadlocks than fur, sat on the sill, looking like a grumpy war veteran and sounding like one, too, every time he croaked. Which was often. Constantly, until Hope came over. A purr like screws in a broken blender rumbled from his chest when she scratched behind a half-bitten ear, wondering what sort of mites she'd later have to pick from her nails.

"And just what the hell is your name, huh?" A faded metal tag jingled from his collar. "'Handsome'. Let me tell you, Handsome, someone's been lying straight to your face for a while now, and I think I know who it is."

The beast clumsily jumped down onto the counter. The knives scattered from the overturned block a second time.

"Do I look like the maid to you?" Hope pedaled her nails in the soft divot behind Handsome's jaw, a trick that had yet to fail in seducing any cat that crossed her path. "Guess you're not that bad."

In the void of the muted morning news, the calming of the windstorm outside, and Oliver's absence, a faint buzzing drew Hope back into the den. Questing for the source of the hum, she couldn't help but press a palm to her diaphragm.

A certain queasiness comes hand-in-hand with the knowledge that you've let something slip your mind. Something important. Something time-sensitive, with a deadline and dire consequences.

Through the thin fabric of her jacket pocket, strewn across the couch, a square of blue lit up.

Don't pick it up.

Don't pick it up.

You have to pick it up.

Hope lunged for the phone, friction burning her knees on the timeworn rug, nearly dropping it before the final ring. She pressed the cell to her ear.

Killian laughed. It was the laugh of a leopard who'd had its fun and was ready to stop playing with its food. "And here I was, beginning to think you'd forgotten all about me, darling."

It was a quick conversation. Entirely one-sided. But the pace at which a thing happens never determines the magnitude of the earthquake with which it shakes one's life to the ground. It was the *how*, the *what*—and in Hope's case, it was a name.

A secret. A disgrace. A name that made her hang up on Killian mid-sentence.

Edward J. Wright. The Old Man with the barber chair.

"I, uh, donated my wife's clothes two years ago," Oliver called, padding down the hall. "I'm not quite the walk-in closet type, so this is all I got, but the dryer should be shrieking bloody murder any second now—"

The flannel hit the floor. Handsome hissed and fled. Oliver froze in place, staring down the barrel of his own gun.

CHAPTER THIRTY-TWO

LOST IN THE WOODS SOMEWHERE

B efore forcing Oliver to cuff himself to the heated towel
rack in the bathroom, Hope made him turn the dial down
so he wouldn't burn. To his credit, he followed her directions to
the capital T until he was on the floor, knowing that
underestimating her would be a grave mistake.

She stood over him, clutching the scratchy robe to her body.
The air was thick with lingering steam, and in the fogged mirror
she saw only an unrecognizable blur holding a pistol the size of
her head.

"I'm supposed to pull into the cop shop at the crack of
dawn. This is the first place they'll send the constables when I
don't pick up the phone. I'm not so sure you've thought this
through."

"I'm sorry." The apology fell flat, dense as peanut-buttered
toast landing face down. "This wasn't supposed to happen."

The accusatory amazement with which he fixed her made a
more effective weapon than words ever could, but the quiet
couldn't last forever. Not when Hope found herself unable to
leave.

Eventually, he said, "Why did you even come here?"

"One last stab at humanity, I guess. Thank you for giving me that much."

"Did this mean anything to you?"

"Don't be stupid. It meant everything. But now everything is falling apart, and I gotta try and find the pieces." She racked the slide on the Glock 19. "I can't afford you trying to stop me, cus I'm—" A pause to swallow ego. "Well, you're probably the only one who can."

"Pieces..." Oliver chewed his lip before looking up. "If—and that's a monstrous, walloping fucking *If*—you can gather these pieces, what the hell are you gonna do with them?"

"Puzzle boxes are your thing, Detective." Hope crouched until they drew eye-to-eye, pretending the hurt in his didn't hurt her, too. "Jigsaws are mine."

"Cut the act," he snapped. "Look, I don't know what changed between now and ten minutes ago, but pulling a gun on your only ally is a flimsy solution, at best."

"Where's the fun in jigsaw without the constant threat of it sliding off the table?"

"So you're gonna burn all your bridges before you run for the hills?"

"Screw the hills. Woods are more my speed."

"Listen to me. You need to let me help you—" Muzzle met forehead. Body went rigid. "You won't shoot me," he said. "You're not the Bowerbird."

"You're right." She lowered the gun. "That's why you're handcuffed to the towel rod."

She curled her finger off the trigger safety, watching Oliver shake his head in disbelief as he tried to make sense of all the debacle's moving parts. He seemed to scatter them across the tile floor, searching for patterns, corner pieces, some sort of bigger picture. He succeeded.

"You know who it is," he said, matter of fact.

"Yeah."

"It's him, isn't it?" His eyes went to her wounds. "Your predator?"

"Yes."

"What exactly are you hoping to accomplish then?" he asked, baffled. "What the hell are you trying to get from all this?"

"You wanna know what I want? What I long for—what I've always fucking longed for? A return to a normal that never existed in the first place. And when what you want is an impossibility, you're doomed to disappointment." Hope stood. "My body rejects its own humanity like a haunted goddamn house, because this skin and bone wasn't built to hold it. Morality is a virus. Virtue, a cancer. Every ounce of me fights to kill it, each hour in the day, each minute in the hour, each second, millisecond, each whatever-the-fuck comes after that..." she trailed off, absorbed in the faraway past, before shaking herself back to the present. "I don't want this. You think I do?" As Oliver shifted, she aimed the gun at his brow. "I just want to be human!"

"But he won't let you, is that it?"

"I won't let me!" Hope straightened up and slammed the Glock on the counter. "If I want to stay alive, I *can't* let me. You thought I was decent, well, I'm sorry for not telling you sooner that you were wrong." She let go of a held-in breath. "Do you know what it's like to wake up homesick for a place you've never known—for a place so unreachable you can't even really picture it? I want to go there, to go home, but I've never been there... so how can I go to a somewhere I've never been without a map, a compass, or a helpful stranger to point me north, or south, for all I know? Tell me, Oliver, how can I go to a home, to a *normal* I've never been allowed to call home without tying a noose around my neck and forcing the universe to *let me*?" Trembling hands

251

lifted the weapon again. "How do I find peace," Hope said, voice concrete-cracking, "when I can't leave my chaos behind?"

"It's not about leaving a part of yourself behind, Hope. I'm sure you figured that one out long before I came into the picture. It's not something that needs to be pinched off or cauterized! It's all just a matter of keeping your... your chaos on a leash. You can shorten it. Lengthen it, even, if you have to. But as long as you've got that leash? That's control over *it*, not the other way around."

"What good is a leash when I've got no collar to hook it on?"

"A step in the right direction."

"I don't have time for steps! I need to do something now, take action now, *right now*, or someone's gonna turn up dead tomorrow."

"That's why you let me help you. That's why you uncuff me, hand me the gun, and get in the passenger seat of my car so we can hunt the prick down. Together. *Legally*."

"A master chaos wrangler then, are you?" Hope scoffed. "From where I'm standing—that is, over you, with your own service weapon—you ain't a master of much."

"It's exactly that attitude of always thinking you're the smartest in the room, hell, the *only* one in the room, that makes you underestimate your enemies. Worse, your friends." He annunciated each word with a punch to the towel rack: "It. Will. Get. You. Killed."

"You're not my friend, Detective."

"I was before you made me cuff myself at gunpoint." Oliver tugged at the chain. It didn't give. "What I'm telling you, and what you are doggedly refusing to hear, is that I'm willing to reconsider that stance so you don't have to go through whatever you're going through alone."

"I do my best work alone." Hope dropped the robe; Oliver turned away. She shimmied into the oversized red-and-black flannel he'd fished from his closet until it fit like a dress. "Less people die that way."

"*You'll* die that way!" His shout clogged the room, boxed in by all that tile. Hope's heart ached at the sheer desperation in his voice. "All this, all that you have, you're ready to chuck in the trash even when you have someone ready and willing and *actually equipped* to handle the mess you're determined to drown in? And for what? Why, Hope? Stop acting like a coward."

"I have nothing!" Hope screamed. "Had nothing. And then the world took that nothing from me, too. So I took it back. I took it all back and then some—I took back my nothing, I took back their something, plus a little extra for my time, and I'll never stop raping and pillaging the world and the vile men who run it for what it did to me, not until it's paid its dues. I won't stop, not until it curses my name in every language it knows." She gulped, her throat abraded by the outburst. "How could you possibly help? You'd be nothing but dead weight, interfering with shit you couldn't hope to understand."

"You've got enough spite to power all Reykjavík, don't you?"

"There's a difference between spite and anger."

"And you're drowning in spades of both!"

"Drowning?" Hope said. "No. I don't need air anymore." Anger was her nourishment; it filled her lungs and guts with coals, and the fire there kept her going. "Anger keeps me sane," she said.

"Sane? Hope, listen to yourself! Is this really what you call sanity? Holding an officer hostage at gunpoint—the only idiot officer still somehow on your side?"

"You're not on my side. You're on the floor."

"Then you've let your anger blind you." Despair brought a hush to his voice. "I'm here when no one else is because—"

"If I had a dime for every man who tried to convince me I'm helpless—"

"Because I admire you."

Three simple words. The first an uppercut, the next a right hook, the last a gut punch that stuttered her psychological clock with its pared-to-the-bone sincerity. How many sweet three-word poisons had she swallowed like bitter pills over the years? How many false *I love yous* or *I adore yous*, all expertly designed to disarm her just long enough to unbutton her blouse?

"I won't do you the disservice of pretending to know what's going on or what you're dealing with," Oliver said. "But what if I can sweeten the pot with something priceless? Priceless, that is, even to someone like you? On a mission like yours?"

Sweat slicked Hope's hold on the pistol grip. "Everything's got a price tag. Ain't any I can't afford on my own."

"I'm not talking about money. I'm talking about a way out."

Her finger hovered on the trigger, shaking.

"You know who's doing this. There's a ghost in your eye every time you look at me. Sometimes I swear I can see his reflection, like he lives there. And I guess he does. Doesn't he? Maybe he's made you a hostage in your own head, but even if he'll take no ransom, we can throw him out together, Hope. All you have to do is—"

"Trust you?"

Oliver's jaw clenched when she snatched the words from his mouth.

"Why would I do that?" she jabbed. "Because you *admire* me? We'll see what admiration buys when you've got a bullet in your knee. Talk is cheap, bud."

"Then give me a chance to earn it."

"No."

"The fact you'd go for the leg and not my head must count for something. It must mean—"

"That I'm not a killer!" Hope spreadeagled her arms in a sweep of exasperation. "That's *all* it means!"

The gun in her hand was a tool to keep Oliver in check. A sort of electric collar. But if that's all it was, why couldn't she set it down? If Hope was not a killer, why did it feel so at home in her palm?

She wanted to tell him. Tell him everything. But it wasn't just Killian holding her hostage. It wasn't just the fact she was a personal shopper for Europe's most depraved murderers of means. There was another part to her story.

The Old Man. The barber chair.

The beginning of it all.

Hope couldn't give up Killian without giving up everything. Giving up herself, her life, giving up what she'd done to survive and all the things she somehow, for some reason, kept on doing long after the Old Man had been vanquished by the justice system.

Oliver accosted her with betrayed awe. But what would that betrayal, already agonizing, turn into if he ever knew the whole truth? She couldn't bear to find out.

This chained-up abandonment, here, might be forgivable. The truth was not. She beelined for the bathroom door.

"Hope, wait."

And she did, in the doorway, harpooned by Oliver's desperation and weighed down by the anchors of her innate want to stay.

"Tell me who it was," he said.

"I've had a thousand opportunities to give you the killer's name. Do you really think—"

"No. Tell me who did this to you."

"That's a loaded question." Hope appraised the pistol. "Should I tell you who deceived me? Who manipulated me? Should I tell you who terrified me, undermined my beliefs, convinced me I was a monster and a deceiver, anyone but the me I thought I was? Should I tell you who used me and beat me, or who cut me till I was more red than white, more animal than woman—should I tell you who tricked me into liking the pain too? Is that what you're asking, Oliver?"

"I'm asking you to tell me who ruined you," he said darkly. "Because I want to help you ruin them back."

A casualty of ruination. Was that what she'd become? Was that what passersby saw, giving her wide berths on the street?

"He'll rot in a dank cell until all the clocks stop, and longer after that. Tell me who did this to you. I will make it happen."

A cold, pleasant shiver played her vertebrae like piano keys. She ignored it. "A cell isn't enough."

"But it is a start," he said. "Who ruined you?"

"I'm not ruined."

At the top of his voice, Oliver yelled, *"Who ruined you?"*

"I did!" Hope cried. "Isn't it obvious? The *who* is the reason you're in handcuffs!" Her voice shrank. Wilted. "That's my little secret, Ollie. Happy now?" She spared one last look at the man who'd foolishly thought her decent, aching for a world where she deserved his kindness. "It's me. Always has been. And if it's any consolation..." She gestured at everything with the gun, at the gun itself with her eyes. "I never meant for things to go down this way."

"No one ever does."

A current of bitter anguish carried her through the den, where she retrieved her guthook knife from under the couch along with her abandoned coat and boots. Hinges hungry for grease whined as she opened the front door.

"Tell me something," Oliver shouted from the bathroom. "Did it work? When you took it all back from the world and put it where it was supposed to be, did it fill you up again?"

Hope was glad to be outside the bathroom, out of eyeshot, distanced from his last-ditch effort to stop her in her tracks.

"No," she called. "And there's only one thing I can do about it." Hope hefted the pistol, measuring its power. All the hell it could unleash. "I'm lost in the woods somewhere, Ollie. Don't search for me."

As the darkness outside swallowed Hope whole, the last sounds heard were the cock of the gun, the click of the door, and Oliver pleading for her to stay.

She didn't.

CHAPTER THIRTY-THREE

THE HOWLING NOTHING

H ope made it ten houses up Sörlaskjól in Oliver's stolen Skoda before pulling onto the seaside shoulder. The gun was an unwelcome guest in the passenger seat. Her cellphone rested on the dashboard until her restless leg-bouncing sent it toppling into the footwell. She picked it up and held it against the wheel, examining the lock screen as if by plugging the right code on the PIN pad she could make this all go away. No more gun. No more Killian.

No more Old Man—no more Edward Wright.

When Killian had said the other man's name on the phone, it was like hearing a cat quack. It didn't belong in his mouth. That name lived in a separate dimension entirely, and the fact that they'd clashed surely meant a wormhole would soon engulf the world. Her world.

Killian had known. All this time, he'd known what she'd done. Her deepest secret.

The morning's first early riser drove by in a busted Subaru, blinding her briefly as a star of headlight bounced off the rearview mirror. Lights went on in kitchens as moms donned housecoats and set coffee pots to brew. Dads joined them at the table for quick breakfasts, tightening their ties. Front doors opened. Car doors shut. Soon, a steady stream of commuters flowed up the road at a leisurely pace, but to Hope it seemed like a funeral cortège. The rest of the world, divorced from hers, continued to spin, ushered forward by time and social mores and entirely unaware that her universe had gone supernova.

The phone chimed, lighting the cab jellybean-blue.

A media message from Killian. Before Hope could stop years of reflexive muscle memory from keying the PIN and opening the text, a photo of a man she thought she'd never see again filled the screen.

The years had been unkind to him, but kinder, at least, than Killian's wrath.

Where she remembered grey eyes made small by crow's feet whenever he did anything other than frown, there were big grandpa glasses with thick black frames. The left lens was spiderweb-cracked. A swollen fig of a black eye grew underneath. The goatee was still there, grey instead of blond, barely discernible beneath the crust of dried, terracotta blood.

The thought of unleashing Killian's starved-wolf fury upon Edward Wright was a fantasy she might've entertained in the past, but the fact that Killian now had in his paws not a wealth but a treasure trove of her closeted skeletons filled Hope with nausea. What else could have made her turn on Oliver so fast? She wasn't sure she could hate Killian any more than she already did, but when she inevitably recalled the image of Oliver cuffed to the towel rack, burned to the wall of her psyche, she despised Killian with a fresh and boiling rage. And now she had to hear him out because he had her by the throat. All he had to do was bite down.

Hope redialed the number and Killian picked up on the second ring.

"I was beginning to worry." The beep of a stopwatch. "Two minutes to spare. Ever one to leave me waiting."

"Not my fault you always show up early." Forcing indifference into her voice when she felt powerless to the point of breaking was an exercise in self-control. "You gonna tell me what you want or should I settle in for another riveting night of cat-and-mouse bullshit?"

"Let's call it cat-and-cat and make it more interesting."

"Let's call it get-to-the-point and make it less fucking tiresome. How do you know him? How'd you find him?"

"You can't even say his name, can you?"

"Answer me."

"Ladies first."

"I don't have time for this."

"You're absolutely right, darling. Time is the last resource you have today." The words came a mile a minute. "The clock has never been less on your side. Twenty-four hours may seem like an age on a normal day, but when it's served as an ultimatum, the minutes tick by like flies with better places to be, richer corpses to bloat, so say his name and we may just shave a few seconds off your kill switch."

"I—"

"Ah, you must've called him by some pet name when you let him fuck you for twelve-hundred pounds a night. Which it... Ed? Eddie-Bear?"

She swallowed thickly. "Mr. Right."

"I wonder if he feels giddy, hearing you say it again after all this tragic time apart. How about it, Mr. Right? Butterflies in your stomach, a rod of rebar in your trousers? Oh dear, how negligent of me. Usually easier to speak without a gag in one's mouth. Must bring back fond memories though, hm? Here we are. There, there. Don't bite."

"Oozing, traitor cunt!" It was a ragged, Glaswegian grunt.

"Blonds. Fuckin' blonds, eh? I shoulda rotisseried the bitch on a rusty pipe in the shed out the back before I ever stuck my dick in 'er. Woulda screamed louder, I bet, and begged a little harder, yeah? Hard to do, isn't that right, you blisterin', gangrenous twat?"

Smack!

Edward groaned. He hacked something wet in the background.

"She's a brunette, to be fair," said Killian, perfectly calm. "Perhaps if you were kinder to the working women brave enough to come within three miles of your cock, you'd know such a paltry thing."

Hope's nails carved crescent moons in the steering wheel leather, unable to inch a word in edgewise and unsure what to say even if she could.

Smack! Edward's howl was pitched across a piano of octaves that didn't belong in a man's mouth unless he'd undergone a certain surgery.

When she finally found her voice, it was breathless. "I'd call you a hideous human being, Kil, but that'd imply you've got some humanity left."

"'Clean and unclean birds, the dove and the raven, are yet in the ark,'" Killian quoted, almost but not quite winded. "But even with all that false righteous anger of yours, I do believe we'll be sharing the same side of the ship in the end."

"I'd sooner throw myself in the sea than live in a small world where God thinks you and me are the same."

Mania drove Killian's curt laugh into higher, wilder territory, spiking nails into her knuckles until she couldn't let go of the wheel. Never had she been anything more than a distant, after-the-fact observer to his acts. Never had she been subject to who or what he was or how he sounded, how very, very *off* he sounded when committing the sins his soul needed to endure the infuriating dullness of the sober, well-adjusted world. She'd never had so much as a bystander's spot on the curb.

Now she was in the audience—and soon she'd be on the stage.

"Tell me why," Hope said through gritted teeth. "Just tell me why, and I'll be there."

"Terror has a voice, darling, and it communicates with those who've ears to listen. It has spoken nothing but your name since the moment you parted the gates and invited me in for dinner."

"Pardon my hearing, but that doesn't sound like a fucking reason. Enough with your pedantic horseshit."

"There has never been a love like ours. You realize that, don't you?" He was just toying with her now. "I know you do. Not under this moon. These particular stars."

"That's cus it ain't love. Whatever it was we had, love's as far from what it is as the moon is from the goddamn sun. Y'know what it is? All it is? It's insanity."

"Since when was there ever a difference, darling?"

"Is this your master plan? Visit an old client of mine in prison and think, *Oh, she'll realize she's still got the hots for me compared to this maggot-pocked cheesewheel*? Well, you're wrong, asshole. As usual. Wrong as wrong gets. Do whatever a sick fuck like you wants to do to that rice-pudding crotched piece of shit, but feel free to leave me out of it."

"That's just the thing. What you request is an impossibility. Don't you remember my last post, when I served as a prison chaplain in Glasgow? Of course. How could you forget? Well, I learned some fascinating things over the years, as it happens— souls behind bars are chatty folk, indeed—but imagine my surprise when the most hated inmate in the prison's history had a story to confess about a naughty little girl named Hope Rippa? Why else would I take poor Edward Wright hostage from HMP Shotts if not to blackmail this Hope Rippa into finally confronting what she did in that barber chair all those years ago?"

When speechlessness was the only answer, Killian doubled down, dropping the pageantry.

"You have twenty-four hours to meet me at the private airstrip." The same one she'd delivered that fateful last order to, east of Sólheimajökull. "One minute past 6:ooam tomorrow and a video recording of the very detailed confession I beat out of Mr. Right with nothing but my left fist will be delivered to the Reykjavík Metro Police, attention one DCI Oliver Ragnarsson, addressed from a certain someone named the Bowerbird in that lovely feminine script of yours. I've become quite the forger, in my time. Do we understand one another? It's time to finish what you started," he said. "Come kill the man who killed your life."

Hope rested her head on the wheel. Light from the muted radio reflected off the butt of the knife handle jutting from her boot.

"How long have you known?" she whispered.

"Mr. Right always did like to brag." Killian didn't gloat. Somber calm filled the hole left behind by his passing mania. "It took just one month after his incarceration at Barlinnie to regale me with the tale of How Hope Became the Magpie."

Hope squeezed her eyes shut until she saw green and purple stars.

When Killian had called in his new client request at the prison in 2010, it wasn't just because he'd needed supplies. He'd been testing Edward's story—confirming a truth he, at the time, hadn't wanted to believe.

"If you love me, why would you do this to me?" she murmured. "Nothing you do has ever made any sense."

Killian responded, introspective and grim. "That's the thing about walking the depths, darling. There is always a way onward, but never a way to tell whether you've gone forward or back, through the howling nothing."

Click.

Hope dropped the phone at her feet. The screen went black. Huddled beneath the wheel, tucked between her knees, Hope Rippa came quite close to crying. Sobbing. She beat the console, the windows, the roof, ready to fold, ready to give up.

But she didn't.

She unfurled from her fetal position, slowly whistling a deep gulp of air through her teeth. Folding down the sun visor, she dabbed at the smoky remains of smudged eyeliner, the faded purple of her lipstick, once a crisp Merlot and now a blurred memory of mauve. She adjusted the rearview, the side mirrors, the seat height; she switched gears and flicked the blinker and turned safely until she was fifteen minutes from Sörlaskjól, following tidy ant-queues of cars inland as they plodded off to their various anthills.

Twenty-four hours. It wouldn't take more than three to get there, and she had nowhere else to go. She turned the radio on, listening to the early-morning news before mention of the Bowerbird Murders made her turn it off. She drove in what felt like circles, trying to think, hypnotized by license plates and red lights, yellow blinkers and the white dashes dividing lanes. She sent reluctant feelers to assess the state of her inner thoughts. The feelers recoiled. How could she dive into that knot of a thousand twisting thoughts, all writhing like snakes mid-orgy on the forest floor? She couldn't get near them. They had teeth and weren't afraid to lunge, busy fornicating and making more thoughts, more sharp, slithering little beast-thoughts that slipped quick into the brush, too quick for her to catch. When she tried, she sliced her hands on the thorns.

She was too tired.

Idling at a red light, Hope picked up the phone when it

buzzed. Behind her, someone honked. She drove on, following a roundabout aimlessly until she gathered the gall to open the message.

> She really should have considered hiding the key to her cage with a tad more finesse. Taped under the staircase railing? How perilously unimaginative, even for a canary.

Hope swerved into the next lane. A red Honda CR-V roared until she straightened into the left lane, trapped between traffic and nowhere to go. Bile and denial rose in equal measure until air was less a guarantee and more a downright luxury. She struggled to stay in the lane as she exited the roundabout onto a quiet street.

A media message. A voice recording.

She pressed play. What else could she do?

"You didn't tell me your canary was a screamer," Killian's recorded voice said, speaking loud over Andi's sobs, muffled by duct tape. *"Who knew we shared the same taste in women?"*

Mid-wail, Hope looked up in time to draw level with the grille of a big white truck, swerve out of its path, and strike a telephone pole head-on.

Glass cracked.

Metal crunched.

Head met airbag and there was nothing but black.

CHAPTER THIRTY-FOUR

THE BARBER CHAIR

AUGUST 2008

I t was the last night on Hope's schedule, the one in the little black book she kept hidden in the inner pocket of her duffel bag.

She'd already pegged another working girl to pass her client list on to like the torch it was, a cute Finn new to the life named Emmie, Effie, Ellie, or some such. She leaned heavily on the young end of the escort spectrum, Hope thought, but it wasn't really her business, was it? She hadn't been much older when she first started out. The newbie would be perfect for the men in the book who were into the doe-eyed, fresh-faced variety of call girl, the kind that gave the *girl* part a much more literal meaning.

It was a profession which Killian had first found admirable and increasingly deemed distasteful the more intimate he and Hope became. A natural progression for any relationship. After all, why keep a stable of legs to straddle when you could not only climb atop a single star stallion, but be no worse off financially—better off, in fact—than you ever were before?

One more night. One more man. One more *someone else* and then she'd be free. She'd be Killian's, totally and completely.

Killian had rankled at the idea of one more night, but ultimately conceded, falling for the lie that a last-minute cancelation for a 'farewell' appointment would cross her best client's name from her book, a devastating blow to the girl soon to inherit Hope's list.

The truth was a surprise—the truth was Edward Wright's goodbye bonus, a wish-you-well-and-miss-you worth £2,000 on top of the standard hourly rate. Not that Hope needed anything more from the filthy-rich horse breeder. She wanted for nothing with Killian at her side, but that was precisely the *why* of tonight.

When all you can give the person who gives you everything is a body to wake up next to in the morning, a body that doesn't leave in the night or refuse breakfast the next day, guilt starts clogging the pipes. Hope yearned to show Killian she could offer something, anything, in return, besides sex and a side of companionship. Maybe a trip to Italy. She'd always wanted to go to Milan, and he'd mentioned a fondness for the Dolomites more than once in the hushed whispers of their pillow talk.

After straightening her pleated miniskirt and slipping back into her heels—Mr. Right preferred them off at the door—she wandered around The Scotsman penthouse Edward had styled as home. While she wouldn't miss the tedious humping or the fifty-something body doing the tedious humping, Hope would miss the suite: its private terrace overlooking swathes of ancient architecture between the hotel and Edinburgh Castle, the eggshell-everything furnishings, the overall sense of grandeur soaking the suite in champagne-bubble luxury.

While Edward showered in the master bathroom, Hope descended the spiral staircase, riding the railing halfway down, savoring a night ill-spent but worth the trouble. So elated was she, floating about like an untethered hot air balloon that'd escaped its basket rider, that when she noticed the normally padlocked office sporting a naked doorknob, Hope didn't hesitate to wander inside.

"Looks like her legs were stitched up... what, twice? Recently, too. Do you see that, man?"

"Think she got away from the Bowerbird or something?"

"Nah, rookie... I mean, who knows? Looks to me like she couldn't get away from flypaper even if she had wings."

"Or a telephone pole."

"Hand me the gauze and bandages, man."

With quite literally a hop, skip, and a jump, Hope slinked into the unlit office before bashing her hip on the edge of a metal table. Hunched over and slinging sailor-speak, she didn't realize she'd knocked over a bunch of shit until she straightened with a groan. Praying to the God she'd just damned to hell that she hadn't broken some Ancient Greek amphora, she plopped to hands and knees and crawled around the table—well, a cart; from down here she saw the wheels—until she reached the fallen items. Confusion set in only when she held garden shears in one hand and a power drill in the other. The confusion doubled upon spotting the array of drill bits and scalpels that'd scattered along with them. Train of thought stalling like a backfiring tractor, Hope stood with the tools in her hands, unable to process why they were here. Had Edward hired some folks to do indoor renovations? Some landscaping on the terrace? Was this their storage closet, and maybe they'd left them behind? Hope metronomed from one tool to the other until a pitiful moan froze her still.

A brunette girl stripped to frilly underwear and a pink training bra begged with glassy, walnut eyes to be set free from the bindings lashing her to a barber chair. She squinted in the meager light flooding in from the hallway, pining away behind a hefty knot of rope gag. What at first seemed to be mud or dirt crusting her body turned out to be dried waterfalls of old blood.

Hope dropped the shears. Hope dropped the drill. The clatter was loud. The drill hit the cart, sending it banging against the wall. The girl muffle-sobbed, and then those teddy-bear browns went wide. A shadow blotted the sun of the hallway chandelier: a shadow in the shape of a man whose arms Hope backpedaled straight into.

"Bunny," Edward lamented. "What have you done?"

"At least she dodged the powerline. And the truck."

"What's the ETA on the police?"

"Jeez, who knows. Those poor bastards got enough of a citywide dumpster fire to keep their hands on the extinguisher for months. Not to mention the missing pair of hands... You hear about that?"

"What, Ragnarsson? Bet you they'll find him slumped in the kitchen with a shotgun—"

"It's cold enough out here without your morbid ass saying shit like that. I met him once. He's a nice guy."

"Woah. Blood pressure's seventy over fifty. Prep the IV, I'll keep pressure on the wound."

"I've held my home open to you for years, and there was only ever one rule." Edward's voice transformed from sad to bitingly cold. He shoved Hope away, sending her stumbling back into the dungeon. "Could you remind me what my one rule was, Bunny?"

"Don't go in the office," she stammered, unsure who to keep her eyes on: the crying kid tied to the chair or the animal who'd put her there. "Never go in the office."

"I like you, lass." Edward sounded legitimately torn. "Quite a bit, in fact. This rule was in place for that very reason. To *protect* you."

"F-from what?"

"The knowledge of good and evil, 'a course," he said. "*My* good and evil. What a dastardly Eve you are, eh? Pinchin' the apple when I trusted you enough to offer free rein of my abode."

While he clucked in disapproval, Hope's own tongue was burnt rubber in her mouth, her mind an oversoaked sponge with no pores left to absorb what he was saying. He sighed at her, shaking his head.

"Unfortunately," Edward began, "however grand The Scotsman's suite, its office wasn't built for two, yeah? I've already spent too much effort conditioning this young lady, here. To begin again, and with you... Well, you don't even need behavioral adjustment, do ye, Bunny? Put a clip of cash in your hand every other week, and you make for fine dressage."

"Please." Hope backed into a second table, this one rickety and wooden. A pair of bloody pliers hit the floor. "I'll do anything."

"Och, sweet wee thing. There's only one thing you can do now."

His fingers glided over a magnetic strip mounted on the wall. They bypassed a butcher knife, and then a machete. They skipped over a paring knife, a cleaver, a stylized Highland dirk. Finally, they made a decision: settling on a glittering blade four inches long and capped with a deadly hook—a tool whose purpose she was ignorant of, but know-how or none, her imagination filled in enough blanks to empty her bladder down her bare leg.

"Please," she said. "I won't tell anyone."

"Isn't that what they all say right before they die?"

"I keep a log of all my meetings," Hope tried. "There's a paper trail. They'll know."

"Who's *they*? Do you have a madam?"

"There's still documents."

"Alibis can be bought," Edward droned, almost bored. "And my bank account is more than up to snuff. No one's gonna miss a whore."

Hope whisked about the room, grabbing the doorknob, the tables, touching weapons and rolls of tarp—everything she could leave fingerprints on, even plucking a few strands from her head to scatter tactically around the room.

"There. I'm an accomplice, see? Why go to the cops if it looks like I'm your little helper?"

"Because you'd look like an escapee by demographic alone."

Edward stalked forward. Hope stumbled back, flailing for a lifeline and finding nothing but open ocean.

"Please, baby," she sobbed. "There's gotta be something I can do. I'm your favorite, remember? Your Bunny. I'll stay, I swear—just give me a way. Gimme something to do. I'll do anything! Please. Please don't kill me!"

This gave Edward pause. He considered the guthook knife in his hand for a time, measuring its heft. After he arrived at some conclusion, some decision, he presented Hope with the handle.

"Alright then," he said. "Turn this into a murder weapon."

"Holy hell, that smell's gonna wake the dead for miles."

"Not to mention the rats. Saw one the size of a housecat just yesterday."

"No shit?"

"Swear on my mother's grave."

"Your mother isn't dead, and even if she was that wouldn't do much to convince me... Christ. Of all the trucks in Reykjavík that could've tipped, it had to be the one carrying twenty tons of monkfish from Akranes."

"The road's a minefield. See the teeth on those beasts?"

"Fangs, man... I stepped on one when I hopped out the bus, went clean through my boot. Look. See? Wild, right? These rubber soles they make us wear, good for less than nothing. And y'know the best part? The damn thing's head didn't even squish. It crunched. Like I bit a raw turnip."

"She's just a kid."

"What does that change?"

A snatch of light streaking over Edward's shoulder caught the metal of the heart-shaped tag on the girl's collar. Connie. Hope bit back a moan of frustration.

"Plshhh," Connie begged, saliva gushing around the gag. "Plshh dnnn!"

"I..."

Hope blocked out the muffled pleading, searching instead for a place to start. To end. The guthook knife trembled in her hand. She'd bled pigs and beheaded chickens on her mother's farm in Georgia, but Connie's collar was thick, covering her from carotid to clavicle. *What I tell you 'bout naming them hogs? Stupid girl. Stupid, idiot girl. If I didn't squeeze you out, I'd never guess you was mine. Go on, now. See how it feels to bleed out a pet instead of a nameless thing. Then you'll learn.*

"I don't know how to..."

"Figure it out. You're a smart girl."

Stupid, idiot girl.

Tears and snot slimed the rope wrapped around Connie's head. Melted mascara stained it black. The blade quaked in Hope's grip as she stepped back, assessing the girl's body as if it were a cake and she was deciding where first to cut. The knife fell. She squatted to retrieve it but her hand was repelled as if by an opposing polarity.

Kill someone? Kill a girl, a little girl? This wasn't some swine on her wretched mother's farm. One misstep and that could've been Hope in the barber chair, wailing around a rope gag. She looked up at Connie. Saw her own reflection. The mirror of fear, of dread, of a desperate want to not die.

A desperate, desperate want.

I can't do this.

I can do this.

I can't do this—

"Crack on, then!" Edward barked, and Hope snatched the knife off the floor.

I can do this.

But how?

After several tries Hope tottered onto her knees, drawing level with the filthy crater of Connie's navel.

Butchering was Mama's domain. She said Hope was too clumsy. Not precise enough to sever the belly without puncturing the intestines, ruining the meat and robbing the house of a paycheck. But that didn't matter now. The only thing that mattered was getting out alive, and if Hope had to gut a young girl named Connie to walk free of The Scotsman with her heart still beating, then she would.

She had to. She had no other choice.

That's what she told herself. Over, and over, and over.

Survive.

Connie released a strangled, gurgling gasp when Hope plunged the knife in her sternum. Body to body, Hope leaned against Connie's shoulder so she didn't have to see the shock in her eyes. As she struggled to rip the blade's hook down from the diaphragm to that filthy navel, parting flesh like thick beige curtains, Hope discovered that not looking didn't protect her from the sound. The sound of tearing skin, the slop of viscera on wood floor, the moist, clogged-drain sputter bubbling from Connie's mouth.

"I'm sorry," Hope breathed. "I had to."

"You didn't," Edward said. "But you did."

He laid a hand on Hope's shoulder to gently pry her from the disemboweled corpse and turn her from it. She still caught a glimpse of the gory octopus slithering from Connie's opened gut.

Hope swallowed her scream, her vomit, her every emotion.

"Head on up to the master bath. Toss your dress and shoes in the second hamper on the right. Once you've finished showerin' off that blood and pish, I'll type up a list of new gadgets to fetch to replace the ones ye broke. In all honesty, they were getting' pretty battered, anyway, yeah? The price'll come outta your bonus this week. That's fair, I think. But in the future? Not to worry. I'll provide the funds and even toss you an extra something for the value of your time—and the risk you'll be exposing yourself to on my behalf... Oh, Bunny, don't cry. At least you're not in that chair, eh? My little survivor. My little helper."

In the future.

"Now, now. Not to worry." Edward patted her head. Stroked her hair. "I'll take care of the body myself. Go on, sweet little magpie."

Limping her way up the spiral staircase, Hope didn't realize until she looked in the bathroom mirror that she still held the guthook knife.

"Property values are bound to plummet around here. They'll be scrubbing fish slime from the blacktop with Brillo for ages... Look, folks are gawking from the windows instead of the sidewalk. That's a first."

"Could be worse."

"How?"

"It could be summer."

"Ugh. Don't make me spew on the poor girl, I had cod for dinner last night and it hasn't exactly come out yet. I swear my wife's trying to put me six feet under by way of an impacted bowel."

"At least it wasn't monkfish... Finally! Constable's here."

"You find a vein yet?"

"Yeah. Get the saline. Yo! Watch the stretcher, man. The girl's had enough of a shit night."

"Wait, check it out. Is she crying? While unconscious?"

"Thank goodness, she's waking up..."

"We've got a fighter in the ring."

"Ma'am, can you hear me?"

Hope winced in the ambulance's light, glaring like a white sun between the moons of the two EMTs' heads.

"When you never shut your mouths, it's hard not to." They chuckled in relief. She groaned in pain. "What was that you said before?"

"You'll have to be more specific, darling," said the one who looked like blond Elvis.

"Don't call me that," she mumbled, hot pain skewering her

head from temple to temple. "The thing... the thing about your mom's grave."

"Oh, the swearing? This clown to your right thinks he saw a rat—"

"After that," Hope said.

"I think she's talking about how your sweetheart of a mother hasn't done you the courtesy of kicking any buckets yet," said the one with a full beaver of a beard.

"Woe is me, 'tis a sad truth."

"Oh, hey, ma'am—I wouldn't move just yet. That pole did a nasty number on your head—"

"She's not dead..." Hope sat up, resisting the EMT's gentle but insistent hands until she had to slap them off. She reached up, fingering the damp bandage around her forehead, the stickiness sugarcoating the side of her face and neck. "She's not..."

"Who's not?" Beaver asked.

"We better get to the hospital," Elvis said.

"He swore... He swore on his mother's *well-kept* tomb." Hope squeezed her eyes shut as if the pressure would sharpen the image in her head.

The graveyard outside the church window. The undertaker's shed beyond. Epiphany sent her into freefall.

"The bitch never died."

"All right, miss, let's lie back so we can get going—"

Adrenaline lightning-struck her. Hope side-swept Elvis's arm, rolled from the stretcher, and in a quick six second's time had the guthook knife from her boot pressed to Beaver's neck. The hook snagged a patch of fur on his Adam's apple. She spat the IV tube from her mouth, having ripped the canula from the crook of her elbow with her teeth. The vein blew.

"You're gonna do a few things for me, Mr. Presley, or your partner's getting a nasty throatful of metal. Got it, bud?" Head pounding, Hope checked on the cop investigating the Skoda Octavia partially wedged in a utility pole across a minefield of dead fish. His back was turned. "I said, *got it?*"

Elvis gulped.

Soon, he was lashed to the stretcher. Beaver sat on the floor, wrists bound behind his back with tourniquets. All it took was the threat of the knife. But Hope needed more than the knife. She needed the gun. And the gun was still in the crashed Skoda half a block up the street, undergoing inspection by a constable with a flashlight.

Vertigo threatened to sweep her feet. Monkfish tripped her every step. The stench assaulted. The cold bit. Her head swam and swam, tilted to and fro just like her body, and then she was close behind the constable, getting closer. The passenger door was open. It dinged away as he examined the glovebox.

When the knife handle hit the base of his skull, Hope heard a few muffled shouts from behind closed doors. Lights went on. Phones were no doubt being whipped out to record whatever happened next; pencils and pads were fetched to take down the license plate. Some would call friends. Some would call neighbors. Others would call 112, and these others were the spring in Hope's stumbling step, her propulsion as she climbed back behind the driver's seat, flipped the car in reverse, and left an unconscious cop and two hogtied medics in the road.

The police couldn't know where Hope was headed. She had time. Clearing blear from her eyes and fog from her brain, she slipped the guthook knife in her boot and the gun in her lap, squeezing the steering wheel, urging the crippled car to 100, 120, 140 kilometers an hour before she finally broke free of the city without a single siren behind her.

Hope rubbed the dashboard, thanking a loyal horse. A thin stream of smoke trailed from under the crushed-can hood. The road beyond the streetlights was dark and dangerously frosty. Snow began to fall.

"Just get me where I'm going," she said. "I'll take it from there."

The dash read 9:00am.

———

The pretty, blond night clerk shot up from behind the check-in desk when Hope barreled through the front doors with a Glock 19 aimed between her eyes. The rolling chair crashed against the accent wall. A massive fish tank mounted under the town slogan—*Fjöðurfjall, Chasing Dreams Instead of Dragons since 2016*—exploded in a rainbow of fins.

Marching up to the counter, Hope smacked a vase of fake lilies to the floor, racked the slide with a vicious *snick-click!* and said, "Take me to Elizabeth Glass."

CHAPTER THIRTY-FIVE

THE FOURTH STATION

Hope paced the concrete floors of the lair—the secret room whose trapdoor lay behind the altar of Killian's church—pondering the phone in her hand. Killian's mother, gracefully riding the line between blond and grey, sat tied to an old chair. It'd almost been too easy, this kidnapping: ushering helpless Elizabeth from the undertaker's lodge to the church without a peep, even after Hope knocked out the night clerk and lashed her to the radiator. The timid hunch rounding Elizabeth's thin shoulders, combined with her immediate cooperation, told the story of a woman beaten into obedience by a husband with a temper, the empty promise of heroin, and a cavalry of back-alley men who traded favors for needles. Watching her now, limp-necked and studying her feet, Hope chafed. She should have been furious at a bitch capable of birthing such a monster, but mothers were as much to blame for the beastliness of their sons as children were guilty of the sins of their fathers. In fact, the only thing Hope felt looking at Killian's mother was pity.

"I'm sorry," she told Elizabeth. "This time, I really did have to."

She dialed the number.

"Does someone need directions?" asked Killian.

Elizabeth tried to scream behind the rope in her mouth—it was a measly, useless sound no one but Hope would hear, but still she gave the chair leg a piston kick. The glare Hope administered spoke what she couldn't—*One more of those and I topple you over*—proving effective when Elizabeth offered a chastened nod.

Hope returned her attention to the cellphone. Collecting her temper. Calming her pulse.

Breathe in.

Breathe out.

"I want proof of life," Hope demanded.

Shuffling, rustling. A cough, as a gag was pulled from mouth to chin.

"Hope, what's going—" Before she could get out so much as a fourth word, Andi's tearful appeal was cut off.

"Someone's been watching too many crime dramas," Killian admonished. "Good enough?"

It wasn't. Not in the least. Hope had no image—couldn't, for the life of her, paint a picture where Andi was in Killian's claws and what that scene might look like. Was she mere ransom, or had she been hurt? Hope dipped a toe in the vile swamp of empathy and lurched back, imagining the depth and degree of terror her former lover must have felt, being abducted from her home the night she was meant to leave for safer shores, and for the very same reason she was leaving in the first place.

Crunching her cheek as if it were hard candy, Hope pressed her knuckles to her mouth, not only to keep her from unleashing an unholy torrent of cusses, but to imagine. Imagine what it was like for Andi, the woman she claimed she didn't love, and maybe didn't, but still cared for deeply.

Had Andi decided to leave in the morning, had she been asleep when the lock turned, when a hand slipped through to unhook the flimsy chain? Had she woken from a dream when the floor creaked under Killian's feet—did she grab for her Pikachu nightlight? Did it cry *Pika! Pika!* when she squeezed it, flashing the room and its intruder yellow?

Did she have time to scream before the rag covered her mouth; did she see the assaulter's frigid stare looming above; did she know to blame Hope when consciousness reluctantly returned, here and there, between gasps of chloroform? She must have been petrified. All the crying and thrashing might've earned her a time out—a blow to the back of the head—but it would have been a mercy. At least until she'd woken up.

"The line dividing me from you has begun to blur," Hope mused, holding the shattered pieces of her calm together with twist-ties and glue. "I gotta do something about that."

"That line dissolved years ago, darling. Can't you feel the abyss left behind by its absence? It vanished the moment you consented to my artistry."

"More like butchery." Hope thumbed the stitches rollercoasting down her thighs. "All you've done is make me your pornography, and I was too young and stupid to notice when it started."

"And yet you proved more than capable and perfectly happy to become my Babylon. All you needed was a Virgil to guide you down the paths of Inferno."

"Spare me the literary blather," Hope sneered. "You're Caligula, not Virgil."

"Even Caligula had his protégés."

"Is that what I am to you?"

"A protégée? No. Once upon a time, perhaps, but today? Today, you'll become my mirror."

"Mirrors break."

"I'd never break you. Not completely. I've little use for a partner who requires reassembly."

"Guess I'll have to break myself then." Hope lit a cigarette. "If only to show you just how shattered your reflection really is."

He snickered. "You've hardly got the gall."

"Actually, I've got more than gall. I've got fear, and fear can be one hell of a motivator." She took a drag. Inhaled deep. Blew smoke in Elizabeth's face, from which she leaned away. "So go ahead and watch me break, cus you won't be able to stop it. Wanna know why?"

Hope slid the gag from his mother's mouth. She held the speaker to her face. It was the first time Elizabeth spoke—and it was not the kicked-kitten mewl Hope expected it to be, but rather a throaty growl with a sharpness to its edge.

Elizabeth said something in Irish.

Biting her cheek soothed neither Hope's anxiety nor her pounding head. What was she telling Killian? Where they were, the fact Hope was armed with a knife and a gun? Laboring to translate her time-lost Gaelic, she relaxed when her brain caught up and cracked the cypher.

Stay strong, my boy. Do not come.

Whatever she says, do not come.

I have that feeling in my bones again.

"What do you mean by 'again', Mrs. Glass?" asked Hope, before Killian could react.

Elizabeth's eyes, as talcum blue as her son's, rose to appraise Hope without moving her slack head a smidge. Small pearls beaded their corners. The tears followed a roadmap of wrinkles. There was, if not a wisdom, then at least a fathoms-deep world-weariness in those eyes which found Hope's impressive grasp of language wholly unsurprising.

Once her sympathy ran out, Hope gagged the old woman again.

"Bet you recognize that voice," she said.

The pause stretched between them was a dynamite fuse,

sparking and spitting in the dark of some cave. But there was no blast. The flame fizzled—but the dynamite was no dud. When next Killian spoke, it was defined by lines of even, measured fury: the distant call of a demon in the cavern, disturbed by the hiss of the fuse.

"You have lost the plot of your own story if you think this will solve your problem."

"It's worth it if I get to decide how your story ends," Hope said. With the gun in one hand and the knife in her boot, a knife already blooded and accustomed to her palm, she found herself eager to smash the lock that kept Killian's anger contained. "So here's what's gonna happen."

Hope laid it out for him, plain and simple.

"You won't kill her," Killian said.

"Maybe not, but I'm notoriously clumsy with a knife. It's funny, actually. Your logic, I mean. You're betting your mom's life on me not being capable of a second murder when you've been trying to prove me not only capable of but biologically built for murder, all this time. Is this where I prove you right, I wonder?" Hope leaned away from the cellphone so Killian wouldn't hear the gulp she swallowed. Excitement. Terror. Two extremes tapping a foxtrot across her head's ballroom floor. "What a shame you won't be here to see your magnum opus in action. That'd be a kind of brutal cosmic irony, wouldn't it, Kil?" She paused to let him absorb her threat. "See, you ain't the only one with a stopwatch. How's six hours sound? Bah. Know what? Let's make it five, huh? With the pace you've been working at lately, that should be plenty of time to pack up and hit the road. D'you hear me, Killian?" Hope paused both for effect and to hone her voice to solid stone. "Five hours before Mrs. Glass is unfortunate enough to experience how successful her son really was in his experiment."

The phone's barrier offered some semblance of safety, and

confidence in that safety, but talking to Killian in such a way—threatening Killian in such a personal, irrevocable way—made balloon animals of Hope's intestines. What the hell was she doing? What was the endgame?

That was the thing. She had no clue.

Excitement. Terror. The coming of an end.

"What a mistake of potential you proved to be."

"And you're just a mistake," she countered. "In every way, shape, and form."

"What, pray tell, shall I do with Mr. Right?"

"Whatever the hell you want. You started this mess with Edward. Find a mop bucket and get to work. Clock's ticking."

"And what about—"

"You'll bring Andi with you unharmed," Hope snapped. "As for Ed's confession? You'll bring that to me, too, on whatever phone or camera you recorded it on. Do I make myself crystal fucking clear?"

No answer.

Hope used images of Andi trussed in duct tape to stoke her outrage. She backhanded Elizabeth Glass and held the speaker close to her drooling mouth so her son could hear the slap and the muffled cry of pain.

"Tick tock, Father Glass."

Guilt may have been a corrosive beast—guilt may, by midday, have eaten Hope's remaining sanity alive—but one does what one must. To save one's people. To save themselves. To bring a fifteen-year game of chess to a head, and say, with impregnable certainty:

Zugzwang.

CHAPTER THIRTY-SIX

ZUGZWANG

The second Killian descended the stairs into the chapel storeroom at just past 3:00pm, Hope raised the gun, he raised his hands, and she demanded to know where the hell Andi was.

"This isn't poker, darling," he said, the pet name ringing hollow of its usual coyness as he examined his hogtied mother. "I'd be a fool to bring all my chips to the table without assessing my odds. Don't fret. She's closer than you think. Mother, are you—"

"Where's Edward?"

"I intubated his stomach with a garden hose, poured three liters of petrol down his throat, and tossed in a few lit matches. As it turns out, you only need one, but who doesn't love a good bonfire on a cold winter's night?" Killian slowly lowered his arms, but Hope did not lower the Glock. "Would you care to see the photos? They're on the same phone as Mr. Right's confession."

Where Hope swore she'd feel an abhorrent tension from Elizabeth, she felt the opposite—less than the opposite: no reaction. Was she high? Was she senile? No. She just knew what her son was. Hope found herself wishing for a quick five alone with the woman to ask when she'd first known what Killian was. What had he done first?

Had he mutilated the neighbor's cat and pinned the crime on a dog? Did he peep on the girls' football team in the showers and set fire to family photos in the coach's office after being caught? Perhaps he was particularly vicious to a peer in grade school, cutting their belly with sharp rocks at recess, convincing them Child Protection and Welfare would whisk them away from mommy and daddy for the abuse if he or she dared tattle-tell?

When was the first time Killian had crossed the border from morbid curiosity acted upon to morbid curiosity gone too far? Maybe, at fourteen or fifteen, he convinced the same peer he abused in grade school—whom he'd not so much befriended as groomed—to skip class one day. Maybe he led them to a graffitied storm drain outlet all the senior cycle kids used to drink their parents' whisky and smoke their siblings' joints, promising an afternoon of quiet debauchery. Maybe, when they arrived, and when the peer's back was turned to examine the moldered couch on the shoreline, the mire of candy wrappers bobbing in the two-inch river of greywater, and the baubles tied to the sewer grate, Killian retrieved the Santoku knife he'd stolen from the kitchen and stabbed them in the back. Maybe he wasn't satisfied, maybe he turned them around to see their face, and stabbed again and again and again, wondering at that titillating look in their eye, and at the sounds they made as they died, and at the sounds the knife made when it went in and out of flesh.

Hope imagined daddy was traveling on business when this happened, and when Killian returned home long after dusk, covered in blood and still holding the knife, Elizabeth must have screamed. Asked him *What have you done?* and *Tell me* and

Show me. And he would show her, leading her to the storm drain where he hadn't bothered to so much as throw a mothbitten blanket over the body. Was she afraid of her own son, then, when she witnessed the evil he was capable of? Did she fear for her own life, imagining what it'd be like to be stabbed to death by her progeny?

No. Hope knew Elizabeth would've piled the corpse in whatever fancy car her husband bought her in lieu of affection, loaded it with cinderblocks, and dropped it in some canal or sea. She would've bleached the knife, burned Killian's clothes, and she'd have done all this with shaky hands and a pale face. But she'd never reprimand him. How, after all, do you scold the Devil for doing what devils are born to do?

"Give me the phone," Hope commanded.

The cell skated across the floor, nudging the tip of her toe.

Unaccustomed to holding a gun on a man, let alone multitasking while holding a gun on a man, it took her a few extra seconds to retrieve the phone without giving Killian a window of opportunity. Opportunity for what?

I swear.

But he'd taken Andi. He'd lied. All his promises were meaningless now, whatever twisted version of trust they'd clung to null and void. Perhaps Killian still saw Hope as distinct from the people he hunted—her own merciless God—but she thought back to the two ravens battling over Hanna's meat.

Hope kept her aim even.

Flicking up and down between screen and man, combing media files for the most recent mp3, she finally found it and hit play.

"In 2008, a filthy, mange-ridden mongrel of a whore named Hope Rippa disemboweled thirteen-year-old Connie Withers on the ground floor of The Scotsman's penthouse suite in Edinburgh, and I was convicted for it a year later after

I got sloppy with the disposal of another disappointing subject. That one was my sixth attempt at breakin' a girl proper, because what are they but horses meant to be ridden—"

Hope paused the audio, not needing to hear more. "This'd never reach a judge's desk, let alone a jury."

"No statute of limitations in the grand old UK."

"No stock in the insane ramblings of a convicted pedophile and murderer neither."

"Nevertheless, you'll still have all those polite Icelandic policemen back at your door, no longer quite so polite. With a nudge like this one, I'm willing to stake my net worth on them seeing right through that sheetrock façade of yours. They will strip it down, and really, *really* search, until that pet detective of yours finds whatever he needs to find, realizing he'd been betting on the wrong pony all along. Ever the recordkeeper, you are. It wouldn't take too long. I wager you hung on to that knife, too. Didn't you? I wager you have it to this very day. Poor, shell-shocked little Hope, helplessly naïve—what else would you do with a murder weapon but wash it in the sink and tuck it in a shoebox under the bed?"

"Has anyone ever told you what a windbag you are?" It was a small and sweet joy, even now, to prod Killian's ego with a toothpick. "You really do talk too much."

He scratched the pad of his thumb with his middle finger's nail. Hope smirked at the sight. The gun trembled in her hand. A thrill shuddered through her: the situation, the setup, the absurdity of all the bush-beating, cat-and-mousing, whiplashed back-and-forthing, frothing her senses to mania. A murderer before her, with nothing to do but show his hands. A hostage behind her, with nothing to do but creak in a chair. And Hope, stood between them in the secret storeroom of one of Iceland's nineteen Catholic churches in one of its six Catholic parishes, armed with a policeman's Glock and a killer's blade, *her* blade, unsure what to do next.

No, not unsure.

She had to destroy the phone.

Killian must have sensed her intention or at least picked up on the beginnings of movement—to throw the phone to the floor and crush it under her bootheel—because he made the slightest tapping gesture with his index finger, a motion that said *Hold on* or *Wait*.

Hope held on. Hope waited.

"Don't you want to know what sound she made?" he asked. "When I broke into her flat?"

"No, Killian. I don't."

"How about when she woke up, trussed like a hog in the cold?"

"No."

Killian looked thoughtful, deigning to take his eyes off the barrel and trigger to wander along the ceiling in thought. She was sure he'd tap his chin were his hands not in the air, ever a slave to theatrics. The show, however, was becoming tiresome, and with no intermission in sight Hope opened her mouth, but—

"What about the sound she made when I jabbed the first needle in her arm?"

When Hope tried taking a breath, there was no oxygen left in the room.

"It was a distinct type of moan. One would've thought I'd just made her climax. In a way, I suppose, I had—and without ever unzipping my trousers." He took one step forward. "When I broke out the second, she mumbled these pitiful little *no*s, kind of like you used to, on those rare occasions I was granted the pleasure of fulfilling your adorable rape fantasy. Do you still finger yourself to such thoughts, I wonder? Or was that a phase that passed once you hit your twenties and graduated to finer desires?"

Hope's battered head swam. The blood on her face had long cooled to a film, but the stench of iron was practically brand new.

"By the third, she'd gone quiet. Nothing to hear there. Except maybe your name, muttered under her breath. How sweet. Or was it sour? Was poor Andi swimming in happier times, or was she cursing you for dooming her to such a fate? Because she knew. Oh yes, she knew who to blame. I was but a middle-man, the guillotiner, whereas you, darling, *you* were the queen who passed the death sentence with a casual flick of the wrist."

Another step. Hope's vision went blurry, and not with tears. Her bandaged temples throbbed.

"I had a fourth, but I didn't need a fourth. I didn't need a third, not even a second or a first, really, but you know me. Prone to—"

"Theatrics," Hope choked.

"Indeed."

"Where is she?" It was a whisper, answered only with a sinister smile that banished her brain fog. "Where the fuck is she?"

"You asked me a question, once, which I never answered," he said, jutting his chin at the cellphone. "Therein lies the answer."

Hope blazed through the gallery. Photos of a beaten man. Edward on fire. Andi drooling in the grass. Then, a black thumbnail—a video.

"*What are you gonna do with the industrial-sized vacuum sealer,*" Killian mimicked, taking yet another step forward, this one the languid stroll of a leopard with cornered prey. "*And what the hell'd they do to rustle your feathers?*"

Unable to look at him, Hope pressed play.

Andi's thin body, curled fetal on the ground, didn't move as the thick, clear plastic slowly tightened around her. The camera zoomed in on the rolling whites of her eyes. The pawing of her hands. Writhing of her legs. The frothy saliva oozing from her lips, bubbling up and bursting against the synthetic material.

"Truth is, your canary did nothing at all. My feathers remain distinctly unruffled—at least by her. Not a plume out of place, in fact, even after I watched her remove your blouse in the park. This was not her fault. It was yours."

The plastic embossed Andi's frame in a skintight death suit. She tried to fight. To thrash. The casing was too strong, the drugs too powerful. Her hyperventilating breaths fogged the bag from the inside.

Puff.

Puff.

Puff.

And with every puff, quickening and quickening, and then slowing and slowing, body going still in its translucent tomb, Hope's fire trickled away and left her sober.

"It's as you said. Boredom with nowhere to go. Lightning with nothing to strike. But then I found it. Where to head. What to hit." He was mere inches away now. "And from where I'm standing, it looks like I struck the bullseye."

Andi stopped breathing. Andi stopped moving. The whir of the machine went silent after a cheerful beep. A green light winked on, marking its job complete.

Hope's scream of disbelief woke patients in nearby cottages. Lights went on, tiger-striping the dim cellar in gold leaking through the slits between wooden wall panels. They might search the garden or the pond, they might even search the church, but they would never find the source. A God-fearing folk, a Killian-fearing folk, they would never tread past the altar—wouldn't so much as climb the first step to the pulpit.

Collapsed on her knees, clutching the phone, rocking it to and fro as if it were a baby gone blue-faced in the night, Hope stammered between strangled gasps. "You said... you wouldn't make... her sing."

"She didn't sing. She wailed, at first, until the Dilaudid kicked in. Hardly musical—"

"You killed her!" Hope shrieked. "You made her sing, you killed her!" She retreated inward, into realms of memory viewed through clear hindsight lenses. "You lied to me. You had to lie eventually, but..."

The word on her tongue was *why*. The word on her tongue was never spoken, not because she'd become lost in her inner cavern, but because she found the answer there, waiting, like a skeleton in the dark. Hope reached out to the skeleton, to its hand, holding a flashlight whose batteries were long dead. But she pressed the switch anyway.

Hope looked up at Killian through eyes clouded with tears. "But when have you ever told the truth?"

"Just because one doesn't lie, it doesn't mean what he puts forth is true?" Killian considered this, pursing his lips. "A fair enough point, though you're as familiar with it as I."

It took Hope's quaking hands minutes to remove the SIM card from the cellphone and snap it in half. With it went Edward. With it went his admission. With it went Andi. *Crack.* Gone, like a broken neck. Like Saga's broken body, contorted inside an oven.

Hope thought of Saga the barista.

Of Gunnar and Katrin, and their cat named Biscuit.

Of Erla Sigursdottir, Kristján Arnarsson, Amelia Symanski, Lilja Ragnarsdottir, Cecilia Kristofersdottir, Khadiija Ali, Jon Jonsson—each of whom may not have liked Hope but definitely respected her—and of poor Hanna, whose first big break turned her into a birdfeeder in the park.

Hope thought, lastly, of Andresína Hammershaimb. The canary in the coal mine in tragic reverse.

Perhaps it wasn't mourning. Perhaps it wasn't grief. Perhaps it wasn't true love down to the tee. But whatever it might've been, it was a force blinding in its intensity, deafening in its clarity, and catalyzing enough in its strength to propel Hope forward without thought, reflection, or consideration of consequence and stab Killian Glass with a guthook knife.

CHAPTER THIRTY-SEVEN

DARLING

I n that hair-split second of flesh and of metal, Hope achieved
a level of intimacy incomparable even to sex itself. There is,
after all, something obscenely personal about stabbing the one
you love. Like a shoulder yanked from its joint she dislocated
from reality, his body heat enfolding hers, his breath
encompassing hers, and she heard, no, *felt* his heartbeat, *thump-
thump-thumping* against her breast.

Elizabeth's blood-curdling wail was but a whisper at the
bottom of a well.

There was a light gasp in Hope's ear, a hitch of breath, and
the smallest of sighs—not a sigh of surprise or pain, but a sigh of
soul-rending *relief*. Reality, long gone and galaxies away,
watched from distant cosmic sidelines. Void cocooned them
together. Abyss wrapped them in shrouds. There was nothing
but them. There would never be anything, anyone but them. No
time to pass. No blood to spill. No regret to suffer, remorse to
swallow, or lives to lose forever.

Reality, a swift and ruthless god, was quick to correct her.

Elizabeth's sobbing scream; Killian's weakening knees. As if
she'd been physically struck, Hope went down with Killian as

he collapsed. His back hit concrete, driving the knife deeper into his sternum and forcing a groan from his lips. If shock was the force widening Hope's eyes until they fogged, then Killian's eyes were their antithesis: clear and lidded, sparkling as they appraised her with something like pride. He was a reverse mirror, of sorts. His mouth shut tight when her jaw hung open, heart steady as hers hammered, body still as hers rattlesnaked all over—except for the killing hand white-knuckling the grip of the blade.

When Killian spoke, all the agony that should have twisted his face poured through into his voice. "Finally."

"You... you..." Hope watched blood pump up around the knife, dripping down Killian's sides to form pools, then ponds, then lakes on the floor. More red in her ledger. But it was too much. She didn't want this red, couldn't stand this red, but still it *drip-drip-dripped*—her pages so saturated they dissolved as if left out on the stoop in the rain.

She searched her crimson reflection for answers, for words, for anything in the vacuum of space inside her skull. "You killed her."

"And now you've returned the favor."

"Why... why did you do this, Killian?"

"Because I wanted to see what would happen." Blood spurted from his mouth with a gurgly cough. He grimaced, letting out a long breath to mask a moan of pain. "As always, you did not disappoint. Impeccable delivery... Perfect timing."

"No," Hope whispered, then solidly asserted: "No!"

"*Come kill the man,*" Killian repeated, studying the ceiling as if it were full of stars, or clouds, shaped like falcons and crows. "*Come kill the man...*"

"I'm not you." It came out high-pitched, a pleading cry.

His response came slow. "Then why haven't you let go of the knife?"

"Because I'm afraid."

Almost a slur, he asked, "Why are you afraid?"

Saga, Katrin, Gunnar, Hanna.

"Why?"

Andi, Andi, Andi.

"You murdered her. You... you *filmed* it. You showed it to me, and you... This is your fault, not mine!" She knew this last was a partial lie. He knew it was, too. "I don't want this," Hope admitted, confused and despising every inch of herself, perplexed by this paradox of love and hatred, adoration and abuse. "I'm not you," she insisted. "I'm *not you!*"

The last word was a sob.

"You're right."

The concession seized her. A beat as long as a northern winter's night, silent and still but for Elizabeth's puttering sniffles. Trust Killian to admit fault when he had nothing left to lose.

His gaze was patient. "But do you understand the difference between us?"

"You're fate," Hope stammered. "You're nature. You're born-this-way."

"And you?"

"I'm..." More blood. More pain. Slippery-slidy pain. "I'm choice," Hope said, at last. "I'm nurture. I'm... made-this-way."

"Made into a woman capable of loving the beast."

"I don't love you." A lie.

"I know."

"I hate you." A truth.

"I know."

"I hate both of us," she said, and he replied: "And yet we were inevitable."

Were.

Killian's arm was weak. Trembling, unsteady. Still, it

managed its journey to her shoulder, and Hope surrendered to his gentle pull, settling in the bend of his arm. Their foreheads met. She clutched his cheek, mewling in despair at the scarlet handprint left behind. He caught her hand before she could retrieve it, keeping it there, syrup-sticky and shaking.

"Do you remember that rhyme? From Aberdeen? The one you couldn't stand... How did it go..."

Hope's heart dropped into her stomach, her stomach into her feet.

"There once was a magpie who killed a finch, but she fell from the tree and into a ditch. Blood on her wings and feathers in-beak, she wondered what to do? To hide or to seek? The finch family would come home soon, by noon; she knew not whether to fight, to flee. Caught by uncertainty, snared in doubt, the wee little magpie did cry out. What had she done, and did she care? However in this world would she fare? The sweet little magpie... red on her claws, she... she..."

"No. Hey. How does it end?" Hope shook him until his baby blues butterflied back open. "Damn it, Kil! How does it end?"

"That's for you to decide, darling." He smeared bloody fingerprints on her jaw's gentle curve before his muscles failed, flopping his hand to the freezing floor. "What else is life but choose your own adventure?"

"You did this to me," she sobbed. "*We* did this to me. You've gotta... You have to help me. You gotta tell me what to do. Where to go. How to live, how to... What do I *do* now? You took everything from me. Everything I had. How do I—Killian!" Another shake, another flutter of lashes. She whined in desperation, barely able to see. "What the hell do I do?"

The *without you* went unspoken, but it was clearly heard.

"You know I can't decide your fate." His cough was coarse.

The spasm brought on a wince; the knife shifted deeper. "Oracles and ravens... knucklebones... tarot..."

"You're not making sense."

"Prayers in the pews and crystal balls... God or no God, your choice is your own. It always has been. Always will be."

"I don't want a choice!"

"And yet it's yours to make."

"Please." Hope grasped his face, staining his cheeks: wet, cold, and growing colder. The tears fell, leaden with helplessness and unpasteurized regret. "I'm more than the monster you turned me into."

"And I'm less of the monster you believe me to be."

"I despise you, Father Glass."

"And I love you," he whispered. "Sweet little Magpie of mine."

Sirens whirred in the distance. Wind howled, slicing through snowfall. A brisk draft swept through the cellar, tousling Killian's sweat-damp hair.

"Answer me one last thing," he spluttered, blood welling up in the corner of his mouth. "Do you think you'll ever recover f-from... what you've become?"

"I don't know." Hope swallowed. Closed her eyes. "I wish you could be there to watch me try."

Killian's smile was knowing, almost wise. He knew the damage this would do, the unerasable scar tissue his death—his murder—would leave behind. "I can't tell you how to go on from here... I can only tell you what to do. Right now. In this... this m-moment."

Hope waited, afraid to so much as breathe despite the urge to shake the answer out of him.

"Kill me," he said. "Kill me and run."

A stab this deep is a long, slow death. He'd suffer for hours. And while part of Hope wanted him to suffer it, to stab him again and again—he *deserved* it for everything he'd done—another part of her couldn't bear the thought.

"Remember the cabin, where I taught you how to dress a deer?" His eyes, barely open now, watched her sincerely. "It's just like that."

"You never had to teach me," Hope whispered, hearing Connie's strangled, gurgling gasp, her tearing skin, the slop of viscera on wood floor. "I'd done it before."

"Do it again."

"No."

"Trust me. One last time."

"Trust you?"

"I spared your detective."

Hope thought, *You murdered Andi*.

Hope thought, *You murdered everyone*.

Hope thought, *You're a monster. You need to be put down*.

She needed to think these things to do what she knew she had to. Not because he wanted it. Because she had to survive. That's what she told herself. Over, and over, and over.

Survive.

"Go on... It's okay. You w-won't hurt me." His eyes rolled, glazing. A dreamy smile broke like sunrise across his face. "You could never hurt me, Hope."

She flexed her fingers, steeling herself to end his anguish. Close their book. Cut the thread binding *me* to *you* and free the world of their evil.

Pressing her lips to his forehead; staring at the indifferent walls. Listening to Elizabeth's pitiful pleas; tasting salt on her tongue.

Hope adjusted her grip. She shut her eyes tight.

"It's okay, darling."

These were his last words.

Elizabeth screamed as she watched her son die. Hope screamed as she killed him.

And then, Hope thought, weeping silently against the dead face of her tormentor, her predator, her ruiner of worlds:

I hate you.

I love you.

I always will.

———

How much time had passed in that basement? Elizabeth sat, half catatonic in overwhelming grief. Hope laid next to Killian's eviscerated body in a similar state, sponge-soaking up the oceanic blood pooling from his exposed insides. Her tear ducts had long gone dry in tandem with the vast hollowness she couldn't feel inside. What would Killian call it? The howling nothing. The great and howling nothing. Move forward, move back. Don't move at all. Can't move at all. There was no more onward.

Red fingerprints painted his eyelids after seven failed attempts to close them. They continued to stargaze the mildew in the wooden ceiling no matter what she did. So she laid there. Watching the ceiling. Pretending they were smashed on Nigori sake, cloudspotting in their private corner of Old Aberdeen's Seaton Park and arguing over the menial differences between falcons and crows.

"You're fucking blind if you think that beak ain't hooked," she mumbled drunkenly.

And you're either spitting mad or hopelessly stupid if you cannot see that those legs are as skinny as yours.

"It's a motherfucking falcon, bud."

No, it's a bloody crow.

"Fucking blind," Hope croaked.

She'd silently conceded that the cloud did, indeed, look uncannily like a crow, but had been too stubborn to revoke her stance. It had only made her angrier at the time. But that was all gone now.

"Blind, blind, blind," she said. "The both of us. Always blind. Walking into walls."

He'd walked off a cliff, this time, and she'd pushed him. Only because he'd shoved first.

Only because of what he did. Was that true? Hope had descended those stairs with the Glock pressed to the small of his mother's back and she'd had no plan. She hadn't assessed all possible scenarios. She hadn't simulated the myriad outcomes. Hope had tied Elizabeth up, threatened her dangerous son, and held him at gunpoint with no escape route charted or exit plan fleshed. If she had assessed, if she had simulated, would all paths have led to this same endgame? Would she have still gone through with it? Would she have *had* to?

We were always inevitable.

Perhaps this was, too. These deaths. Heartbreak was a sort of death, wasn't it?

Blue police lights strobed between the wood-slat walls. Each flash snapped Hope closer and closer to the surface of reality, a spent reel of super eight slapping the camera as a reminder to turn off the film, get up, and go about your life.

What life? What life would be left to live if the police caught her this time, guilty down to the roots of her teeth? Hope shot up and stood, stumbling when an age on the cold floor turned her legs to jelly. Adrenaline pumped into them. Into her brain. She recalled the message Killian wrote on her bathroom mirror.

Fight. Flight.

Your choice.

Which will it be, little Magpie of mine? What sort of monster are you inside?

A valid question. One he'd never know the answer to. One she barely knew herself—she hadn't yet decided.

She looked to the gun on the floor. Fight.

She looked to the pair of weak, smashable panels in the corner. Flight.

Left vacant and dissatisfied with both options, Hope stared at the hatch leading back up into the church. The haven. The house of God finally free of its Devil. Gnawing on these thoughts and puking them back up, Hope remembered something vital in the acrid backwash they left behind.

There was a third option. There'd always been a third option.

CHAPTER THIRTY-EIGHT

STAY

When Hope emerged from the hatch, a man silhouetted by the blue lights of police cars parked in the courtyard opened the church doors with his gun raised. The Maglite in his other fist clicked on, blinding her with its piercing beam. Once she raised a shaking red hand in defense, the beam traveled down her neck, her torso, her knees, coming to rest in a puddle of clinical white at her feet, much like the puddle of gory red gathered there and growing. The doors moaned shut. The shadow stalked down the aisle. Votive candles flickering in a wrought iron stand to his left lit him amber, just amber enough to reveal his identity in the dark. Hope's guthook knife clattered to the stone.

Shouts from outside.

"Search the shed!"

"Stay back, people!"

"She can't have gotten far!"

And she hadn't gotten far. Hadn't needed nor intended to. Not a single officer had thought to check the church. Not a single officer, of course, except the one leading them—the one who may very well have misdirected his subordinates away from where he somehow knew she'd be.

"Oliver." Hope stumbled forward, catching herself on the pulpit. The Bible fell with a *thunk*. "You... found another gun."

"I keep a spare at the station," he said, lowering the weapon slowly but never releasing the trigger—making deductions even slower, because there was only one to make, one he was battling not to arrive at. But he had to acknowledge it eventually.

That the blood was not her own. Not this time.

When he finally gave in and gave up, a man already exhausted to the point of breaking became more tired and more broken, and whispered, "Hope, what have you done?"

Elizabeth's shock-drunk weeping echoed from the cellar. Oliver didn't move. He had ears and eyes only for Hope, and how she wished he didn't, because in those eyes lived a tragic disbelief that physically hurt to behold. The disappointment. The betrayal. The world-rending anguish as the last sparks of hope died in the sky, the final firework fizzling at the end of a long, loud night. Hope for her innocence. Hope for the future. Hope for Hope—all of it, dashed, no more fuses to light. Their tears fell in unison, coming to a mutual heartbreak as the slim dirt trail diverging from the highway of her destiny—an alternative universe in which they might be happy together, free from the afflictions of their crueler realities—dissolved into nothing. She practically heard the rasp of rusty scissors cutting the skinny red string of fate binding their lives.

Snip.

"Tell me you didn't do this," he begged. "Please. Tell me, and I can make it all go away."

"You know I can't do that." Her voice was thinner than her will to keep standing. "I wish I could."

Oliver couldn't stop shaking his head. It wasn't judgmental, only sad. Incredibly, irreversibly sad.

"How'd you find me?" she asked.

"GPS. In my car. How'd you drive here with a concussion?"

"I laugh in the face of medical setbacks," she said, nowhere close to smiling.

The looming hush between them was loaded with things unsaid.

Hope plucked the blood-sodden flannel. It clung, drenched and heavy, to the skin of her stomach. "I hope this wasn't your favorite shirt." A wistful chuckle escaped her. "I imagine it'll be in an evidence bag soon."

"It looks better on you, anyway."

"Even like this?"

Oliver closed his eyes in the trademark way men did when they tried to scrub their minds clean of unwanted sights. He did not, likely could not, respond. Rugburn-pink wrists shifted as he adjusted his grip. Hope imagined him tugging at the towel rack until he bled, leveraging his feet against the tile wall and yanking to no avail.

"I'm sorry," she mumbled.

"For what?"

"Chaining you up in the bathroom."

"I think that's the least of what you should be sorry for."

"I had to do it."

He stepped forward. "No, you didn't. You could have let me help—*none* of this had to happen."

"You don't even know what happened."

"Who do you think has to go down there and see whatever it is you did with that knife, Hope?" The bags under his eyes were dark red and puffy. "Tell me it wasn't you. Tell me it was self-defense."

"No," she breathed.

Faintly, in the distance: *"Did anyone check the church? Where's Ragnarsson?"*

Their clock was ticking.

"One last cigarette for old times?" she ventured. "I doubt I'll get my hands on any smokes in the clink."

After a beat, Oliver nodded sluggishly, as if in a shock state. Hope pulled a pack of American Spirit from the front pocket of his borrowed flannel and couldn't resist the pang in her chest when he tensed, as if she'd concealed a weapon to shoot him. Cut him. Do anything to harm him. It hurt like hell, but she couldn't blame him, and nothing about this endless night-and-day had been anything less than agony.

Slipping the last cigarette between her lips, Hope realized she was one vital ingredient short. "Got a light?"

Oliver couldn't pat his pockets, not with a pistol in one hand and a flashlight in the other. "You know I don't smoke," he said sadly.

Hope's smile was one of serenity and defeat. Her laugh, blank. She spat the cigarette.

Up came the gun. Not because Oliver saw her as a threat, but because he was an officer of the law and she was now a murderer, plain as day, and his colleagues were on the way.

"Show me your hands," he said.

She showed him her hands.

"Kick away your weapon."

She kicked the weapon down the stairs.

"Get..." His voice cracked. A skull on a sidewalk. "Get on your knees."

She fell on them.

Ascending into the chancel and crouching behind her, Oliver gathered Hope's wrists at her back. Hot breath on her neck. Goosebumps all over. Hope traveled back in time to relive the shower, the steam, the warm comfort of Oliver's body fitted against hers, but when she opened her eyes she was cold and wet, not with water but with Killian Glass's blood. Pints of it. Quarts of it. Far too much of it.

For a time, nothing happened. No unhooking of cuffs or sheathing of guns. No movement at all except for the tremble in Oliver's hands as they held hers for the last time. She squeezed them. He squeezed back.

"Your story didn't have to end this way," he said.

"Yes it did."

"You could have stayed."

"I did." Hope gasped; the handcuffs were cold and tight, colder and tighter than she'd imagined they'd be. "Just not with you."

"You could've."

"I wanted to. But I couldn't."

Oliver rested his forehead in the curve at the back of her neck. The contact made her want to cry, but her tank was dry. "Why?" he whispered.

"Because." Hope gazed up into the rafters, seeing falcons and crows. Bowerbirds and magpies. "It was inevitable."

The church doors crashed open, banging against the walls. A swarm of yellow-jacketed officers and white flashlights poured into the nave.

"Ragnarsson!" yelled a fellow plainclothes pushing through a constable tide. "You got 'er?"

Oliver lifted his head and waved his partner forward.

"Yeah." He cleared emotion from his throat. "Over here."

Marching Hope down between the pews, she was greeted by sneering mugs, lowered Glocks, and batons held hard in white-knuckled fists.

"Relax," Oliver told them. "It's done."

They reached the church's threshold. The snow stopped falling. Through a small window in the clouds, a winter sunset bled on the frost. An army of police cars cordoned an army of onlookers, covering their mouths and muttering amongst themselves, equal parts repulsed and fascinated by the all-red spectacle.

With joyless finality, Oliver breathed in. Breathed out, long and shaky.

"Let's go, Miss Rippa."

CHAPTER THIRTY-NINE

BIRDCAGE

The recently renovated and reopened temporary detention center on Skólavörðustígur was a ten-minute walk from the narrow footbridge at the tip of Lake Tjörnin, where Hope had delivered the paraphernalia for Killian's inaugural murder. Café Svartur, where the murder took place, was twenty. The church where she'd found the Penitents was a mere seven down the very same street. Hope knew this no thanks to the paltry window in her cell—it faced the small exercise yard at the back of the ancient complex—but because the office building directly across the road housed Rippa Royale, LLC., no doubt flush with police since the day she'd been booked.

That had been twenty-three days ago. The women's prison three hours east of the city was a medium-security affair, and with no precedent by which to handle Hope's case, the authorities dawdled and argued, unable to agree on a solution to their legal predicament. Given her rap sheet of arrests and connections to the victims, there was no doubt in any judge's mind that she was, indeed, the Bowerbird.

But what to do with such a criminal? How to house her, sentence her, how to keep her from doing yet more damage to their scarred and sundered country? Hope had spent nearly five days chained in the police station's coldest interrogation room, waiting for construction crews to turn a cell into a cage fit enough to contain a monster.

Beetle-Mole had delivered her meals. Sad-Moustache had escorted her to the restroom. Oliver never showed. She wondered if he ever watched on the other side of the two-way mirror, and often found herself staring at her reflection, imagining him staring back. It was unlikely. Impossible. Surely he had his hands full, no, *overflowing* with the aftermath of her supposed reign of terror, and in any case the look he'd fixed her with in the rearview of the police van on the way out of Fjöðurfjall that day—the last time he looked her in the eye—made one thing quartz-clear. He could no longer stand the sight of her.

A platoon of special forces police had transported her to the detention center, and not one of them was recognizable.

The first week at the center came and went with little complaint. The prison boilers were starchy and overlarge, but the mattress was serviceable, and she was separate from the noisy, smelly traffic, drug, and sex offenders that made up the center's miniscule male populace. Sometimes they chucked pebbles at her second-story window, shouting obscenities which barely penetrated the stone, but having made nice with her day- and night-shift guards, Frans and Janus, these disturbances were quick to come to an end. While they were jail guards on paper, they'd been bussed in from maximum-security Litla-Hraun specifically for her safety. Their duty was to ensure other men didn't sneak through the ward in the night seeking vengeance in the form of a swift bullet to the head—or something worse, followed by a bullet to the head.

By the fourteenth day, the pressure of isolation had drawn the walls in closer. Frans slipped her a thin notepad and one of those stubby half-pencils they dish out in psychiatric wards to suicide risks, but Hope was neither a writer nor a doodler, had rarely picked up a pen in the past decade for any other reason than to sign the backs of checks. Computer and cellphone screens were her bread and butter, but the likelihood of gushing one of those out of her jailers, no matter how chummy she was with them on the surface, wasn't even close to slim. It was simply none. The only item they could slip through the bars beside trays of surprisingly decent food, for which she quickly lost her appetite, was a flimsy, fine-toothed comb to yank the knots from her hair, which was becoming more brown than blond and growing fast as crabgrass.

She was due to be transferred to the women's prison for reception and remand at 6:00 in the morning.

It was 2:45am.

Hope threw up in the sink.

Janus fetched a plastic cup of water which she swished and spat, nursing what little was left. Had she traded one fear for another? She'd lived in constant terror of Killian, but there was that saying: better the devil you know. With no idea what to expect, no clue what would happen next, and no ability to envision the rest of her life inside these bars and concrete walls, Hope was close to completely falling apart. Presented with the easy options of fight or flight, she'd chosen to stay, and because she made that bed there was nothing left to do but lie and die in it, too.

Had she assaulted a police officer and stolen his property? Yes. Had she kidnapped an innocent elderly woman? Sure. Had she disemboweled the man she loved and hated in retaliation for lying to her, threatening her, and murdering the woman she cared for? Absolutely. And she'd do it again.

What she wouldn't do again was snap the SIM card that proved, at least to some extent, that Killian was the Bowerbird.

She'd destroyed it out of self-preservation, first—for it contained the Old Man's accusation that she'd killed Connie—and overwhelming, uncontainable rage, second, unable to bear Andi's dying gasps. Had she not acted so impulsively, that SIM card could have potentially reduced what would no doubt be several life sentences to a decade or less with good behavior.

But there was no sense dwelling on her myriad mistakes.

Janus, less a brick shithouse and more a blond-haired, blue-eyed cinderblock mountain of man, lit a cigarette and passed it through the bars. "Probably won't be having one of these in a while, Birdie. Enjoy it while you can."

"Thanks," Hope mumbled. Pretzel-legged on the floor by the bars, she inhaled a drag to the bottommost reaches of her lungs, wishing the cancer she'd probably develop in her fifties would kill her then and there. "I'm not the Bowerbird."

"The boys keep a running tally of how many times you say that in a day on a blackboard in the breakroom. They place bets."

"Let me guess." She exhaled long, savoring every swirl of smoke. "You always win."

"I've never seen men so eager to lose their paychecks."

"I'm sure their wives are proud."

Janus studied her with a depth of intelligence unbecoming of his meatheadedness. "I've been watching these live safaris on that nature channel in the mornings after my shift. South Africa, I guess. They got these wild little cats... Leopards, I think."

"Leopards are pretty big."

"Ocelots?"

Hope shrugged, unsure what he was getting at.

"Ah, I remember. Servals!"

"Servals," she repeated flatly.

"Yeah, servals. Beautiful cats. Jump to high hell, deadly as

312

all death, and here's the kicker—they might not run as fast as cheetahs, but they don't exactly lag behind. Half the size and barely eight kilometers slower. They remind me of you."

"I can't jump very high, bud." She'd never imagined herself in a feline's likeness. She stroked the feather tattoo on her arm. "What makes you think we're similar?"

"There's another program comes on after the safari." His tone darkened. "Some sort of zoo. They call it a rehab center, y'know, for injured cats, but the cages are so... small. And the ones that are too hurt, they never get out." There was nothing threatening in those words, only pity. Despite what Janus might think of her innocence or guilt—the jury was still out on his opinion—there was a doleful melancholy in his expression that Hope felt keenly. "That's the thing about wild cats, Miss Rippa. They've got claws, and fangs, and they're unpredictable." Tender navy eyes traced the cell before settling on her. "They're doomed to cages," he said. "Always cages."

"I've lived my life in a cage, Janus. This one's just a little bit smaller."

Hope floundered both beneath the weight of this fact and the name she hadn't heard in over three weeks—*Let's go, Miss Rippa*—and brought her knees up to her chest as if she could curl up and disappear. The concussion had been long-lasting, but the hairline fracture to the skull beneath her temple was worse, and with it would come months of stress-responsive headaches. Nausea. Migraines. Something else must have been irreparably damaged, something the doctors had missed after the battery of MRIs they'd subjected her to. Maybe it was a tumor. Maybe it was encephalitis. Maybe it was the two-ton burden of karma finally exacting its pound of flesh.

Whatever it was, it didn't matter. She couldn't escape the birds.

A thousand-thousand magpies screamed and cried and

flapped for freedom overhead. Thousands more than the cell could rightly hold. They bashed against the window, got caught in the bars, rained feather showers so thick they coated the floor. Her body. Stuffed her mouth until she couldn't breathe.

Hope stuck her head between her knees. Crossed her arms over her head against their swooping assault.

Make yourself small. Less damage that way. Less sound that way.

Cover your ears.

"Stop!"

Your eyes.

"Stop!"

Your face, your face, they always go for the face.

"Stop, please make them stop!"

Wings. Beaks. Talons.

So loud, never quieting; making a ruckus, a mess, an unstoppable force inside the unbreakable object, a demonic legion fresh from the floodgates as the trumpets of Armageddon rang out from the skies and—

"Hope!" someone shouted. "Hope, snap out of it!"

Hands. Calloused and large. Cracked by winter. They grabbed the wrist they could reach—the right one—shaking it hard and repeating her name until the birds stilled, settled, and faded away. A tornado of wings lost their wind, and as the last dervish of feathers floated to the ground, they dissolved to air before her eyes as she peered through the paltry fortress of her fingers. She realized, almost as an afterthought, that it was not Janus's hand.

Hope peeled her gaze from the floor and very nearly broke when she saw the tortured brown eyes, slicked-back hair, and fishhook scar curving over his upper lip.

"Oliver?"

"It's me." His voice split, cement not yet set and trampled by careless feet. "I'm here. You're getting out."

Getting out?

Hope, gulping spit and unable to speak, rested her head against his through the bars. It wasn't much contact. Wasn't much skin on skin. But compared to the feathers, the talons, the beaks, the squawks, the swipes, the snipes, the shrieks, the screams—she'd take it. *God*, she'd take it.

"Hey. It's all right. You're getting out of this shithole, okay?" Oliver stared until she met his eye. "I swear."

Frans, come to relieve Janus of his shift, flipped through countless keys on a ring. They exchanged looks—Janus baffled, Frans speechless and shrugging—before Oliver stood back to let the guard jimmy the lock free and open the prison cell door.

Hope wobbled to her feet with no small effort, hesitating on the border between imprisonment and freedom. Was this a trick? A prank? Another hallucination, wishful thinking made temporarily real? Frans and Janus waited to one side. Oliver waited, concerned, in front of her.

She said his name, questioning.

"It's okay," he said, certain.

Hope rushed from the open cell and collapsed in a heap into his arms, weeping into his shoulder. His back slid down the wall and they fell together, one hand cradling the back of her head, one arm wrapped as tight around as her depleted body could stand. They stayed that way until Frans and Janus departed. They stayed that way until Hope's tears ran dry. They stayed that way for an hour, maybe more, unmoving in the chill until the head of the guard buzzed into the ward and nodded.

———

After turning the church at Fjöðurfjall on its head, a one Jasper Kolursson from forensics found, during routine cataloguing of Killian's body and its adornments, a handwritten series of letters and a USB in his trouser pocket. In the letters they'd uncovered a detailed plan to antagonize and eventually assault Hope Rippa—implying her retaliation was an act of self-defense—as well as a confession, styled as a suicide note, to being the Bowerbird. Video recordings of the murders and taped phone calls on the thumb drive corroborated the claim. Processing the evidence had taken a long time, and the paperwork to grant Hope's freedom even longer, but Oliver personally oversaw its journey through the bureaucratic meatgrinder to make sure it didn't take months instead of weeks.

Hope was still on the proverbial hook for the tricky business of the kidnapping, theft, and obstruction of justice—not to mention knocking out a constable and detaining two EMTs—but in light of extraordinary circumstances and Oliver's refusal to press charges on his end, she was, so far, looking at one year's probation and a few months of community service.

It should have been a relief. It should have been liberation. But all Hope felt was disquiet, walking circles in her own head around an idea too painful to confront.

We were inevitable.

Had Killian known he would die in that cellar? Did he know it would be by her hand? Did he, all along, know that death was his true endgame—did he plan for it, design it, reinforce the foundations until diversion from that endgame was all but an impossibility?

Was he so adamant to be right about Hope's nature that he was willing to die for it, or had he simply craved death, an end, entrusting her—the only person he'd ever been able to love, in his own sick way—to deliver it?

Hope may have fulfilled this destiny, but she'd ultimately

proved him wrong. She hadn't fought. Hadn't fled. She accepted, she surrendered, she *stayed*, and that proved she was no monster. It set a brick wall firmly between *him* and *her*.

Didn't it?

"Hope?" Oliver waited on the snowbound sidewalk. She waited at the detention center door. "What is it?"

She looked up from her boots. Considering Oliver's dour expression, she wondered how much he knew of the romantic history between her and Killian, but she didn't have to wonder. One look was enough. It said, *Everything,* and it sparked a supernova of devastating shame. At least Oliver wasn't privy to their professional relationship. In that much, she took a scrap of comfort, along with a rasher of guilt.

Her first steps to freedom in nearly a month. The street was deserted at 4:05am. The hour of her release was intentional, and secret, no doubt, to avoid a rioting public.

"Have you ever heard of henhouse syndrome, Ollie?"

"Can't say I have."

"It's like... surplus killing. When a fox breaks into a chicken coop and kills more birds than he can eat."

"Yeah? What about it?"

Hope cracked her neck, exhaling an ounce of tension. "I suppose it doesn't matter now."

As if one wrong move would suck her back behind bars, she picked her way gingerly across the road. She scanned the sky for magpies. The street for shadows in the shape of priests.

"Even in death," Hope muttered, "the only cage he wants me kept in is his own."

They ambled toward a police car. A replacement for Oliver's ruined Skoda.

"You couldn't have known what he'd do before you let him into your life," he said. "You were young."

"And now I'm not, yet I'm still a fucking fool."

"Don't talk about yourself that way."

"What, should I keep the truth to myself?"

"Just because you say it out loud doesn't make it the truth."

"And the truth doesn't care about your feelings," Hope said. "What's your hot take, anyway?" She stopped walking. Oliver took three deliberate steps before following her lead. "What is it you think of me, after all this mess?"

He didn't turn around, instead opting to rub the scar on his neck as if to remind himself: *This, too, I will survive.*

"That's a complicated question," he said. "All I know are the facts. The *real* facts. I know you killed a man, and it wasn't in self-defense. You kidnapped his mother, and you would've hurt her if things had gone sideways. You cuffed me in the bathroom you'd kissed me in only a few moments earlier, leaving me till morning when I offered nothing but help, and then? Then you made me return the favor."

Finally Oliver turned to face her, hands firmly pocketed.

"What do I think of you?" He shook his head and shrugged, utterly befuddled. "I don't know what to think of you, Hope. You had that... perverted love–hate affair with a *monster*. Is that what's in store for you and me if either of us hangs around? Cus I didn't understand it, not when I figured things out while you were behind bars. I still don't understand most of it. I don't think I ever will. I'm not a monster. But the love–hate part? That, I think, I could come to understand. Because I felt it. I'm feeling it. Just a little bit, right now, like the beginning of a headache that hasn't started yet."

Hope held her elbows, hugging herself. She needed it to say what came next. "Do you love me?"

Oliver focused on the inky sky, still shaking his head, as if he'd never stopped since he found her in the church. A weak ribbon of green aurora danced overhead, reflecting in his dark eyes, before fading into the unkind sky.

"I could have," he admitted. "For a moment, maybe I did. But now I'm not so sure."

Hope nodded. The hollowness returned, but it was better than the fear. "I get it."

She kept walking. So did he.

"Y'know," she began, "you never did tell me how you got that scar. What happened to your family."

"Does it matter?"

"I guess not. To me. But it might to you."

Oliver's steps stuttered, as if he wanted to stop, but he forged on. "My wife was killed. My daughter was killed. I almost joined them, but I survived. That's all there is to it."

"That's the least there is to it."

Oliver's exhale was clipped. "How would you explain to me the worst night of your life?" he asked sternly. "Think about it. *Really* think about it. Maybe it was a month ago. Maybe it was fifteen years ago. Enlighten me—would you be *able* to talk about it? Would you want to?"

"No."

"How about scared. Would you be scared? Not just of the memory, but of how I might judge you after you told me?"

"Yes."

"Then it's as I said. That's all there is to it."

Hope followed him to the car, shut down, sinking deeper into her recesses and ravines. Oliver paused at the passenger door, one hand anchored on the roof, the other massaging the temples of his hung head. "I knew him. Did you know that?"

A bungee cord yanked Hope from rock bottom and propelled her not back up to the cliff, but straight up into the sky. She flipped him around by the shoulder to face her. "*What?*"

"I knew Killian."

"Don't say his name."

"I knew him."

"How?" she demanded.

A horror film played in her mind on repeat: Killian on a jet to South Carolina, Killian breaking into a home on a street lined with pecan trees, Killian guillotining a woman, a girl, and finally the man asleep in his basement office, nearly succeeding but ultimately failing and slipping from the window as Oliver bled.

But Killian never went to the States.

"After," Oliver said. "When I came back to Iceland, tweaked out of my gourd, I went to Fjöðurfjall. Lived there for over a year. That... animal. He helped me get clean. He put my life back on track." Oliver dragged a hand down his face. "He gave me my life back and all that time, he was taking others. Right in front of me. A demon straight from Satan's balls, and I couldn't even see it."

Hope's grip loosened, drifting down to his elbow.

"Neither did I," she said. "And I shared his bed for three years."

Oliver leaned back against the car, eyes on the heavens. She wondered if he was cloudspotting before remembering it was dark.

"This wasn't how I planned this conversation," he said.

"You had a plan?" she asked.

He didn't answer, only posed another question to the sky, maybe even to God if He bothered to listen. "Where do we go from here? I have no idea what to do next."

"That's the thing about walking the depths," she said, quoting Killian at the man she could have chosen over him. "There's always a way onward, but never a way to tell whether you've gone forward or back, through the howling nothing."

"Has prison made a poet of you?"

"I wish." A mournful laugh escaped. "After this shit, I'm anything but employable."

"You could always boot me to the futon," he joked, but the humor didn't touch his eyes. "It's not as lumpy as it looks."

"I wanna try," Hope said, touching her palm to the side of his neck, her fingertips to the edge of the scar he couldn't speak of. "But I can't. *We* can't. I ain't ruining anymore lives. I've done enough damage to my own, let alone..." She waved her free hand as if to address Iceland as a whole. "Everyone else."

"You're not to blame for what Killian did," Oliver insisted. "Not to other people, and not to you."

"Maybe not entirely, but I played my role."

Hope smiled wanly. It was the only way to safely reveal her pain. The secret Oliver could never know.

She'd played more than a role—killer, enabler, killer—but she could never admit that aloud. She couldn't bear to see that look of betrayal twist Oliver's face again, corrupt his eyes again, so she sat on the landmine of her shame without saying a word. But still, there was something she had to know.

"An..." She cleared her throat. "Andi?"

"Her, uh, body—" Oliver wetted his bottom lip. "She was taken back to the Faroes," he said, somber. "A cemetery in Mykines. I'm... sorry. I know that isn't enough."

Mykines. Andi's birthplace. The words alone pricked at a tender void somewhere in Hope's sternum; pins and needles of the heart, or whatever remained.

"I'll visit as soon as I can leave the country," she said. Promised. "First thing."

Dwelling in thoughts of Andi, of Andi in the ground, Hope started at the sound of Oliver's voice.

"So," he said, "where can I drive you? Wouldn't happen to be in the mood for shitty sushi and Nigori sake, would you?"

Hope laughed, and then stopped, and then crumpled. Tears stabbed the corners of her eyes. She teetered on the edge of collapse, of sobbing and of screaming, but she refused the tears' fall—refused her emotions' sway.

"I think I'm gonna walk home, Ollie," she said quietly. "I could use some fresh air after all that jailhouse rank."

"That's probably not the best idea for you right no—"

Hope pulled him in as she had in the shower. The kiss was fleeting. Unsure. A featherlight touch, wary of everything. The passion was there, but it was shallowed, hidden behind a shroud of caution neither of them could dispel. And though she remembered the scalding water raining through their mouths, the clouds of steam rolling on their tongues, they did not kiss again.

The pair didn't separate when their lips parted. They hovered, instead, in the frost clouds of one another's breath.

"I don't know what I am," Hope mused. "But I think I know where I am, at least."

"Where's that?"

"Lost in the woods."

"You said that to me once. You told me not to search for you, a few hours before you gutted a murderer. I thought I found you when I saw you standing in that church, but then I saw the blood on you and realized I was miles off-trail." Still, they lingered against one another. "Should I call off the dogs?"

"Probably best for both of us."

"That's the thing. Even after all this, I'm not sure I can."

"And if you don't like what you find?"

"Then I guess I'll be lost in the woods too."

"Well, if you do decide to come for me, bring a flashlight, would you?"

"Hm?" His chuckle was breathy. "Not a compass?"

"There's no way out of these trees, Ollie," she warned, only half joking. "But at least you won't have to sit in the dark."

Exhuming herself from his grasp was like tearing open every

single scar, one by one by one, each opening wide to weep with every inch she moved away.

"I'll see you around, Detective Such-and-Such." She backed down the street, saluting and feigning a casual manner before turning around. "Take care of yourself, would you?"

She kept the tears to herself. She kept the goodbye to herself.

Hope drifted off into the night.

CHAPTER FORTY

ÞÁ ER VON

ONE MONTH LATER

D CI Oliver Ragnarsson slouched in his office at the station, neglecting paperwork in favor of gnawing his knuckle and losing himself in a stupor that might have lasted hours. When other knuckles—decidedly smaller, delicate knuckles—rapped at the door, he was reluctant to emerge from the trance, because at least in the trance he could stay numb. But those knuckles were insistent, and with their second knock came squealing hinges, ringing phones, chattering voices, and laughter, too: the standard sounds of a cop shop post-case closed.

He hated them.

"Come in."

A slight young woman with platinum hair to match her porcelain skin slipped into the room like a phantom, head down, kitty heels quiet, holding a hot-pink sequin folder to her chest so tight he feared it might rupture.

"Do you speak Finnish, Detective?" she asked in Finnish.

"*Kyllä*," he replied. "A bit."

"Oh, thank goodness. The woman at the front wasn't so... inclined?"

"Care to tell me why this woman at the front sent you to my office instead of the twenty desks you passed to get here, Miss...?"

"Lehtinen. Ellie Lehtinen." The name was familiar, but he couldn't grasp why. "It has to do with the missing person's case I'd like to file, if you'd be so kind as to assist."

"Forgive me, Miss Lehtinen, I'm sure your predicament is pressing, but I'm not your guy." He yanked the desk phone from its cradle and started punching the number for Detective Tinna to handle the petitioner, after which he'd call the constable up front to tear him a few new assholes in the politest way possible and free of charge, but this Ellie character, scrunching her mouth and then her nose, as if debating a terribly difficult choice, finally made one and snatched the phone from his hand. Anger and confusion canceled each other out, leaving him stunned.

"I'm sorry!" Ellie stammered. "I, um... Well, I may have lied."

"Please return my phone, Miss Lehtinen. You don't seem the type to last long in a holding cell."

"I have a reason," she said, scurrying back as if he'd shot up from his chair, when in fact he hadn't even straightened from his slouch. "A very good reason!"

"Let's hear it before I page the Chief Inspector."

Ellie scuttled toward the desk, practically sideways, as if she was making herself a smaller target in case he decided to lunge. Faced with such a squirrelly creature, Oliver let her place the dazzling folder on his desk lest she have a stroke if he so much as twitched.

"It's all important information, but I think what you're most interested in will be on page three." Here, her tone descended from its scant squeak of fear into a softer sadness. "It's why... Why I came to you first."

One page. Two pages. Three.

Hope's headshot leered up at him with a classic, savvy businesswoman's smile: half smirk, half glare, daring you to challenge her authority and eager to put you in your place if you did. Oliver launched up from his chair, startling the girl, but he had attention only for the page.

Jotted in the margins in navy blue ink: *Last seen March 19th.*

"What..." he stammered. "What is this?"

"I t-told you," Ellie stuttered, placing his phone back on the desk. "I'm here to file a missing person's report."

"When was she... Where did she..." All his weight tunneled in his wrists, palms planted hard on either side of the folder. "What happened?"

"She took the Learjet to Aberdeen on the nineteenth to scout a new client, but when I didn't receive the call to make arrangements, I snooped through her work schedule." Ellie clasped her hands, fidgeting with her thumbs. "There was no new client in Aberdeen."

Oliver racked his brain for reasons Hope would lie. To return to the closest thing to home she had? To relive memories of, if not happier times, then ones that were simpler, that made more sense than the here and now?

Every notion to surface was swiftly struck down. Each explained why she might have gone; none explained why she hadn't returned.

"She was due to arrive back in Reykjavík four days ago. Her cellphone goes straight to voicemail. Her email keeps pinging back messages, saying the domain name doesn't exist." Ellie was crying in earnest now, all sniffles and hiccups. "I don't know what to do. All she told me was to wait a week before giving you those documents. I haven't looked... I couldn't bear to. Who knows what they are, who knows what..." Covering her face with her hands, Ellie's shoulders shuddered. "Hope saved my life, and now, she's just... gone."

Oliver mindlessly handed the girl a box of tissues, from which she pulled a handful. He couldn't tear himself from page three—but there was a thick stack waiting beneath it.

"Thank you, Miss Lehtinen," he droned. "You've been very helpful. Detective Tinna will take your statement. Her desk's second on the left."

Ellie dabbed at her nose, her eyes. She turned to leave, taking the hint from the dismissal in Oliver's monotone.

"Wait."

She paused in the open door.

"How did she seem?" he asked. "Before she disappeared?"

Ellie's brow furrowed slightly, diving into a fugue-like state of recall to seriously consider the question.

"Mr. Ragnarsson," she began, "I've known Hope for a long time. She always kept me at a distance, and everyone in the office muttered mean things behind her back because of it, but I knew it was to protect me. To minimize her influence on me, I suppose. I think she was afraid I'd become like her, and I guess that makes sense, now." Ellie carefully closed the office door so it didn't make a sound, but she didn't turn to face him. "Many years ago, around when she'd hired me off the street—this was back when Rippa Royale was barely a startup, back in Edinburgh—I came into work early because I had to double-check some expense reports and catalogue her voicemails. It was a Monday. She never liked starting the day listening to drunken clientele requests on the answering machine, but she still beat me to the office. Always first, no matter what. For a while, I thought she lived there." Ellie giggled at a bittersweet memory, heavy on the bitter. "That morning, her eyes were puffy and... flat. Matte, yes? Like someone scrubbed them dry. I pretended to flip through my binder while she wiped her cheeks, and then she waved at me. Just waved. Any other day at 7:00am she was usually barking marching orders for the week, matching shoppers to clients who'd requested service, but... she was quiet. I went to my cubicle, and she didn't come out until nine-thirty. *Nine-thirty!* I should have noticed before, when she waved, but I didn't." Ellie cleared her throat, eyes darting about the carpet as if she were about to divulge corporate secrets. "I didn't notice her engagement ring was gone until she leaned on my desk."

Oliver remembered the ruby ring, the secretive way Hope had worn it around her neck. Had the chain been there when he'd seen her last, tucked into her shirt—*Take care of yourself, will you?*—or had she left it behind, abandoned in an evidence locker? He couldn't remember. He supposed it was for the best.

"What does this have to do with my question?" he asked, not unkindly.

At last, Ellie looked his way and Oliver saw her blue eyes go lifeless. Matte, as she'd said. "She looked the same exact way when she gave me this package." Her cheeks went ruddy. "The night before she got on that plane. When she said your name... well. She didn't say anything further. But I saw it. That sadness. When you look that way, when you feel that way, there's only one reason." Ellie took a breath. "Losing someone you love."

Oliver pinched his nose between thumb and forefinger, squinting down at his desk. At Hope.

Do you love me?

I could have.

What a stupid thing to say.

"Thank you, Miss Lehtinen," Oliver repeated. "You've been... very helpful."

The door clicked closed.

Oliver lowered himself wearily back into the chair, thumbing the edge of the page until a papercut slit it open. The phone rang. He unplugged it. Anxiety whipped his heart into a fever pitch, painfully aware of every *beat-beat-beat*.

Page four was a list of names. As was page five. Six. Seven. Eight. Two columns per sheet all the way to page twelve, the last, and in its bottom-right corner was a poor doodle of a Scotch pine.

Oliver booted up his computer, plugging names into every search engine he knew. A crop of news articles sprouted for the first, Maria Agveropoulos, heiress to a Greek shipping magnate based out of Athens and New York and convicted on three counts of first-degree murder in Glasgow. A second crop, just as fruitful, appeared for Monroe McCord, a corporate lawyer for a major media outlet expatriated from DC to Inverness: two voluntary manslaughters, one second-degree.

Combing through the names, Oliver entered a mix of hits and misses all across Europe, from one in Greenland to twelve in Hungary. The hits were enough to draw assumptions about the rest—murderers one and all—but then there was the question. The gnawing, nagging question, wiggling like a worm in the folds of his brain.

How did Hope know?

Killian Glass was not on the list.

After succumbing to the computer screen's hypnotic blue light, letting it fog his mind so no macabre speculation could find its way home to his thoughts, Oliver eventually closed the sequined folder. The ledger. The docket of the doomed, or soon to be. The package would soon be delivered to Interpol's clutches. Most of it, anyway.

He slid her headshot from the file. There was no need for them to know from whence—or whom—the names had come.

And then he remembered something.

There's this cabin we used to visit, way deep in the Scottish moorlands.

He flipped back to page twelve and its doodle of the tree.

Smack dab in a forest so small and dark it didn't even have a name.

He stroked the scratchy penmanship, too dry and week-old to smear.

South of Auchallater, outside this village called Braemar, 'bout an hour west of Aberdeen.

He shut the folder again, clawing his nails down the sequins.

I wish I could just go there. By myself, y'know? Poof. No more chaos, no more hiding, just... I dunno.

"Peace and quiet."

Oliver chewed his lip. Rubbed his neck. Pulled out the bottom-right drawer of his desk and found the Maglite sitting atop stacks of papers, spent batteries, and Chinese takeout menus. Retrieving it from its nest, he relived the horrid day it was last used: when he discovered Hope soaked in blood by the altar of Fjöðurkirkja, hooked knife in hand, still wearing his flannel shirt.

The scene flew through his head in a series of images rendered in too-vivid Technicolor, an obscure film set to fast and faster forward: 2x, 6x, 8x, 10—

He pressed pause. Pressed stop. Turned off the mental television, left the couch, the room, left the whole damn house, replacing it with a sensation (a kiss), a thought (*Don't leave*), and a request that, at the time, he'd thought cryptic, and now realized was literal.

If you do decide to come for me...

Oliver rose from the chair, powered down the computer, and slipped into his leather jacket on the way out of the police station.

Bring a flashlight, would you?

THE END

AUTHOR'S NOTE

While there has been some chatter in the conservation community related to reintroducing wolves to the Scottish Highlands, it has not happened as of yet. Additionally, the old prison on Skólavörðustígur known as Hegningarhúsið referenced in Chapter 39, has indeed been renovated, but has not been reopened in a penal capacity.

ACKNOWLEDGMENTS

You'd think I'd know how to kick off an acknowledgements section after reading so many to get an idea on how to do it, but once you actually sit down to write, everything feels so insufficient – so I'm just going to jump into my startlingly long list.

Firstly, this story (and myself) would never have gotten off its ass without the keen eye of Sam Kruit of Bowler Fern Editorial, an incredible editor and even better friend to whom *The Monster and the Magpie* is dedicated. She's been groaning at Hope, babying Ollie, and swooning over/shouting at Killian since the time when this book was called Henhouse Syndrome, and, now that I think about it, long before it even had a title. I couldn't have asked for a more excellent, persistent, and truly hilarious cheerleader.

Next up is Amanda Jain, my agent over at Bookends Literary, who's been in my corner from day one and has never stopped fighting for my work. Your support means the world and has helped me believe my writing is actually worth publishing, which is no small feat when you're as self-deprecating as me.

Then there's my critique swap partner and brilliant author, Sue Wentz, whose amazing literary insight, friendship, and support has gotten me through some truly rough times. While I'm at it, let's include the entire crew at Writer's Soapbox! I'd be hard-pressed to find a more wholesome, funny, and kind gang of writers.

Speaking of writer gangs, I'd be an idiot not to mention my League of Stuffed Demons: Devani Anjali, Tyler Clawson, and Paul Davis. From the meme exchanges to the music sharing to the long chats about our projects, our dreams, and life's ups and downs, I'm not sure how I would have gotten through the past few years without your ride-or-die support.

My beautiful friend Layla Olefs, for the endless supply of memes and the biannual video chat dates that keep me sane.

The ridiculously talented Shawn Cosby, for assuring me that yes, it's perfectly normal to have your title changed.

My editor Ian Skewis, without whom this story would have been a nonsensical mess, and not to mention Betsy, Tara, Abbie, and all the other folks at Bloodhound Books who made magic to get this book out there.

An (unorthodox?) shoutout to Drawfee, Secret Sleepover Society, Neocranium, and Mr. Ballen, whose Youtube channels and online communities got me (and continue to get me) through my worst, braindead days.

Jacob Geller, genius video essayist and all-around wunderkind, for the term "howling nothing".

Now, in their place of honor, my family - especially my mom, Irma, who has always had my back ("you got this mama!"), encouraged me to go for it ("you need to learn positive visualization"), and hounded me to "let her read it already" (I didn't), and my dad, Freddy, who was always eager to read my short stories despite not being the source of my bookworm gene!

Rounding out the team is Vincent Dowling, my partner and designated sounding board, whose enthusiasm over fielding my endless writing-related rants, interacting with my ideas, and proposing even cooler ones (oh, and endlessly egging me on to make things as horrific as possible) never ceases to amaze. Really, you should do this professionally.

A NOTE FROM THE PUBLISHER

Thank you for reading this book. If you enjoyed it please do consider leaving a review on Amazon to help others find it too.

We hate typos. All of our books have been rigorously edited and proofread, but sometimes mistakes do slip through. If you have spotted a typo, please do let us know and we can get it amended within hours.

info@bloodhoundbooks.com

Ingram Content Group UK Ltd.
Milton Keynes UK
UKHW040634220523
422126UK00004B/58